A NATURE OF CONFLICT

THE REDEMPTION SAGA

KRISTEN BANET

Some in the world will want you to fail.
Some will want you to fall.
Some won't let you keep moving,
On this journey to something better.
Fight back.
Fight hard.
And remember,
You are not alone.

GLOSSARY

- Ability Rankings - Common, Uncommon, Rare, Mythic. A simple system created to judge how rare abilities are among the Magi.
- Burnout - When a Magi uses all their magical energy and must consume life force to continue.
- Doppelganger - Magi with the sole ability to shape-shift into other human beings. (Legend)
- Doppler – Slang for Doppelganger
- Druids - Female Magi with a plethora of natural abilities. They take over large areas of uninhabited land as caretakers. (Legend)
- Imp - Derogatory term for agents with the IMPO.
- International Magi Armed Services (IMAS) – The Magi's military in case of war against non-Magi or an uprising against the WMC.
- International Magi Police Organization (IMPO) – The Magi's organization for tracking down Magi criminals across the globe.
- Legend – A unique groupings of Magi. They are of equal power and have the same abilities per

group. Incredibly rare. Many non-Magi legends have their roots in these Magi.

- Magi - Humans with magic. They have anywhere from 1 to 5 abilities and a magical Source.
- Reading - A ceremony after a Magi comes into their magic, where a Magi who can 'read' (see Ability Glossary), discovers all the Magi's abilities. This information is then recorded for the Registrar.
- Registrar - A documentation system for recording all Magi and their powers during their teenage years. Viewing a Registrar entry requires approval by the WMC. Magi are required to submit to having a Registrar entry made via a Reading. There are lists Magi can join for public use, such as lists of healers in case of a global crisis, also kept with the Registrar.
- Source - The well of magical power inside a Magi. It's two-fold in how it can be measured—strength and depth. How powerful a Magi is versus how much magic they can do before running out of energy.
- Vampyr - Magi with the sole ability "borrow" abilities from others. They can also become immortal by "feeding" off a non-Magi's life force. (Legend)
- The World Magi Council (WMC) – The governing body over Magi. A group of 15 individuals voted into power every ten years.

1

SAWYER

I t was a nightmare, and Sawyer recognized it as it began. It was too dark, something that had never bothered her before. She wondered for only a second which scene her mind would replay this time.

When Axel took a swing at her, she blocked it and swung back - wild, uncontrolled, untrained. Her hand slammed into his magic shield, something he always kept carefully wrapped around himself once their relationship turned sour and began to rot.

A backhanded blow cracked across her cheek, flinging her to the floor. She was eighteen. She knew how to kill, but she didn't know how to take a hit, defend herself. So much had changed.

Despair began to take over as the nightmare spiraled out of control. She couldn't get away. She wasn't strong enough to defeat Axel; she never had been. She always got it worse when she tried to fight back.

"Fight back," someone ordered, his tone hard, resolved. "Actually fight back. You're in control here. You have the power."

Sawyer looked away from Axel, grunting as he kicked her ribs. She saw Jasper standing nearby, looking horrified but not *interfering. This was their deal. He was going to teach her to take control of her subconscious mind, change the outcomes of her nightmares.*

Seeing him made her remember this was just another nightmare, another lie her past was making up in her head. In her head. She could win here. She could fight.

She grabbed Axel's foot before it came down a second time and twisted his ankle hard, listening to it snap. Axel screamed and fell back. She jumped over him and swung down several times, his shield finally cracking under the onslaught, finally shattering until she could connect with his face.

"Wake up," Jasper commanded. "You won."

She was pulled out of her nightmare in the blink of an eye.

SAWYER GROANED as she woke up, rolling to the edge of her bed to get up and instead running into a body between her and freedom from the confines of her comforter. She pushed herself up and looked down, annoyed with the pale chest between her and her desk.

"Fuck," she mumbled, seeing Zander's flame-red hair, the freckles that covered his face and chest. The tattoos that made his body intriguing – the ones he hadn't had when life separated them years before.

She'd forgotten that he'd ended up in her bed the night before. They had argued. Again. Over something petty, she remembered, something stupid. She didn't remember exactly what that had been, but their arguments tended to end in her bedroom or his, forgotten on the floor with the discarded clothing.

The sex was always fantastic, at least.

She moved to the other side of the bed and left that way,

hoping not to wake him up. She didn't need him worrying about her nightmares. This was between her and Jasper, regardless of how the other guys felt about that. They all wanted to help. Elijah wanted to cuddle her through it - an excuse to have physical contact in a bed. Quinn wanted to watch over her, and that was just Quinn. Zander...well, maybe that was what they had argued about, now that she thought about it. She still didn't remember.

Vincent just wanted her sane.

Easier said than done.

She found sweatpants and a tank top, pulling them on before staggering sleepily to her desk and collapsing into the chair. She reached blindly for the journal Jasper had given her to record every instance of a dream or nightmare she had. She flipped the journal open and groaned as she began to search for a pencil. She heard her door open and close softly. She didn't need to look for who it was. She could feel his magic enter the room.

"Here," Jasper whispered gently, holding out a writing utensil of some sort.

She snatched it and rubbed her eyes. "Good morning," she mumbled, beginning to recount everything of her nightmare on the page. Every detail remembered, every feeling.

"Good morning," he replied. "It's four in the morning. You almost made it through the night."

"Oh goodie," she grumbled, scratching down her thoughts. "Work out in an hour."

"That's right." He chuckled and grabbed the second chair.

She didn't like that there more furniture in her bedroom now. Between the extra chair at her desk, the two couches they had brought up, the TV, and the weapon safe, there was too much goddamn furniture. They had made her room into a place where they could come up, sit down, and bother the piss out of her. She half hated it.

"We've been doing this for two weeks," Sawyer declared impatiently, slamming the journal closed when she was finished. She knew Jasper was going to want to read it, but she hadn't let him yet. "Making it through the night is not a milestone."

"Yeah, it is." Jasper sighed and shook his head. "You can't give up now."

"I always need you to remind me to fight. It's getting annoying."

"One day, you won't need the reminder."

"And then what?" Sawyer snapped. She was in a shitty mood. She didn't know why, really. This wasn't the first time he had come up to talk to her in the aftermath of another nightmare. They had started right after they got back from Texas, and two weeks later, she was losing her patience.

"Then you start winning on your own. Then Axel stops being a threat in your subconscious."

"I'm literally beating the nightmares back." Sawyer snorted, rolling her eyes to the ceiling and staring up at it.

"It works," Jasper said, shrugging. "I did my research, contacted a few other dream walkers. For your specific case, keeping your privacy intact meant this was the best option. The other idea is a therapist."

"Oh, yeah. That's never going to fucking happen," Sawyer muttered, turning a glare on Jasper.

"I know, which is why we're going with this."

A groan from the bed silenced any response Sawyer was thinking of making. She glanced to Zander in the bed as he rolled and buried his face into a pillow.

"I'm amazed you don't find this weird," she whispered,

4

keeping her voice low so they didn't wake up the temperamental redhead.

"I do and don't," Jasper offered. "I don't find it weird that you are sleeping with him, Vincent, and...well, not me. We aren't there yet, but we're in a thing now and have kissed. What I find weird is being in the room while he's there in your bed, sleeping. It's like I'm invading any privacy you two might want. I do it too often."

"You aren't a problem," she promised softly. "We argued yesterday."

"I know. Everyone knows. You two make it well-known when there's something wrong."

"I don't remember what we argued about."

"He slapped your ass as you left the entertainment room. You punched him in the gut for it," Jasper reminded her.

She heaved a sigh and rubbed her face. A snicker from Jasper told her that he found it funny. She wondered who else was probably laughing at them over it. "For fuck's sake," she mumbled.

"Yeah, then you argued about inappropriate physical contact and the rest of us ran off," Jasper finished, smiling. He stood up, looking uncomfortable for a moment. "I'm going to read until our run."

She rose at that and kissed his cheek softly. He turned into it and slowly, tentatively took her mouth for a deeper kiss. She ran a hand over his smooth skin, the flat, defined planes of his chest. It pulled a groan from him.

"That's a sight to wake up to," Zander's voice cut in, sounding sleepy and pleased. Jasper and Sawyer stepped apart and she glared at Zander. "Don't stop on my account."

"I'll see you later," Jasper whispered. His cheeks were flushed, and she knew he was embarrassed. He didn't appreciate Zander's 'who cares who's watching' attitude. It just wasn't for him. "Are we still on for-"

"Movies?" she finished. "Yeah. We're still on for that."

"That's sweet," Zander teased. "You two are actually doing the dating thing. Movies and dinners and kisses. It's adorable to watch."

"I'm going to kill him," Sawyer whispered to Jasper.

"Your call. I'm out of here." Jasper chuckled. "He's all yours."

"He's yours too," Sawyer called as Jasper retreated. She muttered a curse before turning to Zander. "You need to be like that?"

"Why was he up here?" Zander asked innocently.

Sawyer was glad to see he was waking up in a good mood. She knew she was about to ruin it, though. "I had a nightmare. He pulled me out and came up to make sure I was okay."

"You could have woken me up," Zander mumbled, his contented mood vanishing. She knew Zander wasn't going to like that she hadn't just cuddled with him for security... and maybe some morning sex.

"Jasper was in there with me. He knows more than you and everyone else does about them. He's seen them. You don't need to be in every piece of my business." Sawyer crossed her arms and glared at him. "We've been over this."

"How often does he come in here?" Zander demanded.

"Every few nights. A few of those while you've been here."

"No one else?"

"Zander, you're the only person I actually *sleep* with." That was a truth they all knew. Zander was the only person who she spent the night with. She and Jasper weren't having sex and Vincent was...She had shit to work out before she crawled back into that bed, with its black silk sheets. "So, no. No one else." Sawyer sighed, shaking her head. "We've got forty-five minutes until we need to meet for the run. I'm going to get ready and maybe even get down there early. You can sit there and pout, or leave. Your choice."

"I just want you to talk me about this," he mumbled.

"I have nightmares," Sawyer snapped. "Of Axel beating the fuck out of me. Of Henry dying. Of killing people. It's hard to talk about. It's a fact of life for me. It's new enough just trying to let Jasper help me. That was a big fucking step for me. Don't be an ass about this, Zander. It's four in the fucking morning and I'm not in the mood to argue about this."

"Jesus fuck, Sawyer," Zander said with a groan. He threw the blankets off and rolled out of her bed. As he walked closer, his gorgeous, inked form nearly diverting her attention, he opened his mouth again. "I'm sorry for caring."

She looked up at him, all of his six foot five and pissing her off. "Don't you fucking go there with me," Sawyer snarled. "Get out." She pointed to her door.

"Don't-"

"Shut. Up. And. Leave." Sawyer commanded, saying it slowly so it would get through his thick skull.

He glared down at her and she bared her teeth in warning.

"You spend too much time with Quinn," he muttered, his eyes on her mouth.

She twisted the snarl into a grin. "He doesn't shove his foot in his mouth every time he fucking opens it," she retorted. "I appreciate that about him."

Zander didn't say anything after that, collecting his clothes and putting on his sweats before storming out of her room. She ran a hand over her face.

Two weeks of this. Since coming back from Texas, she and Zander found a way to argue over fucking everything, and she was running out of patience. How often they slept together, where they slept, whether she would let him shower with her, who ate off whose plate. Everyone thought it was funny, but she had thought once they settled the relationship stuff it would have stopped.

It had gotten worse.

Sawyer sat back down at her desk and ran a hand over the journal. Complicated. The very thing she had worked so hard to avoid. It was making her annoyed, cranky. She liked simplicity, knowing where she stood, and that was still out of her reach and even more unreachable than it had been.

She flipped through her journal, thinking about the nightmares for a moment. Better than thinking about the rest of her complicated life. She'd had some strange ones after Texas, of children she didn't know, couldn't save. She and Jasper had talked about that for long hours. After a week, they had returned to her normal nightmares: Axel, and Henry, and nameless victims.

She didn't do anything else except stare at the journal until it was time for her to get up and get ready for morning PT. She made it down there before anyone else except Quinn, who - like every morning - was as shirtless as the day he was born. His back was to her, showing her the myriad of crisscross scarring that she didn't know the origin of. Scout and Shade were in the grass, lying out, panting softly from the run he had already taken them on.

"Good morning, Quinn," she greeted him as she walked down the steps of the back porch.

"Good morning, Sawyer," he replied.

"Sleep well?" she asked, stopping beside him and just staring into the woods as well.

"I normally do," he said simply. "You?"

"As well as can be expected." She didn't know what else to say. Quinn knew sleep was tortured for her, and they didn't talk about it. He was accepting he couldn't stop the nightmares; she was accepting she could try.

He turned and looked down at her. As down as he could. Zander was much taller than her, but Quinn wasn't. They were nearly even, her five foot eleven to his six foot two. They were on more even ground in some ways, and in others Quinn outclassed her completely. She was coming to terms with the feral, strange, and immensely powerful Magi she called a friend, even if he could kill her with barely a thought. At least they were more similar in height, right?

"Zander?"

"Nightmare, then Zander," she corrected.

"You might need to beat him up again," Quinn suggested. She would have guessed he was joking, but his tone was so bland and matter of fact that she knew he was being completely serious.

"I'm convinced he likes that more than arguing," Sawyer mumbled petulantly.

"Probably," Quinn conceded. "Maybe that's why he likes riling you up."

"It's whatever. Let's move on from it. How's everything? I haven't seen you for reading in a couple of days."

"Good. I...leveled up? Progressed? I'm now considered a high school reading level. Thank you. I think you are the reason for it." Quinn gave her a very rare smile. "We should celebrate, I think?"

"Are you asking to hang out and celebrate something with me?" Sawyer smiled at him. Now this was a serious step. They had kept everything about books and learning since Texas. He hadn't wanted to do anything else with her and she didn't press him for more. She wanted it. She had a soft spot growing in her chest for the feral Magi who had such secret capacity for tenderness. "I would love that. I'm really proud of you, Quinn. I knew you were going to get better - we just needed to find a reason for you to want it."

"Thank you," he whispered, staring intently at her. "It's still a long road, but you...you gave me a gift. I will always remember it."

Sawyer's heart skipped an odd beat and she had to break eye contact. She'd always found him attractive, but she would never act on it. He wouldn't want her. Their friendship was just beginning, and she didn't think he would want to join the tangled mess of her relationships.

The conversation ended, neither of them finding anything else to say, leaving Sawyer to absorb the dark silence of the world around her. At nearly five in the morning in October, the world was still asleep, but slowly beginning to wake up. She began to hear some birds rustle in the trees and begin their days. Vincent and Elijah walked out, followed closely by Zander and Jasper, who were quietly bickering over something.

Since coming back from Texas, Jasper had convinced them to let him join in on the outdoor runs, to get up to speed with his new prosthetic.

She stretched in silence, Vincent coming to do his own next to her. They exchanged a glance and he sent her a telepathic thought.

"Good morning. How was your night?"

She gave a heavy, over-exaggerated sigh and eyeroll to give him the gist of it. It made him chuckle softly. She should have found it weird to be asked by one of her boyfriends about another, but Vincent was always polite and just seemed to want to see how she was doing with all of it. Everyone on the team could sympathize with the exasperating nature of Zander Wade.

"Well, if you need someone a little less pushy, you know where to find me."

She pursed her lips and looked at him. It was basically saying 'are you serious?' and she hoped he got it.

"I'm just saying." He shrugged minutely.

She finished stretching, shaking her head a little with a smile. The bickering between Zander and Jasper had quieted down, leaving them all in a companionable silence.

"Everyone ready?" Vincent called down after nearly ten minutes.

Once everyone gave affirmatives, he led them out, letting them fall into a line behind him. It was an easy morning, even though they moved faster than normal. It was for Jasper's benefit, as he continued to grow accustomed to running on uneven terrain with his prosthetic. They had picked up the speed regularly every day they ran, giving him a little more of a challenge. His cardio was exceptional, and he was just as tired as the rest of them at the end, but they didn't want to cause him to fall as he got used to it. They hadn't had the chance to work on it before Texas, so this was untried ground for him.

Back near the plantation house, Vincent slowed and stopped them for a cooldown walk for the last five minutes.

"We'll do legs starting in one hour," he announced. "I figure we can try out the new protein shakes first. Elijah?"

"Yeah, I'll get them made up for all of us," Elijah confirmed.

Sawyer looked back at him and wondered how he was doing. He hadn't pranked on her all morning, teased her or anything else. It wasn't that it worried her - it just didn't happen that often. He caught her looking and grinned. She smiled back. That was uncomplicated right there. Elijah still flirted, she still denied him, and things were still good.

Sawyer ended up following Elijah to the kitchen while the others went downstairs or to do their own thing.

"How are you, little lady?" Elijah asked her, as he pulled down a huge tub of protein and several other powders and mixes.

"I'm doing good," she answered, propping herself on the counter next to where he was working. "We haven't hung out much."

"You've been busy," Elijah told her with a teasing tone, grinning. "I mean, how do I compete with Zander?"

She looked him straight in his hazel eyes and made a show of looking down his massive form, the broad shoulders, the huge chest, the fit waist that was still thick. He was a man that a woman could hold on to. A tree to climb, she remembered thinking when she'd met him. A tree she was going to climb eventually because she wanted to. Then she slowly went back up to his eyes.

"There's no competition," she replied innocently. There really wasn't. Zander had that bad playboy thing going for him and a lean, gorgeous swimmer's body. Elijah was a working man who had an easy-going nature that only wanted to see people smile. They weren't comparable men. Not to her.

"I'm sure there is," he said, winking. "But you have yet to take me up on my offer. I know things that Zander could only dream about."

"I'm not so sure." Sawyer chuckled. "He's very good in bed. I'm just so satisfied."

"Too bad he opens his mouth," Elijah reminded her, pointing at her with a spoon he was using to dish out the different powders. Then he went back to what he was doing.

"He says some good things too," Sawyer replied, feeling a little defensive of her redhead.

"How much he loves you?" Elijah whispered, looking at her again. There was something soft on his face.

She nodded. He did say it a lot. Not just during sex, but when they were arguing, and when they weren't. He didn't miss a chance to stop reminding her.

"I mean, he does. It's as obvious as the sun."

"I know," Sawyer mumbled, looking down. She loved him too, but damn, he annoyed the hell out of her at every opportunity.

"Want to hang out later? Get you away from the fan club? Maybe if you and Zander get some distance every so often, it won't seem so rough." Elijah elbowed her, and she sighed.

"Tomorrow. Today, I'm going to the movies with Jasper," Sawyer explained, smiling.

He chuckled and nodded. "All right. Tomorrow. Me and you. Quinn too. We'll head out to the swimming hole before it gets too cold. Still warm enough for it right now. Wouldn't want to pass up the chance to get more hours in."

"No, we wouldn't," she agreed. "That sounds like a good, relaxing day away from the house. Plus, Quinn told me before the run that he wants to celebrate hitting a high school reading level. We'll have fun."

"Yeah, the swimming hole isn't Zander's thing. Mutters about water safety, of all things, like Quinn would let us swim in a gross stagnant pond or something," Elijah muttered, rolling his eyes. "It'll give you some time away from him and Jasper...and Vincent."

"The other two aren't argumentative monsters," Sawyer mumbled with a groan.

The conversation ended as Elijah turned on the blender.

A minute later, a glass was pushed into her hands and commanded to drink. Strawberry flavoring helped cover up the bland powder, but the weird grainy feeling in her mouth was unavoidable. She finished it dutifully as the rest of the team started coming into the kitchen since they heard the blender.

The leg day in the gym was as easy as the run. She partnered with Jasper, keeping a close eye on him as he proceeded through the workout on the new leg. His perseverance to make it work made her a little proud.

"You did good today," she said to him as she grabbed a towel. She frowned and realized it was the last one. She tossed it to Jasper, deciding he deserved it more.

"Thank you," he replied, looking a bit bashful. "It's been a long time since I could do squats without my body protesting. Can you throw a second towel?"

"There's no more," Sawyer said, pointing into the bin where clean towels were normally kept.

"Shit," Jasper hissed. "We need to call her. I thought we already did."

"The nice old cleaning lady you have banned from the house?"

"Yeah," Jasper sighed. "Vincent!"

"What?" Vincent called back before walking over. "What's wrong?"

"We need Estella to come back. We're falling behind on the household chores," Jasper quickly told him. "It's time. Sawyer has settled in. She's not a danger to Estella. Elijah said she was going to start coming back."

"I'll call her later today," Vincent replied casually, shrugging. "Other things came up and I forgot to tell her it was okay for her start her weekly visits again. It's not a problem."

"What's going on?" Zander cut in.

"You were supposed to clean towels." Jasper threw the last one, now wet with sweat, at him.

Zander made a disgusted face and looked at the towel that had hit the side of his face and fallen to the floor. Sawyer couldn't hold back a snicker. "Shit. My bad," he mumbled, leaning down to pick it up. "I'll get them done today, or at least get them started."

"Thank you. I'll ask Estella to start coming over again. Sawyer, I hope you're ready. She's a great little old lady." Vincent walked away after that, leaving the gym with Elijah. Quinn, Sawyer noticed, was already long gone.

"I'm going to get in the shower before you guys," Sawyer announced. She left the gym before Zander or Jasper could beat her to the bathroom that she shared with them. She didn't use Elijah and Vincent's ever, because Elijah left it a constant mess to piss off Vincent. She'd made the mistake of going into it once and regretted it. Quinn had his own attached to his bedroom, something private, and she'd never been in his room or his bathroom. She would never go in without his permission either, unless she had a death wish.

She smartly locked the bathroom door. If she left it unlocked, Zander would get frisky and want to play. While sometimes that was appreciated, today she wanted space from him. She needed it, or one of them was going to get hurt.

She took her time, ignoring one of them knocking on the door. What she hadn't expected when she got out was both of them waiting on her.

"I'm going. You two can fight over it." Sawyer chuckled, waving to the steamy bathroom. As long as it wasn't her doing the fighting, she didn't care what they did.

"I'm going first. When I get out, we're going to the movies," Jasper said quickly, diving into the bathroom.

Sawyer was unable to stop the laugh at Zander's annoyed face. She was still laughing all the way up to her room.

2

SAWYER

She met Jasper in the garage. She'd never been on a date like this, and it excited her in a weird way. A date. It was so simple and also so incredibly Jasper. He'd asked her after they got home from Texas, and things had repeatedly come up to stop them from going. From paperwork over Texas to visiting the kids at the orphanage, stuff just never stopped coming their way.

He was wearing a pair of clean jeans and a simple button-down shirt, looking put together and a bit preppy. His sense of style was something she normally didn't go for, but it looked good on him, the button-down just a little too small. Like every guy in this house, Jasper was a specimen of male fitness. She looked down at herself and wished she'd gone for more than the black jeans with fake distressing and a tank top that made her small chest look semi-decent. He was even wearing nicer shoes than her. She'd gone for a 'nicer' pair of black boots and he was wearing perfectly clean trainers.

"I'm driving," she declared, spinning her keys on her

finger when she looked back up from her outfit. She looked to her gorgeous Audi that waited for her. She hadn't taken anyone for a ride in it; she didn't go anywhere anymore. That one visit into town and the bad taste in her mouth from Texas left her wanting to stick close to home.

"Are we going to get pulled over?" Jasper asked nonchalantly. "Well, are *you* going to get pulled over again?"

"Let's hope not!" Sawyer laughed and unlocked the car. She slid in and waited for him. She watched him look over the car slowly before getting in, then taking in all the interior detailing and electronics once he did slide in.

"I've been staring at this car with Zander, wondering if we would ever get to ride in it," he admitted softly, a pink blush over his cheeks. "It's a stunning car."

"I'm quite taken with it myself," Sawyer teased.

"You didn't let me finish," Jasper whispered. "It matches its stunning owner."

"Oh, Jasper, um, you don't need to..." she mumbled and gave up trying to find words. Oddly, her face heated up. Compliments like that weren't ones she was familiar with. She didn't have a plan to handle it, a way of shrugging it off.

"Did I render you speechless?" Jasper was teasing her now. *Jasper*, of all people, was teasing *her*. "It's okay. I'm probably very bad at this. I never really..." He trailed off, covering his face and she could relate.

"Me neither?" Sawyer replied, turning her car on. She hit the button to open the garage door closest to her and began to pull them out. "Not like this. Dating, compliments. Never was something I did."

"I don't want to be Zander," he informed her. "I don't want to fall into your bed and be a pain without us testing the waters, learning more about each other. Sure, we grew up together, but we've been apart for a long time too."

"Do you know how to just fall into bed with someone?" Sawyer wrinkled her brow and frowned at Jasper. He wasn't the type.

"No, but I think the possibility is there." He chuckled.

"I thought so," Sawyer huffed. "The possibility, by the way, is not there. You're too nice of a guy to just fuck a woman and think it makes everything okay."

"You screwed Zander and thought it would make everything okay," Jasper reminded her.

"I'm not nice," Sawyer retorted. "I'm fairly certain I'm an idiot actually. I mean, what woman in her right mind would try to get Zander to settle down?" She was mad for thinking, for any moment, that any of this was going to work, but they told her it would, and she was going to try it out. What did she have to lose, really?

"The one who knows he will for her," Jasper whispered. Sawyer kept her eyes on the road. "It's always only been you for him. He would have fucked his way into an early grave if we hadn't stumbled onto you."

"That's reassuring." Sawyer sighed.

It took them thirty minutes to get to the movie theatre and Jasper was extra sweet, jumping out to get her door before she even had a chance to think. More things she wasn't used to. "I let you drive but I'm still getting your door," he told her.

She laughed and patted his chest, letting him feel good about it. She wasn't going to give him a hard time. Something about all of this had her feeling young and stupid and she loved it a little. Just a moment to pretend they were two normal people on a normal date to the movies.

"What are we seeing?" she asked.

"No idea. I figured we could just pick at that moment."

"I've heard about some Idris Elba movie," Sawyer offered. "It's a disaster-romance, survival thing. Plane crash, wilderness."

"We'll do that then," Jasper agreed, nodding as a smile spread over his face.

She grinned at him and took his arm with hers. Together, they walked to the counter, and she let Jasper buy tickets. He took her to the concession stand, got them both drinks and some popcorn. She felt out of place, in a different reality for it all.

Movies with a boy. She didn't even do this as a teenager. She damn sure didn't do this sort of thing with Axel. They had partied in expensive clothing. He'd danced her around the world, shown her things she never would have seen otherwise. He had wooed her with money, power, and adventure.

But Jasper was normal, and she loved it. She was going to fall for her amputee childhood friend because he was going to woo her with real life.

They settled into their seats, and he leaned over to her. "We are the only people in the theatre," he whispered.

She sat up and looked around. Sure enough, there wasn't another soul in sight. "What does that mean for us?" Sawyer asked seriously.

Jasper didn't answer, just wrapped a hand around the back of her neck and pulled her in for a kiss. Sawyer's eyebrows went up, but she decided to hell with it. She relaxed and deepened the kiss, letting her tongue explore his mouth, taste him. This was what Zander had interrupted earlier. She moaned into him and heard a groan in return. When it ended, she enjoyed how dark and turbulent Jasper's stormy blue eyes were. There was a heat there she didn't normally see in him. It was enticing and beautiful, her golden boy looking at her like she was the only thing he'd ever wanted. He nearly looked like he would take her there in the dark theatre, as the lights dimmed for the trailers to start.

As the movie started, he pulled up the arm rest between them and pulled her into him a little more. She shifted, getting comfortable, his arm casually over her shoulder.

Halfway through the movie, she wasn't paying attention to it. Jasper was thoughtlessly creating trails of goosebumps on her arm and that was driving her mad, in a good way. She turned to him during the movie's sex scene and kissed him again.

The movie forgotten, she grabbed onto his shirt and nearly climbed on top of him. He pressed a hand to her lower back and held her as they made out. His other hand rubbed her thigh slowly, long strokes up and down the outside.

"We should watch the movie," he whispered huskily. "We'll get thrown out if we keep this up."

"Fuck the movie." She went back to kissing him, nibbling on his bottom lip as he groaned. She could feel how hard he was and rubbed him through his jeans, which prompted him to grab her wrist.

"We definitely can't do that here." His voice was gruff, undone, and heated. It sent a shiver down her spine, realizing there was a passionate man underneath her golden boy.

"You're right," she agreed softly. "I just…"

"Sawyer," Jasper moaned and kissed her again. She noted that he kept her wrist tight in his hand, refusing to let go. "We still have to go get lunch after the movie."

"You are committed to this date thing," she teased.

"I really am." He chuckled. "Does it bother you?"

"No, I find myself quite liking it," she admitted, whispering the words against his lips.

They kept their hands to themselves for the rest of the movie. Not their mouths, though. Jasper kissed her temple and nibbled on her ear at one point, making her nearly whimper. Something about a hot breath over her sensitive ear sent her wild. She didn't tell him that, though. It was a weakness she didn't want him to exploit. Zander already knew and used it to his advantage every time he had the chance.

"There's a Mexican place I think you might really enjoy," Jasper told her as the credits started to roll. "Want to try it out?"

"Would love to," she answered, untangling herself from his arms. Even their legs had gotten wrapped up in each other. She stood up and he followed. She was feeling a little hot and bothered by the dark encounter of going to the movies. She had realized why other people her age would do it. That was a place where anything could go, it seemed.

At the Mexican restaurant, they were seated in a booth and ordered before any conversation got restarted.

"Congrats on testing out of the GED," Jasper began. "I'm proud of you."

"I knew most of it," Sawyer replied, shrugging. "It wasn't hard for me. Sure, I missed a couple years of school back in the day, but none of it was overly complicated."

"Thinking about college?"

"What would I go into?" She frowned, taking a sip of her water.

"Criminal justice?" he offered. "Our job. There's a few

colleges in the country that offer programs specifically for IMPO hopefuls."

"How popular are those programs?" Sawyer was disbelieving. Not many Magi wanted to be an imp. She'd never planned for it, that was for sure, even before she'd become a thief, then assassin.

"Not very," Jasper admitted. "I think last count there were only fifty Magi in the US who graduated with the major."

"No shit," Sawyer snorted. "The WMC isn't exactly popular."

"No, they aren't," Jasper conceded. "They are our ruling body, though. We do vote for them."

"From a few very specific pools of Magi deemed worthy to hold a seat on the Council," Sawyer reminded him. It was a corrupted system. Over time, the fifteen seats of the WMC were a revolving door for maybe twenty or thirty Magi families, all the richest and most powerful of the Magi community. Families who could trace their roots back to Rome, to Alexandria, and further. A normal Magi didn't grow up thinking they were going to become a Council member. They were born and bred for it, the next line of the dynasty for that family.

"True," Jasper agreed. "You aren't wrong. There's problems with the system, certainly, but it's been our system for millennia, since before the Roman Empire, though that's when it really gained most of its power."

"Correct me if I'm wrong." She chuckled. "There used to be several councils, all over the world. Not one singular world council but regional."

"You are correct."

"Why don't we still do that?"

"Because those councils used to go to war with each

other constantly." He took a deep breath. "And install themselves in regions as gods."

"Ah, you're talking about the Greeks," Sawyer realized. "I know we have a hefty amount of evidence that the Greek Pantheon was either based on Magi or founded by Magi, but what if they were already around and Magi just pretended to be them?"

"Sawyer the scholar?" Jasper laughed. "Really?"

"Look, I just had to write a paper on this for my damn GED," she huffed. "It's been on my brain."

"You should go to college. You're intelligent enough and you have a thirst to know more," he pressed.

"After all of this, then," she negotiated. "If I can get through the next five years, get my pardon and have a clean slate, I'll go to college and do it right. Third time's the charm?"

"Third time?" Jasper frowned at her and she grinned.

"Yeah, third time trying to be a functioning adult and member of society. The first was...him. The second was with Charlie in New York, the third time is this."

"Well, damn. Eventually you'll get it right, I hope," he teased.

Their food arrived, and they tasted what each other got. Sawyer was in love with her fajitas, but she had to admit that Jasper had chosen well with the shrimp tacos.

"Anything you want to talk about?" he inquired when they were finishing up with their food. "I'll admit I'm not ready to go back to the house yet."

Sawyer opened her mouth and closed it again, thinking about what she could possibly ask Jasper about. His life after they left her at the orphanage? She'd gotten the gist of that. They didn't like the IMAS; Vincent recruited them to the IMPO for his team. They chased down serial killers, crime lords, and presumed dead assassins, though the last one had been an accident they had stumbled on. It was a mistake she'd made that she didn't get pissed off thinking about anymore. He would party with the guys when they finished a case, have some fun with a random person.

"You guys seem very...solitary," she mentioned carefully. "It's just you five. You don't really talk about other friends. Sure, James, your...*our* handler is brought up, but he hasn't visited to hang out since I've been here. Estella, the cleaning lady I haven't met yet. No one else."

"We are," Jasper admitted. "We are. It's the curse of the job, really. You were right on the plane to Texas. We show up in an area, we cause hell, turn everything upside down, then disappear - and that's important. Imagine if we had a bunch of friends in our community. Imagine then that someone like Axel found out. Or god forbid we didn't catch a killer before the case went cold or we became targets. Teams like ours, we're expected to lay low and keep our shit under wraps when we're off the job." Jasper sighed, shaking his head. "It gets lonely, but you end up best friends with your teammates, or it all falls apart and the team is dissolved by the IMPO. We live in a bubble and we're let out when they need us, basically."

"How are other teams?" Sawyer continued casually.

"There's a general consensus that we don't really see each other unless something big is happening or we run into each other at different IMPO headquarters around the world on accident. There aren't many of us, though, so it's rare. You're most likely to see other Special Agents in New York. There's always a few teams moving through the main headquarters for some reason or another." Jasper frowned, looking thoughtful. "You aren't the only reformed criminal in the organization. There's a few others. You are the most infamous. You should know that while you aren't outed publicly, every single Special Agent definitely knows your name, who you are, and who you have been. They also know you're on this team. So, if we run into another team and they're rude, stand-offish or anything, that's why."

"That didn't answer the question," she pointed out. She did tuck all the information away, though. It was good stuff to know, and she should have asked earlier. "Do they settle down and have kids? Do they live just like we do here in Georgia? Like, what is the 'normal?'"

"We're normal, for the most part," he explained. "Our formation wasn't. The members of the team aren't, but our lifestyle is. Special Agents normally retire or step down to a lower position if they want to settle and have kids. Normally."

"Any other women in the community?" Sawyer used a fork to poke around her food.

"A few. A lot of cases like you, one tough-ass woman who works on an otherwise all-male team. Some teams are more even, but there's just less women in the IMPO and even the IMAS."

"Obviously," she mumbled. "Not many women like me."

"There are no women like you Sawyer, only close," Jasper retorted. "I've run into other agents with the IMPO. Sure, we have tough people, but I've never met someone who has lived as much as you."

"Most people don't want to live as much as I have," she reminded him. "Hell, I don't want to have lived as much as I have." Before he could respond, she changed the subject. "What were you and Zander bickering about this morning? Before the run?"

"He wanted me to talk to him about your nightmares,"

Jasper explained. "I told him that if you weren't, then I wasn't going to. He didn't appreciate that."

She had been hoping it was nearly anything else. "I'm going to stab him," she blandly commented.

"Please don't. There's no hospital close by."

"He can heal himself," Sawyer reminded him. "It wouldn't be fatal. It might become fatal, if I have to repeatedly stab him."

"You two are the worst," Jasper said while chuckling. "Is this how it's always going to be? I won't be surprised, honestly, since it's how you've always been, but I thought age and time would calm you both down."

"No, I think it's gotten worse. I'm pretty sure it's worse, really," she said, nodding. She was pretty aggravated by it. "He's pushy, and if he keeps pushing, it's going to land him in an early grave, I swear."

"And you?"

"He'll aggravate me to death. Mutually assured destruction, this relationship."

"Vincent's easier, I'm assuming?" Jasper smiled, leaning back in his seat.

"No, Vincent's not easier, he's different. You, you're easy. Ignore my old occupations and your rigid sense of rightness and we're fine."

"We don't need to ignore them. I meant what I said in Texas," Jasper whispered. "How is Vincent different?"

"He just is," Sawyer sighed. She wasn't sure how to explain what was going on with her and Vincent. "Why do all of you keep asking about the others?"

"Because we're all friends and we're with you?" Jasper answered, shrugging. "It's natural for us to want everything to go smoothly with this? To be concerned about how you are and each other. Zander and I used to talk about you, when we were teens. When a boy was mean to you, we would talk about it and promise not to do or say what he did. When you argued with Zander and cried on my shoulder over it, I would tell him to stop doing it later. When you ignored my...attempts at flirting, I asked him for advice."

Sawyer blinked several times. That was much more than she'd been expecting. For her, it had been ignored, all of it. Her awkward, conflicted teenage feelings and their...well, there had been something going on with them, but that hadn't been what she'd expected.

"We planned all those years ago to both date you," Jasper murmured. "This is just...what we always wanted. I'll admit, though, that seeing you again in New York, it was the last thing I wanted to think about. Then there were the nightmares and I didn't know what the fuck to do about those. I didn't know what they meant at the time." Jasper pushed his plate away. "So yeah, I worry about you and Zander. I worry about you and Vincent, because if one of them hurts you, I'll probably lose you too. If Zander had broken our friendship with his antics as a teenager, we would have lost you in a different way than we did."

"Jasper," she breathed out. "Do you really see this as tied together like that? Each of you?"

"Yeah," Jasper confirmed. "I do."

She considered that. They wanted it to work with all of them and that was...looking difficult. It was still new, though, so Sawyer didn't want to get fatalistic over it yet. No reason to freak out because everything was new and strange and they hadn't found their footing yet.

"Don't worry about it," he said quickly. She blinked and looked back at him, having stared at her food while she thought about it all. "It's...Sawyer, I want to be with you and we'll do this at our pace. And you'll do your thing with Zander at the pace you two decide. Same for Vincent."

"And Elijah," she reminded him softly. She knew he was part of this little deal, this idea that she could be with whoever she wanted whenever she wanted. "I don't think that will ever happen, by the way. He's a great friend, though."

"Elijah is a great guy," he agreed. "Ready to head out?"

"Yeah," Sawyer decided. "Yeah, let's get home."

Jasper took her hand when they left the booth. He paid before they left and once again opened her door for her to get in the car. She was going to light a cigarette before getting in the car, but Jasper gave her a look as he held her door open.

"I don't really like that habit," he said patiently.

"I know. I'm sorry. I won't smoke on our dates," she told him, sliding the smoke back into the pack. "I can't imagine kissing me after one is very nice."

"I notice, but you don't smoke often enough to make it really bad. I don't like it, but I like kissing more, so I'll survive."

She made a mental note to get breath mints, so he didn't have to worry about it anymore.

When she hit close for the garage door at home and shut the car off, Jasper leaned over and kissed her again. She leaned into it, meeting him halfway, until a knock came on the car. She growled and looked through the front windshield, seeing Elijah grinning at them, his arms crossed.

"Now, young people," Elijah began, putting on the most 'dad' voice she'd ever heard. "You know better than to make out in the car when the little lady needs to come home before curfew."

29

"Killing. All. Of. Them." Sawyer bit out, glaring at Elijah. Jasper just jumped out of the car and ran to open her side. This caused Elijah to laugh. She climbed out of her car and continued to glare at Elijah. "What the hell?"

"I was passing through. Running out to grab something from town, saw you two pull in, and wanted to fuck with you. Didn't expect to catch a make out session. Bonus, honestly." Elijah was still grinning as he explained. She was considering strangling him when Jasper wrapped an arm around her waist and pulled her along. "Feel free to stay and continue. No reason to run off now."

"Pervert," Sawyer growled. "Go watch porn."

"It's not as much fun," Elijah called after them.

"We're never going to have any privacy in this house, it seems," Jasper muttered, yanking her out of the garage and into the area leading to the dining room and kitchen. "Sorry."

"You have nothing to be sorry for," she grumbled. "There's just too many damn men in this house and you're all horndogs."

"I mean..." he leaned in close. "Can you blame us?"

"Yes," Sawyer answered, looking into those heated, stormy blue eyes. She saw a pink blush on his cheeks. He was embarrassed by Elijah as well, she knew it, but damn if it didn't look good on him. "I'm going to relax for the rest of the day, maybe catch up on my Netflix for the first time in months. Want to join?"

"No," Jasper sighed. "I need to get to work. I'm behind in one of my classes."

"Classes?" She frowned.

"I'm still in college." He chuckled. "Yeah, I know. I do a lot of distance learning. I've got more than a few degrees at this point, but it keeps me busy during the slow times, and I love to learn."

"Have fun with that," Sawyer told him. "I'm off to Netflix."

"Enjoy your Netflix," he chuckled. He kissed her cheek before letting her go, and she smiled back at him as she left him there.

3

ZANDER

*Z*ander knew she was back from her date with Jasper and hadn't yet come to see him. He sat quietly in his shared office with Jasper, stewing. They hadn't spoken since she'd thrown him out in the morning. He was frustrated. She refused to let him in, refused to share herself with him when he told her practically everything about himself. His wants and fears. He trusted her and he felt like it wasn't returned.

"Jasper-"

"If you are asking about the date, it went really well. We had fun. Movie was all right, and the food was delicious. If you're asking about her nightmares, don't continue." He looked up from his notes, and Zander glared at him.

"I'm glad the date went well," Zander replied. "Seriously. Real glad."

"I hope you are, since it gave her a moment out of the house, away from the explosive problems you two are having," he commented casually, looking back down to his notes. "Stop giving her a hard time, Zander. She's going at her speed, not yours. You've already convinced her and pushed her into this, into getting physical with you. Don't push her further. She'll start to shove you back harder."

He took a deep breath, looking for a way to tell Jasper how he was feeling.

"She's in her room, watching Netflix," the golden boy told him. "If you want to talk to her."

"She threw me out this morning," Zander muttered. She probably didn't want him up in her room at that moment.

"She didn't tell me that." Jasper sighed, putting his pen down. "Why?"

"I might have been an ass."

"What did you say?" Jasper pressed.

"'I'm sorry for caring,'" he repeated.

The curse that flew out of Jasper's mouth was impressive. "Go fucking apologize," he snapped. He flipped his notebook closed and glared back at Zander. Zander looked away as Jasper started to nail him to the wall over it. "Jesus. Zander. You...God, all this experience you have with women and you say something stupid as hell. *Again*. What the actual fuck is wrong with you?"

"I just want her to trust me with it," he mumbled.

"She will!" Jasper yelled. "In her time! Holy fuck. Go! Now!" Jasper pointed to the door. "Jesus, you just can't stop, it seems."

Zander ran out before Jasper could get angrier with him. It wasn't too often that Jasper raised his voice and yelled. He was a passive, decent guy - and normally right.

He didn't go to Sawyer's room though. He went across the hall and into Vincent and Elijah's office.

"Hiding in here?" the Italian asked as Zander walked in. "Come on."

Zander quietly went behind Elijah's desk and sank down.

"He's right," Vincent continued. "You should apologize to her."

"I just want her to trust me," he whispered. "Ya know?"

"Oh, yeah. I get it." Vincent sighed and put his book down. Zander saw that he looked tired. Not haggard like he used to, not worn out, just a little tired, like he'd gotten up too early. He seemed healthier now than he had before Texas. He was healthier-looking than he ever had been before they caught Axel. "She doesn't spend much time with me. We play a lot of chess. She doesn't tell me too much. The stuff she does tell me is stuff that also relates to me. About my nephew, about what she knew of Axel's organization." Vincent smiled softly. "She does trust you, though."

"No, she doesn't," Zander snapped.

"She lets you sleep with her," their CO reminded him. Zander swallowed and looked away. "She won't sleep with me."

"Why?" Zander asked. He'd forgotten her mentioning that in the morning and now that he thought about it, he didn't see her and Vincent together late at night. He also didn't pay too much attention to her activities with the others. He knew of the date because it had to be planned and it was something to tease them about.

"Because last time she tried to kill me," he answered. "She's scared that she'll do it again in another PTSD flashback. She has stuff to work out and it's inconvenient, but we need to live with that. She needs to get through her own problems."

"Fuck," Zander groaned. "You really have a way of putting things into perspective."

"You have a way with making small things into big problems. You're also short tempered and abrasive. You're as much of a fighter as she is, and while the arguments are funny, you need to stop." Vincent's tone grew hard at the end. "Hide in here until you're ready to go see her. Elijah is off getting Estella."

"Any advice?" Zander asked.

"Find an activity to do with her that isn't sex or arguing," Vincent answered, shrugging. "Might help you two find some common ground again. Work out, spar...don't spar, too close to fighting and it'll just lead to sex. Video games? I'm not sure she plays, but she might? You can introduce her to it?"

"Like chess?" he added sarcastically. He was being petulant, and he recognized it. He wasn't even sure why he'd decided to fuck with Vincent like that.

"Get out," the Italian ordered, pointing to his door. Zander glared at him, but Vincent didn't show any emotion. "I don't have to deal with the pissy attitude either."

He groaned and walked back out of the office. Thrown out by Vincent now. Fantastic. Just what he needed, to piss off everyone in the house. Now he just needed to find Quinn and Elijah to make the day complete.

He was constantly shoving his foot in his mouth. He was normally better at women, Jasper was right, but Sawyer always got to him. He wanted more, and she just shut down. Talking about anything serious was impossible, and when he tried to show affection, she practically ran or yelled at him.

Zander thought about that part. Slapping her ass hadn't been the smartest thing to do. He hadn't been thinking.

He really did have some shit to apologize for. Like always. It was becoming a pattern.

He made the long walk up to her attic room, noting that her cold magic now reached the bottom of the stairs up into the attic. It was a long way to bleed out. He'd expected it to stay in the attic, but he was constantly forgetting just how powerful Sawyer really was. She also had some serious depth to her Source, able to use her magic much more than he or Jasper could before burning out.

He knocked on the door and waited as patiently as he could. He wasn't going to screw up before he even got started by just barging into her room.

"Come in, Zander," Sawyer called out. He slipped in and closed the door quickly. There she was, laying on one of the couches and watching Netflix like nothing was wrong.

"Heard the date went good," he started, suddenly a bit worried he was going to mess this up.

"The date was wonderful," Sawyer confirmed, not looking at him. "Come sit down and tell me what's on your mind."

"I wanted to say I'm sorry." Zander sighed and sat down on the couch, lifting her feet to put them in his lap. He knew she hadn't gone out in sweatpants and a tank, so he assumed she must have changed to have a lazy day. "For being an ass. I shouldn't be slapping your ass and claiming it's how I show my affection. I just like your ass and wanted to touch it. And I know you're having a hard time with the nightmares still and I don't want to make it worse."

"You can't make it worse," Sawyer replied. "You can't make it easier or harder. It just is. Jasper has the magic to get in my head and help me through it. You don't. That's all."

"I just..."

"You want to be in everything," Sawyer finished. "I know."

"Do you want to play some video games?" he asked, hopeful. "It's what Jasper and I do to kill time and hang out without it getting too complicated. I get to be competitive and he gets to just unwind."

"If you get a system set up in here, yeah." She chuckled and looked down at him. "Call of Duty?"

"You know...?" Zander was a little shocked.

"I taught self-defense to kids and helped them with their homework," she reminded him. "You think I didn't spend my fair share of time playing video games with them?"

"Well, shit." He laughed. He hadn't thought about that. "We'll finish what you're watching, then set it up."

"You're forgiven, Zander," she told him suddenly. "But I'm tired. Of the arguing, of the foot-in-mouth syndrome, the nosiness. I'm tired of being tired. As for the ass thing, I don't know why it pissed me off at the time. I had to ask Jasper what we argued about yesterday, I couldn't remember."

"Are you saying that I could do it tomorrow and you might not get mad?" Zander asked incredulously. How was he supposed to work with that? He decided he just wouldn't. It was degrading, looking back. Slapping her ass was treating her like a piece of ass and she was more than that.

"Oh, well, nearly everything you do frustrates me more than if anyone else did it," Sawyer admitted a little guiltily. He saw a pleading smile on her face, as if she was begging for him to understand. "Sorry. You *are* an exasperating man."

"I'm sorry," he mumbled, beginning to rub her feet.

"Yeah, well," she huffed. "This is what real relationships are, right? Bickering, figuring stuff out?"

"I think so?" He hadn't had one in years. Girlfriends in high school were the last attempts at steady he had. After he'd been with her just that once, he'd decided he wouldn't go steady with anyone else. Only her. It was only ever her.

"We might need to ask someone else?" She laughed.

"We might," he agreed.

"You should know, I'm avoiding you tomorrow," she declared. "I need space, ya know? We're always right next to each other, and I think that might be part of the problem. Well, Elijah thinks it might be and I think I agree with him."

"Sure," Zander whispered. He wanted to be around her for every minute of the day, but he could see how living with three men who all want her could be smothering. All four, if she and Elijah finally went through on the flirting.

Five if Quinn could figure out he was already half in love with her.

After her show was done, he set up a system to play on. He handed her a controller and was grinning when Jasper walked in and joined them, sitting on the other couch.

This was what he wanted. Companionable moments where they were good and normal and together. He just needed to learn how not to shove his foot in his mouth. He was thankful that Sawyer was quick to forgive if someone admitted they had fucked up.

He would change for her. He wouldn't bother her about her nightmares; he wouldn't touch her in ways that made her feel like property. He could change. Most things. He was certain they were going to hit something that he couldn't change, but he was damn sure going to try. He loved her too much for his own idiocy to ruin what they had.

4

SAWYER

The next day, Sawyer was ready to go out with Elijah and Quinn for some relaxation. Between her nightmares, Jasper, Zander, Vincent, and finishing her GED, life had become exhausting. Her GED was finished, for which she was thanking the gods, whichever ones she could remember.

"Meet us out there," Elijah had told her when he'd left after the morning workout. She'd showered, relaxed, and let her muscles stop protesting before deciding to head out. Plus, nine am had been too early to go swimming - a little too cold - but the afternoon sun was still very warm at this time of year in Georgia, touching the eighties and making everyone sweat.

She walked out by herself, a tank and shorts over her bathing suit. She wasn't sure if Quinn or Elijah would wear one, but damn it, she would. She wasn't a complete heathen like them.

When she got to the waterhole, Elijah was already there, nude and laying out on her favorite rock. Sawyer sighed and jumped up next to him, maintaining enough distance that he couldn't reach her. She was over the casual nudity. It was a scene she'd seen often enough at this point: the barrel chest, the thick corded neck, the massive, broad shoulders. The thick, muscular thighs, the defined, lovely abdominals.

She could stare at it all day, so she ripped her eyes away before he could tell she was staring. So far his eyes had been closed, but that could change.

"How are you?" she asked, pulling off her tank and shorts and hanging them from a branch so they remained safe and dry. Unless Elijah or Quinn threw them in, which was a serious threat. She put her phone on another rock, far away from the water, so it didn't have a chance to get splashed. It sat next to Elijah's phone. The cellphones were sacred and would be safe.

"Doing better now that you're here," Elijah flirted.

She adjusted her swimsuit, a simple, all black bikini that let her get the best tan without going nude. "I'm glad to brighten your day," she replied before lying out next to him. "Where's Quinn?"

"Not here yet," he answered, waving around. "Obviously. He probably lost track of time while scribbling down those notes you've convinced him to do."

"I didn't convince him to do anything except try a little harder for me," she retorted. "He's doing better, from what I understand."

"Oh, yeah," he agreed. "Since you got involved, he's jumped a few years in the mandatory stuff. He's more confident about it. I just want him to remember to relax every now and then."

"You care for him so much," Sawyer noted. "He'll be fine though."

"I know." Elijah chuckled. She closed her eyes when he rolled to his side towards her. "How are you?"

"I would be better if you didn't interrupt my date yesterday." Sawyer teased, grinning. She wasn't mad about it anymore.

"I didn't interrupt your date," Elijah corrected. "I interrupted the post-date make out session in the garage."

"Prick," she said, reaching to swat his chest. She closed her eyes to soak up the sun and lost track of the time. She had probably fallen into a light sleep. A laugh woke her up and she felt water splash over her legs. She sat up and narrowed her eyes on the water.

The sight was breathtaking. Elijah was in waist-deep water, dripping wet in the afternoon sun. His cheeks were flushed with excitement and the heat. Quinn dove under the water where she couldn't see him.

"Get in the water, Sawyer!" Elijah called out to her, grinning like a mad fool. Right before Quinn pulled him under. Sawyer tossed her head back in a laugh as Quinn dragged Elijah into the deeper end, and when Elijah tried to get air, Quinn just shoved his head back under.

"Save me, Sawyer!" Elijah called out, between laughs.

"She isn't going to save you," Quinn growled, wrapping an arm around Elijah's waist. He forced Elijah back under.

"Quinn, be nice to the poor boy!" Sawyer yelled out, smirking. It was impressive that Quinn, leaner and smaller than Elijah, could take down the cowboy.

"He likes it," Quinn retorted. She saw that he didn't let go of Elijah though. Elijah took the chance to grab Quinn and drag them both under.

She sighed happily and enjoyed the sight of them roughhousing. She had little to no understanding of the friendship between them, but it was fun to watch the manliest men she knew play like boys. She knew they were nearly always together; they were keyed into each other's moods and protective of each other.

She laid back down and closed her eyes again, just listening to them laugh. She dozed back off.

She dreamed of sunny days. Of a happy moment with Henry, pushing him on a swing set. She had been pretending for him to be happy, to be excited for him to get out of the house and play. Looking back, it was one of her happiest memories, though at the time, she remembered aching. Her ribs had been bruised and she'd favored them for weeks after it.

But Axel would never ruin a good day where she took care of his son. He would let her out of the house, under close watch, to push him on the swing. She was burnt out, no magic left. All she could do was enjoy the moment with Henry, and it had become a small bright spot through a dark hell.

Then she and Henry made it home and he was sent to his room.

And she was alone with Axel. Her world went dark the moment she was alone with him.

She sat up and groped around, not sure what she was looking for, her heart racing. The sun was bright and hot, and the air was humid, but now the shade from trees was over her resting spot. She pushed to a standing position and nearly slipped off the rock.

"Sawyer?" Elijah called. "Sawyer, what's wrong?"

She gasped for air, trying to stand up straight. It had been a long time since waking up from a nightmare had rattled her like this.

"Sawyer." Quinn's hoarse whisper cut through and a hand grabbed her upper arm. It steadied her.

"A nightmare." She rubbed the scar on her chest with her free hand. "It's okay. I'll be okay."

"You are working with Jasper?" Quinn asked. Splashing of water told her that Elijah was also getting out.

"I am," Sawyer sighed. "I am and it's not going as quickly as I want it to but hell, at least I was able to wake up this time before..."

"Before?" Elijah inquired. "Sit."

She fell back on the rock, ignoring the shooting pain from landing too hard.

"She doesn't have to tell you," Quinn snapped, glaring around her to Elijah.

"She doesn't," Elijah agreed. He sat down next to her. "You can if you want to, though."

"I don't," Sawyer curtly informed him. "I would like to pretend it hasn't ruined my nice day."

"Whatever works," he murmured. He bumped shoulders with her and she sighed. "Go find one of your boys, let them make the day good again."

"Oh, for fuck's sake," Sawyer groaned, swatting Elijah on the chest. Quinn was laughing a little. "Can we just...forget about it?" She waved her hand, hoping to dismiss the entire conversation. Sex was the last thing she wanted. She couldn't even find the humor in the suggestion.

"If that's what you want," Elijah said, then they let silence fall.

Sawyer's mood had soured, and she got up. She grabbed her clothes down and pulled her tank on, then her shorts. She didn't say anything as she walked away, hoping the long walk back to the plantation house would clear her head.

"Can't have sex," Sawyer mumbled to herself, alone on the trail. Not after that nightmare. She'd sent Henry to his room, and while she was burnt out and magicless, Axel had raped her.

What a fucked up time that had been in her life. Over and over, she looked back and wondered if she could have changed things. Let that first assassin kill Axel. Tried to run earlier instead of being naïve enough to think that Axel loved her. Found and escaped with Midnight before she was killed, but then Sawyer wouldn't have been there for Henry. She could have taken Henry and disappeared later, but her fear of Axel's retribution had been paralyzing and her love for Henry had been too much for her to even consider walking away without him.

She was back at the plantation house and in her room when she realized that she forgot her phone back at the swimming hole.

"Fuck," Sawyer muttered angrily. She stormed back out of her room and outside, but didn't bother using her magic to make the trip to the swimming hole faster. She wanted the angry walk. Maybe it would burn off the soured mood and lighten her heart again.

She was close to the swimming hole when she heard the moan. She frowned but didn't stop walking closer. She did stop when the view of her favorite rock came into sight - and the two men on it.

Chest to chest, they were staring at each other. Quinn was laid out on the rock, Elijah propped up on his hands over him. Quinn grabbed Elijah's messy hair and pulled him down, and bit his lower lip, tugging on it roughly.

Sawyer watched Quinn roll them over, a growl erupting from his chest. She winced in sympathy at the hard impact Elijah had with the stone. It didn't stop, though. Elijah grabbed the feral Magi and swung him back down as well. It continued like that for several moments, and she didn't like the aggressiveness about it. She wondered if she should step in and stop the fighting, but when she took a step forward, another thought crossed her mind.

They were wrestling for dominance.

And the cowboy finally won, it seemed, when he grabbed Quinn's hips, forcing him to stay down.

Sawyer's breath caught at the sight of Elijah kissing his way down Quinn's chest. She had walked back in on them having a tryst. Quinn raised his head to watch the cowboy as well, panting. She didn't blame him for wanting to watch either.

Her heart raced, and she wasn't entirely certain as to why. There was something immensely erotic about the sight of Elijah licking over Quinn's abs on his way down to his incredibly hard cock.

She was captivated, but her mind was screaming for her to turn around and walk away. She had known they were close and that Elijah played both fields.

This was not what she had been expecting.

She flirted with Elijah constantly and he flirted back. He was with *Quinn*. They were *lovers*. She just kept watching, realizing it was a serious turn on to watch Elijah make Quinn's head fall back as he took the head of Quinn's cock into his mouth.

Quinn's head rolled to look in her direction and she locked her gaze with the ice-blues of the feral Magi. Fear ran through her for getting caught just stunned and watching them. She would kill a person for walking in on her and a lover. Guilt at her accidental voyeurism filled her chest. This wasn't her business and she had no right to stand around and get off from it.

She didn't say anything, just turned and blinked away. Out of sight of the swimming hole, she ran. She flew into the back door of the plantation house, out of breath. She didn't even get her phone. She'd completely forgotten about it the moment she had seen them.

"Fuck," she gasped, placing a hand on her chest. She hadn't been in the mood thanks to the nightmare, but that sight had woken up her sex drive in seconds. She never thought two built, gorgeous men getting off together would do anything for her. "I need answers."

She walked to Vincent's office and through the door, not bothering to knock or use the door knob. She startled Vincent enough for him to mess up the papers he had in front of him.

"Are Quinn and Elijah in a relationship?" she demanded, pointing towards Elijah's desk like he was there. "Am I flirting with a taken man?"

Vincent's eyebrows flew up, but he remained silent.

Sawyer waved dramatically to Elijah's desk. "Am I stepping on something that I shouldn't?" she snapped.

"No," Vincent replied carefully. He stood up slowly and walked to her. "No."

"There's a 'but' there, I can feel it," she said angrily. She was not a whore who stole boyfriends or lovers from other people. She wasn't going to be the thing that ruined whatever those two had going on, and she was honestly getting very pissed off that Elijah constantly flirted with her. He was with someone else, someone she respected. They were all supposed to be friends and he was...

"You should talk to Elijah and Quinn about Elijah and Quinn." Vincent sighed. "I can tell you that it's not as bad as you think though."

"He's with Quinn and also in this stupid deal," Sawyer yelled.

"He's not...fuck," he mumbled. "Sit down. Tell me what happened."

"I saw them!" she roared.

"Excuse me?" he sputtered. "You *saw* them together?"

"Yeah. I left my phone out there on accident and went back to get it. I must have snuck up on them accidentally." She took a deep breath as she explained, trying to calm down. "Quinn saw me." She felt faint at that and sank into the chair in front of Vincent's desk.

"Sawyer, there's no way, under any circumstance, that you can sneak up on Quinn," he told her plainly. "If you saw them together, he let you see them together. He would have felt you coming the moment you stepped foot in the woods."

"Oh my god," she groaned. "He's going to kill me. Quinn is going to kill me."

"No, he's not." He chuckled. "I think you should wait to talk to them before making any assumptions."

"I can't look them in the eye anymore, that much is certain. Vincent, I saw Elijah sucking-"

"Don't tell me what you saw. Please." Vincent waved a hand to cut her off. "Please don't." He muttered a small curse and went back to his own seat. "They should have told you about their arrangement earlier. It's not like it's a secret that we're trying to keep or anything. I just felt they should tell you, not me, Zander, or Jasper. It's their thing."

"Arrangement?" Sawyer frowned at the choice of words. Not relationship.

"Yes. Arrangement. Quinn is, or at least was, feral. We all know it. He can't go out and pick up some chick from a bar, Sawyer. Or a guy if he's in the mood for it. I'm not sure he cares either way. Whatever floats his boat at whatever moment he's considering it. Elijah and Quinn are best friends, nearly brothers in spirit, and their bond is deep. I'm not sure I even understand it." He took a long, slow breath. "But they are not in a relationship as far as my understanding goes. I think the best term would be fuck buddies."

"Oh." Casual. Friends with benefits. That changed things a little. It also made more sense. Quinn didn't seem like the type of person who would commit, and not because she thought he was noncommittal. He probably just saw the sex as a separate thing from the friendship.

"Yes. Oh." Vincent chuckled. "Why did this freak you out, Sawyer?"

"Because Elijah is in this little deal," Sawyer admitted. She had intentions of eventually sleeping with him. She couldn't resist one day saying yes to his flirtatious ass and seeing how it went. "I don't know, really. I don't do men who are with other people. I'm not the other woman and never will be." She thought a little harder. "I don't want to hurt Quinn."

"I don't think I'm the person to explain this to you," Vincent whispered. "They will be fine. You will be fine. I can't really help past telling you that you aren't getting between them by flirting and maybe being with Elijah."

"Yeah, I'm beginning to realize I may have overreacted," Sawyer replied. "Actually, I feel kind of stupid now."

"If it helps, when I found out after they started, I accused Elijah of taking advantage of Quinn." She heard laughter in Vincent's story. "Quinn was young, barely twenty. He was obviously unaccustomed to our ways of doing things, and I found him and Elijah in bed together. I accused Elijah of seeing someone he could easily get in bed with."

"What happened?" she asked, shifting to get more comfortable in the chair.

"We were living in a smaller place, a temporary location.

We had to move. Quinn nearly brought it down on my head for making the assumption," he finished.

"See, that sounds much more like Quinn than what I had been thinking. I'm so happy I didn't accuse Elijah to his face for trying to cheat on Quinn with me." She would have. She was feeling a bit idiotic. She knew better than to jump to conclusions. She'd been worked up by the scene and bombarded by new implications of what it meant for her and them, the friendship she had with them.

"Yeah, thankfully you came in here and didn't do that."

Sawyer was still uncomfortable though. The sight had turned her on and she'd violated their privacy. She was embarrassed over her actions. She was disturbed that she was turned on when she'd just had a nightmare that should have warned her off sex for at least a week.

"Sawyer?"

"I'm fine," she answered. She looked over to the chess board. "Want to play?"

"Why?"

"It would give me something to do for the day." She didn't have much else to do and she hadn't spent time with Vincent in a few days outside of their workouts.

"Want to go get out of your bathing suit first?" He stood back up and went to set the board up.

"No, I'm good," she replied, moving to sit on the black side of the board. When he sat down on the white side, he didn't start.

"Something else is bothering you," he commented. She knew better than to play evasive with Vincent. He would get what he wanted before the game of chess was over. It's how he'd gotten her to admit to not sleeping with him because of the nightmares. Because of what she had done the last time they were in bed together.

49

"I had a nightmare while just laying out on the rocks. It really got to me," Sawyer told him. "Between that and seeing them, I've had a weird day. It started good. Now I'm not sure what it is."

"Okay," Vincent sighed. "I take it you won't tell me what the nightmare was?"

She decided to throw him for a loop. If she was going to get shocked and surprised today, then he would too. So she gave him the information he didn't think he would get. "I was playing with Henry," she whispered. "It started as a happy memory. I woke up right as it took a dark turn."

"Dark turn?" Vincent repeated back to her. She looked into his eyes and saw that little bit of haunted and broken there.

"I brought Henry home. Axel was feeling randy. I sent Henry to his room. Axel raped me," she explained. She frowned, considering a perverse thought. "Is it rape if I let him, even if I didn't want it?"

"I think it was," he answered in a strangled, choking way that made her wince.

"It was a long time ago," she reminded him, hoping it accounted for something, anything.

"For you," he mumbled. "I've only known for a couple short months."

"I'm sorry. I shouldn't unload this kind of stuff on you." Sawyer groaned and leaned back in the chair. "It's unfair. He's your brother." This was why she wasn't sleeping with him. She didn't think he deserved all the horrors of Axel Castello, once a brother he loved.

"He hasn't been my brother for a long time," he said with conviction. "You're my friend, though. I'm always willing to hear it. Always. You understand?"

"I'm not always willing to share," she replied. "*You* understand?"

"Better than most here." He pushed a pawn forward. She looked down and mindlessly pushed one of her own. "I'm always willing to listen when you're willing to share."

Complicated. Sawyer hated how things were always so goddamned complicated. She and Vincent didn't have the same level of pain between them like before, but it was still there. They had this complicated history they would never escape, which led to a complicated relationship and complicated feelings.

"Thanks," she said.

They played silently after that and Sawyer appreciated the peace. She was beginning to find refuge in Vincent and their chess games. They were quiet, thoughtful moments in a world of chaos and explosive personalities.

"Check," he announced.

"Of course," she mumbled. She'd only won once so far, and it had been sheer luck. She moved her king in hopes to save herself, but she knew it was about to be over.

"Would you...like to come see me tonight?" he asked, refusing to look up from the board.

"I don't think it's a good idea," she answered. "I don't want to hurt you."

"I figured I would ask." Vincent sighed and moved his Queen. "Checkmate."

"Vincent," she whispered. "I really don't want to hurt you. You have to understand that."

"I do," he said. There was something closed-off about it. She didn't know where to go from there, so she stood up and began to walk out. "Wait, Sawyer." She looked back at him and felt awful for the sadness in his eyes. "I'm fine with waiting, but I do want more than this. More than chess games and work."

"I don't know what to give you," she admitted. "I don't, Vincent. All I have is nightmares and I don't know how to... Jasper is helping. Once I feel like it's safe, I'll come back to your room, Vincent. I'm not trying to avoid you or put you to the side. I'm just scared of hurting you."

"We have a trip to New York coming up," he reminded her. "We leave in a week. I...bought us tickets to something. I was hoping you would go out with me to see it."

"I would like that, actually," Sawyer told him honestly. "Really. And thanks for the reminder about New York, I had forgotten. Other things on my mind."

"I think everyone has. It's just a standard visit so they can give us an evaluation on how the case in Texas was handled. It shouldn't be anything serious."

"Let's hope," Sawyer huffed.

Vincent walked over to her and she took the chance to see how he looked, to really appreciate it. He was so put together now. His white button-down shirt was pressed and tucked into slacks that were also perfectly pressed, with that clean fold down the front. He'd shaved in the morning, that was also obvious, even with some stubble already coming back. He even had his dark, curly hair styled. She wanted to mess it up.

The idea of ruining his image made her want more.

When he was closer, she grabbed his shirt and pulled him the rest of the way. She ran her other hand through his hair, thoroughly ruining his styling. He kissed her roughly, realizing what she was trying to do. Her back hit the door and she let him pin her there, with no escape. Well, she could escape by phasing through the wood, but she liked to pretend he had her at his mercy.

"I don't like you put together." The words had all sorts of implications.

"Then mess me up." Vincent chuckled, kissing her neck.

She did, untucking his shirt and unbuttoning it deftly. She was annoyed with the undershirt keeping her from his skin, so she pulled that out of his pants too. She slid her hands under it and ran her nails over his abs, making him hiss with need.

Someone tried to open the door, causing it to whack her on the back of the head. She growled at the pain as Vincent backed away so she could get out of its way.

Elijah walked in and laughed the moment he saw them. "I was looking for you, Sawyer." He held up her phone. "You left this at the swimming hole. I see you're busy with Vincent though, so here. I'll go. You two kids enjoy yourselves."

Sawyer snatched it and shoved it into her pocket. She looked back to Vincent and he just nodded. *Oh shit.* He wanted her to talk to Elijah about *his* sex life.

She was nervous as fuck now. "Wait," she blurted out.

Elijah raised his eyebrows.

"Sawyer needs to talk to you," Vincent explained. "About you and Quinn."

"What about Quinn and me?" Elijah frowned.

"I saw..." Sawyer took a deep breath. She really had no idea how to broach this topic. She just jumped straight in. "I saw you sucking his dick. Which isn't a big deal, you do you, but we flirt and...well, I thought there was something going on between us and it threw me for a loop."

5

ELIJAH

E lijah stepped all the way into the office and closed the door after she closed her mouth. That wasn't what he'd been expecting. He figured he would walk in on her and Vincent doing something, though he figured it would be chess, not what looked like a make out session.

Tit for tat, he thought. He seemed to catch her in positions she probably didn't want him to, and now it seems she saw him in one. Well, Elijah wasn't sure how he felt about her seeing him go down on Quinn. He knew he was a little mad at Quinn. Quinn would have known she was coming for a long time before it even got started. Elijah was fine with a little voyeurism, but it needed to be acknowledged by all parties beforehand. And why hadn't Quinn told him *after* that Sawyer had seen them?

"What did Vincent already tell you?" He assumed Vincent already told her something. She would have either stopped Elijah and Quinn for an explanation or gone to one of the guys for an explanation. She wouldn't have sat on it and stewed alone, not when it came to any of the team. She was too direct for that. Sawyer wasn't going to keep secrets or allow them to be kept from her.

"That you guys are pretty much friends with benefits." Sawyer raised her hands. "I'm cool. That's fine. It's not my business, ya know?"

"But we flirt and you..." Elijah was looking for the whole story.

"Jumped to conclusions that I shouldn't have before talking to Vincent," Sawyer admitted. "They don't need repeating."

Elijah went to his desk and sat down on the front of it. He felt a little bad. He should have told Sawyer before she saw anything. It would have kept this very strange situation from happening. He wasn't sure why he and Quinn hadn't talked to her about it yet. Busy? Meeting her, her past, her joining the team, her and Vincent, Texas. There had been so much going on that it just never seemed important.

"Quinn and I aren't a couple," Elijah declared. "He and I find physical comfort in each other, but it's only ever strengthened our friendship, nothing else."

"Yeah, I've pretty much gotten that," Sawyer replied.

"I don't think you do, not really." He sighed. She was defensive as hell. He wondered what else was bothering her about it. "You thought if I do anything with anyone else, I'm cheating on Quinn and you don't think that's okay."

"I mean, I have three boyfriends, so I realize the hypocrisy of the thought I had. And really, it's not my business." Elijah crossed his arms and just kept listening to her. "I just, for a second, was very confused. About everything, me and you, you and him. It's fine, though. Not my business and I'll make sure not to act like there's anything wrong with it because there's not."

"Sawyer, if you get it, what's eating at you?" he asked,

grinning. He was figuring it out. There was a blush spreading over her cheeks and she glanced at Vincent, who shrugged. Elijah looked at Vincent, looking completely ruined. Shirts untucked and pulled up high enough to see his abs, his hair looking like he rolled out of bed.

He wanted Sawyer to admit it.

"Nothing that needs mentioning," she told him, hard. She narrowed her eyes, her face still flushed.

"Yup." Elijah's grin felt like it was going to get stuck there. God, this woman was great. She was tough and direct and then completely out of her depth and didn't know what to do. She definitely wasn't going to admit that she thought seeing him and Quinn get busy was sexy as hell. He knew she did based on her flustered reaction.

"I'm sorry for invading your privacy and seeing it," Sawyer said quickly. "It wasn't my intention. I actually went back for my phone."

"You could have said something, and we would have stopped. You didn't invade anything, just caught us in a moment. Everyone here has done it at least once. No harm, no foul," he said, making it sound like a promise. "It didn't weird you out though? Two guys?"

"I don't really care if you are two guys, two girls, or two apes," she replied, crossing her arms as well. "I cared because you're two of my friends, and I flirt with you and I didn't know if I was going to ruin something I didn't know about."

"And you aren't going to ruin anything because there's nothing to ruin." Elijah confirmed. "It's okay. We're best friends, Quinn and I. We don't have sex that often. We just both crave some physical affection and that's the extreme end of it." He shrugged. "Sawyer, I've had sex with other people for years and he's never been possessive or had a problem with it. If anything, he encourages it. If he ever found someone else he trusted to be with, I would probably adore that person. They would need to be someone special for him to trust them, especially a woman."

He was pretty sure he already knew the person Quinn would trust enough. Elijah already adored her.

"Well, that's good to know," Sawyer announced, nodding in a formal, prompt way he figured she got from Vincent. "I'm going to get out of my bathing suit now."

"Have fun," he purred as she walked out. He loved the bathing suit on her and he so wished to see what she looked like without it. He'd seen her naked before, but he hadn't gotten the chance yet to commit it to memory, and he wanted to. He saw the scars, but he wanted to *know* them.

"That was interesting," Vincent remarked mildly.

Elijah resisted the urge to tease the Italian for the disheveled state he was in. He could barely contain a reference to his new nickname for their CO, the Italian boy toy. Since he didn't want to mess with Vincent, he directed his thoughts to Quinn. "I'm going to strangle him," he said nonchalantly.

"Quinn?" Vincent frowned at him. "Why?"

"He damned sure knew she was there and never bothered to mention it. I would have preferred not to get blindsided." Elijah told him. "I'll get him back tonight. He's coming inside. The nights are getting too cold for him."

"I'm glad to know he's not out there freezing."

Elijah just nodded, silently agreeing with Vincent. Quinn very rarely slept indoors, even in his own room. He only came inside consistently during the winter, when it was too cold for a simple fire to keep him warm or too much work, since Elijah knew that Quinn grew up in Northern Canada, tucked away deep in the wilderness. He knew how to stay warm, but he was getting lazier with the conveniences of the civilized world. Every year, Quinn came inside for the winter earlier and left during the spring later.

Lots of things about Quinn were changing. He used to give Elijah a warning when someone was going to walk in on them, once he knew it wasn't normal to walk in on someone having sex. Gave them both a chance to semi-prepare for it.

Elijah was half mad Quinn hadn't said anything and beginning to get very curious as to why. Why would Quinn let Sawyer walk up on them?

He sat down in his chair and continued to ponder it. Quinn would have known well ahead of time that she was coming, so before they even had gotten started. Quinn had initiated it. He'd been hard and willing, and Elijah was more than happy to help a friend out, so he'd gone along with it.

Quinn was being a sneaky shit and that made Elijah curious.

"I'm going to shower," he announced, walking out before Vincent could say anything.

He headed for his bathroom and caught the distinct sound of Sawyer and Zander bickering up in the attic. Elijah chuckled, looking up to the ceiling, directly underneath them, and waited to see if it would escalate. Zander was going to lose his girl if he didn't learn how to install a filter between his brain and mouth. Elijah hoped it didn't happen, but he also wasn't going to fix Zander's problems for him. The guy was emotionally immature and inexperienced with relationships.

Elijah chuckled. Zander and Jasper were exact opposites. Elijah wondered how in the hell they had remained friends for so long, and Sawyer being in the house only made those differences more apparent. Zander:

experienced in the bedroom but awful at pretty much everything else, which was made worse by his rash behavior and recklessness. Jasper: no experience with the bedroom, or none that mattered, but he was an intelligent and decent fellow, if a bit shy about it all and insecure.

Elijah stripped and carelessly tossed his clothes on the floor. He didn't really like living like a slob, but it was one of the few ways to get at Vincent. He thought Vincent was anal about folding clothes and being neat at every possible opportunity, and Elijah needed him to loosen the fuck up. It was a stark reminder that he was Axel's brother. Vincent wasn't an OCD, narcissistic neat-freak like Axel, and Elijah wanted him to stop pretending to be.

Once the water was hot, he stepped inside and sighed happily. A hot shower after a day at the swimming hole was pure bliss. The only thing that would make it better was her there to help with his back.

The thought made him hard. Elijah groaned and looked down at himself. He'd just gotten off in the woods. The damn thing had no right to demand more.

"Fuck," he mumbled, wrapping a hand around it. He stroked himself slowly, hoping to just get it done and over. One thought stuck in his mind through the entire thing. Sawyer watching him with Quinn. What if the tables had turned? What if he watched her and Quinn? Or Quinn watched him and her?

Or he had them both?

The mere idea finished him, and he leaned back on the wall of the shower. He thought he knew why Quinn let her sneak up on them.

And everyone calls me the pervert.

Elijah finished washing and moved to his bedroom. He

picked up a sketchbook off his dresser and sat down at his desk in the quiet.

"Turn on station, genre, Country," Elijah told his sound system. "Volume, four." He called a pencil to his hand with his telekinesis and opened the sketchbook. Sawyer was on every page, and he was about to add another. He had another sketchbook full of Quinn. Another full of his family, which now had updated versions, since he'd seen them in Texas.

The horrified look on her face when she had woken up from her nap in the sun.

The look had freaked him out. It's why he needed to draw it, put it on paper. Get it out of his mind.

When he was done with the details of her wide eyes, looking at something he couldn't see, he closed the sketchbook and placed his hand over it.

"Elijah. Quinn is in and wants to cook more of the venison." Vincent's voice politely interrupted his silence.

He groaned. He needed to enchant the sketchbook before he went down.

Enchanting was about intent and power. His intent was that the sketchbook couldn't be opened by anyone except him. He pushed his magic into the sketchbook, a lot of it and it was like filling an empty bowl with power, or wrapping something in paper, depending on what he was doing. This was a wrap, an external enchantment. He was powerful enough that nearly no one could break past it. Quinn could, but would respect his privacy, but none of the other guys could even attempt it. Elijah made this enchantment to keep nosy Sawyer from discovering just how much he watched her, looked at her, thought about her. She would be able to break it, if she was inclined, but she would need to work for it and then he would know she was trying.

She had enough on her plate without him adding another person to the dance around her bed. And Quinn. He had to look out for Quinn, so he didn't get lonely if they all fell for Sawyer, who desperately seemed to want none of them to fall for her and was just accepting her poor fate.

Elijah tucked the sketchbook into a drawer and left his room.

He found Quinn rubbing down several large pieces of venison, steak cuts.

"We need to talk after dinner," Elijah warned him.

"Okay?" The wolf-like Magi frowned at him and Elijah raised an eyebrow. Quinn shrugged and went back to what he was doing.

Dinner went well. He was always happy to cook anything Quinn caught for the team. They all enjoyed it, since it broke up the monotony of Chinese takeout and whatever they could buy for groceries. Elijah wondered why no one had commercialized venison yet. It was delicious, and Quinn had tricks about how to treat the meat that made it more tender than some of the best beef.

"I'll do dishes," Sawyer announced, pushing her plate away from her. "It's my turn, I think." Elijah watched her leave. She'd been quiet for the meal and that was unusual. He collected the plates she couldn't carry and followed.

"What's on your mind, little lady?" Elijah asked, throwing out the scraps they had leftover before putting the plates on the counter next to her.

"I was on the Dark Web earlier. Argued with Zander about it. Nothing important."

"Why are you on the Dark Web?" he groaned. He knew

she shouldn't be doing that. *She* knew she shouldn't be doing it.

"Truthfully?" Sawyer shrugged. "Boredom and a touch of curiosity."

"You know, next time you're bored, you know where my room is. Come see me. I promise not to be annoying like Zander," he whispered, sliding a hand over her lower back.

"You mean you won't make me scream in frustration?" she gasped. "I fucking hope so. Two people like that and I might start killing people again."

"I would make you scream from a lot of things, but I'll never leave you frustrated." Elijah kept the comment light, teasing and flirtatious, but he was confident in the truth of it. Her cheeks turned a little flushed and flustered, and she swatted his abs with a wet, soapy hand. "You walked into that one, Sawyer."

"I seem to walk into all of them with you," she said while chuckling. She waved him away. "All right, you get out and let me do this. Fucking pervert. Distracting, incessant pervert."

He laughed as he left her to the dishes. He grabbed Quinn in the hallway, who willingly followed him without a single word.

Elijah took them to Quinn's room and locked the door once they were inside. He paused, unlocked the door, let the wolves in, then relocked it. Shade and Scout jumped up on Quinn's bed and curled into furry balls, their tails covering their faces.

"You couldn't warn me?" he asked immediately.

"Warn you?" Quinn frowned at him.

"That Sawyer was there at the swimming hole while we were getting down and dirty? While I went down on you?

She didn't see anything else." Like Elijah flipping Quinn over and taking him from behind.

"Oh!" Quinn's face turned to shock, and a bit of 'oh shit.' It was an expression people didn't see on Quinn very often. "Um."

"Words," he muttered. "Use them."

"I didn't think you would mind?" Quinn said cautiously, a little confused. "I didn't think it was a big deal?"

"You know it's a big deal. You know that people need to be aware of these things," he replied, groaning. "You know that. And her! We hadn't told her anything was physical between us. Quinn, you blindsided her. She freaked out. Thought we were a couple and that I was going to cheat on you with her."

"I don't..." Quinn frowned now. "I don't think like that."

"Yeah, she remembered that part after." He huffed. "Quinn, come on. There's another reason, and you need to tell me."

"She and I don't spend a lot of time together now." Quinn sighed and sat on his bed.

"You spend a lot of time together," he retorted. "You're together nearly every other day, pouring over books as she helps you with your education, since she does better than Vincent."

"Yeah but that's work," Quinn snapped. "It's not anything else. I want to...take her hunting, and swim more, and other things. I don't want to be another piece of work for her and I want more than a teacher."

"She's your friend, too. What did you want by her seeing us?" Elijah murmured. He would have faked some confusion, but the wolves would have told Quinn it wasn't real. They were probably reporting Elijah's every scent to Quinn.

"I let her walk up on us..." He took a deep breath. "I hoped she would join."

Elijah heard it, filed it away for a later moment, and then started to laugh. He fucking knew it. "You should tell her you think of her that way," Elijah told him, grinning like a fool.

"She looks at me like a little brother," he growled.

"I don't think she thinks of you that way. She finds you attractive too." Elijah reminded him, sitting down next to him. "She's just a woman with a lot on her plate, and she can't read your mind, Quinn. You were also pretty fucking abrasive when she first got here so she probably sees you as off limits, probably thinks you aren't interested."

"She's different from other women," he whispered. "Other women would have joined."

"She is?" He thought that Sawyer was just a fantastic woman, but not overtly different. Unique in her own ways, but still very much a woman.

"Different from women I know...knew," Quinn explained. "A Druid would have joined, and I thought, Sawyer is powerful and she's taking what she wants now - she would join. Hopefully."

"Sawyer isn't a Druid." Elijah growled, suddenly angry that Quinn was even still thinking about the women who tore up his body and ruined his self-worth. That left him feral, uneducated, and alone. Who had done their best to destroy him. "I would hope she's fucking different. She gives a damn. They didn't."

"She's afraid of me," he continued. "She won't want to be in bed with a male who could hurt her. Axel was more powerful than her and look what he did."

Elijah cursed. Quinn was so perceptive, but past the fact that he and Axel were more powerful than her, there was literally nothing else in common. He knew that fighting the comparison was a losing battle, though. Quinn was looking at relationship dynamics with her like a pack structure and power was important in a pack structure. Her history with powerful men...well, there was no denying it, and Elijah was partially impressed that Quinn was thinking on it when he thought of her. It meant Quinn was considering emotions, thoughts and feelings when he thought of her.

"Why are you thinking about Druids?" He changed the topic. "And just remember to let me know if Sawyer is about to walk up on us. I can handle it differently. Be prepared for it, at least."

"She liked it." Quinn chuckled. "Shade followed her scent. She liked the scene."

That much Elijah had figured out on his own. He didn't miss that Quinn changed the topic. "The Druids," Elijah reminded him. "You haven't willingly talked or even thought about them in a long time."

"Something is going on that has me uncomfortable. I can feel Druids to the south using their magic to its full potential. It just has me itchy. It hits like waves, every few nights, two or three Druids, full power, washing over the land." Quinn shrugged. "It has nothing to do with me, but it's unusual. It's just making me itchy and won't let me stop thinking about them."

He was uncomfortable just hearing about it. Quinn was immensely strong, dangerously powerful, and to feel anyone's magic from that sort of distance was something no other Magi could probably do. Elijah sure as hell didn't feel anything and he was one of the most powerful Magi in the house, nearly even with Sawyer.

"Would other Druids here in North America feel anything?" He rubbed his hands together, as his mind whirled. Were they all so powerful to feel each other across the globe?

"Of course. Probably every Druid on the planet would know something is going on down there, and they probably know what. I'm not going to ask any of them." Quinn let out a growl when he was done. "They wouldn't tell me anyway, since I hate them so much."

"I know you do," he whispered. Quinn had so many reasons to hate Druids. The scars on his back were a visual reminder of it every day.

"Anything else you want?" Quinn asked, looking to him. Druid talk was over, Elijah knew it. Quinn wasn't going to want to stick on them for longer than he needed to.

"No. I really just wanted to give you a hard time over Sawyer," he admitted.

"Sorry," Quinn mumbled. "I won't try that again. I don't know why I thought my idea would work."

"Don't think I wouldn't find it amusing. I would probably give my left testicle for a time like that. Just next time tell me before you try to make it happen. And maybe her." Elijah chuckled, covering his face. Quinn was so bad at these things. At least he wasn't fighting with her like Zander; he just had no confidence in being someone important to her. He had no confidence in anything that had to do with 'civilized' people. If she were a Druid, Quinn would have already found a way to express himself and got her in his bed, but she wasn't, and that made all the difference, since Quinn hated Druids and women because of them. She was the farthest thing from a Druid Elijah could imagine.

Whether it ever happened or not, Elijah knew those two would also be friends, and he hoped Quinn saw that as being important to her.

"I'm going to bed," he declared, standing up and

stretching. Quinn wrapped an arm around his waist and held him so he couldn't walk away.

"You want her too," Quinn whispered, knowingly.

"I do," he confirmed. "You've known that."

"You don't want her like I want her," Quinn corrected. "You want her the way Jasper does, or Vincent."

"And what's that mean?" He demanded, turning to look down at the other Magi.

"You know exactly what I mean," Quinn said before releasing Elijah. "I want her physically. You want her...feelings."

"You have lost your mind," Elijah teased. Then he left the room before perceptive and strange Quinn could call him out on anything else.

Yeah, Elijah wanted her more than just as a friend, or friend with benefits. Something he hadn't wanted from another person for a very long time. He just didn't want Quinn to talk about it. Or anyone else, including Vincent, who said things in Texas Elijah hadn't wanted to hear.

He was fine continuing to lie to everyone else about it. And he knew Quinn was now also lying to himself. Quinn wanted more than just her body too, but Rogue Wolf had no idea how to love a woman.

6

SAWYER

"Are you ready for New York?" Vincent asked Sawyer the moment she walked into his office. She'd come down at his command, since he'd had a question. She didn't understand why he couldn't just ask the question he wanted through his damn telepathy, but she had come downstairs anyway just for him to do so.

On further consideration, she would have needed to come downstairs to answer it anyway. She was still irked that he just hadn't asked it using telepathy and given her the chance to think of an answer on the way downstairs.

"Yeah? Why wouldn't I be?" Sawyer frowned at him. "We leave tomorrow. Of course I packed already."

"Good, that means we can relax for the evening." Vincent chuckled humorlessly, his eyes rolling to the ceiling. "Elijah is already begging me for a movie night or even a night at the bar before we go. Something for the entire team to do since we've been a bit scattered outside of workouts."

"Fantastic," Sawyer mumbled. "Let's do the bar. We don't go out enough and I haven't been yet."

"I'll let him know. Go get ready and pass on the word to your other guys. I'll tell Elijah and Quinn," Vincent ordered. This was something of a common occurrence now. Sawyer handled Jasper and Zander while Vincent took care of Elijah and Quinn. She would trade him if she thought he would accept. Again, she didn't know why he didn't just tell everyone telepathically. "And Sawyer?"

"Yeah?" She looked back at him before she left his office.

"No weapons in New York." Vincent's smile was knowing, and she glared at him for a moment before walking back out of the room. Like hell was she going to New York in front of a ton of imps and military men without her blades.

"I'm serious, Sawyer. Don't make me have to check before we leave for the airport."

She cursed and made a mental note to take the twelve-inch daggers and throwing knives out of her bag. She didn't want to get reprimanded over it and forced to leave them behind anyway. And that's what he would use his telepathy for? To remind her to take her blades out of her bag?

She hit the second floor and went straight for Jasper's door first, feeling both of them through the door. She knocked twice before pushing it open to see Jasper and Zander lying on the bed with controllers.

"What's up?" Jasper asked as she walked in and looked around. She didn't go to anyone's room very often. They normally came to hers, which she preferred. Her space, her domain, where she would feel more comfortable. Jasper had gone for blues throughout the room, falling into more blue greys, stormy like his eyes.

"We're going to the bar tonight," Sawyer said, looking around. "Nice room." Hers was also in blues, though she had since changed her sheets and comforter to dark greys and blacks. She was slowly making it more her and less whatever they had originally come up with.

"Thanks," he said back quickly, jumping off the bed.

Zander followed him more slowly and stalked over to Sawyer. "We're going out, huh?" he asked, grinning.

"We are going to the bar," she repeated. "The entire team. Something fun to do before we head to New York."

"Vincent's getting soft. He hates doing things the night before anything important. Says we should get our rest." He laughed. "I'll go put on something nice. Please wear those leather pants."

Sawyer groaned with exaggeration after he kissed her cheek and walked out. She rolled her eyes to Jasper, who smiled innocently.

"I'll get ready now." He pulled off his tee shirt and she took a hissing intake of air at the sight. "Are you just going to stare or are you going to get ready, too?"

"Christ," she mumbled. She kept staring at his bare chest though. Her eyes trailed down a little. She'd seen him shirtless before, but she was living in a house with men who were expected to stay in peak physical condition. She appreciated the sight every time she got the chance, now with a lot less reserve than she had before. She blinked a couple of times and smiled innocently back at Jasper. "I can see why you aren't worried about losing a leg. The rest of you makes up for it."

The comment made his cheeks flush with that pink she loved. "Get out of here," he told her, stumbling over the words a little. "Before you make me more embarrassed."

"You started it," Sawyer reminded him, pointing at the discarded shirt. Teasing Jasper about his sex appeal: new favorite pastime, and hopefully it would get him to accept his beauty. He was such a good boy, but she wanted more of that man she knew was underneath. "Maybe you should keep your clothes on if you don't want me to notice what's underneath them." She turned and began to walk out.

"I'll remember that," he called out as she was leaving.

"Please, forget it whenever you want," Sawyer called back, laughing through the words.

She changed in her own room, and she did pick out the leather pants, sliding into them. They hugged and held the best parts, and smothered the less desirable ones. She chose a black tee, not wanting to go all out on her outfit. She pulled her hair from its ponytail and shook it around, then went to her shared bathroom to see what she had done.

"I need to brush that," she sighed. She grabbed a brush off the counter and began to tame her hair. It was too long, too curly, full of thick waves that made a mess of things when it got wet and didn't get brushed soon enough. She was beginning to wonder if she should cut it all off, but the idea left a bad taste in her mouth. Her long hair was the most feminine thing about her, except for the tits, ass, and vagina.

She felt she was looking presentable when she left the bathroom and walked down to the kitchen, finding Elijah there with Quinn, *both* ready to go.

"Quinn, you're coming?" Sawyer tilted her head in some confusion. She knew Vincent said the entire team, but she had yet to ever see Quinn go to town for any reason. Even if by chance he needed something, someone else would go pick it up for him. If they could, they would order it online on a rush delivery.

"I am," he answered. She looked him over slowly. He was wearing *jeans*. And *real shoes*, loafers, not just the uniform boots she'd only ever seen him in. Hell, most of the time, he was barefoot. She didn't even want to consider the dark button-down shirt he was in. She felt like she was looking at a different man. He must have noticed her shock at his appearance. "Yes. I can dress myself when it's called for. No, it's not comfortable."

"I..." She didn't have anything to say to that. Anything she *could* think of was just going to shove her foot in her mouth.

"Looks good, doesn't he?" Elijah chuckled. "I wish I could convince him to get dressed up more often."

Good? She was impressed. He looked *human*. Quinn looked like he belonged in a group of friends at a bar and not in the woods by himself. It was a good, if weird, look on him.

"Are we waiting on Jasper and Zander?" Vincent inquired patiently as he walked in.

"We are," Sawyer told him. He walked over to her and she leaned into the soft kiss.

"You look good," he whispered. "I love when your hair is down."

"It's a pain," she replied. "I'm considering cutting it all off."

"Please don't," Quinn cut in. she looked over to him, her eyebrows rising. "I like the long hair."

"I'm on his side," Vincent told her.

"I like the hair," Elijah said finally, but then shrugged. "Though, it's your hair. Cut it, don't cut it, whatever. You'll still be the hottest thing this side of the Mississippi."

"Elijah is the smartest man in the room tonight," Sawyer declared. "Because you guys and your opinions about my hair really don't play a factor into whether I'm going to cut it or not." If she got tired of it, then it was going, whether they liked it or not.

"If you cut your hair, I'll be upset," Zander said, growling, as he walked in.

"Why?" she huffed, turning to him.

"I like seeing it on the pillows," Zander explained, grinning.

She narrowed her eyes on him. Of course he had some reason like that. It astounded her that she thought he was attractive when he could be so piggish.

"Let's just get to the bar before these two start a fight," Jasper interjected quickly. "Please."

"All right, you heard Jasper's plea. Let's get moving," Vincent said it all with a laugh. Sawyer was happy to see their 'leader' in a better mood than she'd ever known him. Since coming back from Texas, he only had small moments of darkness. He didn't seem to be crushed under the weight of the past as much. Sure, she had some stuff to work out and that meant he was getting a little ignored, but that was a necessity to her. He didn't seem to be taking it too hard since she accepted the date he had planned for New York.

She drove herself, taking the Audi while the guys took two Range Rovers. She didn't plan on having more than a couple of drinks, if that. She would stay under the limit to make the drive home.

At the bar, the one she had the weirdly fond memory of getting a drunk Vincent from, she realized she had beaten the others and went inside on her own. It was a quiet, run-down little country bar in the middle of nowhere, with beat up wood furniture and tattered upholstery. She assumed everyone inside were locals that she just hadn't met yet. She found a booth and slid in, waiting on the guys.

She was in relative silence for only a few seconds before Zander's cheery hello to the bartender announced the arrival of the rest of her team.

"How did you beat us here?" Vincent asked as he slid in next to her.

"I speed," Sawyer answered. "Not like crazy-ass Elijah, but I like to go fast."

"I should have remembered," he said in an 'aha' sort of voice. "The speeding ticket."

"Let's pretend that never happened." She moved further into the booth so Jasper could sit on the other side of Vincent. It left Quinn, Zander, and Elijah trying to fit on the other side. The scene was comical.

"Drinks!" Elijah declared, slapping his hand to the table. "Sawyer, you should have ridden with us. Jasper and Vincent are the DD's this time. Now you need to worry about staying sober for the drive home."

"Exactly," she retorted. Driving home was an excuse not to get hammered.

Drinks were brought, and Sawyer had water to start, pouring it from a pitcher whenever she was getting low. When she finally ordered a drink, she went strong: a Jack and Coke.

The team mostly talked about New York, their favorite things to do up in the city while they were there on required visits. Sawyer knew the bars and theatres they were talking about, but she had never visited them. She had stayed under the radar so well up there because she hadn't gone to those places. They were places where Magi regularly hung out openly and reveled in their magic and the security that normally came from being a New York Magi. Magi trouble didn't hit New York, thanks to the overwhelming presence of the World Magi Council and their two dogs, the International Magi Police Organization and the International Magi Armed Services. The cops and the military. She hid right under their noses for a long time because she didn't go to the places that the team was talking about.

"Want to dance?" Vincent asked her quietly, after nearly an hour of sitting, drinking, and chatting.

"Sure," she agreed. Jasper let them out and slid into the corner of the booth. Vincent took her hand and led her to the middle of the room.

Other older country couples were also dancing, but it all felt weird to Sawyer. This wasn't her thing. She wasn't much of a dancer. She appreciated being asked, though. Like Jasper's date and holding the doors open, this being asked to dance in a dingy little country bar felt normal.

Vincent kept it easy on her, just hands on waists and shoulders, spinning in a slow circle. She knew he could probably waltz like his brother, or any other ballroom dance, but he didn't get her to do one. For that, she was thankful.

"I really do love your hair long and down," he whispered in her ear.

"I like my hair," Sawyer admitted. "It just gets hot and hard to deal with."

"If you cut it, I promise I won't hate you for it," Vincent teased.

"If you tried to hate me, you would be sexless before the end of the day," she threatened in a light, joking tone. She meant every single word of it though.

"I believe it," Vincent mumbled. "Your body. Do as you please with it, of course."

"I'm glad we have an understanding," Sawyer said politely, as if a deal had been struck.

They finished the song and Vincent took the middle seat of the booth, letting Sawyer be on the outside so she could stretch her legs out. She ordered a second Jack and Coke and finished it before jumping into the conversation at the table. "What do I need to watch out for in New York?" she asked, looking down at Elijah and then turning her eyes on Vincent.

"They know who you are, what you've done, and why," Vincent whispered, his voice low to retain any amount of privacy. "Remember we recorded you after leaving the hospital?"

"They've all seen it?" Sawyer asked, her eyebrows nearly coming off her forehead. She remembered them setting up the camera, remembered that she forgot about it the moment she started talking.

"No," Elijah cut in. "All of the Council, yes. All of the top ranking IMPO officials, yes. The tape, at the very least. But other teams know your name versus your old alias and title. They don't know any of the personal details from the… video. Just in case."

"Just in case I go rogue." Sawyer looked down at her empty glass. Her stomach turned at the thought. She'd already known that people knew about her, at least privately, in the organization. She was about to meet those people. People who didn't know her but knew of her. "I'll have another one of these. We might need a third DD that isn't me."

"I will," Elijah told her kindly, pushing his drink away. Zander took it. "You look like you're going to be sick."

"I'm considering it," she muttered. She got up. "I'm going to the bathroom, then the bar for another drink."

"We'll be here," Jasper called after her as she walked away.

Sawyer got to the bathroom and went to the sink. She splashed her face with cold water and stared at herself in the mirror. So far, she'd only been around people who knew her, who'd witnessed her and Axel's absolute hate for each other, who'd seen her own confession. She'd stayed away from the lower ranking IMPO agents in Texas, just because she hadn't wanted a problem. She hadn't realized just how much and how many people knew about her. So many. So many who had never even seen her, but were probably already judging her.

She left the bathroom, heading straight for the bartender.

"Whiskey, whatever you got," she told him. He just nodded back to her. She missed her bartender back in New York for a moment.

When the drink slid in front of her, she sipped on it before turning to look at her team back in the booth. They were talking quietly, except Quinn, who stayed very silent, just holding a glass of water. Elijah must have said something, because laughter started to ring out from the table. She smiled at the scene.

Beautifully normal.

She finished the whiskey and left the glass on the bar. She had to pass through a few tables to get to the booth, and she weaved through them easily.

Until a hand took a solid squeeze on her ass.

At that exact moment, Vincent looked over to her. His eyebrows climbed up his forehead as she felt her temper flare.

Sawyer turned slowly to the offending hand: a young man, probably a local farmhand by the look of him. He was grinning, looking innocent.

"Don't do that, okay?" she warned.

"Don't know what you're talking about." He chuckled, and a few of his friends laughed. There were four of them total.

She shrugged, realizing that it would be too much effort to push the issue. She wasn't there to get into a fight, so she turned back to her guys and began to walk away.

"Yeah, hot stuff, walk away."

Sawyer took a deep breath. Trouble followed her everywhere, it seemed. An easy night out at the bar on a Friday. That was all she wanted.

"Everything okay?" Vincent asked her as she sat next to him.

"Yup," she answered. "No biggie. Farm boy got handsy and I've decided I really don't care tonight."

"Okay." Elijah raised his glass of water. "We'll leave it alone."

The only person at the table she was worried about doing anything was the one pinned on the inside and looking a little drunker than everyone else. Zander was glaring at the table like he was going to set it on fire. Sawyer was thankful that his abilities were telepathy, healing, shields, and *water* control. All pretty passive.

"Fuck that," Zander mumbled.

"What the fuck?" one of the guys roared. "How the fuck did that happen?"

Sawyer spun her head to the table and saw their drinks were tipped over, all of them. Because every drink in the room had some water in it, Zander was able to cause trouble. The laps of the farm boys were drenched, their shirts stained with beer.

"What the hell, Zander?" she hissed over to him. "I said fucking leave it. Guys get handsy. I wasn't in the mood for some shit."

"Just fucking with them," he replied, a grin overtaking his face.

"Which one of you did that?" one of the young men demanded, looking in their direction. "Fucking Magi."

"Forget about it," Elijah warned. "You got your little grope in, we spilled your drinks. It'll teach you not to feel ladies up without their permission, little twat."

"Why don't you come out here and fucking say that to my face?"

"I did," Elijah answered. He was holding back a chuckle.

Sawyer rolled her eyes and turned to glare at Zander, like nearly everyone else at the table.

"Are you fucking serious?" Sawyer asked him.

"Jesus, man. Our first night bringing her here and you're trying to get us in a fight," Jasper accused.

"You also just got us cut off. You know the rules. No magic," Vincent reminded them.

"I'm going to kill you," Sawyer promised Zander in an emotionless tone.

"They deserved it," he said, without a single bit of regret in his voice. "It was a harmless lesson to keep their hands to themselves."

"You all just going to ignore me?" the farm boy demanded.

Sawyer looked back over to him. "Yes. You don't want this fight." She gave him the same emotionless tone she'd given Zander. She and the team would wipe the floors with the young country boys. It wouldn't even be hard.

"We can fucking take you," he postured.

"No." She was laughing at that. "You really can't. Magic or no magic."

"We'll go," Vincent announced. "No trouble. It's done and we're leaving."

Sawyer stood up and let Vincent and Jasper out.

"You aren't going anywhere," another farm boy called out.

The one who had groped her shoved Vincent.

That was the last straw. No one touched her guys. *No one.* Without a second thought, she slugged him and sent him to the floor, out cold.

"Well," Elijah drawled out, looking down at the farm boy. He looked back up, a grin on his face. "I guess we're fighting."

"What the fuck, you cunt?" one of the buddies roared and swung for her. She blocked as Zander and Quinn both jumped out of the booth behind Elijah. Jasper grabbed one before he could get his friend from Sawyer's grasp. She had the one who swung at her by the shirt and flung on the table. She brought a fist down and knocked the boy out before he could even think to stop her.

It was over in seconds. The team stood around in the middle of a ring of young men, all on the floor. Sawyer took a quick moment to make sure none of them were seriously injured. She didn't hear any screaming from the ones that were still conscious, so she figured no broken bones.

"Get out before I call the cops," the bartender yelled. Sawyer thought it was a heaping helping of silly since they were cops, technically. "Now! And don't fucking come back. I'm done with the trouble you all bring."

"They fucking started it," Zander yelled back.

"I don't care," the bartender snapped. "They'll be banned, too."

"Yup," Sawyer declared. "I'm going to kill you, Zander." She stormed out, her temper gnawing at her. She had told him not to fucking do anything. To let it lie. So a guy groped her ass in a bar. Who fucking cared? Shit like that happened and they needed to be on a plane tomorrow. Zander didn't need to go and start some shit.

"Sawyer!" He ran after her. She didn't turn back to him as she unlocked her car and began to open the door. Zander pushed it back closed. "Sawyer, he'll let us come back in a couple of months and this will be forgotten. It's nothing to get pissed over."

"You know what?" Sawyer snapped, looking up at him. "Get in the car. We're going to have a fucking talk, Zander Wade." She pushed him off her door and watched him go to the other side.

"You got him? Good to drive?" Vincent asked loudly as he walked to his Range Rover.

"I got him," Sawyer growled. She got in her car and tore out of the parking lot before Zander even had a chance to put his seat belt on.

"We got kicked out of the bar - where the hell is anger coming from?" he demanded.

"I told you not to do anything!" she roared. "I didn't want the fucking drama tonight, Zander. You couldn't keep your fucking shit in line, and decided to do whatever you fucking want, like you always fucking do."

"I fucked with them a little, big fucking deal," he argued. "Vincent isn't going to reprimand me for it. Neither will Elijah. This shit ain't a big deal. It's not the first fight we've gotten into at a bar and it won't be the last. You even threw the first punch!"

"The fight isn't the fucking problem," she snarled. She was holding the steering wheel hard enough to make her knuckles pale, nearly white. She ground her teeth in frustration.

"Then what is?"

"That I asked for you to drop it!" Sawyer screamed. "I

don't need you fighting for my fucking honor, Zander. I don't need you to get possessive and fucking weird over someone touching my ass in a bar. They were a bunch of young and drunk guys. I have an ass. It was going to get groped. That's fucking life. I decided it wasn't fucking worth any trouble and you fucking ignored me."

"Really?" he huffed. "You don't need someone fighting for you? You would let those fucks get away with disrespecting you? Well, you might, but I sure as fuck won't."

"Then we're going have some fucking problems," she snapped. On another night, in a different life, she would have done something. She would have nearly broken the hand that touched her without her express permission. She hadn't wanted any of that tonight. She had wanted normal. To just sit with her friends and her lovers and just have a drink. Zander had decided to throw that away and they were going home early. "I want to keep my fucking head down and if you can't comprehend that then we aren't going to fucking work."

"Jesus fuck, you are hard to like," Zander retorted. "Your way or the fucking highway. I get it. Whatever. You want everyone to step in fucking line with your wants and needs, whatever. I'm not some fucking lap dog for you, though. I'm not going to just take your goddamn orders and hope you aren't pissed off by something I do. I'm not going to take this shit. If everything I do pisses you off, then I guess this isn't going to work."

They finished the drive home in silence. She sat in the car as Zander got out the moment she parked in the garage. She heard the door to the house slam shut.

Lap dog.

Follow orders.

Hope not to piss your master off.

Sawyer jumped out of the car, her mind reeling. She walked into the house, her temper still riding her, but she didn't go up to her room. She stomped into Zander's room, having heard the door slam to that as well.

"I don't expect you to follow orders," she angrily spat out. It made her sound like fucking Axel. That was her life with Axel. Follow orders and pray to whatever gods she could remember that he wasn't in a bad mood and looking for a fight. "I expect you to fucking listen to me a little, though."

"Whatever, Sawyer," he mumbled, pulling his shirt off. His back was to her and she glared at the back piece he had. A dragon, angry and fiery, destructive and dangerous. Like him. For all his passive magic, his personality was the dragon on his back, not the sweet, warm healing he could do. "I get it. You need control. Vincent does whatever you say. Jasper does whatever you say. I won't."

"It's not about control!" Sawyer roared. "It's about respect!"

"Respect?" Zander snapped, turning to her. "You think I don't respect you?"

"You damn sure don't act like it," she retorted.

"That's the stupidest thing I've ever heard come out of your mouth." He looked a little dumbfounded. "Sawyer, I respect the hell out of you. It's why I won't let some trash country boy think he can feel you up and get away with it."

"That's not..." she growled, trying to find what he thought was respectful about taking a piece of petty revenge she hadn't wanted.

"Then what?" he asked softly, stalking over to her.

She narrowed her eyes at him. "You wanted that shit because it offended you," Sawyer answered. "Not because you care about me. I would have appreciated you just letting it drop."

"Why can't you be any other fucking woman?" Zander was looking pissed off again. "Any other woman would have been happy that someone was going to stand up for her."

"I don't need you to stand up for me," she reminded him.

"What if it's the only way I can show I fucking care?" he demanded. "Because I'm not Jasper. I don't do little cute dates. Sawyer, I did this for you as kids, remember? We used to fight together."

"Times change," she bit out. They were fighters, her and Zander, they always had been. She was tired of fighting. Him. The world. Her past. She was so fucking tired of it. "I'm going to bed."

"Sawyer," he called after as she walked out. "Sawyer, don't run from me."

"I'm not running," she replied. "I'm ending this idiotic argument."

"Then end it by fucking listening to me," he argued.

"Then don't fucking start it by listening to *me*." She turned back around to him. She was going to leave, but he'd gone and opened his mouth again. "One simple thing was all I wanted tonight. Normal. Drinks with everyone. A moment out of the house and something nice before we go to New York, where I have to meet a ton of people who are going to think I belong in a cell, not on a team. I specifically said to drop it. You didn't."

"I don't have it in me to watch someone do that to you."

"You've done it to me!" Sawyer declared, waving her arms around like 'what the fuck?' and just feeling astounded by the hypocrisy.

"You didn't like it and I haven't done it since," Zander retorted. "Remember? We fought, we fucked. I realized you didn't like getting your ass groped and slapped. Haven't done it since."

She was even more angry that he had a point. He'd changed his behavior for her. Didn't treat her like a piece of meat he could touch however or whenever he wanted.

"I also stopped asking about the fucking nightmares," Zander continued. "Sawyer, let me tell you how pissed I am that you yelled at me - your boyfriend, your childhood friend - for touching your ass, but you were willing to let it go with a fucking stranger who probably thought you were a whore he could pick up." He took a deep breath.

Sawyer closed her eyes. God, he was *right*. She hated when he was fucking right.

"I'm sorry," she whispered. "For not understanding how that would make you feel."

"And I'm sorry for picking a fight you didn't want. It's going to happen again, though. I won't let people treat you however they fucking want. I won't let you think it's okay to be treated like that just because you don't want trouble. Why? Because I fucking love you."

"Do you mean it?" she asked.

"After," he answered.

She would have laughed. She was still angry at him, but that was their code that this argument was over. She ran a hand through his hair and pulled him down for a kiss. The argument would continue...after. Tomorrow. Next week. The next time one of them pissed the other off.

But she couldn't resist having him in her life. Even against her wishes, he fought for her. That meant something to her, even through her anger.

He popped open the button of her leather pants and shoved them down, all without breaking the kiss. She undid his jeans at the same time, with one hand, still holding his face to hers.

Her leather pants fell to the floor, then her thong. His jeans were next, and she was pleased that he'd gone commando and was hard as steel, those piercings a promise for this to be good. He pulled her shirt off and the bra went across the room. She stroked him, making a groan leave his gorgeous lips. She shoved him back until he hit the bed and fell on it.

She straddled him, his legs going off the bed, and kissed him harder, their tongues warring for dominance like they always did. Nothing Sawyer and Zander did was soft. He flipped them over and pushed her higher on the bed. She thought he would start fucking her there, but she tossed her head back in ecstasy when he placed his mouth over her core and stroked her clit with his tongue. She ran her hands through his red hair and held him there as he devoured her. Zander hadn't eaten her out yet, and she was glad he knew how. This was a skill she needed to remember he had. He shifted so her legs were over his shoulders and he shoved his tongue into her. He ate her out as roughly as they normally screwed.

"Oh, Zander," she moaned, unable to take it. The fight. The anger. The argument. Aphrodisiacs for them. Every time they argued or fought, they had explosively great sex.

When he shoved in two fingers, she came. A scream of pleasure tore from her chest and her body clenched on him. He continued to rub the sweet spot and lapped up everything her body gave him.

"Perfection," he growled once her orgasm had finished. She was panting softly as he crawled up her body and thrust into her, hard. He set a relentless pace and Sawyer just wrapped her arms and legs around him.

It was hard and fast. Brutal. There was nothing tender about it. Zander was braced over her, and she was captivated by green eyes as he drove into her like it was the last thing he would have before his death. Like the sex was a part of the argument they just had. The piercings he had were creating sensations in her that she knew she would never get used to. She could count each barbell of the ladder as he dragged them out of her and shoved them back in. The Prince Albert slid over her g-spot every single time he thrust.

He leaned back and picked her up with him, staying deep inside her as he did so. Her back hit his headboard and she relished in the small amount of pain from it. He pounded up into her and used gravity to get even deeper. She bit down on his shoulder but was unable to stop any of the noises that he was bringing out of her. This was *fantastic*.

His hands moved down to hold her ass, squeezing hard.

Sawyer felt like she was going to catch on fire. It was so much. His body grinding against her clit as he drove up and up into her. The pain on her back, the rough wooden headboard scratching at her. Her nerves were firing back every sort of sensation possible as he fucked her harder than she thought possible. She wondered if there would ever be a limit to how hard they could make it.

She shattered and took him with her. He groaned in her ear as he filled her. Sawyer was not of their world anymore. She could barely see. Her vision was blurred and focusing on anything past his pale, tattooed shoulder as they both rode out their orgasms was an impossibility.

Zander laid her down and she just curled into his pillows. Her body was blissfully boneless. He laid out panting next to her, neither of them getting under the blankets.

"Stay here tonight?" he asked her.

"I'm not moving, and you're crazy if you think I am," Sawyer answered, laughing softly. "You're stuck with me tonight."

"I'm never stuck with you," Zander retorted, rolling to his side.

She looked over at him, feeling better. She was too tired to be angry. In this moment, she just didn't care. He could go out and get himself arrested, and she wouldn't be able to summon the energy to get even mildly annoyed. "I'm stuck with you," she teased.

"I mean..." He shrugged. "I've made you sticky, but I don't think it works like that."

"Gross," Sawyer groaned.

"Get the lights."

"You get the lights," she huffed. She sure as fuck wasn't getting up at this point. The next time she was getting out of bed would be in the morning.

"Sawyer, please. I can't feel my legs."

"Neither can I, and it's *your* fault!"

Twenty minutes later, Zander got up and turned the lights off.

7

SAWYER

New York. Sawyer walked out of the airport and smiled at her city, glad to be back. After the great sex with Zander, they had woken up and left for the airport. The flight had been quiet: a simple rundown of the itinerary, then everyone took naps since they had left for the airport at three in the morning. They didn't need to be at the main office until Monday, and it was Saturday afternoon.

"Are you going to see Charlie?" Jasper asked, walking next to her to their rentals. They both threw their bags in the trunk of the little Ford Focus and slammed it closed. They needed to wait on the rest of the team, whose bags were late getting off the plane. The team had been forced to fly commercial for this trip.

"I am, tomorrow," she answered. "I called him earlier in the week. He and I are going to get lunch then do my class together. I can't wait to see all my kids." Sawyer was thankful for this trip for that reason. Her old life. She fucking missed it sometimes. Other times, she was glad that those kids now didn't have her darkness around, and she was getting a real chance to find her own salvation.

"One of us will need to go with you," Jasper reminded her. "We're lax at home, but here in New York, you can't go anywhere alone."

"Yeah," Sawyer sighed. "I remember the warning you've already given me ten times before we got off the plane. Stick near you guys. No going off alone. Don't talk to other agents, or anyone else, without you guys. Do nothing that could possibly get me in even the whiff of trouble." She took a deep breath. "And nothing about any undue personal relationships."

"Sorry," he mumbled, looking down at his feet. "I know you're listening - I'm just worried."

"Be worried about Zander. He tends to punch everything and get into fights," she commented, throwing a side-eye at her red-headed lover.

"So do you," Jasper countered.

"I am smart enough to decide not to fight when it's not necessary," she rebutted.

"Sure," he said, a smile coming over his face. "Until you punched that guy without warning."

"He shoved Vincent. And I had warned him. I told him he didn't want the fight. So did Elijah and Vincent."

"Would you punch someone like that for me?" His smile turned into a bashful grin.

"I would do it for any of you," she replied.

"Without our permission? Even if we asked you not to?"

"Oh, damn it." Sawyer smacked his stomach. "Yeah, I get it. Can't get mad at Zander when I would do the same thing. I understand."

"I just heard the argument last night," Jasper whispered,

keeping his voice low enough that Zander couldn't hear them. "I noticed he didn't call you out on it, but I'm going to. You don't get as angry at me as you do him."

"I expect this kind of thing to come from Vincent," she muttered in annoyance, crossing her arms.

"He's preoccupied with this trip and this date I hear he's taking you on." He chuckled.

"Do you know anything about that?" she inquired. She didn't. Vincent was close-lipped about the entire thing.

"More than you," he informed her. "It's on Tuesday. He'll tell you more tonight."

"Ah." She nodded slowly. He'd better. "What's taking them so long?"

"I don't know," Jasper said, shrugging. He leaned on the car and Sawyer decided to kill the time and have a smoke. It wasn't a smoking section, but she couldn't wander off to find one, or smoke in the rental, and she'd just gotten off the plane. She was having a cigarette, fuck the rules.

Jasper tried to take it from her as she lit it and she jumped out of his range.

"Don't mess with me," she warned him. "I'm going to smoke this cigarette." She even had breath mints for after it.

"If someone comes over to tell you to stop, you will," he ordered.

She nodded. If some security guard said anything, she would put it out, but not for Jasper. He knew she wanted her post-flight smoke. She was doing good at not smoking as often since Jasper and Zander didn't like it, but she wasn't ready to completely quit the habit. Plus, she knew she was smoking more often than she used to before they caught her. She needed to cut back in general.

"We're here," Elijah said as he led the rest of the team

over. Quinn and Zander were pulling a cart that had three large wooden crates with holes. Kaar, Shade, and Scout were inside them. "These our rides?"

"Yeah, they gave us some cheap shit this time." Jasper groaned. "Normally we get better."

"Yeah, but we're still in the dog house, so this was expected. They gave us a nice hotel, though, and James is waiting on us there. He texted and said he needed to tell us something. Like why Quinn was forced on this trip." Vincent took the keys for the second Focus from Jasper and popped the trunk.

Sawyer watched them load in bags and put her smoke out when everyone else was ready to go. Kaar, Shade, and Scout were freed from their crates and she saw that the wolves were wearing collars, something she'd never witnessed before. Shade had red and Scout had blue. Kaar immediately flew into an open door to one of the cars. The bird didn't ever pay any attention to her. She barely saw the damn thing.

"Quinn was forced to be here?" Sawyer asked Elijah quietly before loading in with Jasper and Zander.

"Yeah. He's never been asked to come to New York." He looked concerned. "This time, they demanded he and, in turn, the wolves come. He wouldn't leave them in Georgia by themselves, so they had to come."

"Then they put us on commercial?" Sawyer was pissed. She pulled out her mints and threw one in, crunching down on it, making it explode in her mouth and taste too strong. "Kaar, Shade and Scout had to ride in crates. Quinn was uncomfortable as hell with all of it, and Vincent wasn't very pleased either. Are they trying to be assholes?" She would have never put Midnight in cargo on a flight. Ever. She felt for her guys, knowing the pain of having an animal bond that couldn't be treated right due to other circumstances.

"Yeah," Elijah answered. "They are. You'll meet them Monday."

"Fuck," she muttered and jumped in the car. Scout was next to her, split from his brother and Quinn in the other car. She wrapped an arm around him and he leaned into her. "I got you, boy." She scratched through his thick fur, behind his ear, and relaxed him enough to lay down and put his head in her lap.

The drive to the hotel was a slog. Saturday traffic in New York was flooded with tourists, locals out and running errands, and taxis doing whatever they wanted. Sawyer stared out the window, taking in her city. They wouldn't pass by her area, the Bronx and gym, on the way to the hotel, but she knew she would see her New York home soon enough. Tomorrow.

It was almost too soon. She was a little nervous in a way that she never had been about seeing her friends in New York. Her *family*.

Liam still refused to talk to her, and that was something she hoped to work on. She talked to Charlie every couple of days, finally convincing the old man to text her and send her pictures of her kids at their lessons, now run by him and Liam.

They pulled in front of the hotel and Sawyer released Scout before getting out. Scout ran for Quinn, who was already out of that Focus, and she didn't like how he shook. Both wolves looked uncomfortable and upset. So did Quinn. He was wary and anxious, his back straight. Sawyer walked to him and gently touched his arm.

"Are you okay?" she whispered, keeping it low enough

that other people walking by had no idea she even said anything.

"I hate...big cities. New York is..."

"Bigger than most," she finished for him. "You weren't like this in Dallas."

"We weren't in Dallas very long," Quinn said, looking down to his wolves. "We were just passing through. We're going to be here for a week. In this big hotel, no escape. No space. I had to collar my brothers so no one shoots them."

She watched his nostrils flare and his eyes grew a little panicked. She just kept rubbing his arm as Elijah walked over and did the same on Quinn's other side. She knew why the wolves had to have collars. She had always thought of it as practical, marking them as a Magi's bonded animal and not a wild one running through the streets.

Now she hated it. Those two shouldn't be wearing collars. They weren't fucking house pets.

"Valet will park the cars," Vincent told them as he walked over. "Everyone get their bags?"

"I loaded them up," Zander called out, pushing one of those luggage carts over, ignoring the bellhop next to him. "We're good."

"Perfect." Vincent led them inside, Kaar perched on his shoulder - a clear sign the raven belonged to him.

Sawyer stayed with Quinn and Elijah. They flanked the feral Magi, and she could see and feel just how tense he was. She wondered how much, or how little, it would take to set him off in the massive, crowded city. She remembered how Quinn hadn't been with the team when they caught her. Now she understood why he'd been left in Georgia.

The hotel was gorgeous: dark marble, gold accents. Lush furniture was placed about for anyone who wanted or needed to sit down. Sawyer particularly liked the pillars throughout the high-ceilinged lobby. It was regal and enchanting, but also dark and elegant. Deep blacks, brilliant golds, exquisite detail, statues around the room and other expensive art pieces. She could glance at them and know they were unique and authentic.

There had been a time in her life that she would have stayed at a hotel like this. This place had money and rich clientele. There was nothing fake about it. She would have picked easy marks during her off time while she had been just a thief - that first year or so with Axel.

Vincent checked them in, passing out keys. Quinn was going to room with Elijah this trip, and they gave the team rooms made for Magi with bonded animals, with beds for them, bowls for water, and access to the roof, where they had built a garden for the animals to go on walks or out for a fly.

"You and I both have our own rooms," Vincent explained on the elevator. "Quinn needs Elijah with him. Zander and Jasper can bunk up. You aren't allowed to room with any of us, though."

"Boss' orders?" she asked, frowning at her key.

"No," Vincent sighed. "Mine. I don't want anyone to think there's something going on. You could room with any of us and nothing would happen, not this close to the WMC, but I don't even want them looking in our direction over it."

"I get that. I appreciate my own room." Sawyer stepped off the elevator the moment it dinged and went straight to her door. Room seven eighty-nine. It was close to the end of the hall. Turning, she saw that Elijah and Quinn would be across from her. Vincent would be on her left. Jasper and

Zander were on Elijah and Quinn's right, diagonal to her. She memorized that. If she needed anyone, she could walk through a wall to get to Vincent, and it would be fast to get to anyone else. Did she expect trouble in New York? No, she didn't, but she was going to be ready for it anyway.

Which was why she'd still tried to sneak out of the house in Georgia with her knives. Vincent hadn't been okay with that.

She threw her bags on her bed in the large hotel room, and immediately walked back out of the room. Vincent was walking out of his room at the same time, having done the same thing. "Weren't we meeting James?" she asked.

"In the hotel's bar," Vincent replied, chuckling. "Once everyone drops their bags and Quinn gets the wolves to settle for a nap up here, we'll go."

"What's he need?"

"I don't know," Vincent admitted. "He probably just wants to check in. He hasn't seen you since the Atlanta incident. Probably wants to check up on you before the madhouse of the WMC and the IMPO digging through your head to make sure you're stable, like they will the rest of us."

"We're good," Elijah declared, walking out of his room.

Quinn followed him, looking just a fraction calmer than he had. "They should be comfortable. The hotel had food ready for them," he mumbled, looking back inside the room quickly.

Sawyer's heart broke a little. He was so not okay.

On their walk to the elevator, as Jasper and Zander jogged to catch them, Sawyer wrapped her arm in Quinn's for a moment. "They will be okay," she whispered gently to him.

"I know," Quinn responded. He held her arm tightly, like a lifeline. She was okay with it. The fact that he was letting her touch him was big. Touching him to comfort him? That was out of their world.

Down at the lobby again, Sawyer let him go before the doors opened. They passed through people wandering around the lobby, ignored anyone asking for their help, and just followed Vincent straight to the bar.

"The WMC paid for a place like this?" Sawyer mumbled to herself.

"They all stay here," Jasper explained, having heard her. "James must have convinced them to do something nice for us, since they fucked with us about the flights. With Kaar and the wolves, we can't just stay at a regular hotel. We needed one that catered to Magi."

"How much does it cater to Magi?" Sawyer asked as they entered the bar.

"The walls are enchanted so people can't walk through them, to permanently harvest Source as it bleeds off us and keeps energizing shields between the walls," Jasper continued. "It's insanely complicated. Probably expensive to have done. This is the only place I've been where it's done."

"It would have to be complicated and expensive." *Or everyone would do it.* Sawyer sighed. That wasn't something she'd expected. Every Magi bled off magic. Their Source constantly refilled and expended energy, a cycle. Burning out wasn't permanent because the Source continued to produce magic, but it took time for a Magi to completely refill. When Sawyer had been wearing an inhibitor, the natural bleed of magic - a radiation, really - had been the only way her body hadn't killed itself with excess, and it had been tough to deal with.

To use that natural radiation of magic from any Magi to reinforce shields and enchantments...that had to have been done by someone powerful, very powerful. Or several people, a dozen or more, working together with clear intent. It said even more that she hadn't noticed the magic in the walls. Now she focused on it. It was everywhere. The building held so many Magi, and had so much magic in the air, that it was easy to hide.

"Sawyer?" Jasper leaned over her shoulder and she shook her head.

"I was just thinking about it. I didn't even notice," she told him.

"Most people don't until they're told."

They found James sitting at the bar. The older man grinned as they walked up, shaking Vincent's hand before pulling him into a half-hug. Sawyer raised an eyebrow. He *hugged* Vincent. Those happy grey eyes fell on her and she held back a groan.

"Sawyer," James said pleasantly. "How are you?"

"I was better in Georgia," she answered blandly.

"And she hasn't changed at all, it seems." Their handler laughed.

"No, she really hasn't," Elijah confirmed. He was wearing a shit-eating grin, his eyes darting between her and James.

James shook his hand, then Jasper and Zander's. When he got to Quinn, he gently touched his shoulder. "I need to speak with you in private on Tuesday. There's an important meeting for you on Wednesday and I want you prepared for it."

"What?" Quinn growled out the word.

"I can't tell anyone else about it. I barely convinced them to let me talk to you. They were going to blindside you with it." James's voice dropped to a whisper. "I'll tell you more Tuesday. If you want to head back up to your room, you can."

"Thank you," Quinn mumbled. With that, he turned and left, not another word or thought for them.

Sawyer watched him go, confused and a little scared.

"James?" Vincent asked, full of concern.

"I can't say anything," James repeated. "It's nothing bad. He's not in trouble. It's...fuck. It's IMAS related. And I can promise, he'll still be IMPO and on your team after Wednesday. They aren't taking him."

"I don't like the sound of that."

Sawyer saw the agitation all over Vincent's face, but their handler only shrugged at them. "I can't say anything else. It's between Quinn and I...And the WMC, IMAS, and our bosses."

"Christ," Vincent snapped. "Buy us drinks and tell us the rest of what's going on here in New York."

"Oh, the rest is easy. You aren't due for anything until Monday afternoon." James picked up his own drink off the bar and took a sip. "First, they want to say you did a great job in Texas. You really did. You found a cell of openly violent anti-Magi residents. You secured an unregistered Magi who illegally took a position of authority over non-Magi." He waved a hand "All of that. I'm proud of you all myself. People wondered if you could handle things since Axel had been caught and you now had Sawyer. I didn't worry."

Sawyer narrowed her eyes on him. He was so easy, nonchalant about it all, as if they hadn't been disturbed and haunted, and the entire thing had been easy. He hadn't been there. He had no idea what Texas was like.

She looked at the bar and waved a bartender down. "Whiskey," she ordered. "On his tab. Whatever you have. Cheap." She pointed at James.

"Are you sure, ma'am?" The bartender, an attractive dark-haired man, pointed to several bottles they had behind the bar. "We have an impressive collection of some the rarest whiskeys, scotches, and bourbons on the planet. You should pick one, try out something new. On *his* tab." The bartender winked at that last part, and Sawyer instantly knew that in another life, she would have a new best friend.

"You have several varieties of Macallan there," she noted. She hadn't had a taste of Macallan in a long time. Years.

"The twelve-year, the eighteen-year, and the thirty-year," he confirmed. "Have you tried a Macallan before? On *his* tab, I would recommend the thirty-year single malt scotch whiskey. It's aged in fine oak."

"I'll take it. On the rocks, 2 ice cubes." Sawyer chuckled. "How much?"

"You might not want the answer to that. The bottle runs over three thousand dollars." The bartender laughed. He slid her drink over to her slowly, and when she took it, his fingers grazed hers. "Come back any time."

"Sorry, I'm only in town for the week."

"Could be a fun week," he retorted.

"I'm not the girl you want to take home," she whispered kindly before walking away and back to the group, who had wandered to sit in a quiet circular booth. She slid in next to James and held up her drink. "Thank you."

"Oh? Did I buy that? You're welcome," he said, chuckling with her. "What is it?"

"Macallan, thirty-year fine oak aged," she informed him, taking her first sip. Heaven in her mouth. It was delicious. "Runs about three thousand a bottle, so I have no idea how expensive this drink is."

"Christ," he huffed, looking at the glass. "Vincent."

"Sorry," Vincent said unapologetically. "I'm about to flag

a waitress down and order one of those for everyone at the table. On your tab."

"What did I miss?" Sawyer looked between them. Vincent was threatening James? Happened often enough, but only when their handler was the bearer of bad news. More bad news.

"Monday will be good, Tuesday will be awful, and Wednesday will be a nightmare," Elijah said.

"Monday, we get our backs patted for Texas. Tuesday, we'll be separated for mental health evaluations." Jasper sighed. "Which we knew. They will ask a lot of personal questions, they always do, and you just need to get through it without acting insane."

"And if that's awful, what is going on Wednesday except Quinn's meeting?" Sawyer looked from Elijah to Jasper, then Zander. Zander sank into his spot further, looking grumpy. Vincent groaned.

"They are going to review whether you should remain with the team. Based on our, and especially your, mental health evaluations."

"Oh." She felt the dread settle in her chest at that thought. "Is there smoking allowed in this bar?" There went her idea of cutting back.

"Yes," James answered politely. His humor was gone.

She pulled out her pack and, with barely shaking hands, put the cigarette in her lips. She didn't get a chance to get her lighter. The end lit up on its own. She mumbled a thanks to Elijah as she pulled something that looked like an ashtray closer to her.

"Well, that's not going to happen," Zander announced. "We're keeping her. Or we'll do what we threatened when she was in the hospital."

"I'll make sure to warn them," their handler muttered,

looking a bit angry now. "You do know they will eventually fire me and put someone stricter on you guys, right?"

"Shit." Zander grunted.

"Yeah, *shit*," James retorted. "I'm doing everything I can up here. Literally, they are pulling this out of their asses. You did fine in Texas. Sawyer, they will be aiming at your PTSD and your history. Looking for a way that may give them a reason to put you into care, without your magic. 'Get you help' is what one said. We both know it'll be a prison sentence until the contract runs out."

"You're buying me another one of these," Sawyer said, lifting her glass. Then she finished it off and left the table again. She only made it three steps.

Then security flooded the bar.

Sawyer went still as the team stood up and walked over to her as well. James said a curse as IMAS soldiers took guard positions all over the room and yelled clear as they methodically made sure there were no threats in the room.

Sawyer's anxiety sky-rocketed. Were they here for her?

"Rome is here," James whispered cryptically.

Rome? She had no idea what that meant.

"D'Angelo?" Vincent asked softly. "Really?"

"She's just coming off a vacation. Why she's here in the hotel, I don't know. The Councilwoman has a residence here in New York. But this is definitely her entrance. She's the only person who I can think of coming to town right now with this sort of security," James explained quickly. "This should have nothing to do with us."

"Should," she repeated.

"They aren't here to arrest or capture you. It would be a violation of the contract," their handler continued. "Let's just watch and wait for a moment."

Sawyer did just that, her eyes glancing over the soldiers.

They were huge and well-armed. They each were in similar all-blacks to what the team wore on cases, but with key differences. Their pants were more military or cargo in style, with huge pockets on the thighs as well. They wore long-sleeved black thermals and Kevlar vests. Each carried a type of assault rifle, and Sawyer was going to guess it was an M-4, since it was standard military fare. They used the same sidearm that Vincent had given her before Texas, the Sig. On their upper arms, there were rank patches, which were also dark grey and black in design. She had no idea which patch meant what.

"At ease," a soldier told them as he walked closer. "We're just securing the room. Agents, you can go back to your drinks."

"Thank you, Captain," James replied, seeming much more comfortable. Sawyer had no idea where 'Captain' lay in the IMAS rank structure. "Whose presence are we expecting?"

"Councilwoman D'Angelo," the soldier answered professionally. Then he loosened up and smiled. "Can't tell you anymore, but I don't think it has anything to do with you. You can enjoy your night. Hoo-yah, brothers." He looked to her. "And sister."

With that, the captain walked back to a group of soldiers in the middle of the room and began barking orders about where they needed to be. Sawyer raised an eyebrow at James, then turned it on her team.

"Explanations?" She didn't say anything more, just expected one of them to start talking - and immediately.

"Don't know anything about IMAS?" James frowned at her and then turned a mock glare on Vincent. "You should have taught her something about them before coming to New York."

"Captain is an officer rank in IMAS, O-2 specifically." Vincent droned on, "Which means they are one rank over the O-1, Lieutenant. There are seven enlisted ranks and seven officer ranks. I'll run you through them all later. That Captain is probably in charge of Councilwoman D'Angelo's security team. It's befitting his rank and it's a prestigious assignment, so he must be very good at his job."

"Or very good at kissing ass." Zander snorted in disgust. Even Jasper was glaring at the soldiers around them. "You rise to the highest rank of your incompetence in IMAS. By the way, the brother and sister shit? Yeah, they are all super motivated like that."

"Harsh," Elijah mumbled. "And there she is." He nodded towards the bar's entryway.

Sawyer looked back over and watched the beautiful woman walk in. Some things were startling about her, right off the bat. She looked young, nowhere over forty, but her hair was a long, silky silver, like the steel of a blade. She didn't have the wrinkles to match the hair color, which made Sawyer wonder if she went grey early in life. The councilwoman didn't even look their way, only went straight for a booth in the very back, where a member of the waitstaff was already waiting for her.

"I think I'm going to go to bed," Sawyer announced. "The bar seems less appealing with all of this here."

"I'll walk you," Jasper offered. "I don't want to be here either. Zander?"

"You all can go," James said, waving them off. "I'm not comfortable with more talk about what's going on with this many ears and one of the opposition sitting in the room."

"Opposition?" She frowned at him.

"She was vocal that you should be executed in the hospital," he whispered. "Go, before she notices any of you.

She wanted the team disbanded, arrested, and tried for treason for sticking up for you. She threatened me a good bit too, but others convinced her I was just the messenger. You don't shoot the messenger."

Sawyer left at that, the team hurrying after her. This woman had wanted her *dead*.

New York suddenly sucked.

8
___

SAWYER

Sunday came quickly, and Sawyer ran out of the hotel with Jasper on her tail. She barely waited on him to get his seatbelt on before hitting the gas.

"Excited?" Jasper asked, looking over to her as he secured the seatbelt.

"Obvious?" she asked back.

"Very." He chuckled. "Miss them?"

"Yeah," she sighed. "I have. I know everyone is doing all right, but I just..." She trailed off as they drove through New York. "You know, seeing that Councilwoman in the bar last night, what James had said about her, it freaked me out. I'm glad to be going to see my kids, and Liam and Charlie. They wouldn't want me dead, ya know? Good people who gave me a chance. A reminder there is some good in this city."

"I get that," Jasper replied. "Don't let the Councilwoman get to you though. She is going to lose this battle. The majority of the WMC is in your favor and they have little to no reason to mess with you, unless you give them one. James is just warning us that if we step wrong, they *are* watching."

"They're in my favor because the contract is in their favor," Sawyer whispered.

"Excuse me?" Jasper frowned at her and she closed her eyes for a moment while they were at a red light. When she opened them, it was just turning green and she hit the gas.

"You know that me on this team is just something they can do until they need me, right?" She tapped her fingers on the Focus' steering wheel. "The contract was clear. Did you read it?"

"No," he admitted. "Only Vincent and James were allowed to look it over."

"Jasper, they are keeping me alive and giving me my freedom in five years because I'm their assassin. One day they'll need someone dead. And now they have someone they can call to make that happen."

"They would never," he sputtered.

"They are," she pressed. "The WMC is just as corrupt as any other government. The thing is, I'm either their assassin or I'm in jail. I made the choice. Sure, it's awesome being IMPO, learning what you guys do and helping people like in Texas, but it's not the main goal of the contract. It's a secondary goal. It's their way of saying, 'Yes, you can be useful while we don't need you.' It keeps me out of prison, per contract terms. But it's not what they want."

"Does anyone else know this?" Jasper leaned back in his seat and stared at her. She could see him from the corner of her eye and didn't like his expression.

"I think Elijah? I might have made it clear to him on accident - or he figured it out."

"Then why are they trying to pull you off the team?"

"Because they're assholes?" Sawyer didn't really and truly know. She didn't know who all the players were and where they stood on her situation. She couldn't make guesses as to who felt what and why. She could make one guess. "There must be factions. Pro-Sawyer puts that person as wanting the WMC to have a pocket assassin, which doesn't look good. Anti-Sawyer means I should get locked away for my life, but the WMC doesn't have an assassin, which looks better for them from a PR standpoint. There could be other standpoints, but those would be the main two, and there's only fifteen people on the Council."

"I was thinking the same thing," he agreed. "It's a complicated situation."

"Yes."

"How long is this drive?" Jasper changed the subject.

"Depends on the traffic." She looked around. There was a lot.

It took them an hour to limp into the Bronx and get to the gym. Sawyer stretched her legs the moment she got out. Atlanta's traffic wasn't this bad, and she was mentally wondering when this trip had become a competition between the two cities. New York was her home. Fact. Her kids were here. Liam was here. Charlie was here.

She also knew she could never *live* in this city again. Not with the WMC knowing who she was. Not if she wanted her friends in the city to be safe in the long run. Her old enemies would come out of the woodwork eventually, and since she'd been caught, her identity exposed, the risk was too high.

Atlanta was safer. The plantation house far from the world was even better.

"You ready?" Jasper asked, standing next to her in front of the gym.

"Yeah," she whispered, staring at the front doors. She walked up and pulled the front door open, a small ding announcing her arrival.

"Sawyer!" Charlie laughed, practically jogging her way.

She wrapped her arms around the older black man and they held on to each other. July was the last time they had stood in the same room. It felt like an eternity ago, even though it was only a few months.

"I've missed you, old man," she whispered, tears prickling her eyes. She clung to him hard, refusing to let the moment go so easily. "The calls aren't enough."

"No, kid, they really aren't," Charlie said, his voice full of emotion. "Let me look at you." He pulled away, his hands on her shoulders.

She smiled at him, unable to stop it. He was a good man, and the only person she'd ever even considered close to a father. He'd found her on death's door - and his door. She had been trying to break into the gym to use the showers, anything. Her injuries had stopped bleeding during her trip up to New York, but they had gotten infected. She had been dying, and he just picked her up, put her in his bed, and got to work. He only had one power, to heal, but he was very good at it.

He looked her over for a very long time. She just waited. He would need to make sure that his decision to sell her out to Vincent's team was really agreeing with her.

"You're still hitting the gym. Your shoulders are more defined. They forcing you into more upper body work than I did?" Charlie grinned, patting one of her shoulders.

"We have a schedule," Sawyer said, shrugging. His hands slid away, and she reached over to pat his massive belly. "Still not on a schedule?"

"I'll have you know, I'm very healthy." He chuckled, hard enough that he shook. "There's no heart attacks in my future."

"Good. Where are they?" She looked around. She didn't see any rugrats running around.

"Liam took them on a field trip this morning," he said, leading her to the back. "I figured you and I can go on lunch, then we'll hang out with all of them when everyone is back."

"I like that idea," Sawyer whispered. Field trips? She'd never done that. She brought them here after school; she helped them with their homework, played games with them, taught them how to defend themselves. But a field trip? "Where did they go?"

"Hayden Planetarium," he replied. "You know the one."

"Yeah, it's famous," she mumbled. She missed this gym, she thought as they walked through it. "Anyone staying in my room right now?"

"Nope. Still exactly how you left it. I'm going to keep it that way, too. You ever need a place to crash, you have one here. This is still also your gym as much as it is mine. Only let the kids crash there if their parents need them to stay over. They respect your things, and a few of the girls have taken to making sure the apartment stays clean."

"Charlie." Sawyer swallowed. That was sweet. Tears were still in her eyes as they made it to his office on the second floor. She appreciated Jasper's silence through it all, just letting her and Charlie pretend it was just them.

"They want you to come home," Charlie explained as he sat down behind his beat-up desk.

"I know," she whispered, looking down at the floor.

"But you can't."

"But I can't." She fell into the chair in front of his desk.

"I know, and I understand, kid. I do. I haven't explained it to them yet, but they'll be okay. It'll be good for them to see you, though. Even if you can't come back up here to live, because you're scared to, you can come visit."

"I agree," Jasper cut in. "We'll talk about scheduling some trips for the team to visit so she can."

Sawyer turned to him as he closed the office door and sat in one of the extra chairs. That wasn't what she'd been expecting from him. She hadn't been expecting him to get involved at all, really.

"Thank you," Charlie replied. "I would appreciate that."

"Me too," she offered, still watching Jasper. What was his game? He'd never really liked what she did up here. He just shrugged, but didn't say anything more.

"How's everything else? I heard about some thing in Texas? And a man named James has been stopping by and bothering me. Says he can keep me updated on how you're doing?"

"You know James?" Sawyer glared to Jasper, who just looked confused, then looked back at Charlie. "Really? Blond, greying hair? Grey eyes? Laugh lines, wrinkles. Probably in his late forties?"

"Yeah, that's right," he confirmed.

"That's our handler. He is the best person to talk to if you want to know where we are and what we're doing. If he offered to keep you up to date, then he's trying to do something nice," Jasper said, stretching out his legs before crossing them. It exposed part of the new prosthetic.

"Okay, and where did that come from?" Charlie pointed at the leg.

"Happened during the Atlanta incident," she told him. "As for Texas, it happened. It was...weird. Anti-Magi group, serial killer, unreg Magi. Charlie, it was fucking weird."

"I bet it was." He hummed and crossed his arms, leaning back in his chair. "How's the other teammates? You're still getting along with everyone? You can be honest with me, if you haven't been on the phone."

"I'm getting laid now," Sawyer said perversely. "I haven't lied to you about anything. You know what's going on with my love life. It is what it is."

"We'll order food here, and you can keep telling me how it is. Lot of men and not a lot of you," Charlie teased.

She narrowed her eyes at him. "Why don't you tell me how the gym is still up and running?" She sure as hell wasn't funding it; she didn't have any money.

"Your men released all your funds to me and hooked me up with an accountant that properly invested it, so the money can continue to pay for the gym and replenish in the market. After getting Liam's college paid off, they thought it would be easy to handle it."

Sawyer turned back to Jasper.

"Zander is the computer guy, remember?" Jasper shrugged. "He might be a prick that doesn't seem very smart, but he knows his way around the web. Vincent knew someone for Charlie to meet. We wanted him to surprise you with that."

"I wish people would just tell me what's going on half the time," Sawyer muttered in annoyance. She dropped the annoyance and looked back at Charlie though. "I'm glad. I would hate to see this place go under."

"Fight Nights are going really well for me, too. We started charging admission and we moved them to weekly." He chuckled. "There's one every Friday, if you'll be in town."

"We should be gone before then," Sawyer sadly told him. "Sorry. I wish. Right now I only get to beat up on Zander."

"A pity," he laughed. "Let me order something for us to eat. Kids won't be back for another couple of hours."

She listened as he got them subs from a local joint only two blocks away. They would send a kid to run the food down. She pulled out her wallet and checked for some cash. She still had a little bit left, sitting on it just in case anything came up. She pulled out a twenty for tip, while Jasper pulled out enough cash to pay for the meal.

"I can pay," Charlie whispered hotly at them.

Sawyer laughed at the hilarity of the comment.

"No, we're treating you," Jasper replied sternly. "No worries."

Charlie just hung up the phone, since he was done making the order, and glared at them. She was still laughing as the food showed up and she told the kid to keep the change from what she and Jasper gave him. The boy must have only been eleven, and he was getting something close to a thirty-dollar tip for twenty dollars in subs. They had made his day.

"It always feels good to do that," Charlie said through chuckles as the kid tore off to enjoy his prize.

"Right?" Sawyer agreed, grinning like a fool. "Harley was a runner when I found her, remember?"

"I could never forget."

They ate quickly, laughing over small stories, telling Jasper all about the children Sawyer kept finding.

"She would bring them home like strays, young man. You have no idea. It was like every week she was in the city, she had another one sitting at my table, eating my food, with bruises that needed healing."

"Thank goodness I never brought home actual animals?" She shrugged as Jasper silently chuckled, his shoulders moving as the only sign.

"I'm sorry we took you away from this," he told her. "Really. It freaked me all out when we first pulled you out, but you really have done amazing things."

"She's a treasure."

Sawyer just shrugged.

"Why New York, though?" Jasper frowned. "Why, after you tried to escape Axel, did you come up here? You didn't know Charlie yet."

"I actually survived them dumping me into the ocean off a cliff." Sawyer sighed. Her eyes unfocused. She thought back to the hellish, fevered time from Charlotte to New York. "Two bullet holes in me. My chest cut open to the bone. My hip wound was practically a gutting." She closed her eyes and remembered. Why New York? "I pulled myself out of the water. I stole a car. Dropped it off, stole another car. Robbed a gas station for bandages and whatever I could get my hands on for the injuries." Why New York? "I was hoping that I could get to New York and try to see if the IMPO, since I made the deal with that team, would protect me. I was out of it. I had no idea what was on the news." Sawyer opened her eyes again. "I got here, barely alive. I saw the news. Heard what people were saying. Shadow: dead. IMPO team: dead. Axel willing to commit major acts of terrorism to get what he wanted." She looked down at her hands. "I had nowhere to go. My deal with that team got them killed. I stumbled on the gym, tried to break in. Charlie found me."

"The rest is history," Charlie finished for her. "Her wounds were severely infected. I put her into a coma for a week to treat them and keep the fever down. I had the right instincts about not taking her to a hospital. She mumbled in her sleep. Told me things. When she woke up, I learned the full story."

"I'm sorry for asking," Jasper whispered. "I didn't mean for this to take a dark turn."

"It's fine," Sawyer forgave him. "It was years ago. And look at me now. Charlie helped me get healthy. Then he taught me how to fight, not just shove the pointy end of a dagger into someone. He helped me achieve this physique. I changed." Sawyer smiled at her golden boy. "Then you guys barged in and ruined everything."

"I would say Axel ruined everything and we fixed it," Jasper countered.

"Men, you all tend to ruin things," she retorted.

"I'll give you that," he conceded.

Sawyer's gentle smile turned to a victorious grin. Jasper was much easier to beat in verbal wordplay than Vincent.

"Wow. He's whipped," Charlie muttered, looking between them. "They all that bad?"

"Fuck no," she told him. "I fucking wish."

That brought more laughter from all of them.

"Charlie!" Liam's clear young voice rang out.

Sawyer nearly jumped out of her seat. Her heart began to race. For years, she only had two close friends. Two. Charlie and Liam. Liam had learned about her much later; she told him after what happened with Axel in LA, and he'd still wanted to be near her and in her life.

He'd hated her since before Texas. Refused to speak to her - all her news about him came from Charlie. He was twenty now. He hadn't answered her call for his birthday.

She was terrified of seeing him.

"Does he know I'm here?" Sawyer asked quickly.

"No, I wanted you to be able to surprise them all," Charlie answered, opening the office door. "Coming down!" he roared back.

Sawyer followed him out of the room with Jasper. She wasn't used to being nervous like this, but it was becoming more common. Nervous for a date with Jasper. Nervous for a conversation with Elijah about him and Quinn. Nervous about seeing Liam.

Too goddamned nervous.

"I have a guest, as well!" Charlie announced as they walked into the main area of the gym.

Sawyer stepped out from behind them and saw her kids. All of them. She swallowed back her emotions. They were all there. Ages seven to twenty. All going wide-eyed at the sight of her.

"Hey," she called out softly.

"SAWYER!" It was like all of them had screamed her name at once. The younger ones came running immediately, and she was jumped. She grabbed two, hugging them tightly before getting two more of them.

As the younger ones jumped around, even bothering Jasper since they remembered him, Sawyer looked up to the teenagers. Liam hadn't moved at all. None of them had. Some looked a bit pissed. She wondered how much Liam had talked to them, how much he'd expressed his own anger at her to them.

"Let me talk to the older kids," she told the younger ones. "Keep Charlie and Jasper busy for me, please."

"Yes, Sawyer!" one girl saluted her. Others giggled and laughed. They cleared a way for her to get to Liam and she started it off by glaring at him.

"Workout room. Now," she snapped, pointing to the room where she would hold her lessons.

The teens smartly listened. She followed them and locked them all in together.

"You said you weren't coming back," Trevor started off, angry and glaring at her. "That's what you told Liam."

Sawyer closed her eyes and rubbed them gently. When she looked back up, her temper was firing up as well. She was *not* going to be talked about or chastised by a bunch of teenagers. "Liam knows more about what's going on than the rest of you. He understands why I'm not going to live in New York anymore and is just angry."

"Don't talk about me like I'm not here," Liam said with a growl.

"Don't spread rumors," Sawyer retorted, turning on him. "You know better. I opened up and gave you the full story, Liam, and what do I get in return? Your petulance? Your anger?"

"We needed you here and you decided you weren't coming back!" Liam yelled.

"You called me a coward!" she roared. "I explained it all to you and you called me a coward!"

"Explained what?" Jessie asked, her arms crossed. "What does Liam know that we don't?"

"That I'm a retired assassin called Shadow," Sawyer said it without thinking. The moment the words were out, there was no taking them back. She watched Jessie's eyes go wide. "Fuck." She hit the wall with her open palm, pissed that she'd just said it like that.

"Sawyer..." Liam sounded a little guilty. "I didn't want to expose you."

"So instead you made them think I was just running?" she hissed at him. "I guess it's time to tell a story. Gather round, kids. Let me tell you about a girl called Shadow." She said it sarcastically as she leaned onto the wall. "Because her life and 'death' is why I'm in a deal with the WMC for the next five years to stay out of prison. Because my life as her led to me having enemies all over the world. The biggest one, the one I used to work for and the one who thought he'd killed me, found me earlier this year. That's why I was pulled into protective custody. They found out who I was when I nearly died in August." She bared her teeth at them, frustrated. "So *forgive me* if I think I shouldn't be a constant presence in your life right now."

"You..." Trevor blinked a couple of times and sank to the mat. Two other young men did as well, looking a bit dazed. "You used to kill people."

"I still do," Sawyer whispered. "It's why I teach self-defense, though. Charlie taught me how to not kill, and I wanted to teach others who find themselves in places like I was once in."

"You used to get hit," Jessie realized. "You were once one of us."

"In a way," Sawyer mumbled. "I was in a relationship. He taught me to be a thief. Then he taught me how to kill. Then he forced me to kill. Blackmailed me into it, using the lives of others. I'll never let another person unable to defend themselves be put on the line because of me." She took a deep breath. "I won't let you end up like the people I've failed before. So I won't come back to New York. Not permanently. I'll visit. As often as I think I can. But, between old enemies and my political trouble, I can't stay here."

"Coward," Liam whispered. "You are scared of us getting hurt and don't trust us to protect ourselves like you trained us to."

No one else said anything. Sawyer began to think only Liam really thought that way. Maybe it was because he'd known her the longest and had been the closest to her. The first. She'd killed his father to save him from the beatdown she'd witnessed.

"Don't," she warned. "Don't say that to me." She was not a coward. She would not be talked to like that. That boy had no idea what kind of things he was claiming he could protect himself from.

"Seriously, Sawyer!" He was angry again.

Sawyer narrowed her eyes. Was she going to need to prove it to him that this was out of his depths? "Mat," she ordered. "Get there."

"Yeah, let me prove it to you," he huffed. "You don't need to worry about us."

She grinned as he pulled off his shirt and threw it. The kid was turning into a man. She hated it a little, even though she was also proud of him. She just needed to remind him of the difference between a Magi and non-Magi. She had fucking magic.

She blinked directly in front of him and captured his arm and twisted it behind his back. She hadn't even given him a chance to react to her suddenly appearing across the room. Others gasped. They had never seen her magic. She had never shown off in front of her students. She kept it to Fight Night, which they were banned from attending as minors.

Liam tried to toss her over his shoulder and she rode it, sublimating before she hit the floor. He was still hunched over from the toss when she solidified and grabbed him. She tossed him instead, though she could have kneed him in the face too. She didn't want to injure him.

He stayed on the floor, staring at the ceiling in shock.

"I used two of my abilities," she whispered. "I have five, four that matter. I can move through solid objects, phasing, and cloak as well. The last isn't something you need to worry about. I used to have an animal bond. She's dead." Sawyer's voice went cold towards the end of that statement. "Now, here I am, one of the most infamous assassins that walked this earth. I'm telling you that there's a possibility that you can be used to hurt me, by people with different and possibly more powerful abilities than me. If you can't trust my judgement, Liam, then you are a fool."

"Shit," Jessie whispered. "Sawyer...what did he do to you?"

"The scar on my lip. The scar on my chest. The scar over my hip. My left ring finger," Sawyer answered, not looking away from Liam. "He dropped me for dead in the ocean. I should be dead. You don't need all the details."

"We tell you all of ours...because we trust you with them," Jessie reminded her.

"Get up, Liam," Sawyer told him, ignoring Jessie's comment for a moment. As Liam stood up, she turned to the younger girl. "He took my animal bond and used it to keep me in line. Did you know a Magi can feel the pain their animal does? She was a little black house cat." She sank to the mat and stretched out her legs. "He killed her later on. Some of you understand what it means to take the beating so someone else doesn't have to. That was my life. For years. He said kill this person and I did. So he couldn't hurt a young boy the way he had killed my cat." Sawyer waved a hand at all of them, her left, to remind them of the missing finger. "That's why I did this. Made this. Taught you all. To stop you from being me. Forgotten by a broken system, ignored by those around you. I wouldn't watch others go through what I did. And I won't let more children die for me. And that's what you are. Children." She looked up at Liam, who was brushing himself off. "You understand now? I won't let you, or them, be another Henry. I won't. I trained you to protect yourselves, yes, but not to get dragged into my life. Not to get dragged into the criminal underbelly of the Magi world."

The possibility was slim that they would ever be in danger, but Sawyer wasn't willing to risk any of them, for any reason. Non-Magi children, all of them. They wouldn't stand a chance if someone glanced their way, trying to find her.

"I'm sorry," Liam whispered. "I just miss you."

"I know," she whispered back, standing up. "I'm just not sure how to fix it."

"I'm not sure how to do all of this without you." He waved to everyone else in the room. "I'm barely older than them. I'm only-"

"Only twenty?" Sawyer's heart broke. "So was I when I met you. I have faith in you, Liam. I do. You can make this even better. Help kids by doing the right things. I've got it all set up for you."

"Will you come back?" he asked, and she hugged him. They held on to each other for a long time.

"I'll always come back," she promised. "I just won't stay."

"That's enough."

"It needs to be." She laid her head on his shoulder. Gods, why was he so tall now? "You'll always be my little brother." She wondered if she ever told him that she considered him the younger sibling she never had. Now she would, every chance she got.

"All right, big sis," Liam replied with an embarrassed chuckle.

She felt a flood of pride and happiness at his words. "Let's get the kids in here for a lesson," she decided. "Go on, tell them to get in here. I've learned some new things from my team while I've been gone, and I'll teach them to you all. Hurry. I can stay until dinner, then I have plans."

"Sweet!" Trevor jumped up and ran for the door.

Sawyer looped an arm around Liam's shoulders and leaned on him. "You can do this, Liam. I believe in you. You don't need me."

"I'm sorry for being so angry," he repeated.

"Don't be sorry. Just don't let your emotions rule you like that." She chuckled. "Still something I need to work on. It's an ongoing thing, believe me."

"We're all just works in progress. I think that's the saying I heard in Philosophy class." He grinned, and she nodded.

"Yes, we are," Sawyer agreed. "Who we are, what we do. Everything about us. Like your self-defense training." She scooped up a younger boy running to her as Trevor let them in. "Hey, little man. Have you been good?"

"I have, Miss Matthews!" he answered. "Have you?"

"I've been trying." She laughed and watched as everyone got into place. "I've been trying, little man."

9

VINCENT

V incent knocked on Sawyer's door bright and early Monday morning. He needed to make sure she was ready to go, and he hadn't heard from her yet. He would have used his telepathy, but the enchantments in the wall prevented him from doing so.

"What?" Sawyer called out, sounding groggy and unready.

"We need to leave in twenty minutes. Everyone else is down at breakfast." He said it loud enough that someone down the hall looked at him with a frown and put a finger over their lips. Chastised by a stranger. He leaned on the wall next to her door, wondering why she was taking so long. She was normally up before anyone else, since she could never sleep through a night unless she was exhausted.

The door swung open and her head poked out. He crossed his arms and smiled at the tangle of near-black hair that she had falling over her face. She had bags under her eyes, and Vincent hazarded a guess that she had only gotten to sleep right as they needed to get up. Or she tossed and turned all night. It sent a bolt of worry through him, but he wasn't sure asking would get him answers.

"Fuck. Why didn't you try earlier?" She glared at him.

"I did," he answered. Three times in the last two hours. "I got no answer and don't have a key to your room."

"Shit." Sawyer slammed her door closed, and he could hear her rustling around. Five minutes later, she stumbled out of her room.

Vincent sighed as she closed her door. "You could have gone for something more formal," he teased, smiling as he said it. She'd gotten her hair back into a ponytail, looking more managed than it had. It didn't have knots in it, at least, but it was still curly and voluminous. From there, she went standard uniform. Black cargo pants, black t-shirt, work boots.

"Sorry, I don't own a suit," she retorted, looking over him with a sneer. Vincent raised an eyebrow and began walking to the elevator. She was in a bad mood today, that was certain. He just decided to ignore the comment and sneer. Zander, Elijah, and Quinn were also in regular uniform. It wasn't a big deal.

Inside the elevator with her, he heard a soft sigh.

"Sorry. Two nights in a row without any sleep. I shouldn't be an ass," she whispered, leaning on the back wall of the elevator.

"I figured you weren't getting any," he replied, looking back at her. "Do you not own anything formal?"

"No," she answered. "I don't. No dresses, no suits. Lost all the ones I wore when I was younger, never wanted or needed them since."

"I'll take you out later today, then," he offered. "You'll need something for our date."

"Oh?" Sawyer smiled. "After my morning bad mood, you still want to do that?"

"I've seen your morning bad mood at its worst, and it didn't scare me away," he reminded her. She had tried to kill him once. He wasn't going to get pissed off over a mood caused by a lack of sleep. He had better things to use his energy on.

"Touché," Sawyer conceded, bowing her head in mock defeat. "Are you the fashion guy of the group? Do you know anything about dresses?"

"Are you okay wearing one?" He chuckled, moving back to lean on the wall with her.

"Yeah, just no heels." Sawyer motioned to her long legs. "I don't like being taller than the guy. Hard to do when you're five foot eleven and heels are normally a solid three to four inches. Most men don't like women to be taller than them either."

"I didn't know that was something that bothered you," Vincent said honestly. He could see why it would bother her, but it seemed like such a mundane, and slightly insecure, thing. She seemed like the type of woman who completely owned her body. "They would make your legs look longer."

"It's...just a thing," she deflected, shrugging. "I'm really not a big heel wearer and my legs don't need help looking long. I'll get a pair of flats."

"We can make that happen," Vincent agreed softly. The elevator dinged for the lobby and he led her out. The team was already at the front of the hotel, waiting on them, and Vincent couldn't stop a smile as Zander offered Sawyer a small breakfast sandwich. He had asked one of them to make sure they got something for her to eat, and he was glad it was Zander. It was a good way for him to do something nice and harmless for her. Hopefully, the simple food offering wasn't going to set off some argument about letting her take care of herself or something.

"Thanks," she murmured, taking it from him.

Vincent and Elijah got the keys to their rentals. Outside, Vincent raised an arm and Kaar landed. He'd been letting his raven fly free, only a small ankle tag to make sure people knew the bird belonged to a Magi.

"Hey, boy," Vincent whispered, bumping his forehead. "Have a good night?"

Kaar puffed up and sent some annoyance Vincent's way. Kaar didn't like how busy the city was and people kept shooing him off the patios when he tried to take a break from flying around. He was annoyed that they were getting in the car again. He was annoyed that no one was giving him treats.

"All right," Vincent huffed. "Needy-ass bird."

That comment got Vincent an obnoxious caw.

"Dick," Vincent mumbled, opening a car door and letting Kaar jump in. "Quinn, did you bring any of those seeds this guy likes?"

"I did. Here." Quinn pulled out a bag and Vincent took it, taking seeds out and holding them for Kaar to eat out of his palm. When Vincent went to hand the bag back, Quinn declined it. "Keep it. He's your bird. You and he need to work out your issues."

"There are no issues between Kaar and I," Vincent retorted. Not many. The bird was just a loner, and while they were bonded, they weren't particularly close. He had no problem with a self-sufficient animal. He didn't need the closeness Shade and Scout had with Quinn. Kaar would rather spend all day flying around than sitting at his desk with him, and that was okay.

"Sure." Quinn moved to the other car and got in. Vincent narrowed his eyes at the other car, where Quinn and Scout were hiding. Shade jumped into the door Vincent had open. Sawyer followed the wolf. He shut the door on his clown car and looked at Elijah over the top, who just shrugged.

It was a quiet drive to the IMPO main headquarters. The WMC, IMPO, and IMAS owned three massive buildings just a block away from the United Nations. The WMC sat in the middle, with large steps up to the front door. The IMPO and IMAS were more understated, looking like office buildings from the outside.

He chuckled with Elijah more than once on the drive though, as Sawyer whispered obscenities at Kaar, who was trying to eat some of the biscuit that made her sandwich. Vincent sent a thought to the raven, asking him to stop, which only made him ruffle his feathers and jump on the center console to try for the seed bag now in his pocket.

When they parked, Vincent looked at his bird. "Did you not eat anything last night?"

Kaar sent something like a no.

Vincent pulled out the bag and gave the bird more seeds to appease him, then got out. Kaar went straight to his shoulder once out of the car.

"So…" Sawyer helped Shade out then looked at him. "What is really happening today?"

"We're going to meet some big people from the IMPO, our bosses, and they are going to pat us on the back for a job well done in Texas," he answered, shrugging as best he could with the giant bird on his shoulder.

"That's really it?" She frowned at him. He knew she didn't trust it. She probably figured this was going to be a long day of backhanded compliments. He was willing to bet she was right, but he didn't want to say it out loud.

Games. This was all games.

He was tired of them, truthfully. He enjoyed the ones he played with her - the word games, the chess games, the attempts to outmaneuver each other into revealing more about themselves. But he was tired of the IMPO and the games he was about to play.

"Let's go," he told her. He turned to the rest of his team, all making sure their shirts were tucked in. Quinn was even smoothing out Shade and Scout's coats to make them look nice. Scout shook it back out and Quinn growled at him. The wolf didn't shake out Quinn's hard work the second time. Vincent gave a smile at the scene. Those three were so out of place in the middle of New York. "Everyone ready?"

"Yeah, boss," Elijah answered, adjusting Jasper's tie. Jasper had gone with a suit like Vincent, aiming for professional. Vincent was glad someone had joined him in the pursuit of looking presentable. "We're ready."

"Everyone stay on your best behavior," Vincent reminded them, giving a pointed look to Zander. He was the worst at these things, and he grinned back at Vincent as if there was already trouble in the making. The gauged ears, the neck tattoos, the full sleeves of ink. Zander was always looking to stir things up with those who ran their organization.

"How much trouble can we really get into?" Sawyer asked as they started walking to the front door.

Vincent scoffed and looked at her. "You don't want to know." He pulled open the door and let her in. He followed, letting the guys go in behind him.

The AC of the IMPO lobby hit him immediately. He didn't look around, keeping his eyes on the reception desk. He could see Sawyer out of the corner of his eye, though.

She was taking everything in, her observant, quiet way of making sure she knew everything about the room. He wondered what she was thinking, wished he could read her mind, like he always did.

"Vincent Castello," the receptionist greeted him with a purr, standing up. A pretty blonde named Sara. Vincent knew her well. "It's good to see you again."

"It's been a long time, Sara," Vincent said, reaching out to shake her hand. She held it too long, her fingers drifting over his palm when it finally ended. He sighed internally. Ex-lovers. They never knew when to quit. When he'd been younger, he'd fallen for her for a moment, taken her out, slept with her, and realized she was just trying to get with the 'ex-criminal' agent everyone had been talking about. He never made the mistake a second time.

Now he was falling in love with an assassin. He had horrible taste in relationships.

"You have a meeting?" She asked, looking down at her scheduling book.

"We do," he answered. "With-"

"Director Thompson. I've heard about Texas. I thought this was next week," Sara cut him off. "They should be expecting you. Is that her?" She nodded towards Sawyer, who was further from the group. She was a dark figure in the room. People hushed as they walked past her, gave her looks. She seemed not to notice, but Vincent knew otherwise. He watched her longer than he should have, because Sara asked again. "That's Shadow, right?"

"Sawyer," he bit out. "Her name is Sawyer Cambrie Matthews. Use it." Hearing her old moniker pissed him off and made him uncomfortable. He wasn't going to let anyone stand near her and remind her constantly of a past she hadn't asked for. A past that was still trying to claw its way through their lives and ruin what they were trying to build.

"Sawyer." Sara's tongue rolled over the word like she was trying to get a flavor for it. Vincent didn't like it. "Weird name."

"It's her name," he repeated. He didn't find it weird. He found it and the story behind it as sad and interesting as the woman herself. It was given to her by a nurse as a newborn since her mother didn't have the chance to name her before she was left an orphan. "We have to get to our meeting. Buzz them and let them know we're on our way."

"Of course," Sara replied absentmindedly. Vincent kept his eyes on Sawyer, who met his gaze.

Elijah coughed softly, taking his attention away from their assassin.

"What?"

"Don't get uppity with them," Elijah whispered. "I don't like how she used Shadow either, but we can't be fighting the whole world. It's her title. It's the name that's famous. No one knows Sawyer, but they don't trust Shadow."

Vincent held back a curse. Sawyer met them at the elevator. Zander went to her immediately and whispered something Vincent couldn't hear. He saw her eyebrows raise and then she nodded.

"It's fine, Vin," she told him. "Shadow, Sawyer. It doesn't matter. I am who I am."

"You aren't Shadow anymore," he reminded her. She *couldn't* be Shadow anymore.

"I'll always be Shadow to some people. Dead or alive. Let them use it."

He got into the elevator, refusing to respond to that.

Once the team was inside, it was Zander who broke.

"Why? Why should we be okay with them using that fucking name?" he demanded, turning to glare at her.

"Because they might be scared of Shadow enough not to fuck with Sawyer," she answered, crossing her arms. "Or you guys. They might be scared enough of me to not fuck with you guys."

"I don't like that," he growled.

"You don't have to," she snapped. "It was my fucking professional name. You want to know where Shadow comes from? They *never* saw me coming. I was the dark shadow of Axel's retribution. I was always near him, in the dark, ready to kill anyone who fucked with him. Or so they thought. In a world of white Ghosts, I was the reason people were afraid of the dark."

"Stop," Vincent cut in. "We don't have time for this." He didn't want to hear them bickering about her history, not in this building. At home, they could all argue about the use of Shadow. Maybe in the hotel, but not here. It would ruin them. "Sawyer, I'll stop caring for now, but we'll continue this discussion later. Zander, don't start a fight. Jasper, keep him in line. Quinn, you keep doing you." Meaning, staying quiet and unnoticed. Vincent was impressed with Quinn's control through all of this, and the wolves'. "Elijah...make sure we don't lose all our friends on this trip."

"I got him," Jasper confirmed, throwing an arm over Zander's shoulder. "You need to stay with me, the amputee, since you're the medic."

Zander cursed at him.

"Can do, boss," Elijah said, chuckling. "And you?"

"I'm going to play fucking politics," Vincent mumbled. He realized he didn't give Sawyer any orders. Politics. "Sawyer, stick with me or Elijah." He needed a fucking cigarette. He was annoyed he didn't have one before going inside.

"We got this," Elijah said plainly. "No reason to stress today, seriously."

"Sure," Vincent sighed. He thought so too, but he *hated* the idea of people calling her Shadow. That had thrown him. He was trying to regroup. He needed control for this, and getting thrown for loops by his own emotions was not something he needed.

They left the elevator on the top floor. They had stopped a couple of times on the trip, but everyone saw them and decided to get a different one. Vincent ignored Director Thompson's receptionist and went straight for his office. He knocked once.

"Come in, Special Agent Castello," the director called back.

Vincent opened the door and let his team in before entering. His eyes fell on Director Thompson, an older man in his mid-fifties. Salt and pepper hair was combed to the side, with a goatee with the same graying. He wore a perfectly pressed black suit, like he always did. They had met before, on several occasions. Vincent had to appeal directly to him to join the IMPO years ago. No one else had given him a chance. Then he and James had to convince him to let Vincent form the team.

"Director," Vincent greeted him. "You wanted to speak to us about Texas."

"I wanted to personally say good job," Director Thompson replied. "You found yourself in a situation we hadn't expected. Stevenson, the 'sheriff,' had some things to say, but nothing serious. We handed over names of the more violent anti-Magi people to non-Magi law enforcement groups. We already made moves to relocate any Magi living in the area. All thanks to your team."

"And the killer?" Vincent walked closer to the desk.

"Cory Stevenson will be placed under care, probably for the rest of his life," the Director replied softly. "But execution is off the table."

"That's good," Sawyer whispered, cutting off something else from the director.

Whatever Director Thompson had been going to say was silenced. Vincent looked over to Sawyer, who had found a spot near a large fireplace. The office was expansive with couches, a small bar, the fireplace. It was half lounge area and half office and took up nearly a quarter of the top floor of the building. Vincent would guess that there was even a private bathroom and a panic room attached to it.

"Shadow herself, in the flesh," Director Thompson said cautiously, as if he expected Sawyer to blink across the room and kill him for speaking to her. When she didn't respond, he spoke to Vincent. "You know, Special Agent Castello, I've always been somewhat proud of your little ragtag team of trouble and strange, but you really crossed a line there."

"I merely held the WMC to the contract provided to her." Vincent stayed calm.

"You replaced the team that died for her originally," Thompson retorted.

"I'm in the room," Sawyer called out softly. "And there's no need to remind anyone here of anything that has to do with me. We're all well aware of it, all the time."

"She speaks," Director Thompson scoffed. "Are you as arrogant as I've heard?"

"There's no one in this building, excluding Quinn, who can beat me in a fight," she replied, sounding bored. "Is that an arrogant statement when it's a statement of fact?"

Vincent closed his eyes, frustration washing over him. Arrogance was her shield, her defense. Confidence was her way of keeping people from starting the fight to begin with. Using it against the director was not a good move.

"I would say you have less reason to be, since you've been caught and exposed," Thompson reminded her.

Vincent held back a groan.

"Not by you, and not in a fight," she said. Vincent could swear he heard a laugh in her voice.

"Does she follow orders?" the Director asked him.

"She does," he confirmed. "She's just arrogant. She has reason to be." He didn't like admitting she had the right either, but he wasn't going to lie to the director or himself.

"Does she?" Thompson sounded offended. "What does an infamous criminal have to be arrogant about?"

"She hid in New York for four years, right underneath our noses. I would say the arrogance was well-earned." It wasn't Vincent who said it, but Jasper. Vincent was nearly surprised, and Kaar ruffled a little bit, feeling Vincent's near-shock. He would have expected Elijah or Zander to make that comment.

"See." The director picked up a glass from his desk and took a drink. "This is why I wanted you guys to come see me. You all did a fine job in Texas, including you, Shadow. *But* people aren't happy about this. Actually, there's some who say that this might be your attempt, Castello, to take your brother's place."

Vincent's eyes went wide, and he heard curses from the guys, but it was Sawyer's laughter that stood out.

"Vincent Castello is nothing like Axel. Fucking believe me. If he was, I wouldn't fucking be here, that's for damn sure." She was still laughing as she walked closer. Vincent looked at her again, the swagger in her step, the shake of her head as she laughed. "Why would I ever serve anyone like Axel again?"

"Why *wouldn't* you?" Director Thompson asked. "He gave you wealth and power."

"I can have wealth and power on my own," she scoffed, looking insulted. "I did when everyone thought I was *dead*. The wealth, at least. Power was never really my thing. All Axel ever gave me was scars and nightmares."

"Sticking to the story you told them?" Thompson asked quietly.

Vincent narrowed his eyes at the director.

"It's the truth," Sawyer stated plainly.

"Axel confirmed it, and you don't want to see the tape of that interview," the director told them. "But that doesn't mean everyone is willing to believe it."

"Do you?" Sawyer asked dangerously. Vincent felt the room grow colder. The sharp edge of her magic as her temper was rising.

"I do," Director Thompson told her gently. Vincent saw her jerk to a stop, no longer approaching the director to get in his face. "I personally went to the orphanage in the Atlanta area and confirmed your childhood with Special Agents Wade and Williams. I personally looked into the man who 'adopted' you and the Reader who did your reading that you claimed sold your information to Axel. Both were dead three months after encountering you, by the way, and we'd had reason to believe that Reader was dirty for years."

"Whose side are you on?" Vincent asked him. If he believed her story, what was this about?

"The IMPO's," Director Thompson answered. "If you keep doing a good job, like you did in Texas, I'll look out for you. One fuck-up, though, and I'm shutting this down. Do you understand? I can't let mistakes slide. I have to protect this organization from the whispers of WMC and criminal corruption."

"You can fucking *try*," Sawyer told him harshly.

Vincent heard grunts of agreement from his team. He didn't like that his team was going against the director, but he agreed with Sawyer.

"I'll succeed," Director Thompson snapped back. "One step out of line on a case. One broken protocol. I have some sympathy for you, but I won't let you take down the IMPO with you if you fuck up."

Vincent knew that was going to come up. Everyone was looking for reasons to break this team up, behind closed doors where he couldn't see who was for or against them. Now he knew where the director stood. He'd gone out and confirmed her story on his own and decided he would give her and the team *one* chance.

"Thank you, sir." Vincent stood back up. "Is there anything else?"

"No. Keep out of trouble tomorrow at the WMC. Is that clear?"

"Yes, sir," they all replied, except Sawyer. Vincent looked at her and she shrugged, remaining silent. It was almost like she was saying she only answered to Vincent and the team. Vincent was proud of having her respect like that, and terrified of the power that came from it.

LATER IN THE DAY, Vincent took Sawyer out shopping. They had left the IMPO building the moment the director released them. They'd gone back to the hotel and just relaxed. Elijah, Zander, and Jasper went to the pool.

Quinn disappeared to the rooftop with Kaar and the wolves.

He'd grabbed her and brought her to the mall before she could go hide in her room.

"I hate this," she muttered.

"There's a dress code for the show we're going to," Vincent reminded her. "I would like to get you something. A gift." It would be a gift to himself, really. He wanted to see her in a dress.

She narrowed her eyes at him as they walked through the mall. He just gave her a small smile, trying to pretend there was nothing but the obvious answer. "Isn't this something we shouldn't be doing? Doesn't this look bad for the team?"

"No, I always take one teammate out while in New York for something nice. Depends on who needs it. Zander and I went to see a Broadway performance. Hamilton. He had a good time." He chuckled. "It's a fun performance, which he needed."

"But people think I'm yours now, and not in the bedroom sense," Sawyer reminded him.

"You're not wrong." He sighed, his mood deflating at that. "But I won't let them completely run my life through rumors."

"Good," she said, grinning. "What's the dress code?"

"Black tie," he answered. "I was thinking something simple and black for you."

"Oh, amazing." Her voice had a false excitement. "Are you going to tell me what the show is?"

"No." He couldn't tell her the show, or she would find any reason not to go. It was a risk, a dangerous one that could backfire on him, but he was going to try. He hoped she understood his reasoning when he finally did tell her.

Vincent stopped in front of a little boutique and pulled her in. It suited his needs. He found an attendant quickly and Sawyer groaned when he started talking. "We're looking for a simple black cocktail gown for her. Needs to pair well with flats. It can be as short or long as she's comfortable with. Nothing sparkling or jeweled - it's not her style. Simple and practical."

"Know my style?" Sawyer inquired, elbowing him.

"I know you," he teased.

She laughed at his response then followed the attendant away.

Vincent found a seat near the dressing rooms and watched Sawyer, with an armful of gowns, walk out of view.

"I'm ready with dress number one," she announced. She stepped out and Vincent couldn't breathe.

He always thought she was capable of looking beautiful, since she was in a unique way. He's always found her physique to be enticing and dangerous. She owned the space around her, even in sweats and a sports bra, even when she was trying to hide.

The floor-length mermaid gown made her look like a dark goddess. The attendant must have convinced her to release her hair from the ponytail, since it fell in thick and uncontrolled waves over her bare shoulders. The neckline plunged, revealing the small amount of cleavage she had. The waist was pulled in and gave her a curve to her hips that he'd never noticed.

His mouth was dry. She was stunning.

"Well? It shows off the scar on my chest, but any dress would, I think. That one or any of the others." Sawyer stepped in front of the mirror and he noticed that she glided in the gown - no swagger, but rather, more proper. She turned away from him to look at herself and his eyes went straight for her toned ass. "Vincent? What do you think? Will it work for the thing?"

He just kept staring at her. A simple change of clothes had changed her. Her posture was different. No more simple, easy slouch to her shoulders, as she kept herself relaxed. They were square and her back was straight. It made the more feminine features of her face come out, which he could see in her reflection in the mirror. The defined cheekbones she had, the fuller bottom lip, scarred or not.

Stunning.

"Vincent?" She turned to him and he almost couldn't breathe. The spin was perfect. Who was this woman? He'd never expected Sawyer to be good in a gown. It was like she lived in them and he knew that wasn't the case.

"Yes." He was decided. Even if she didn't wear it for their date, he was buying it for her. That gown didn't belong on anyone else. "How much?"

"Four thousand," the attendant whispered to him.

"We'll take it."

"Excuse me?" Sawyer snapped. "You aren't buying me a four thousand dollar dress."

"Consider it an early birthday present," he told her, pulling out his credit card. To himself. It was an early birthday present to himself. She wouldn't sleep with him, which hurt like hell, but he could enjoy her in that dress for an evening.

"Damn it, Vincent," she muttered, and walked back to the dressing room. She yanked the tags off before shutting the door and handed them to the attendant.

"Were the others as good as that one?" he asked the attendant before she ran the charge.

"That one was my favorite for her," she answered softly.

"It's a gorgeous gown. She wears it well, though it reveals the scar."

He hadn't even noticed the scar. She walked out and dropped the dress on the counter for it to be packed away.

"Thank you," Sawyer mumbled.

"No problem. It looked great. You deserve to have something nice."

"I have nice things," she retorted. "Like my Audi. My BMW."

"But no gowns. Nothing nice for you to wear." Vincent took the bag from the attendant after sliding his credit card away. In a softer voice, he continued. "Nothing that makes others realize you're beautiful, like I think you are."

"Don't get romantic on me now," she whispered, taking the bag from him. "Save it for the *date*. Plus, I know I'm not an ugly duckling. I just don't care about looking good over comfort."

Vincent laughed, shaking his head.

Next was shoes, which Sawyer tried on a simple pair of black flats and decided that was it. He watched her buy several other items, even getting a bit curious when she went to the stockings and got a pair of lacy thigh highs.

"You know a lot about dressing up for a woman who cares more about comfort," he mentioned nonchalantly. He wanted to see what sort of information she would offer him in exchange. He wanted to learn more.

"I've played 'pretty date' or 'hired whore' for work before," she replied casually. "If I needed information about a job, or a way into the building without cloaking, I could dress for it."

"Really?" Vincent was curious.

"I got inside a mansion for one of my hits by pretending to be his brother's escort." She shrugged.

"I'll remember that," he murmured, thinking about the possibilities.

"Don't. I hate that shit." Sawyer huffed, rolling her eyes. "The things I used to do were easier and safer with as little human interaction as possible."

Vincent raised an eyebrow, but he would give her that point. He didn't question it as he paid for everything she was going to wear with the dress.

"Ready to go back to the hotel and relax for the day? Tomorrow will be rough on you and then we'll have a late night. You might want to get some extra sleep tonight, pass out early." Vincent tried to make is sound casual as he walked out of the mall with her.

"You noticed I haven't been sleeping." She called him out.

"Yeah." He wasn't going to lie to her.

"It's all of this." She waved around, and he guessed she was referencing New York. "I'm worried about tomorrow. About what the WMC is trying to do."

"What do you want to do to stop it?" He was always so curious about what she wanted, what she thought would work to solve a problem. He was desperate to get inside her head and knew he never would truly know what was going on in there.

"Fight them for it." Sawyer's tone was hard. Her face was emotionless, but he knew she meant it. "They can take me off this team over my cold, dead body."

Vincent didn't have an argument against that. He knew she meant every word.

10

QUINN

Quinn met James in the IMAS lobby on Tuesday morning. The team was headed for the WMC for mental health evaluations. He was alone for whatever this was.

"Quinn. How are you?" James kindly greeted him.

He liked their handler. James was a good male who looked out for them as if they were his own children, even though they were adults. Quinn never knew or had a father, but he privately wished James could have been that person.

"Confused," Quinn admitted. "Why am I here?" He held onto Shade's collar with his right hand, letting his fingers scratch the wolf underneath where it was itchy. Scout stayed pressed to his left side, nervous and tense. The wolf didn't want to be touched, though, and had never let Quinn really touch him when he was nervous. He knew that Sawyer could soothe Scout, but he didn't have her around. Scout liked and trusted that woman a lot.

"They need you to hear them to." James sighed. "Come with me. I only know very rough details."

"I'll listen," Quinn promised. He walked with James to

an elevator, but instead of going up, they went down. He frowned at his companion for the meeting, but James didn't offer any more information.

They went down three floors, deep underground and left the elevator. Quinn was more comfortable with this than he was on the street above. He could feel the earth on the other side of the walls and knew that if anything messed with him down here, if anything threatened his life, he could bring the building down. Not only could he bring the building down, but he and those with him would be perfectly safe. It would be easy.

"Now that we're down here." James pulled him to the side. "This is about Druids."

Quinn snarled in response. He should have guessed. His temper immediately flared, and he started to seriously think about how easy it would be to bring the building down.

"They need you," James whispered. "Quinn, there's Druids down in South America that are believed to be killing off villages of people, destroying land. I don't know many details."

"Where?" he demanded. He could already guess, but he wanted to know for certain.

"The Amazon rainforest," James told him. "Right now, I'm telling them that you will only give them what you know about Druid powers, you will only work in a consulting position. I don't want you going in that rainforest. From what you told me before-"

"I won't go in that rainforest," Quinn growled. "Ever. I'll tell them what I know, then we're done. I'm not going after Druids. I'm not getting involved in whatever is going on down there."

"You knew something was going on?" James asked, looking confused.

"I could feel it all the way in Georgia," he answered.

"Okay." James looked shocked but recovered quickly. Quinn knew he wasn't normal. He knew Elijah had been shocked by the information as well, knowing he could feel Druids that far away when they used the full strength of their magic. "Let's go meet these people."

James led him to a meeting room and Quinn went in before his wolves, so he could make sure the room was safe, that no threats were there.

It was full of soldiers of various ranks he didn't care about. He knew them. He could understand the patches with chevrons and stars. He just didn't give a shit. He was the most powerful Magi in the room and therefore the dominant one. They would listen to him or he would leave.

"Let me introduce you all to Special Agent Quinn Judge, son of Fiona, a Druid of Northern Canada," James announced. "You requested his help with your current mission."

"It's good to meet you," one man said as he stood up. Quinn didn't shake the hand offered when the colonel stepped in front of him. "I'm Colonel Fischer, Harold Fischer."

"I hope I can help." Quinn kept it short. He hoped he could help them not get themselves killed. Nothing more.

"We think you can," the colonel mused. "What do you know about the Amazon rainforest?"

"It spreads over nine different nations of South America, but that's not what you want to know," he answered and corrected Colonel Fischer in the process. "You want to know about the Druids that call it home."

"Ah, James must have given you a quick rundown," another male said from the table.

"No. I knew something was happening down in that

region concerning Druids for a few weeks. James just told me that's what you wanted to talk about," Quinn corrected him too. He didn't normally play word games like Vincent or Sawyer could. He didn't understand much of the nuance of language, but he knew when someone was flat out wrong. That male had been wrong.

"What can you tell us?" the colonel asked, going back to his seat.

"That whatever you are planning will probably lead to a lot of people dying. I would recommend just not getting involved."

"Is he serious?" a third man cut in, looking at James. "Does he know who he's talking to?"

"He is serious, and he does know who he's talking to," James replied darkly. Quinn knew his handler took him seriously. James would never disregard anything he said. "Quinn?"

"The Druids in the Amazon have always been more aggressive than most. They are wilder than Druids in other areas of the world. It's probably the isolation and environment," he explained. "If you think they are out there killing innocent people living in the area, then you must be thinking that you want to go in and put them down. You will only get more people killed. You should just evacuate people living near their borders and make a deal with them that lets them extend further out."

"How would you know? You're from Northern Canada," the colonel asked. Quinn and his wolves could all smell the indignant anger, as if they threatened him personally.

"Druids all over the world talk. I was raised by them. I heard things, learned from them."

"How do they talk?" Quinn didn't see who. Female.

"The animals. All of them," Quinn said nonchalantly. To

him, it was normal. Shade and Scout frequently brought him information from any animal willing to share with them. Normally, his wolves just heard the birds and reported that. Birds were full of rumors. "You think only bonded animals have any intelligence? They might grow more intelligent than most, but that doesn't mean everything else is stupid."

"You're kidding," one scoffed. "Who is this kid?"

"The most powerful Magi in the Americas, excluding the Druids and the Nymphs. Probably the world," James reminded the stranger. "You wanted him here, you wanted to know what he knows. Expect that he's only going to tell you the hard truth."

"Well." The colonel grabbed a remote and hit a button. Quinn heard something turn on and a projection hit the far white wall. "We're planning a deep recon mission that has a 'kill on sight' objective if a Druid turns aggressive on them. Right now, two villages have gone off the grid with no trade contact. Magi and non-Magi in the area are saying that the Druids have been overtaking their fields and destroying their homes as they push the boundaries of the rainforest back out." The map on the projection had spots with village names. Red areas where farms had been destroyed. "If my men can't kill a Druid to stop this, what can?"

"No one," Quinn answered. He only knew one person who had before. Him. No one would ever know that though unless he told them.

"You have," a woman called out from her spot. He glanced over to her, shock racing through him. He'd been too confident too soon. "You have once before. It's why I wanted you here, to listen to this, and join the mission."

"How do you know that?" Quinn asked, anger flowing through him, a rage he had forgotten he was capable of.

Human women. They always seemed to know too much. This black haired, cold-eyed bitch looked like she thought she knew *everything*.

He instantly hated her.

He held back the want to kill her where she sat. He chained it down. Six months ago, he wouldn't have. Six months ago, this woman would have died the moment she'd pissed him off. He was only holding back now for...he didn't know exactly why. He knew he didn't want to be a monster, a feral, too-powerful beast...was that the reason? Did killing this bitch make him a monster?

"I worked protection for a Magi scientist who studied them," she answered. "It's why I'm here. The scientist is also here, answering questions. We went to Northern Canada about two years ago. We've met Fiona. You have her eyes, Rogue Wolf. You killed the Druid she had wanted to take over her territory when she passed."

Quinn snarled. His mother spoke to outsiders about *him*? Told strangers and outsiders his given name? How fucking dare that raving bitch in heat. If Quinn remembered his mother right, she probably slept with the scientist in exchange for talking to him.

"If you want to live through the rest of this meeting, you will call me Quinn," he growled. That was the line. He wasn't going to hear Rogue Wolf from that bitch's mouth again. "Did she tell you why I killed that Druid, or how?"

"No," the woman answered. "No, Quinn, she didn't."

"Then don't presume you know fucking anything," he commanded. He wondered why fucking females always thought they knew everything. This bitch knew *nothing*.

"He's killed one? Colonel..." One of the younger men at the table looked shocked.

Colonel Fischer watched him thoughtfully. "I would love for you to go with the team-"

"No," Quinn told him finally. He felt bad for the people in the Amazon, but he wasn't going. "I'll consult from here."

"I want you on the mission." The colonel looked angry. "If you are so powerful then you can help my team go in and save these people."

"I am powerful," Quinn confirmed. He pushed his magic out, his Source letting it flow from him with ease, and called the earth to his command. The basement shook. He knew the building above them was shaking. The entire block of New York probably thought a small earthquake was happening, maybe even half the city. He ended it after four seconds. He'd counted, carefully.

The room was silent.

"But I am not helping you put down Druids," Quinn finished.

"You'll follow orders. I outrank you," the colonel snapped. "James, you know I can force this. We need someone like him down there. This situation is getting out of hand."

"You won't find anyone else on the planet like Quinn," James told him softly. "And I'm not going to force Quinn to do anything he doesn't want to do."

"So that's it? We just let these Druids walk all over us? Take people's homes? Run them out of the fucking jungle?"

"Yes," Quinn answered. He wasn't going down there and picking a fight with a group of Magi that could kill him. Not when they already wanted to. He was their enemy for a reason.

"Is there nothing I can do to get the world's expert on Druids to go down and help my team stop this? You've even killed one before."

"No." Quinn wasn't going anywhere near their kind. Not *again*.

He turned and began to leave the room, ignoring one of the soldiers cursing at them. James followed him but said nothing. Quinn could smell James' worry and pride.

On the elevator, the handler did finally speak. "If they agree to drop the idea of you going, are you willing to give them more information?" he asked softly.

"Yes," Quinn answered. Shade and Scout were pressed against his legs. They hadn't liked the idea of going near any more Druids. They hadn't liked the fear Quinn had tried to bury at the thought of it.

"Rogue Wolf?" James tested the name and Quinn snarled at it.

"The name my mother finally gave me when I grew into my abilities. Before that, for most of my life, I was just 'boy,'" he explained to his handler. "Don't use it."

"Does anyone on the team know it?"

"Elijah," Quinn answered softer. "Elijah knows nearly everything." Not everything. Not the parts that really mattered.

"I won't tell anyone else. I'll talk to them when you're gone and let them know that you are comfortable consulting them here or over conference call when you return to Georgia."

"Thank you, James," Quinn whispered honestly. He ran his hands through Shade's dark fur, looking for comfort and hoping to comfort his wolf all the same. He couldn't talk to James about the things he needed to get off his chest now as memories flooded back to him. He didn't want to talk at all. He wanted his pack. He wanted his males around him while he was feeling raw. Raw from the city, raw from the meeting. They would be the balm he needed.

"Go back to the team," James told him. "I got everything from here."

Quinn did just that, heading straight for the WMC building, and forcing the idea of Druids in the Amazon out of his mind. He tried to ignore the memories of his mother, and of the Druid he killed. He felt the uncomfortable sensation of his heart being ripped from his chest at one memory that decided to haunt him before he found the team.

He wished he could forget the reason he'd killed her.

He went to a floor of meeting rooms, directed there by a receptionist. He knew one of the rooms had been assigned to the team to wait in while they were called into appointments. He entered the team's designated room, 2-C.

He found Vincent, who pointed him silently to Elijah - Vincent's way of saying he knew something was wrong, but he would respect Quinn's closeness to their cowboy. It showed Quinn he had a good pack leader, a good alpha who led a group of alphas. He grabbed Elijah and was nearly panicking as Elijah followed him to a dark corner of the room.

"What's wrong?" Elijah sounded sick with worry. "My bud, what's wrong?"

"Druids," Quinn answered. "They want me down in the rainforest to deal with Druids."

"What did James say?"

"He's not going to let them force me. They can't anyway, but there was this one bitch who knew my *name*." Quinn touched his own chest, pointing at his heart. "*My name.* She met my mother and now they know I've killed one of them before. Stupid bitch blasted my life out there to the entire room." He wished he'd killed her. He should have ended the bitch, put her out of her fucking misery for it. He couldn't remember why he'd stopped himself.

"Holy shit," Elijah mumbled, wide-eyed in shock.

Quinn's fury beat in his veins. He debated on going back and taking the building down on their heads. He wanted to, he wanted so bad. "They want me to go Druid hunting. Apparently Druids down in the Amazon are acting up. I told them that going in was going to get more people killed." He was snarling as he spoke, unable to hold down his feral rage.

"We're not letting you go to the Amazon," Elijah whispered. "We're not. I'm not letting you anywhere near that place, Quinn."

"The Druids down there are even wilder than my mother," Quinn told him. His mother was crazy. Druids tended to go mad from isolation. He knew what no one else did. He was raised by her. The scars on his back were evidence of how far the madness could go. He didn't want to know how much crazier the Amazon Druids could get.

"Elijah is right," Vincent called out softly. "You aren't going anywhere near that. IMAS can get their own men killed. James and I won't allow them to get you killed, too."

"They can't make me," he growled. "I'll fucking kill them if they try."

"Let's hope it doesn't come to that, but if it's needed... Quinn, you can quit. You aren't beholden to this organization like Sawyer is. You don't need to work for them, or follow their orders." Vincent walked closer. Quinn let him. He trusted Vincent and his other packmates. He might have gone to Elijah first, but Vin was their leader, even if he wasn't the most powerful Magi in the room. "If you decide to quit, if that's what it comes to, you will always have a home with us. It doesn't matter if you're on the team or not." Vincent gently touched his upper arm. "We got you, brother."

"Thank you." Quinn's heart swelled. Vincent had called him brother. Their leader was changing, relaxing, growing closer to those around him. "What about Sawyer?"

"You quitting the team shouldn't have anything to do with her. Don't worry. We aren't letting anyone take her either." He made it sound like a promise. "Quinn, this isn't the end of the world."

"He's right," Elijah agreed. "It's not. It's shitty that some bitch knows who you are, knows some of your past, and tried to drag you into an IMAS mission, but it won't ruin everything. I mean, everyone here knows what you did after you left the Druids, and it's never been an issue."

"Yeah," Quinn sighed. He slaughtered part of a non-Magi biker gang that thought to mess with him. He hadn't realized at the time what he'd done was wrong, protecting himself in the most violent way possible. Vincent and Elijah explained it to him when they found him. It had never been held against him, but it was a bad introduction to the world around him. "I'm just so angry. Why did they think I would be interested in going down there?"

"We can tell you're mad." Elijah chuckled. He didn't get the joke, but Elijah sobered and continued, "They aren't thinking about what you want."

"No." Vincent sighed. "It's about what they want. They think you'll make sure their mission succeeds. They don't care about *you* at all. That's IMAS. Get in line and follow orders. Expendable." He shook his head. "They can't treat you like one of their grunts though. You're a Special Agent with the IMPO. You outrank most of them."

"Where is everyone else?" Quinn asked, ending the

topic. He didn't want to discuss Druids anymore. Period. He wanted to know where the rest of the team was.

"All in their reviews and mental health evaluations. Elijah is done, and I still need to have mine," Vincent explained, going back to sit down.

"Yours is going to suck," Elijah reminded him. "And Quinn, you don't have one. They only brought you up here for the IMAS thing, it seems."

"Good." Quinn bit out, sitting down next to Vincent. Elijah sandwiched him between them. He liked it. Shade and Scout had gone into a corner for a nap and Quinn had two brothers flanking him while his wolves rested. It was comfortable. It eased his anger.

"I'm not looking forward to mine," Vincent admitted. "It'll be nearly as bad as Sawyer's is probably going."

11

SAWYER

Sawyer tapped her foot impatiently in the small office. A guard had put her in the room nearly an hour before and left her there, as if she really didn't have anything better to do. She didn't, but anything was better than this. The sterile, small, white office was beginning to annoy her. The lights were too bright, the furniture too uncomfortable.

It was a tactic, and Sawyer cursed herself for not realizing it sooner. Push her into a state where she couldn't hold anything back or consider her words before she spoke. Realizing that, she calmed down and waited patiently. The tension and anxiety left her body as she mentally prepared herself for it. She had considered this would just be a meeting with a doctor who would ask uncomfortable questions, fishing for something that needed fixing. Now, she knew it was much more. They needed her to fuck up and were willing to play games with her head to make that happen.

Sawyer could play games, too.

She went to the same headspace that saw her through

every piece of torture the world had thrown at her. She was doing this for someone else. Her team. They needed her to succeed. She would take the abuse: the uncomfortable chair, the bright lights that were too hot, the wait.

She shut it all out and just sat there. She would give them nothing.

Another twenty minutes rolled by before the door behind her opened. She didn't turn to see the Magi entering. Sawyer was stronger, that was immediately obvious, and it was all that mattered. This Magi would lose if a fight was needed. That gave her confidence.

"I'm Doctor Staub," he announced, walking into her view. She looked at him with a blank face. He was a mid-forties, attractive, if plain, man. Brown hair, brown eyes, easy smile. "You must be Sawyer. It's a pleasure to see you today." He extended a hand and she stood up slowly. She had him by two inches, which didn't faze him. He must have already known. Most men were intimidated by a woman taller than them, Sawyer knew from experience. She shook hands with him, then sat back down.

"Nice to meet you," she replied as he went behind the desk.

"I'm sorry for the wait. I was with another patient who took much longer than I'd expected. I would have scheduled you for later if I had known," he lied. Sawyer knew it was a lie. He was fidgeting with a pen; his breathing had changed from comfortable to uncomfortable. He'd over-compensated in information, like he was making an effort to cover up any holes in the story that could lead to questions later.

It had been a long time since she'd met a liar *that* bad. She wasn't the best at catching the signs of a lie, but he'd been so obvious. Not even Quinn was *that* bad at lying, though he rarely lied at all and they were all tiny white lies that people told to protect their own privacy.

"It's no trouble," she promised him.

"I had some time yesterday to look over your mental health record and the case you were recently on." Dr. Staub began, looking away from her quickly, down to some papers he'd carried in. "I'll cut to the chase. You are a victim of abuse-"

"I'm a survivor of abuse," Sawyer corrected. She wasn't a victim anymore. She survived. She won. She lived. "Get it right."

"F-f-forgive me," he mumbled. She had obviously thrown him with that. "Survivor. Do you feel that the trauma you experienced changed anything you did in Texas from what you would have normally done?"

"I'm not sure," she answered honestly. "I've been molded by my life and my own resilience, moral code, and beliefs. I'm not sure how I would react differently because there was never a situation like it before I was...Shadow." She said it carefully.

"You became Shadow at sixteen, according to records." Dr. Staub wrote something down as he said that. "Eight years ago. Long time to be an assassin."

"Shadow didn't exist when I was sixteen. I killed my first person at eighteen. Shadow came after that." Sawyer took a deep breath. "I stopped being Shadow at twenty. So, two, maybe close to three years, of being an assassin. Not the last eight."

"Then why do records say that trauma began at sixteen?" Dr. Staub frowned at her.

"Have you watched the tape?" she asked, frowning back. She had no idea what her paper record said. She didn't even know who made it. The team would have never let anything wrong get into it, that was certain, so it had to have been an outsider.

"What tape?" he asked back.

"Ah." Sawyer rolled her eyes and kicked her legs out, getting more comfortable. She slouched back in her seat and stared at the doctor for a long time before offering more information. "I did a video 'interview' for the IMPO and the WMC about my time with Axel. It explained everything. At sixteen, I was only Axel's thief and his... girlfriend." She wanted to choke on the word, but it was the right word. "He tortured and blackmailed me into being his assassin when I was eighteen. He used my animal bond and then a child."

"The scars and missing finger," Dr. Staub noted.

"That's right."

"Do you feel like you ever want to hurt yourself or others?" Dr. Staub asked.

She wanted to be insulted by the question, but it was standard fare. "No," she told him. She didn't say anything else. That was a question that did not need elaborating on. She was also a better liar than Dr. Staub. She had moments where she most definitely wanted to hurt other people.

The questions went on as Dr. Staub tried to find something wrong with her. She dodged and evaded most of them, giving him half-truths or plain denials. It was why she didn't want Jasper to get her a therapist for her nightmares. She would only lie to them. She didn't share her life with strangers. She didn't have panic attacks. She didn't have flashbacks. She didn't have moments of crippling pain or unbridled rage that led her to hurt people for hurting others.

"You have nightmares," Dr. Staub pointed out eventually. "A small note in the report from the case. The killer said he dream walked and saw that you had some fairly vicious nightmares."

Sawyer narrowed her eyes on him, the first time she'd given him anything except a blank face. "Yes. I have nightmares."

"Do you sleep through most nights?"

"I've never needed much sleep," she countered.

"I'll take that as a no," Dr. Staub mumbled.

She held back a rush of anger. This wasn't his business. This was hers and hers alone.

"I think you might have some PTSD from your past, whether you admit it or not." Dr. Staub sighed. "I wonder if this sort of job is healthy for you. Nightmares can progress to flashbacks and render you unable to make the best decisions while working in sensitive situations. Since it's been so long, you probably haven't received the appropriate care. Are you seeing anyone about the nightmares?"

Fuck.

"Yes." Sawyer answered. This was a corner and she was backed in. She hadn't thought that they would talk to *Cory* about her. That kid had lived a fucked-up life, and he'd seen some fucked-up things in her head. She still didn't want to know why he was there or what he thought about them. She had enough nightmare fuel.

"Who?"

"My teammate, Special Agent Jasper Williams. He can dream walk and has been entering during my nightmares and helping me reshape them, change them. He's talked to several experts anonymously about my situation and has a detailed care plan created."

The door clicked open.

"I was hoping you would get something out of her.

Thank you, Dr. Staub. You may go," a feminine voice called out. "I can handle it from here."

"Of course." Dr. Staub stood up and smiled kindly down at Sawyer. "We'll make sure you get the help you need." He began walking to the door and Sawyer heard him whisper, "She's all yours, Councilwoman."

Sawyer didn't react, but it didn't stop her anxiety from sky-rocketing.

"I'm an empath," the Councilwoman whispered after she closed the door. "You have reason to be worried."

Sawyer turned slowly to see the woman at the door. Silver hair, younger face. Councilwoman D'Angelo from the bar.

"Do you know who I am?" she asked.

"Do you know who I am?" Sawyer asked back.

"That's a yes, then." Councilwoman D'Angelo strolled behind the desk and sank into the chair elegantly. She leaned back, and Sawyer could swear the woman probably crossed her legs. She wasn't going to get back up until the conversation was over. "Shadow."

"D'Angelo."

"Councilwoman, to you."

"Then call me by my fucking name," Sawyer snapped. "I have one. It's Sawyer."

"Sawyer. I'm Dina."

Sawyer scoffed and then burst out laughing. She tossed her head back, her shoulder shaking from the hilarity of it. "Dina, angel of learning, D'*Angelo*. Oh, your parents had a fucked sense of humor." She continued to laugh after she said it.

"My parents, Michael D'Angelo and Charmeine D'Angelo?" The Councilwoman didn't sound amused, but those names made Sawyer laugh more.

"Christ," she huffed out, trying to breath. "Talk about ego. Angels, the family of Angels. Love it. I thought Axel had a self-image issue, but that shit takes the cake."

"Are you making fun of my family to get on my good side, piss me off, or just because you can't control yourself?"

"I'm making fun of them because it's easy and I couldn't fucking care about your family," Sawyer answered. "Pissing you off is an added bonus." She knew better than to say that, but she was already in for a penny on the nightmares. Why not go for a pound on the Councilwoman?

"I knew I wouldn't like you," Dina snapped. "I told them you probably had a general lack of respect for authority and you wouldn't come to heel."

"I think I've come to heel fairly well," Sawyer replied. "But you're right. I don't respect most authority, especially when they decide I should die before they even let me open my eyes."

"You know, then, that I was of the stance that you needed to be handled quickly and quietly. That the WMC shouldn't tarnish their name and reputation by having an assassin in our employment."

"The WMC doesn't need me to tarnish its reputation. You are all very good at doing that without my help," Sawyer reminded her. "The WMC has always had rumors of corruption from the general populace. I know a bit more than that. I know Axel used to have people embedded into the offices of several Councilors, on payroll to push agendas that suited his purposes. I killed one of them when they went rogue on him and tried to get out." Sawyer sneered at Dina. "Don't talk to me about protecting your reputation. You didn't even think I deserved a fair trial. You don't think it's a right we, as Magi, deserve. You would have sent an executioner to my hospital room and taken my head off.

You only protect the reputation of the WMC when it suits you."

Dina was paler than she had been, and that pleased Sawyer. She wasn't going to take the bitch's self-righteous, moral high ground bullshit. Ruin their reputation? They didn't have one to stand on.

"Now, I'm fucked," Sawyer whispered, leaning forward to brace her arms on her knees. "I know what I've done, and I'll own up to it every fucking day. Because I promised a group of guys, the IMPO, and the WMC that I would try. I'll pay for what I did, no matter the reason, every day of my fucking life, and I know it. But don't think I won't fight for those days just because they will be hard. I might go down, but I'll go down swinging."

"I'll have you in a prison cell eventually," Dina replied coldly. "I won't let a *monster* walk around like a *hero*."

"If you think I'm the monster, I would love to know how you consider Axel."

"You're both monsters," Dina said, ending in a hiss. "You sit there, outwardly calm, but I feel the rage inside. You are a bomb waiting to go off, aren't you? Ready to bite the hand that feeds you, ready to go feral like that Quinn Judge. I've been wondering when he'll pop for years and backfire on the IMPO. He doesn't even have your background. He's just unnatural and a threat to the peace and prosperity to the Magi."

"Don't," Sawyer snarled. Quinn was not going to be a punching bag. He wasn't going to get trash-talked by her. "Don't fucking talk about him. He has nothing to do with this."

"Him. Vincent Castello. Elijah Grant." Dina smiled. "Jasper Williams and Zander Wade. They all have something to do with it. They all proved they would rather help a *murderer* than help their government. And they are going to go down with you. That I can promise."

Sawyer took a deep breath and pulled back the anger, pushed it down where it wasn't visible anymore. She'd given Dina an in. She wanted the guys left alone.

It made Dina laugh. "Hide it away, but I know. You want me dead for threatening them? I knew it. Once a violent monster, always a violent monster."

"You don't know a goddamned thing. You don't know what it's like to know that if you fail, people will die," Sawyer growled. "You don't understand the desperation or the fear. You don't know what it looks like to see the corpse of a boy at your feet and know that if you had just killed better, faster, then he would be alive. That if you had let a man beat you just a little more, then he would still be alive. I'll trade *anyone* for the people I care about. I'll kill anyone to keep them. If that makes me a monster, then so be it. I'll keep being a monster. I would rather be a monster than a slimy politician."

"Where are you going with this?" Dina asked softly.

"The only way you're keeping me away from my team is over my dead body. You don't have a reason to execute me that doesn't go in direct violation of the contract we made. If you try to break the contract, I won't hesitate in doing whatever I need to do so that my team and I survive. Because *that's* what I do. Survive. It's not about killing people, being an assassin. Every decision I have ever made was one that would lead me to the ultimate goal of surviving. I'm also not some teenager trying to protect a child anymore. This time, I won't fail." Sawyer stood up. "Now, if that's all, I'm going to go back to my team. I have nightmares. You would too if you were beaten and raped on a constant basis, knowing that if you didn't allow it, innocent people would get hurt. Put that in my fucking review and shove it."

Sawyer turned on her heel and walked out of the room, leaving the Councilwoman alone.

If she wanted to a pick a fight, Sawyer needed to be ready to fight back. Which meant the team needed to know that a fight was coming their way.

She ignored the guards who watched her. She could only imagine what she looked like, dressed in all black, her uniform, as she went through the halls.

"Excuse me," one called out. She stopped and saw another guy walking down the hall towards her. Taller than her, in shape. Not a guard, since he had no weapons on him, she guessed absentmindedly. "Are you Sawyer?"

"I am," she answered cautiously.

He spit in her face. "That's for the dead that you're disrespecting by being here," he told her.

As he turned to walk away, Sawyer saw that everyone was watching. This guy was pulling a stunt. Spit in her face, prove that he was willing to say what no one else was. Then he was going to walk away as if she wasn't the second most dangerous thing in the building. Ignore that she might have something to say about it. He was either ballsy and stupid or a coward, scared to hear what she might have to say.

She decided what she thought.

Coward.

She was about to fuck up. On purpose.

She grabbed his arm and stopped him from leaving. He looked down at her hand and she didn't give him anymore time to think about what was going to happen. She turned him back to her, grabbed his collar and slammed him into the wall. He tried to push her off, glaring, but she kept the hold. He pushed himself off the wall a few inches and she just shoved him back into it.

"The dead?" she asked softly. "You mean the people I killed? They were all criminals too. Did you know that?" She kept her voice low. "They were all dirty. They were cut down because they betrayed Axel. I was just the blade."

"No." He was breathing hard. She wondered if he was scared yet. "The IMPO team that was blown to hell because of you."

"The IMPO team that wanted to get me out," she whispered. "That one? The first? I went to them with everything I had on Axel, so they could stop him. Axel was one step ahead of all of us. That team knew what they were getting into. So did I. We thought we could do it."

"And Jon Aguirre's team?"

"He played a game and lost," Sawyer explained. "He wanted to bait Axel out. Axel doesn't get *baited*. He embedded his Doppler whore into the team and then tried to blow up not just that team, but Vincent's too. Missy always did like explosions." Sawyer released a slow breath. "I won't hold on to the death of people who made their own decisions. I won't carry those around anymore."

"Heartless bitch," he snarled at her.

She pulled him off the wall and slammed him back into it, letting the back of his head knock hard enough to make a crack. "You know nothing about my heart," she hissed.

"Sawyer," James called out. "Let him go."

She side-eyed her handler and released the guy, pushing him away for good measure. "He spit on me," she explained, her lips pulling back in another snarl. She was hanging out with Quinn too much.

"I heard, so I came running." James was breathing pretty hard, she realized. She would guess he didn't get enough cardio anymore. "Cayden, go back to your team. Don't fuck with mine again."

"I can't believe *you* would want to protect *her*," *Cayden* groaned. She committed that name to memory.

"What's he mean?" Sawyer asked, ignoring Cayden's glare.

"I was the handler for the team that died. Four and a half years ago. It's why I made Vincent's team." James explained it quickly and professionally. Curt. She realized her humorous handler was being curt.

She also hadn't liked his answer, but that wasn't a conversation for the public. She wished she had known that sooner. "Later," she told him.

"Yes, later. Now, you can't just kick the shit out of anyone who spits in your face," James gently reminded her, a smile taking over.

"I didn't kick the shit out of him," Sawyer retorted. They were both ignoring everyone now. "If I had, he'd be in the fucking hospital like that fucking sheriff from Texas. *Come on.* I just made sure he couldn't spit in my face and walk away without explaining. Cowards do shit like that. I was making sure he couldn't be one. Can't have cowards working for the IMPO and upholding Magi Law."

"Smart-ass," James snorted. "Let's go before someone tries to arrest you."

"Don't I have immunity as a Special Agent to some things?"

"You're a Probationary Agent," James reminded. "And those immunities don't apply when you attack another member of the organization."

Sawyer groaned and followed him to a small hallway. It was where she'd been heading originally. The team was somewhere back here in a room as they all waited for their own appointments and meetings.

"In here," James ordered her.

"Going," she mumbled, feeling somewhat like her dad had caught her fighting with kids in the schoolyard. It was an odd sensation. She'd never experienced it before. Not even Charlie treated her like that. He just let her do whatever the fuck she wanted.

She pushed into the room and saw the rest of the team waiting there.

"How was it?" Vincent asked her immediately, standing up from the long table in the middle of the room.

"Awful. Councilwoman D'Angelo came in and fucked with me," she answered without pause. "She's trying to pull the entire team down."

"Excuse me?" James shut them in the room. "You were supposed to only be meeting Dr. Staub."

"Yeah, well, she showed up." Sawyer growled. "She hates me. There's no changing that. She wants the team to go down for their threat to leave the IMPO and hide me when they considered executing me. She definitely wants me in a cell, probably right next to Axel."

"No." Quinn snarled. "James."

"I can't fix all the problems you guys keep dropping in my fucking lap," James snapped. "Quinn with IMAS. All of you versus a fucking WMC Councilwoman, which by the way, you all started. The Director of the IMPO is breathing down my neck. He wants this team to be the pinnacle of perfection. No slip-ups." He ran a hand through his hair. "Sawyer then decides to attack an agent in the halls. Quinn threatened an IMAS Colonel and his staff. Do any of you have good news? Any at all? Is there something you have done on this trip I can actually use?"

"My review went well," Vincent answered. "They only asked questions about how I felt with Axel being in prison. They didn't question my loyalty."

"My review was easy, but it always is. They've never looked too deep into me." Elijah didn't seem concerned. "Jasper? Zander?"

"Yeah, it was whatever," Zander spoke up.

"They asked about how I was managing the leg," Jasper added. "Nothing serious."

"So their targets are Quinn, for whatever IMAS wants, and Sawyer to..." James looked at her and she shrugged back at him. "Well. I think we all know why they don't like you."

"What was that about her attacking someone in the halls?" Vincent narrowed his eyes at her and she shrugged.

"Stupid asshole spit in my face. I put him on the wall. I didn't hurt him. Just held him and talked for a minute. What's this about Quinn and IMAS?"

Sawyer listened to all of them try to explain at once but eventually James won out. He explained that IMAS wanted Quinn to go to the Amazon rainforest to help handle a situation with potentially aggressive Druids. Her blood ran cold. Her problems with the Councilwoman were political. Running off to fight Druids? That was life-threatening in a much more real sense.

"No," she declared. "Absolutely not." She spun to Quinn. "You're not going."

He crossed his arms. "I don't want to go, so it's not going to happen."

"Good." She nodded, accepting that. "I wouldn't let you anyway. Not alone, that's for damn sure."

"With that settled..." Vincent said, smiling to Elijah like there was a joke. "Are we done here for the day?"

"Yes," James confirmed. "I'll clean up these messes."

"Wait." Sawyer shook her head. "You and I need to talk."

"There's nothing to talk about," he retorted.

"What's wrong?" Vincent looked between them, confused.

"She found out I'm the handler for the...previous team." James answered.

Sawyer crossed her arms like Quinn had. Intimidating was what she was going for.

"It's not a thing, Sawyer," James stressed. "It's not. I don't blame you for them, I blame Axel. They knew what they were getting into. They knew things could go south. Maybe not in that way, but they knew. Honestly, looking back, I'm glad you still somehow got out. We all knew you were a kid in too deep. Your messages to us made that clear."

"I'm not a kid anymore," she told him.

"You all are. Mid-twenties? Children." James scoffed, grinning. "Four and a half years. I've had my time to grieve. You just keep doing right and stay out of trouble."

"Easier said than done," she muttered, grinning herself. She was light-hearted. If he wasn't mad at her, then she wouldn't be mad at herself.

"Let's get out of here," Zander said in a tone that irked her. He was complaining. "Before we find more ways to make James upset."

"I'm not upset!" James laughed. "Frustrated as hell that you're my team, certainly. Go. Vincent, you're taking Sawyer to a show this trip?"

Sawyer noted that James didn't say on a date and that was telling. Did their handler not know?

"I am. Make sure no one gives us a hard time, please." Vincent answered. "We'll make sure nothing looks too suspicious."

"Thank you for that." James left them then and Sawyer let out a long sigh.

"Today has sucked. He doesn't know?"

"It would put him in a bad position," Jasper explained to her. "We'll keep this between us until things look less...fragile."

"I understand," she whispered, just staring at the door James left through.

"Let's go have a good night," Vincent murmured as he walked closer. "We leave New York on Thursday. We're already halfway done."

What a trip it was already. Sawyer was looking forward to getting back to Georgia. The WMC could be assholes in New York. She didn't care as long as she was going back to Georgia with the guys.

12

SAWYER

Sawyer showered and took the extra time to blow dry her hair once they were back at the hotel.

Another date with another boyfriend. She was going from politics and fights with her 'co-workers' to a date with Vincent. Her boyfriend. It didn't seem right.

"That's a word I'm never going to get used to," she mumbled to herself as she straightened her hair. She figured, with the dress, wearing her hair down would be nice. She hadn't straightened it since before everything. Before Atlanta, before they caught her. She wondered if Vincent would notice.

He would. She scoffed, rolling her eyes at herself in the mirror. He would notice and probably have something to say. What, she didn't know, but Vincent noticed everything.

"The show begins at eight," Vincent had told her when they got back to the hotel. "Meet in the lobby at six thirty." She desperately wanted to know what he had planned that required evening wear.

She started getting ready at three and spent the entire three hours getting ready. It was methodical. She made sure everything about her outfit was perfect. The long, simple black gown, the thigh highs, since she hated wearing pantyhose but needed something. She even applied some makeup, having picked out just a few items. Eyeliner, eyeshadow, and a touch of lipstick, just enough to nearly hide the scar on her lip.

Not like it would have changed anything. The dress showed off the scar on her chest and that was going to draw attention to her. It always did. It was one of the main reasons she avoided dressing up. A tank top with normal people was one thing but the scar was so at odds with the dress.

She didn't see any of the guys on her way downstairs at six thirty-five. There was no reason for her to be running late other than her own slowness. She was feeling nervous.

Sawyer saw him in the lobby. The tux was perfection and all black. She smiled at the fact that his hair, dark and curly, wasn't styled to perfection, but loose and clean. He didn't shave either. Vincent's classic stubble gave him the rough handsomeness that Axel had never had.

"You look stunning," he whispered as she got closer.

"You do too," she replied. She didn't say anything else. He was going to have to point out she was late.

"You straightened your hair. I love it," he said, running his fingers gently through it. It was so intimate for where they were, the hotel lobby where so many people could see them. "Your hair was straight the night we met. I liked it then too."

"The night we met..." Sawyer thought about that. "Fight Night. I remember seeing the scar on your chest. You tried to hit on me."

"I did."

"An act?" she asked, as they started walking out of the hotel.

"At the time, yes. I would have handcuffed you that night," he admitted, chuckling. "I won't tonight, promise."

"That's good to know," Sawyer said, chuckling herself. "Will anyone else?"

"Elijah likes handcuffs in general, so he might try again one day."

She had no idea if he was being serious or not by his nonchalant tone. She didn't want to question it. Elijah could keep his fucking handcuffs to himself if it was the case. She wasn't interested.

"So what are we seeing?" She let him get the door and waited for him outside.

"You'll see," he answered simply.

She narrowed her eyes on him playfully, a smirk toying on her lips, but he ignored her to open the car door for her to get in.

Once they were driving she asked again. "Vincent, what are we seeing?" She was more serious this time. She really wanted to know. "I don't really like surprises."

He let out a suffering sigh and side-eyed her a little. "La bohème," he answered, tentatively.

She didn't respond, taking that in. That was an opera. That was an opera she'd seen with Axel. It was one she sang a song from in her car the night she drove Vincent home and he'd been drunk.

"Why?" She barely got the word out.

"Because I want it to be a good memory," he whispered.

"For who?" She didn't like how strangled she sounded. Why did this upset her? It was just an opera.

"Us."

She felt that tension at the back of her eyes. That precursor to tears.

"We don't have to go." He stopped them at a red light. "We can do anything else."

"No." She took a deep breath. "I just need more of an explanation."

"I don't want this to forever be something that belongs to him. He already haunts your nightmares, Sawyer, are we going to give him this too?"

She didn't know how to respond. She looked down at her hands. She curled her fingers on her left hand and noticed that, closed in a fist, from a certain angle, she couldn't see that her ring finger was missing. She could pretend that it never happened, but it would always be there.

Vincent was taking her to something he loved, hoping she would enjoy it more since it was with him and not Axel. He was hoping to take something out of Axel's power, erase some of the pain. The opera never tortured her. It was a memory that could be reworked into something else, unlike her missing finger. She could give it to Vincent. He was right...Axel had enough of her. He didn't deserve this anymore.

"We can see the opera together," she said, looking back up to the road. The tears in her eyes blurred her vision. What Vincent was doing meant so much. She didn't let him in on her nightmare issues, but he was finding his own ways to make them work, to give them something. "I understand your reasoning."

"Did I screw this up?" He sounded concerned.

"No," Sawyer answered. She gave him a small smile. "No. We'll see the opera and we'll have fun. We'll have a late-night dinner, or order room service. Something like that."

"Thank you. I knew you possibly wouldn't enjoy this but...it's something we both know and..."

"I actually liked the opera; did you know that?" she cut him off. "The first half a dozen times, it was like this. Dressed up, beautiful. I was in love with the music and voices and the performance. I was slowly learning Italian." She looked at his profile. He was listening to her, glancing over to her as he drove. "Nothing ever happened there. It's just a date. I'm okay with you deciding this should be ours now. You're right. He doesn't get this too. Not anymore."

They finished the drive in silence. He took them to the Metropolitan Opera House and led them in after parking. She had never visited before and just took in the scenery. As they entered the theatre, she took in a breath at the deep reds and golds of the room. He took her left hand and they entwined their fingers, hiding their hands between them so no one saw it.

"This is gorgeous," she whispered, in some awe. She had seen beautiful theatres before, but she never got used to them. Years since her last opera, it felt like she was at her first one again.

"It is," he agreed. "I want to bring Quinn one day. I think he would be mystified. I considered this trip, but I don't think he's ready for all of this."

"I think so too." She chuckled. A grin took over her face. "He's not ready for all of this. Does he even own a suit?"

"No, he doesn't. Let's find our seats."

Once seated, Sawyer leaned onto Vincent's shoulder. She didn't put her head down on him, just relaxed against him, shoulder to shoulder. They watched others take their own seats, silently waiting for the show to start.

They kept their hands together. His thumb rubbed the back of her hand and she tried to grab it when it began to tickle a little.

"Stop that," she mock-whispered.

174

"No," he said plainly, holding her hand tighter. "Tell me something."

"What?"

"Which is your favorite opera?"

"La traviata," she answered.

"Good choice."

"I like to think so." She smiled and saw one taking over his face as well. "This was a very good idea, Vincent."

"I'm glad. I should have warned you earlier."

"No. I might have looked for a way not to come, but you're right. This shouldn't be his."

"I like it being ours," Vincent whispered, leaning closer to her.

"I do, too."

The lights went down and the show began. They held hands through all of it, only separating for the intermission to use the restroom. They took each other's hands the moment they were back together, only smiling as the intermission ended and singing began again.

At one point, Sawyer closed her eyes and just took it in. The male singer was powerful and experienced. He took her away, on a journey to somewhere else. Vincent squeezed her hand, bringing her back, and she just leaned over and kissed his cheek gently. In the dark, she wasn't concerned about anyone seeing them.

He turned into the small kiss and captured her lips for a longer one. Nothing overtly passionate, but her breath was taken away by it anyway. She wanted him. She ran a hand up his thigh teasingly to let him know.

They didn't need to say or do anything else. The look Vincent gave her told her everything she needed to know.

When it was over, they practically ran back to the car. Back at the hotel, she went into his room with him and kissed him harder, grabbing his tux to hold on. He held her hips to his own.

"No room service?" he asked in a husky voice that made goosebumps over her skin.

"No," she whispered.

"Are you sure?"

"Yes."

One of his hands slid up and found her zipper. He tugged it down slowly and she stepped back so the dress could fall in a pile of black fabric. He looked her over hungrily and she felt beautiful. She didn't feel this way very often, truly beautiful.

Then he reached for her again and ran a hand over one of the gunshot scars on her stomach.

"Missy," she finally gave him the answer. She wondered why she hadn't told him yet. It didn't matter. He was still looking at her like she was the most beautiful woman he'd ever seen.

"I don't care," he whispered. Then he kissed her again and she melted. She slowly undid the buttons of his jacket and he shook it off. She worked on his shirt next. She took her time, as he kissed over her jawline to her ear. She moaned as he nibbled on her earlobe.

When his shirt was gone, she pulled him by his waistband deeper into the room. He growled at her when she backed into the bed. He leaned down and reached around her thighs, pulling her off balance to fall back. She watched him undo his pants and pull off his undershirt. He seemed a little shy, and she wondered if he was nervous. They weren't drunk this time. This time, they were both very sober and there was no grief weighing over them.

"Come on," she called out to him, moving up into the center

of the bed. He stripped quickly after that and moved over her. He removed her black thong reverently. It was the only way she could describe how slowly he did it, kissing the small bit of flesh he revealed while he did. "Vincent," she sighed out.

"I'm taking this slow," he told her. "I don't know when I'll get another chance."

"Okay." She moaned as his mouth connected to her core. He was gentler than Zander had been. Vincent was slow. He appreciated her like a fine wine. She ran her hands through the dark curls of his hair and watched. She came for him, not with a scream, but a whimper, and when he came up, she was caught in the dark olive gaze that she loved. It was all Vincent.

He didn't hesitate to kiss her as he slid in slowly. She could taste herself there, but that didn't bother her. She wrapped her arms around him and let him push her again to another peak. Slow and easy.

Vincent was like a dark harbor in the storm. He was also the storm. Or maybe their lives and pasts were the storm. He picked up the speed and strength of his thrusts and she clung to him, burying her face in his neck.

"Sawyer," he purred in her ear. He hooked one of her legs, pulled it up and the next thrust was deeper than the previous. She screamed out his name in return. She hadn't thought he could do that.

She continued screaming at the new angle. Just hung on for the ride as he kept up the pace. Her next orgasm was like the high note of the song, a crescendo that was climatic and powerful.

He didn't stop, pulling her leg to wrap around his thigh. He moved to lie to the side and they were still face to face as he continued at a slower, softer pace. They were a tangle of limbs as he pushed to finish, holding her tightly as they both panted softly.

Once he was done, they untangled, and she laid her head on his chest. She was feeling good. It wasn't explosive like Zander, but it didn't need to be. Vincent knew how to make her body sing in the ways he wanted it to. She wished she could appreciate it more, without the nightmares. This had been wonderful.

"Sleep here? I know you haven't been."

"I will. I normally can't sleep in new places," she whispered, not wanting to ruin the peaceful and contented feeling that had settled over them. She should go back to her room. She knew she should, but she didn't have the heart to say no to him, get up, and leave. She wanted him. She wanted to cuddle and see how he woke up in the morning. He was hers and she felt a moment of guilt for neglecting him as she handled her own issues. "I'll stay tonight."

"I just want to make sure you get some sleep," he whispered back. "You don't have to."

"Yes, I do," she said, running a hand over his rough, stubbled jaw. Her eyelids were already dropping. She hadn't been getting any sleep in New York. New places, new bed. But now she had something comfortable, even when it wasn't something she should have.

She was asleep in seconds.

THE OPERA. The music, the lights, the setting, the singers. Sawyer was in love. She felt a hand trail over her back and smiled to Vincent. He was smiling back to her. She loved his smile. It was

small and yet genuine. He wasn't holding back, he just didn't have the over-the-top nature of Zander.

When it was over, he helped her stand and led her out of the building. He ushered her into the back seat of a car and pulled her into his lap as the driver took them home.

Driver.

Sawyer tried to pull away, confused, but he held her too tightly. They didn't have drivers.

Because it wasn't Vincent. The man whose lap she was in already had a tight shield around him in case she tried to fight him. She couldn't break that shield.

"We've had a good night so far - don't fucking ruin it," Axel snapped. "I'm not in the mood for the argument. Henry doesn't need to see us screaming at each other."

"You mean he doesn't need to see you beat me," she retorted, bitter and angry. She couldn't sublimate away. He'd be able to hold her with his control over the air. She couldn't blink out of the car since she couldn't focus on anything outside the dark windows.

Trapped.

He wrapped a hand around her throat and yanked her closer. "Tonight, you're just going to get in my bed. I'm not in the fucking mood."

Sawyer wished she could fight back. She wished so much that she could kill this man and take her Henry anywhere else.

She tried, throwing a wild, untrained punch. He slammed the back of her head into the window. Her world went dark.

SAWYER WOKE up and tried to fight the hold. She needed to get away from whoever was holding her. She needed Axel to let her go. She struggled, but the son of a bitch wouldn't release her. Her magic would be useless. It always was.

Always useless to fight, but she that didn't mean he needed to touch her like this.

"It was a nightmare, Sawyer," Vincent whispered. "It's okay."

The words penetrated her sleep haze and she hated herself. Again. It's fucking happened again.

"Fuck," she growled. She didn't try to leave his chest again. Her cheeks were cold from tears.

"What was it? What happened in the nightmare?"

"Where's Jasper? He's supposed to come in for me and help me." She didn't want to tell him.

"The enchantments in the wall probably stopped him from knowing," Vincent explained quickly. "He would have if he knew. I promise. He's most likely asleep and has no idea. It's okay. You didn't try to hurt me or yourself. You just cried until you started waking up. What was the nightmare?"

Why wouldn't he just drop it? Sawyer knew the answer. He cared. She'd promised herself to work on this and without Jasper, she knew Vincent was the best option to talk about it.

"We were at the opera."

"You and Axel?"

"No, me and you. You became Axel on the drive home. It had been a good dream and turned bad," she told him. That was really all there was to it. "Did I wake you up?"

"No, I haven't slept yet."

"Why?" She didn't like the sound of that. Axel used to fuck her and leave her in the bed to sleep, but he stopped sleeping next to her once they soured. Vincent was now doing it.

For the same reason, neither Castello would ever sleep in her bed. They both thought she would kill them. One knew she would if it ever happened, the other she never wanted to hurt. Both in equal danger.

Her stomach rolled, but it was too empty to lose anything.

"I wanted to make sure you were going to be okay," he whispered, kissing her forehead. "If you can, go back to sleep. I'm just reading a book. It's no worries."

"Why?" she asked again. He hadn't given her the answer she expected. She didn't know if sleep was possible, so questioning him was a better option than trying.

"Because I can. Go back to sleep. You were only out for a couple of hours. You need more. I'm fine."

"Thank you," she mumbled. She closed her eyes and just stayed curled into him. She didn't get any more sleep, angry that her good dream of music and the opera with him had turned sour. She didn't like the new trend of her few good dreams turning bad. She didn't have them often, if ever. She just wanted them to stay good.

She needed Jasper to help her. She *needed* him. She couldn't do this 'fight the nightmares' thing on her own. She didn't know how to make herself lucid enough during them. She got sucked in and went back to a time when she didn't know how to fight back like that. She'd been great at slipping a knife between someone's ribs, but not at defending herself.

"I wish he'd never hurt you, beautiful," Vincent whispered. He probably thought she was asleep.

"Me too," she murmured. She felt him jerk. Her guess had been right. "I wish none of it ever happened, but it is what it is. Now I'm here. With you and the team. That makes up for it a little."

Silence.

"Do you want to just watch TV?" She didn't miss how he didn't say anything in response to her statement.

"Room service?" she asked. "Dessert in bed."

"Good idea," he chuckled. She got up to use the restroom while he ordered. When she was back, he just pulled her into him as he finished up the call.

Twenty minutes later, Vincent answered the door and pulled in a little cart with some cheesecake. She sat up and took a slice from him. He put on an old Western and they ate cheesecake at one in the morning together.

"This is nice," she whispered. "I like this. Midnight dessert in bed."

"I do too," he agreed, reaching over to dip a piece of his into her chocolate sauce. She reached over him and did the same to his strawberry sauce. "Feeling better?"

"A little," she admitted, looking back down at her cheesecake slice, half eaten. "Thank you."

"Sawyer, I'm going to do whatever I need to, remember? Anything. I meant it. If that means you want to work stuff out before we go further, then I'm okay with that. If that means I stay up all night just to make sure you're okay, then I will." He sounded so passionate about it.

She looked at him and gave a weak smile. "Thank you for that. With how...with everything else, it's nice to know that you just accept things."

"It's hard," he said, swallowing. "I want everything to be...better, good. Elijah used to do all of the 'feelings' stuff. I'm taking a page out of his book on this."

"You're doing wonderfully," she assured him, leaning to kiss his cheek. "You and Jasper are both great."

"Not Zander?" He chuckled as he asked. She gave him a blank stare. "I'll take that as a no."

"He and I just...it's constant. New York has at least distracted us from arguing."

"He loves you and he's trying," Vincent reminded her.

"I know," she sighed. "I love him too."

"Have you told him?"

"No," she mumbled, stabbing her cheesecake. "It'll go to his head and I'm afraid he'll take it as..."

"As a sign that he can keep trying to run you over a bit, that everything is perfect."

"All of that, and I'm just not ready," Sawyer leaned back onto the headboard. "I can admit I love both of them to you but not to them. It's weird."

"Nothing about this is normal."

"Thank you for listening. About Axel and them, and... just everything."

"Anything," he whispered, kissing her forehead. "I meant it."

"I know," she whispered back. "Now, cheesecake and movie. Maybe even a little more sleep. What time do we need to be there tomorrow?"

"Noon. We have plenty of time. It's why I chose last night for the theatre. They've been performing for the last week, but tomorrow we wrap up and then pack up. We fly home early Thursday."

"Thank fuck." She threw one of her legs over his and he tossed an arm over her shoulder. They shared bites of cheesecake for another hour and her eyelids began to feel heavy again. She fell asleep leaning into him, still propped up to watch the movie.

13

JASPER

Jasper was having a late breakfast when she stormed up to him. To anyone else, it was a nonchalant walk, but Jasper knew when Sawyer was upset. He could see it in her eyes. Something was bothering her, and he was going to answer for it.

"What's wrong?" he asked immediately.

"I had a nightmare last night and you didn't show up," she told him. "I know it's probably the enchantments, Vincent assured me of that, but I'm still a little agitated."

Jasper blinked several times. She talked to Vincent before him? That hurt in a way he didn't expect.

"Why Vincent?" he demanded softly. He shouldn't have been asking. It was her business, but he'd thought she trusted him with this. Now Vincent was also taking her on dates and talking to her about her nightmares. Jasper felt something important slip from his fingers.

"Because I was in bed with him when I woke up," Sawyer explained, sitting down next to him in the hotel's restaurant.

"Oh. My...my bad," Jasper mumbled, stabbing a fork

through his omelet. Of course she had been. They had gone on a date and finished it off like most people would. It was actually a good step for them, since she'd been scared of hurting Vincent. Which meant the nightmare in bed with him again was going to set her back, not make her feel better. "The walls are exactly why I didn't know. You can..." Jasper took a deep breath. "You can stay in my room tonight, just in case."

"That's a good idea," Sawyer replied, nodding thoughtfully. "I'll trade with Zander. We leave tomorrow. It's a health and safety thing and there will be two beds. Good idea."

"Yup," Jasper mumbled. "You should get breakfast if you had a...late night." He noticed her lack of plate and she pointed across the room. He looked to where she directed and chuckled. Vincent was bringing over two plates, followed by Elijah, Quinn, and the wolves. He slid one of those plates across the table to her and she started eating after a murmured thank you.

"How are you this morning, Jasper?" Vincent sat across from him, without any awkwardness. Jasper didn't mind Zander at all, but something about Vincent's casual nature to the morning after being with Sawyer irked him.

"Good," Jasper answered, maybe a little curt. "You?"

"He's probably on cloud nine," Elijah cut in, before Vincent could even open his mouth. "Sawyer's Italian Boy-"

"Stop that," Sawyer cut him off too. "None of that, Cowboy. You ever want to try the ride, you'll keep your thoughts about everyone else to yourself at breakfast."

"Oh shit," Zander laughed, walking up too. "Shut down."

"That hurt a little," Elijah mumbled. Quinn patted his back in some sympathy but even Jasper could tell he was either uncomfortable doing it or didn't mean it.

185

"You deserve it," Vincent muttered.

"Little lady, tell me you don't mean it," Elijah begged, reaching across the table for her.

"Every word, big boy," she teased, giving a grin. Jasper couldn't stop his own smile at the banter that took over the table. Vincent looked up at him, frowning.

"Are you really okay?" Vincent's telepathic voice invaded Jasper's thoughts. He just looked away from the Italian. *"We're going to talk later."*

He finished his omelet and let the waitress take the plate. They were all ready to leave once they finished eating. Jasper walked out the front of the hotel, their CO hot on his heels.

"Jasper," he said sternly. "You got something on your mind. I can tell. You think too much."

"It's nothing," Jasper answered, crossing his arms. It was a him issue, not a Vincent issue. Vin had nothing to do with how he felt annoyed that Sawyer hadn't found him when she had a nightmare. It wasn't Vincent's fault for thinking a date in classy New York and a night in bed were a good idea to help them be together.

He just found Vincent a threat to his place, honestly. He hated it. He wasn't wild Zander, and he didn't have Vincent's weird connection to her. He was just the smart, inexperienced one. Inexperienced in dating and *everything* else.

"It's obviously something," Vincent said quietly. He heard a lighter strike and watched Vincent take a long drag off his post-breakfast cigarette.

"You can't smoke here." Jasper groaned. "Smoking section is thirty feet that way." He pointed out to his right and his team leader just shrugged in response.

"Who's going to stop me?" Vincent chuckled. "Come on.

You can stand with me. Give it another two minutes and Sawyer will be out here too, with Elijah on her tail. Maybe the entire team."

"I figured Zander, not Elijah," Jasper commented, walking with him to the smoking section.

"You and Zander don't like her smoking mouth. She's using breath mints now, because she won't quit the habit just to appease a guy." Vincent ashed his cigarette, flicking it several times out of habit, while Jasper just considered what he said.

Vincent was a people watcher. He judged how they reacted to the world around them, how they behaved, how they solved problems, all of it. If anyone knew the dynamics of the house, it was him.

"You're right. I don't like her smoking too much." Jasper sighed. "It's going to kill you and her. And Elijah."

"We're all going to die anyway," Vincent reminded him. "Might as well die feeling relaxed and not murderous."

"You didn't answer my question about Elijah," he pointed out.

"He's got a crush on her," Vincent answered. "He smokes more now as an excuse to be in her space, but doesn't want to pull the trigger and make it more serious."

"That...makes sense. Now I remember. We talked about this in Texas." He crossed his arms and leaned on the wall of the building.

"We did, and nothing has changed between those two yet. They either will or they won't." Vincent shrugged. "Why are you upset?"

"It's really nothing," he said, looking down at his feet.

"Sure." Vincent chuckled. "When you're ready, talk to me."

"I will," he promised. If it continued to bother him,

seeing them be relaxed and knowing she was giving Vincent the same secrets she gave him. That still seriously bugged him. He was the person she trusted with that, not Vincent. If that kept bugging him, even though they were all on the same team, he would talk to both of them. This only worked if they communicated. Jasper didn't want to lose his piece of her and he didn't want Vin to get cut out, since he was important to her.

"Here they come," Vincent chuckled, pointing. Jasper turned and looked back over his shoulder to see Sawyer and Elijah laughing about something. She was already pulling out a cigarette and Elijah was stealing one from her as well. She didn't use a lighter, as Elijah lit them both, and they were smoking by the time they got to Jasper and Vincent.

"You both rushed out here," Sawyer pointed out immediately.

"I needed some air," Jasper admitted. "Vincent decided to pollute it."

"Stop complaining, Golden Boy," Vincent ordered, but Jasper knew by his smile that it wasn't serious. He wasn't worried about the secondhand. They were both fucking around. "Where's Zander and Quinn?"

"Quinn wanted the wolves to get up to the roof and do their business one more time in the animal area," Sawyer explained. "Zander is...fuck if I know."

"I'm here," Zander called out.

"Constantly late today, it seems," she corrected herself.

"We're fine," Jasper cut in quickly before an argument could start. "We're not running behind."

"Yeah, we don't have a meeting for another two hours," Vincent added. "At this time of day, traffic shouldn't be too horrendous either."

"Traffic is always horrendous in New York," she scoffed.

"Sometimes it's like the first level of hell and sometimes it's the ninth, but it's always hell."

Jasper couldn't stop himself from laughing at that.

"How was the opera last night?" Elijah asked, looking between them.

Jasper stopped laughing and realized he should have asked that earlier.

"Good," Sawyer declared, grinning. "Quite lovely."

"She looks good in a gown," Vincent told them, with his small smile. "Very good."

"I'm suddenly jealous," Zander commented. Jasper saw Zander look down Sawyer's leg, so he reached out and swatted his friend on the chest.

"Stop undressing her with your eyes and find a reason to take her out in a dress." Jasper shook his head at Zander's groan to what he said.

"Fine. Sawyer, there's this restaurant in Atlanta."

"I call that," Elijah cut in. "You aren't taking her to my favorite place."

"For fuck's sake, Vincent. Did you have to tell them about the dress?" Sawyer wore an exasperated expression and Vincent was just chuckling softly, refusing to look at her.

Jasper felt a pang of jealousy. Vincent had seen her in a gown.

The light banter kept going until Quinn came outside, his wolves following dutifully. They loaded up into their small rental cars and Jasper drove with Sawyer sitting next to him and Quinn with Scout in the back.

Jasper lost his patience with the traffic in minutes.

"You can let me drive," Sawyer reminded him for the third time since they got into the car.

"I actually can't," he repeated. "You don't have the

insurance and cover from the IMPO in case you damage anything."

"I've been allowed before. By you. To the gym," she retorted.

"I wasn't supposed to let you do that." He mentally cursed himself. He had let her drive the rental when she shouldn't have. He had actually forgotten, thinking it would just be easier for her to drive to the gym she knew by heart how to get to.

"Fine," Sawyer groaned. She turned in the seat and looked to the back. Jasper tried not to watch her, but he could see her out of the side of his eye. "How are you, Quinn?"

"Ready to go home," Quinn answered. "One more night."

"That's right. We just need to have this meeting, pack up, and wait for our flights."

Jasper was excited about it too. New York sucked. He hated it here. This was definitely one of the worst trips they had been on, but it was never good. Zander was normally getting into trouble, or underhanded shit was done to Vincent. People tried to convince Jasper and Elijah to leave the team before the Castello took them down with him.

It wasn't a healthy place for any of them.

Jasper got them parked with thirty minutes to spare for the meeting. Vincent, Elijah, and Zander had beaten them, but no one teased him for going slow. They had only been first because they pulled out of the hotel first.

"We ready?" Vincent called out. "James says this is going to be a general rundown. We're going to get rated for the bonus for the Texas job, then get a bit of real time off. He's gotten us a three month break, that much he's told me about. No cases unless it's an emergency. Everyone will get vacation time."

"That sounds great. They threw us out to Texas without a chance to catch a fucking breath," Elijah said, emphasizing it with a groan.

"I know," Vincent said, nodding to them all. He started walking towards the building, Kaar landing on his shoulder, and Jasper fell in with the team to follow. Vincent continued talking as they got closer to the WMC's front door. "But we did well. Sawyer did well. He hasn't heard anything about what went down yesterday…" Jasper and the other guys all looked at Sawyer, who rolled her eyes. "So he doesn't think anything will come of it."

"Good. That asshole spit in my face first."

Jasper should have known she wasn't going to feel very apologetic for it. He wished she would, but he could also understand why she didn't. A stranger running up on her, already in a bad mood, spits in her face over things Sawyer was already doing her time for. Things she had no control over, not really. He might have started a scuffle too, if he'd seen it. He knew Zander would have, even Vincent or Elijah. Definitely Quinn. Quinn knew the insult of being spit on, without anyone having to explain it to him.

They went to the assigned meeting room, Vincent pulling the door open and holding it for all of them.

Everything was wrong.

Jasper stumbled at the sight of several high ranking IMAS officers standing to one side of the room. Sawyer cursed, and Jasper looked over to see her glaring at Councilwoman D'Angelo. He grabbed Sawyer and pulled her to a stop. He couldn't have her running over to get into the Councilwoman's face.

The building shook and Elijah grabbed Quinn, hauling him out of the room.

"What the fuck is going on here?" Vincent roared at James, waving at the guests in the room.

"I didn't win. They got here ten minutes ago, and I couldn't warn you," James answered. Jasper didn't like the look on their handler's face.

"Special Agent Castello, bring your team to heel."

"I'll give you a fucking heel, bitch. Straight up your fucking ass," Sawyer snarled, and Jasper yanked her further away, Zander grabbing her other arm to help. Jasper was thankful one of them was retaining a bit of control. He wouldn't have been able to stop both of them. He didn't even want to think about how Elijah was doing with Quinn out in the hall.

"Sawyer, sit down. We need to think," Jasper whispered harshly in her ear. "Now is not the time to start a fight."

She relaxed immediately, and he didn't like the cold mask that settled over her face. This was Shadow. This was calculating and calm. He'd gotten her to just redirect the temper and that terrified him.

The room grew colder by the second.

Zander led her to a seat and Jasper looked back out the door to see Quinn and Elijah whispering to each other.

"Get in here. This looks bad," he said quickly.

Quinn growled, but Elijah nodded. "Let's go," he said sternly to their feral Magi.

Jasper held the door for them. Once they were seated, he took his own. He threw a glance at Vincent and James, sitting next to each other. Vincent was just as cold as Sawyer, just as closed off. She sat on his other side.

A Castello and Shadow, both cold and emotionless. It was an intimidating sight.

"Now that everyone is calm," Councilwoman D'Angelo began, calm and collected. "We'll discuss why we're here."

"We requested, nicely, to have Special Agent Quinn Judge come on a mission with us. We were rudely denied."

Jasper looked at the rank of the IMAS officer speaking. General. He was one of the three highest ranking members of the International Magi Armed Services. Jasper didn't recognize his face, but his name badge read Kitchner. General Kitchner? Jasper knew the name. General Kitchner was in charge of the Spec Ops division of IMAS, which made him a very powerful man.

"I'm not going to the Amazon. It's a deathwish," Quinn growled out. "If you were smart, you wouldn't either."

"You don't have a choice," Councilwoman D'Angelo declared. "You will be going."

"Then I'll quit the IMPO," Quinn retorted.

"Then I won't feel bad at all for removing Sawyer Matthews from your team. You are the one with tracking, correct? If you aren't in the IMPO, you would no longer be able to catch her if she runs."

Jasper held back a curse, but Zander couldn't. This was bad. Sawyer was stronger than everyone on the team except Quinn. Having him gave them an easy answer to what would happen if she fought against them. They all knew she wouldn't, but they needed the cover anyway.

"I forgot you were using that to let us keep her." Vincent sighed. "If Quinn goes to the Amazon and does the mission, she stays with us."

"With an inhibitor while he's away," D'Angelo added.

"How about no?" Sawyer scoffed. "I'm not wearing one of those, Vincent. Quinn isn't going to get himself killed for whoever the fuck this is either." She gestured to the General and Jasper winced. They still hadn't taught her the ranks.

She had no idea how powerful General Kitchner was politically.

"You might not have a choice if you want to stay out of a cell. He might not either."

"I'll go to the Amazon." Quinn cut in. "I'll go without a fight. No inhibitor for Sawyer. She deserves her abilities to protect herself."

"You don't have that option. While you are away, she will wear an inhibitor. If you quit to get out of this assignment, we will remove her from your team." D'Angelo just smiled.

Jasper just kept his eyes on her. Sawyer was angry, but that didn't show. They could all just feel it. Then her eyebrows went up, and it sent a wave of confusion through him.

"Send us all to the Amazon," she declared. "Send the entire team, myself included."

"We don't need all of you." The General sounded bored.

"You need bodies to throw at the Druids. We're five decently powerful Magi who work well with Quinn. Your chances of success only go up," Vincent corrected him. "He knows us and would know how to use us against the targets. Secondary to that, we're IMPO and we can investigate and explore diplomatic options to lessen casualties or eliminate the need for them."

"No," Quinn growled. "You'll all be in danger."

"We're all in danger anyway," Sawyer told him. "It doesn't matter. You aren't going down there alone. Not under any circumstance."

"I don't like this idea. There's a chance you can disappear in the area and we'll never be able to find you," the Councilwoman said.

Jasper ground his teeth. He didn't like this idea either. It was stupidly dangerous. Staring hard at Vincent, he silently begged for what was going on in his head.

"Roll with it," Zander said suddenly. *"I trust Sawyer and Vincent to know what they're doing. Let's hope they bring us in on it."*

"We'll make this easy for you, on one condition," Vincent continued the conversation.

"If we all live through it, you back off," Sawyer finished.

"Excuse me?" The Councilwoman looked shocked.

"There's a likelihood I'll die on the mission, just like everyone else. Quinn, what's the mortality rate for something like this?" Sawyer was smiling, but it didn't reach her eyes.

"At minimum? I would say half of those who go in and try to fight will die."

Jasper's blood ran cold.

"So for the odds worse than a coin toss, I'm going to make you a deal," Sawyer said to the Councilwoman. "If I walk out of the jungle alive, you back the fuck off. If I die, you win. You get exactly what you want. Shadow out of your way."

Silence.

The room grew colder.

Jasper shivered at the sharp, cold edge of Sawyer's magic. It was a wild cold, at that, like the tundra, thanks to Quinn's temper simmering underneath Sawyer's, even more dangerous than hers. Formidable. Jasper saw a few of the IMAS soldiers grow uncomfortable. They were rubbing their hands together, shifting around, trying to stay warm, even though the cold wasn't real.

Only Elijah seemed completely comfortable. Jasper would have guessed it was because his magic was so warm, thanks to his fire manipulation. The only thing that made him worried about Elijah was that he was a little pale. Sick-looking, but it couldn't have been cold-induced. He didn't know why.

His eyes fell on Sawyer last.

Jasper stared at her. She was willing to throw her life away to keep them together. It was a tough position. He didn't want any of them in danger. None of them wanted Quinn dealing with Druids at all, much less alone.

He loved her for the dangerous way she threw herself into protecting others. She was making sure they all made it or none of them did. Team and family, or nothing at all. Not a single one of them forgotten or left behind.

This was what made her so *good*. Too bad no one else saw it outside the team. None of them had yet, or ever would, earn Sawyer's unique brand of dangerous and deadly love.

"We'll need your answer, Councilwoman," Vincent finally whispered.

"Yes." It was quiet. "If you all go on the mission with the IMAS team, you'll be there on an investigatory and diplomatic mission. They will be assigned as your protection, and if need be, the extermination team. If Sawyer Matthews survives the mission, than I will no longer press to have her removed from the team and her contract with the WMC voided."

"No matter if the mission is a success or failure. If she lives to the point where the mission is over, you will no longer press to have her removed from the team and her contract with the WMC voided." James' tone was hard. He left no room for argument. "Because this could very well be a failure and it won't be her fault."

"Put that in writing," Sawyer commanded. "Now."

D'Angelo glared at her. Jasper swallowed his nerves.

"Fine."

He wanted to curse at their luck. One simple trip they couldn't screw up if they wanted to have some time off. Now they were going to the goddamn Amazon.

The room emptied slowly, leaving the team to quietly accept their fate.

"Quinn, can we do this?" Jasper asked softly.

"I don't know."

"Little lady, you're lucky I love you," Elijah whispered.

"I'm lucky you all give a shit about me," she replied. "Fuck. We're going Druid hunting."

"It's all we have," Vincent reminded them. "She wanted us backed into a corner."

"Was that your idea or Sawyer's?" Jasper asked.

"It better be Vincent's," Zander snapped. "Sawyer wouldn't-"

"It was mine. Vincent asked if I had any idea how to maneuver around them. D'Angelo hates me. I gave her a way for me to die, and maybe you guys, since you all are traitors to the WMC in her mind for protecting me. But it comes at a price. If we go down there, we'll be *known* for it. If we live, it'll look bad for her to fuck with us anymore. She knows that."

"Jesus fuck, Sawyer!" Zander yelled. "You could get killed."

"So could Quinn!" she roared back. "He doesn't fucking deserve to be used against me like that. He doesn't deserve to have me used against him to make him go on a fucking suicide mission."

"So we're all going!" Zander's rage made Jasper's ears hurt. "Did you even think to ask for us to have a few minutes to discuss this before it?"

"Damn right we are!" she screamed. "We're going to go

down, fucking live through it, and fucking earn some goddamned peace. Did you stop and discuss threatening the WMC to keep me from being executed while I was practically in a coma? You could have all become criminals when *you* made *that* threat. We all do what we need to do to protect who we care about. Don't fucking put me on some pedestal to be protected no matter what and let Quinn or anyone else fucking die for it. I won't be with a man who does that."

Jasper coughed and sputtered.

Vincent dropped the pen he was holding, the color fleeing his face.

Elijah jumped up and pulled Zander back, who looked struck.

Sawyer just stood there, her face set, her shoulders squared.

"That's…" Zander trailed off.

"Hot tempers," Elijah said quickly. "You both have hot tempers. Sawyer, he's just worried about you. I don't blame him. I'm worried about all of this. I'm personally glad we're all going down there with Quinn." Elijah continued quieter to Zander, "She's not a princess. She doesn't need to be protected, Zander. She needs equals. Be one of those. She did that for all of us. It'll be dangerous for her, for us, but we're doing it together instead of leaving someone out to hang, her or Quinn. Those were our options. Her or Quinn."

Jasper heard desperation in Elijah's voice. Oh God, he hadn't even thought about how hard this was on Elijah. His brother in his heart and the woman they all loved in their own ways, even Quinn, who was slowly walking to Sawyer. They didn't say anything. Jasper watched them touch foreheads. They were all watching the two most dangerous people on the team have a tender moment of friendship and camaraderie. Both were ignoring the rest of them. He wondered when the tender friendship had gotten that deep.

"I couldn't choose," Elijah whispered to Zander. Jasper barely heard it. "Don't make them choose, either."

"I didn't mean it like that. I thought we should have a team discussion. I'm trying to ask why we didn't go the right way."

"You've done the same thing on us and we backed you up," Elijah whispered fiercely. "Her quick thinking this time is going to hopefully keep Quinn alive."

"I don't want Quinn to die, Elijah. Come on. I just…"

"You love her and don't want her hurt. I know. You two can hash it out later, but right now we need to focus on this shit storm."

Jasper watched Zander nod. He sank back into his chair next to Jasper and leaned on him.

"We're going to the Amazon." Zander sighed.

"We're in for a bad fight," Quinn declared. "We need to prepare."

"We'll have Sawyer sign this deal with Councilwoman D'Angelo, then I'll get someone to portal you all directly home," James said quietly. "I'm sorry."

"It's not your fault." Sawyer sighed. "We were bound to lose a fight with the WMC eventually."

"Losing this one means we're dead," Jasper spoke up.

"No, my old friend, it means I'm dead," Sawyer corrected him. She looked peaceful for a moment. "She doesn't really care about any of you past me."

By her expression, he guessed she wasn't scared to die for them.

He found that a hard bone to swallow.

14

SAWYER

Sawyer signed the damn deal and watched Dina do the same. They didn't shake over it. Sawyer wasn't going to touch the bitch. She didn't say anything until Dina and the rest of the assholes were gone again.

The fucking Amazon rainforest. Of all the places they could be going, that was one she'd never expected.

"How are you?" Quinn asked softly, staying close to her side.

"I'm good," she answered. He hadn't left her side since he bumped foreheads with her. The gesture from him was as intimate as a kiss. She'd been touched. She knew in that moment she'd made the right decision about making sure they all went with him.

"Thank you...for standing beside me through this."

"I would never let any of you sacrifice yourselves for me," she reminded him. "Not when I'm capable of fighting with you."

He didn't say anything else, just tentatively put an arm around her waist and held her for a moment. He was gone faster than she could blink.

"Everyone ready to leave?" James was stiff, and Sawyer felt guilty.

"I'm sorry about this," she told him. "I really am."

"Just come back. All of you. I don't want to lose another team." James didn't say anything else, just walked out of the room.

"Do we follow him?" she asked, frowning at the team.

"Yes." Vincent went after him and they were all scrambling to catch up. "James. Wait. What's the plan? You know more than we do."

"I'll get you this portal home and back. Twenty-four hours is what I can buy you to prepare. It's what they would give Quinn, and that's not changing. You'll fly out from here to Brasília. The mission is being run by the colonel you met, Quinn." James stopped at the elevator and Sawyer nearly walked into Zander. She didn't. She felt a little bad for threatening their relationship, but once again, they were being thrown into something that put their personal lives secondary. First they had to secure their actual ones.

"Is there anyone available to portal us?" Elijah asked, but Sawyer was also interested. They loaded into the elevator and James hit a floor that she hadn't gone to yet.

"I have someone who will do it in a heartbeat, even if he isn't cleared to do it," James explained. "Sawyer, you taught someone some very bad habits."

"Excuse me?" She brought her eyebrows together.

"You'll see," he sighed. "He's still causing a bit of trouble. He failed a drug test only last week."

"Oh fuck, no way," Sawyer gasped. "No! Travis?"

"He's on probation since he was caught with marijuana in his system, but he'll do this for me," he explained. "Since I got him this job when the team caught you. We didn't want to leave a Magi who could make portals for you in an unsafe position. He was a potential target for Axel to exploit."

"I mean, I knew-"

"He doesn't know from me who you are," James cut her off. "But with you in the city, I'm positive someone has told him. It's why I didn't mention it earlier. I wasn't sure if you were ready or willing to see what his reaction could possibly be."

"He was the first person who saw me after Axel and I ran into each other in LA." Sawyer rubbed her face. "He didn't know. I never told him."

"Well, now it's time to confront that," he told her.

The elevator's ding startled her. They walked off and down a hallway into a room full of cubicles. James led them to one in the back corner and Sawyer felt like it was a small funeral procession.

"Travis, I need you. Come with me," James demanded. Sawyer met Travis' eyes as he stood up. His eyes were clearer, more chocolate than mud. No sign of being bloodshot. His hair was still a little long, a little ragged, but it was healthier as well, fuller. He'd even put on weight, maybe a little too much.

"Sawyer!" Travis seemed startled.

"Hey, man," she replied, smiling. Neither of them were following James, who was walking to another room.

"You...I've heard some things."

"Most of them are probably true."

"So...you were Shadow. I was the Magi that made portals for an assassin everyone thought was dead."

"Yeah, I am Shadow. Yes, you were a Magi I paid to portal me around after everyone thought I was dead. No," Sawyer dropped to a whisper. "I didn't kill anyone while you worked for me. In case you were wondering. I stopped doing that sort of work a long time ago."

"I wasn't wondering," Travis whispered back. "I just...I mean, I know why you never would have told me. People here just look at me funny. When someone first told me, I freaked out. I didn't know if you wanted to talk to me while you were in the city, so I didn't ask James to let me see you. And it's not like you were ever bad to me. If anything, you always helped me out, so I just ignore what others say about you." He smiled. "Plus, I'm in trouble with or without you, it seems."

"I've heard. How's being sober?" She grinned. "Should have realized they wouldn't appreciate you smoking pot while working for them."

"It was a good weekend party with some old college friends. I had the week off too. I didn't think they would drug test me the day I got back," Travis grumbled, rolling his eyes.

"You should have-"

"Sawyer. Travis. Get moving," James snapped, looking back at them from the room he'd gone into. Sawyer realized it was just her and Travis standing there still, and others in the office space were staring at them.

"What's going on?" Travis asked in a hushed tone as Sawyer walked with him to James.

She heaved a sigh, her chest getting a little tight. "We're going to need you to make a portal for us to get home and get ready for an IMAS mission we didn't want. It's political. You don't want to get dragged in."

"I'll do it," Travis agreed softly. Once inside, he went into the professional mode that she was used to. "Have a photo for a location? I need to visualize where I'm putting this thing."

"Here," Vincent spoke up. He handed his phone to Travis, who flipped through pictures on the screen.

"Good enough. I'm feeling south Georgia? Not the farthest I've ever done," Travis mumbled, nearly to himself. Sawyer raised her eyebrows.

"It's not nearly the farthest you've made," she reminded him. "LA and New York were longer."

"Don't tell anyone. They don't believe I can make them that far." Travis shrugged. "They normally keep me within a few hundred miles, nothing over a thousand and nothing over oceans."

"They underestimate you, and while that's a topic we need to discuss, the team only has twenty-four hours." James sounded annoyed. "Sorry, you and Sawyer need to catch up next time."

"Roger that," Travis sighed. They could all feel his magic begin to fill the room and concentrate to one end. Sawyer looked around - there was nothing in the room, not even sockets for electricity.

"What do you do in here?" she asked James.

"Portals. This is a room just for portals to be made," James answered. "This is where you would enter the building if they ever offer portals to you for travel, but they like making things hard on you and the team. Nearly every other team of Special Agents has one or two dedicated Magi who can make portals."

"No fucking way," Sawyer mumbled, shaking her head. "They really do like shitting on us."

"It's been like this since before we got you," Elijah added from the back. "They've always loved dicking around with us. You being around just made them up their game."

"Portal is ready," Travis called out. "Am I going in too?"

"Yes, so you can portal them back tomorrow. Guys? Got a

place for him to sleep?" James looked around. Sawyer shrugged.

"He'll be fine on a couch," she answered. "Right, Travis?"

"Sure," he groaned. "Go on. You know the drill."

She chuckled and walked into the black abyss.

In Georgia, she was happy with the heat. It was the first thing she noticed, that the sun was still warm in the South. On the other side of the cold trip through the portal, she moved out of the way so no one else staggered into her.

Vincent was next, holding Kaar in his arms, and Sawyer couldn't stop a chuckle as Elijah barreled into him when he didn't move in time. This led to Zander and Jasper hitting them both.

"Get out of the way for the wolves," Sawyer told them quickly, pulling Jasper and Zander by their sleeves.

Quinn held both wolves by their collars when he nearly fell out of the portal. Shade and Scout were tripped up and nearly fell themselves. Travis came through last and closed the portal quickly.

There were some chuckles all around at the ridiculous trip.

"Let's get ready," Vincent said. "We don't have much time."

Sawyer felt the moment of humor at the team vanish, leaving them all sober and silent. They all walked inside together but split up quickly. Sawyer went straight up to her room. Weapons. She was going to weapon up first, then worry about other necessities for the mission.

Inside her closet was a safe. Elijah had installed it once they had finished inventory of her gear. She opened it and sighed.

So much black. So many blades.

She pulled out her favorites first, the long, sharp twelve-inch daggers. She laid them out on her bed. Two, her standard weaponry. Next she grabbed her throwing knives. They would be good in a pinch.

"Let me help," Quinn said as he walked into her room. "I'm going to meet with everyone on the team to make sure you're prepared. You are first."

"Why?" she asked. It didn't hurt her pride for him to come in and help; she was just curious.

"Because we haven't finished your go-bag," Quinn explained. "The bag for survival missions like this. I need to make sure you have the appropriate clothing, shoes, a fire-starting kit. I know we covered some of this, but I need to make sure."

"Okay." She held her hands up, a gesture that she wasn't going to argue with him. She was out of her depth on this. She was only prepared mentally, but the rest...well, that's why they were at home.

"Weapons. Good. Bring all of them. You never know what might come in handy, and I'll see that you always have something to use." Quinn walked into her closet and grabbed more of her blades. She took the kukri from him and laid it out. That was one that could do serious damage. "You won't need this."

Sawyer watched Quinn pick up and show her the black mask.

"No, I won't need that," she agreed. "Put it back. It'll stay in the safe where it belongs."

"This protected your identity when you worked as an assassin."

"Yeah. Let's not go there."

He wasn't wrong, but she wasn't willing to discuss it. Not when they had things to do.

"Looser clothing is best," Quinn continued. "Cargos, any

color. Black might be too hot for where we are going, but the fit is more important than the color. The leathers you wear will be sweltering."

"Okay." She went to her dressers and began pulling things out. T-shirts, tanks, cargos. Nothing overly tight that would cause sweat to sit on her skin or restrict air flow. She grabbed a duffel bag and began loading it up. "How much?"

"We can't go with too many bags. One bag, whatever you can fit in it for clothing. Your weapons will go in the second bag with survival gear. I haven't taught you any rope work, but I'll give you rope just in case. There's some things we can cover on the trip with the entire team." She didn't like how harried his voice was. He was stressing out.

"Quinn." She reached out to him, where he was still making a walk between her bed and her closet, pulling things out and shoving them into a pack. When she touched his arm, he stopped immediately. "We have twenty-four hours. Then we have a long flight. We'll be fine."

"We're going in nearly blind."

"Wouldn't be the first time for me," she told him.

"This hunt is much more dangerous than ones you've ever been on," he whispered, seeming scared.

Quinn, stressed out? Scared? That fucking terrified her.

"We can do this. As a team," she promised him.

"I wish you hadn't agreed to this." He sighed, shaking his head. "You're right, we can do this as a team, but I...I agree with Zander. I don't want you to get hurt. Not just you. Anyone here on the team. You're my pack, and for you to be here and safe while I'm off in danger...It would have put me at ease, I think. As this draws closer, I'm..." He touched his heart but said nothing more.

"Worried. You're worried," she whispered.

"Yes. I know the word," he growled softly, giving her a

look as if she was stupid. "I'm learning to express my emotions better. I think it's your fault."

"What else is my fault?" she smiled as she asked it. She had noticed he was expressing himself more. From his protective nature in Texas to asking her to celebrate reading, and now this. She noticed.

"I didn't kill a bitch like I would have used to," Quinn said and then slammed his mouth shut.

"What?" Sawyer sputtered.

"There was a female in my meeting with IMAS. She wasn't there today. She knew things about me. Before I met you, I would have just killed her for knowing those things, for just pissing me off. I didn't. I think it's your fault," he explained in a growly tumble of words Sawyer almost couldn't understand.

"Good to know." She nodded slowly. "Why?"

"I don't know," Quinn answered honestly. "But you have changed everything here, so it must be your fault."

"I haven't changed anything!" she huffed, crossing her arms. "I haven't!"

"Everything," he repeated. "And not in a bad way, just one that confuses me sometimes. It's okay."

"I didn't mean for all of this to upset your life, Quinn. There was a time when all I wanted to do was leave, and now we're doing all of this so I can stay." She sighed and sat on the bed, watching him. She had changed everything. She'd upset his entire life. She was fucking his friends, in her own tangled mess with them. She had invaded his privacy and forced herself into his education.

"There was a time I wanted you to," he whispered. "Not anymore. You belong here. With us. You are a warrior like we are. An alpha female strong enough to take what we throw at you and what the world throws at all of us. I knew you were strong the moment we met. It took me those first couple weeks to see how you fit in and grow comfortable with it. Since then...you're my packmate, Sawyer, and you prove that every chance you get by being my friend and supporter. Don't feel bad for the changes that came with you. I don't."

"That's probably the most you've ever said to me at once," she noted. And the nicest. "Thank you."

"Thank you." He grabbed her packed bags and left the room.

She stayed seated. That was interesting. He was changing, and in good ways. She loved that he talked to her more about how he felt. She wanted to know more about him. The mystery that surrounded him, his dangerous personality that fought and protected fiercely.

Quinn was back before she knew it. She stood up, confused.

"If we survive this, I want to take you hunting. Me and you. Not even the wolves." He said it quickly, and she nodded.

"Okay. We can do that." She smiled and shrugged. She didn't know what was wrong, or what had brought about the invitation, but she would accept. She would always accept an invitation to do something with one of the team in a heartbeat.

He nodded as well, then tentatively wrapped her in a hug. She very gently wrapped her arms around him. It was awkward and tense, but Quinn was hugging her and that was crazy.

"Good." He released her and left again. She just stood in her bedroom, confused.

Quinn just hugged her. Talk about change.

She left her room, not trying to follow Quinn, but

looking for something to eat. Checking the time on her phone, they still had twenty-three hours until they had to be back in New York. She could eat, get some sleep in her bed. Those would all help prepare her for this. She knew better than to help in any other way. Quinn was covering that, and he was the expert.

In the kitchen, she ran into a shocked little old lady.

"Estella," Sawyer greeted her. "Sorry, we're back early and only for the day. We have a thing."

"Well, Miss Matthews-"

"Sawyer." Estella, in the three times Sawyer had met her, had not once called Sawyer by her first name. She was going to keep trying.

"Miss Matthews, it's good to see you. I hope the boys haven't given you too much trouble. I was just restocking the fridge and making sure there was nothing expired."

"Got any salads?"

"I brought a few for you. Here you go." Estella pulled out a boxed, premade salad and Sawyer took it slowly.

"Not going to ask what's going on?"

"No. I'm not going to ask. It's IMPO business and not mine. I just keep the house clean and make sure the boys have a nice place to come home to. I don't need to know the rest." Estelle just smiled and continued cleaning the fridge.

Sawyer walked into the dining room. That was the longest interaction she'd had with Estella yet. The other three times were even less noteworthy.

As she ate quietly, Zander sat down next to her. "Sorry," he whispered.

"Me too," she sighed.

"We're so bad at this." There was some humor and desperation in his words.

"It's okay not to be good at something," she reminded

him. "We'll figure it out. I shouldn't have lost my temper enough to threaten you like that. I would never leave you over something petty like just caring about me."

"You were right. I flew off the handle because of it. You made the right call. I just didn't like not being a part of the discussion."

"We both did fly off the handle. As for a discussion, there wasn't one, Zander. I'll try not to make decisions like that often without the team. I just needed an answer right then and there. This is what I came up with," Sawyer explained, shrugging.

"It's not a bad decision. This is the right call for the team." Zander shrugged too. "I just...can't imagine a world without you in it and that's always a possibility. This just makes it even easier for me to lose you. I love you."

"I..." Sawyer opened her mouth, about to tell him how she felt, then decided against it. "I know." She didn't know what stopped her. She loved him, but something was stopping her. "We'll keep working on this. We've argued like mad before. We always have, and we've argued when we've agreed. It never ruined our friendship and I don't think it'll ruin this. We're working on it. This...relationship thing is new."

"I know. Still, I'll keep apologizing. Don't think I don't know that I'm abrasive and loud about stuff." Zander smiled, and she grinned, nodding in agreement.

"I'll keep apologizing too," she promised him. "Plus, when we don't want to argue, I can always kick your ass in COD instead of the gym."

"Bring it fucking on," Zander taunted.

"I'm glad to see you both are still talking," Jasper cut in, walking into the dining room. He sat next to her and she quickly kissed his cheek.

"Of course we are. Zander and I just like to yell at each other."

"Don't I know it." Jasper gave an exaggerated groan and Sawyer chuckled while Zander laughed from his seat across from them. "Hot tempers and not thinking before you speak. You both have it down to an art."

"I'm not as bad as him," Sawyer pointed out. She would not be lumped in with Zander.

"I'm pretty terrible at it," he agreed. "I'm trying."

That was all Sawyer needed to hear. She was going to keep trying too.

THE TIME HOME TO prepare for the trip passed too quickly. Sawyer had gotten just the bare minimum of sleep, alone in her own bed.

They were back in New York too fast. James told them he collected their items from the hotel and was going to store them until they came back.

No one said the obvious: *if* they came back.

He gave them dog tags, a pair for each of them. Sawyer didn't understand why, so she asked.

"I know we have them for identification, but why two?"

"One goes in your boot," Zander answered, seeming uncomfortable. He took it from her and knelt to slide it inside her boot, then did his own. "In case..."

She got it at that. In case her legs were detached or all that was left. She put the other on the chain provided. She dropped it into her shirt so it didn't get in her way.

The mood was somber as they arrived at the airport, where a C-130 waited for them. Sawyer was anxious. This was it. She looked down and reviewed the sheet Vincent handed her at the last minute. Ranks and patches for IMAS so she could identify who was in charge and who was a grunt.

"So, these are the IMPO agents we're stuck babysitting?" A lance corporal laughed as he said it and Sawyer, standing on the tarmac, turned to glare at him.

Jasper grabbed her arm and shook his head slowly.

"I outranked you when I was in IMAS, kid, so shut the fuck up," Zander yelled over to him.

"Don't talk to my soldiers that way," a female voice barked out in anger. "They are not for you to order."

Sawyer glanced over to the woman speaking. Sergeant Petrov. The patches gave her the Sergeant, with Petrov the last name over the woman's chest. She narrowed her eyes on the ice-blonde, dark blue-eyed bitch. "Tell your soldiers to respect their superiors and there wouldn't be any trouble," she retorted.

"I will," Sergeant Petrov replied, stepping closer. Sawyer didn't like that they were the exact same height in their combat boots. It wasn't easy to stare into the eyes of this woman. She wasn't used to it. "They won't make any more comments when I'm done with them, but none of you can go and curse at them either. I won't have discord in my ranks."

"I'm not in your ranks," Sawyer scoffed. "You can't be the ranking IMAS enlisted soldier. You definitely don't outrank me."

"I'm in charge of this group of soldiers and if you cause problems with them, I'm going to put an end to it," Petrov threatened, pointing to the ten or so men and women all dressed in camos nearby. The lance corporal was in the group.

"Fine," Sawyer grunted, shrugging.

Petrov barked an order for her soldiers to follow her, and Sawyer stayed where she was.

"Don't mess with Petrov," Jasper whispered in her ear. "She's the only female who passed the trials to join Spec Ops. They just haven't let her join one of those teams yet because she's got a vagina and not a dick. She's just as much a badass with a reputation as you, though, so please don't start shit with her."

"Bullshit," Sawyer chuckled. "No chick has a reputation as good as mine." Sawyer felt her arrogant streak rear its ugly head. She wasn't going to be scared of some blonde.

"He's not kidding," Zander warned. "Petrov is known to be super by-the-book. She doesn't tolerate people stepping out of line. You follow the rules and don't draw her attention. She's been known to bust people pretty hard for fucking up."

"Sounds like she just needs to loosen up," she decided.

"I don't know what you three are talking about, but get on the plane so we can get this started," Vincent whispered harshly as he walked past them. "Jasper, keep them out of trouble."

Sawyer laughed at Jasper's groan. When he glared at her, she only shrugged. "We're about to meet our impending deaths. Might as well laugh at something," she told him.

He pulled her onto the plane, his shoulders shaking at her humor about it all.

"She has a point," Zander said, chuckling as well.

Sawyer found a seat next to Elijah, who threw a friendly arm over her shoulder. They were all quiet as the soldiers finished loading onto the plane as well.

She took a quick headcount. Their team, six people. Three officers from IMAS, a colonel, a captain, and a lieutenant. Nine. Then thirty-six enlisted soldiers, in groups of twelve. Each group included a couple of higher-ranked enlisted members that would report to the officers.

Sawyer didn't like the strict and rigid structure of IMAS, she decided. It seemed annoying to deal with.

"I hope we're all ready," Vincent told them from his place. "This is going to be a bumpy ride."

"I have to get up and do a presentation for everyone during the trip," Quinn added. "It'll be everyone's chance to learn exactly who we're going in to mess with. Pay attention."

They all gave him an affirmative. This was going to be a long trip.

15

ELIJAH

Elijah kept his arm around Sawyer as the plane took off. He found it comforting. He had Sawyer on one side, Quinn on the other. He was going to enjoy it while it lasted. One or both might not survive the trip. *He* might not survive the trip.

None of them said anything as the soldiers joked and laughed. Elijah wanted to strangle all of them. They had no idea what they were getting into. This wasn't a game or a joke. He didn't like how relaxed they were, and he hated hearing a few of them joke about the team. They didn't say anything too rude, just wondering why they were going to babysit the imps.

Damn war dogs. He'd never liked them. He knew that he and Vincent had gotten lucky finding Zander and Jasper in the organization. They hadn't been fitting in, and they had suited Vincent's vision for the team. Best thing Elijah had ever gotten out of IMAS. He thought most of them were just brutes.

An hour later, Quinn stood up. He watched his feral friend walk over to the colonel and whisper something.

Colonel Fischer seemed to give a suffering sigh and nodded.

"Attention on deck!" someone screamed as the colonel stood up. Absolutely no one stood up, like they normally did for the call, but everyone did fall silent, their heads snapping into Colonel Fischer's direction. Elijah was impressed. A little.

"As you all know, we're going down into the damn jungle to deal with a Druid issue. Now, I'm certain we can handle this well enough on our own, but I've been granted an IMPO Special Agent who is an expert on Druids...and his team." The colonel added the second part begrudgingly. "He's going to give us a briefing on what we need to expect in the woods, so eyes up and get focused. You'll only get this information once."

"What makes this fuck an expert, sir?" a young man yelled out. "Why are we listening to imps? We're fucking war dogs!"

"I grew up with them," Quinn called back. "None of you can say the same. As far as I know, no one on Earth can say the same. But if you want to be fertilizer for their land and meat for their animals, you're welcome to it and I'll sit back down. My team and I don't want to be here. We have the intelligence to realize this is stupid."

Elijah sputtered. Quinn had never called someone out like that before. He and several of the team exchanged glances. They all knew Quinn was pissed. They had put his wolves in cargo with the other animal bonds for the trip, and that was on top of this trip already happening.

"This isn't good," Sawyer mumbled.

"Quinn is trying to make them realize how serious this is," Elijah whispered back. "It won't work, but he's going to try."

"Get started, Special Agent Judge," the colonel ordered. Elijah wanted to knock that smug look off his face.

"Fifty percent of the men and women on this plane will die if we enter into a conflict with a Druid," Quinn began.

Elijah felt a cold shiver go down his spine. He wasn't sure if it was Sawyer sitting next to him or his own worry. Quinn never gave out odds unless he fully believed in them.

Silence.

Elijah was hoping the war dogs were figuring it out now. The imps on their plane weren't fucking around, Quinn especially.

"It won't be the Druid who kills you, though I promise she'll have a hand in it," Quinn continued. "Druids are beefed-up versions of Magi with an animal bond. A single Druid can kill everyone in this plane if she sneaks up on us. She can communicate directly with the animals around her. She has a type of naturalism that doesn't just allow for the small growth of plants, but rapid growth and movement you can't account for. We'll be fighting in a world that will only be on her side. The Amazon rainforest will be our enemy. It will naturally hinder our progress, and it's dangerous enough without her. Imagine the entire thing coming alive with the express purpose of killing you, and you'll begin to understand why this mission is ridiculously stupid."

Elijah winced. Quinn wasn't playing around. He could feel the feral, wild magic radiating off of him, biting at anyone who tried to ignore it. He didn't like how angry Quinn was. It was dangerous, but there was nothing Elijah could do to stop it. Absolutely nothing.

"So what will we be fighting?" a soldier called out.

"The trees," Quinn answered in an emotionless tone. Elijah knew there was no humor in it, but the war dogs didn't.

Laughter rang out from the grunts. Even the colonel was chuckling. "Insects to large predators. Druids bond to nearly everything in their domain. Even if they aren't bonded to it, it'll follow the Druid's call to protect their home. We will be seen as an outside threat. Most of you will die to the plant and animal life. The Druid may not kill any of us with her bare hands."

"Which brings me to my second point." Quinn began to pace in front of them. Elijah didn't like how caged he looked, like a captive animal waiting for a handler to come in and try to feed him, so he could bite the hand. "Killing her quickly will stop most of the conflict. The foliage will stop immediately, no longer fed by her magic. The animals will be harder. Most will go back to what they were doing, but some may need to be put down. They won't just pass on with the Druid. The bond is different in most cases. Only about five or ten animals will be fully bonded to the Druid and pass on with her. The rest will be connected to her, but not fully dependent. This is a quirk of Druid magic." He took a deep breath. Elijah met his blue gaze. This was the hard part for him. Quinn loved animals, no matter what. It didn't matter if they were loyal to a Druid, animals in Quinn's mind were innocent. Elijah agreed. "I know you've stored tranquilizers for this mission. I recommend keeping them on hand. With a rest, many animals will be fine to get up and run off, continue their lives. No need to kill unnecessarily."

"You make it sound like we're going to war with the jungle," Colonel Fischer noted. Elijah still didn't like the humorous expression on his face. "Do you have no faith in us as some of the best soldiers in the world?"

"None at all," Quinn answered. "During this mission, I need you to make an agreement with me. I will rarely give orders, but when I do, I need them listened to. They could very well save your lives."

"I can allow that as long as you don't abuse the power," the colonel told him.

"Thank fuck," Zander mumbled.

"Problem, Private Wade?" the colonel glared over to the team. Elijah sighed. Of course the war dogs knew Zander and Jasper had been in their ranks.

"Special Agent Wade," Zander corrected. "And no. Just glad you're going to listen to the most powerful Magi on the plane, so we don't all die to the idiocy of IMAS arrogance."

"How I wish I could court-martial you," Colonel Fischer grumbled.

"I bet you do," Zander taunted.

"Stop," Vincent snapped. "We can't argue with them constantly. Colonel, you deal with yours, I'll deal with mine. Make sure they'll listen to Quinn if it's needed."

"Certainly. Keep your IMAS rejects. We don't need 'em," a captain cut in. Elijah nearly stood up. War dogs were all making that taunting 'oh' noise. Quinn snarled, and his magic lashed out. The plane shook like it hit turbulence.

"Captain." The colonel turned to glare at his second in command. "We'll talk later."

"Yes sir," the captain said, snapping a salute.

"Is there anything else, Special Agent Judge?" The colonel looked back to Quinn, who shook his head.

"Give me your plans and we'll adjust as needed," Quinn told him. "I need to know what you're prepared for."

"All right." The colonel took Quinn's place in the front of the plane, looking down at the rows of soldiers. Quinn sat back down next to Elijah on their side seats, less cramped than the area the soldiers were sitting.

"We'll be fine," Elijah whispered to him. "We'll follow

orders and get your back if any of the war dogs fuck with you. You're in charge of this, and we won't let anyone question that."

"They will get us all killed," Quinn whispered back. He didn't like how pale Quinn seemed.

"At least it'll be all of us," Vincent mumbled.

"First, war dogs, this is a diplomatic mission," the colonel called out to the soldiers before him. "We're to stand down until hostilities have begun and act in protection to the agents who will lead the diplomacy. The IMPO team, led by Special Agent Judge and Special Agent Castello, will be investigating the causes for recent Druid aggression and hopefully finding a peaceful solution. This is the priority. It's been what several experts advised when confronted with the situation."

Colonel Fischer waited for the groans from the soldiers to end.

"We'll be taking a convoy to Manaus, checking on the first village on the drive. From there, we have boats for the river on standby. We'll be going deep into the jungle to check on the second village that has stopped trade. Non-Magi governments originally brought this to our attention. There's a couple of Druids that live in this area. One or both could be the source of the problem, but we don't know more than that. Most in the area have never even seen the Druids that live there. No one in the area has contacted a Druid in a decade."

"They probably replaced an older Druid for the area," Quinn whispered. Elijah nodded slowly. "They were probably more isolated before that and just don't have the inclination to meet the locals."

"Once we learn the status on the villages, we will move deeper, and hopefully find the Druids and talk to them.

That's where all of this can go to hell." The colonel ended. "There's not really much else. We've been briefed. Everything in this area will be a threat if we end up in a fight. If we end up in a fight, aim for the Druid to end it."

"If we run into more than one, we're all dead if there's a fight," Quinn called out. "Don't forget that. If we can convince one to stand down before a second Druid gets involved, it'll be much easier. Fight the first, and any others are less likely to listen to us, though."

"Good point," Colonel Fischer agreed. "Everyone, get some rest. We'll be on this flight for a long time. Seventeen hours and counting."

Elijah heard Sawyer groan and heard the thump of her letting her head fall back to the plane.

"This is going to suck," she mumbled.

"Yeah," Jasper sighed. "This is what we've signed up for."

Elijah looked at Quinn. Their eyes met, and Quinn sighed as well. Those blue eyes were worried.

"I'm happy you're all here but I also hate it," he said under his breath.

"I know." Elijah knew so well, but he didn't see another option. Sawyer's idea kept them all together, and if they lived through it, they were going to get a long vacation where no one could fuck with them. It wasn't perfect, but in Elijah's mind, it was good enough. He wasn't giving either of them up.

"Did you bring your sketchbook?" Quinn asked, changing the topic. "We'll be traveling a lot."

"Yup." Elijah reached into a thigh pocket of his cargos and pulled out the small sketchbook. It was in a small cover that also had a few pencils and pens for him to use.

"Good. I'm going to get some sleep. You do that then get some as well. It'll help you relax."

Elijah was chuckling at the parental orders from Quinn. "Yes sir," he teased, leaning over to whisper it in Quinn's ear. He didn't care if soldiers were watching. Quinn just loosened up a little and smiled, leaning back as much as possible and closing his eyes. Elijah leaned over to Sawyer and whispered in her ear next. "Find any hotties out there to add to your growing number of playmates?"

She hit him in the gut and he grunted, chuckling. She grinned at him as he rubbed the spot. "Four is enough for me."

"Four?" Elijah purred it.

"You count," she said, still grinning. "For obvious reasons."

"The obvious reason that you want to save a horse and-"

Elijah grunted, laughing as she thumped his gut again. Messing with her was so much fun. He wished she knew that he meant every word. She didn't know, though. She had no idea how hard he was crushing on her. To her, this was friendly and fun. To him, it was becoming more serious. He wanted her like he'd never wanted before. Not even Quinn, whom he did love in a way, like best friends, had gotten Elijah so hard.

"Maybe if I could take you seriously, we would actually talk about it," Sawyer murmured to him. They were all trying to keep their voices down. Whispered conversations were happening all over the plane, to preserve any sort of privacy.

"Maybe if you just took me up on my offer, the conversation wouldn't even need to happen," he retorted, grinning.

"Maybe I have enough other options and you need to work for it harder?" she taunted, crossing her arms. He loved the confidence. She knew she was in absolute control and fuck, that made him hard.

"You two can hash it out later," Vincent whispered to them. "People are listening."

"We're just messing around," Elijah said, chuckling. "But all right. We'll be quiet. You hear that, Sawyer? Close your eyes, go to sleep. Stop being sexy and distracting me."

"Shut up," she laughed out, louder than anything on the plane. People looked over, confused. She covered her face, shaking her head as Elijah covered up his own laughter. It even got a small chuckle out of Vincent on her other side.

An hour later, she was asleep. He pulled out his sketchbook and stole glances at her, doodling her serene face. Sleeping Sawyer was peaceful for the most part. He loved it. It would change if she got hit with a nightmare, but when she wasn't dreaming, it was obvious. She just relaxed in a way that she didn't while she was awake. Her face softened.

An hour after that, Elijah pulled out her carry-on pack. He remembered her sharpening her blades before Texas. He could do that for her. Aside from her, he had the most experience in the care of a blade. He grabbed her kit and began to work. A war dog about five feet away in his own seat watched him, but Elijah ignored the soldier. He focused intently on making sure her blades were perfect, ready for anything. Something nice he could do for her. When she woke up, he would tell her that he was handling it and she could continue to relax.

"Why black blades?" the war dog asked. Elijah looked up and frowned. Did they not know who was on the plane with them? The soldier was Corporal Curtis.

"They belong to her." Elijah tilted his head in Sawyer's direction.

"But why black?" Curtis had a mix of fascination and confusion on his face.

"Sawyer Matthews, probationary agent of the IMPO, once known as Shadow, has always used black blades," Elijah answered. "I don't know who made them for her."

"No way," Curtis laughed. "You're kidding."

"He's not," a female voice cut in. "I should have realized earlier. That's her, huh?"

Elijah found himself looking at Sergeant Petrov, the blonde that Sawyer was mumbling about when they loaded on the plane. She sat a row behind the corporal, on the end, her legs stretched out as much as they could be. She had long legs like Sawyer, but he liked Sawyer's more. She wore a thoughtful expression, one that had a small amount of respect in it.

"She's not what people think, but yeah, that's her," Elijah mumbled, going back to sharpening the dagger.

"And those are her weapons?" Petrov looked down at the blade.

He sighed, nodding. He didn't miss the very slight Russian accent from the sergeant. Interesting.

"Yes," Sawyer answered. Elijah tensed but she just leaned forward, looked down at what he was doing, and smiled.

"You can get back to sleep, I got this," Elijah told her. He was nervous about her seeing him handle her weapons without permission, but she didn't seem annoyed. He was trying to do something nice for her. He hoped she recognized it.

"Planning on it," she chuckled softly, leaning back again.

"Interesting," Petrov whispered.

They all left him alone at that. He knew the information would now spread like wildfire through the soldiers. An

225

assassin and a Druid's son were on this 'weak' IMPO team they had to 'babysit.'

Elijah finished with her weapons over an hour later and carefully put them away. He leaned back, between his two favorite people, each touching one of his shoulders, and passed out.

16

SAWYER

Sawyer thought getting from Brasilia to Manaus would be a relaxing point in the trip.

It wasn't.

The logistics were a nightmare: over forty people in their party, nearly half with animal bonds coming on the trip, and then there was the gear. It was all evidence to the fact that Sawyer was right for working alone for so long.

"Who has a fucking bear for an animal bond?" she asked, crossing her arms she waited with Quinn and Vincent for their animals.

"I don't know, but don't fuck with whoever that belongs to," Vincent replied.

"Must be a powerful Magi," Quinn mumbled. "Must be hot down here for her as well."

"Her?" Sawyer frowned.

"Bear is female," he explained. Sawyer didn't want to know how he knew.

"Her name is Anya."

Sawyer twitched at the voice. Fucking Sergeant Petrov.

She turned to see the blonde and didn't like how patient and put together she was.

"Good for her," Sawyer responded. "Yours?"

"Yes," Petrov answered curtly.

Sawyer went back to looking at the crates being unloaded. The largest crate was opened, and Sawyer swallowed her fear at the massive brown bear that walked out and roared immediately.

"Anya," Petrov murmured, walking over. "Sh, love."

The bear just rose on its hind legs and Sawyer tensed. The damn thing must have been nearly ten feet tall. Even Quinn took in a hard breath as his wolves jogged over to him. A caw could be heard, and Sawyer flicked a glance up to see a dark bird fly up, then dive down. Kaar landed on Vincent's shoulder with a level of force that had her wondering if the bird broke Vincent's shoulder. Vincent just grunted and glared at the raven.

Sawyer swallowed her jealousy.

There was no little house cat running out to her. There never would be.

Sawyer turned away and began to walk to Jasper and Zander, who were preparing their SUVs for the drive.

"This is a fucking circus," Zander mumbled when she got near. "Not even the animals. Just IMAS. Unless it's Spec Ops, IMAS is a hot mess all the time."

"Good to know," she said, helping load their bags in. "How long is this drive?"

"Forty-seven hours," Jasper answered.

She cursed several times.

"Yeah," Zander agreed. "All of that. But we'll finish one of our mission objectives on the trip, so at least it's not a total waste. It'll add time to the trip, though."

"IMAS is really always like this?" She couldn't believe it.

"Yeah," Jasper confirmed.

Sawyer pulled out a cigarette and walked about ten feet away to smoke so she didn't bother Zander and Jasper. Vincent walked over only a minute later, smoking his own. Elijah found them before they were finished and had one as well.

"This all sucks," Elijah mumbled.

"Amen," Vincent whispered.

Once the drive was started, they all knew there was no going back. Sawyer sat in the front of one of the team's two SUVs, five hours in, trying to just get back to sleep. It was a non-stop drive, so she would take over for Vincent at the eight-hour mark. Zander and Jasper were switching in the other one, while Elijah and Quinn didn't have to drive at all. Quinn because he couldn't drive, Elijah because he was making sure their inventory was ready for the twelfth time.

At the eight-hour mark, everyone got twenty minutes out to stretch their legs. Sawyer had gotten no sleep. She and Vincent smoked and switched.

Another eight hours. Another smoke and switch.

Sawyer was able to get four hours of sleep this time. She would have gotten more, but she was able to jerk herself awake, out of another nightmare. Those were starting to get on her nerves.

The mood was somber. She and the guys didn't talk. Elijah slept in the back for a good portion of the drive as well, or doodled in the sketchbook she wasn't allowed to look at.

"Are you sure I can't look? You never share it with me," Sawyer asked for the fifth time.

"Positive. My sketchbooks are private." Elijah didn't sound amused, but no one on the trip was. It was too damn long and too damn hot.

"He's quite good," Vincent told her, yawning. "Very good. He's crafted art pieces before. Designs them in that sketchbook then makes them in his free time at the house."

"I haven't seen any of those either," she replied. "Come on, Elijah. Share something with me that isn't weapons." She didn't have an artistic bone in her body. She could appreciate art but wasn't an artist.

"No," Elijah groaned. "But if I lose it, grab it. It's important to me."

"Why bring it on the trip?" She frowned at his comment.

"Something to do," he explained. "Plus, if I see something but can't get a picture, I can sketch it out later. It could be helpful."

"Like Stevenson's ring," she remembered.

"Exactly." He ended the conversation by saying nothing more, and she stopped asking.

She thought about him for a minute, pouring over his sketchbook behind her. He looked so concentrated, so intense as he sketched whatever he was working on. The flirty goof of a cowboy was so intent on what he was doing.

Like he had been sharpening her daggers for her.

"Thank you," she whispered out to him. That had meant a lot to her, and she hadn't told him yet. It was like a weight she didn't have to carry, knowing her blades were good for a fight. He'd covered her for it, did the work for her.

"For?" He looked up, confused.

"Getting my blades ready for the mission," she answered. "I haven't said thank you yet so...thank you."

"Of course, little lady." Elijah gave her a smile that she could only describe as a little shy, which struck her as odd. He wasn't shy, not at all.

At twenty-four hours, they went off the beaten path towards the unnamed village in the rainforest. At the twenty-eight hour mark, Sawyer was driving again. Vincent and Elijah were both asleep when the message came through.

"Village is only twenty minutes ahead."

Fucking Petrov had goddamned telepathy.

Sawyer reached over and hit Vincent on his thigh. He jumped and frowned. She repeated the message. He was blinking to wake up as he reached back and whacked Elijah hard enough to make her wince.

"Village," Vincent mumbled. "Coming up."

"God, I hope this isn't bad news."

It was.

Sawyer didn't notice when they drove in, not immediately. As the convoy rolled into the village, everything was quiet. It was mid-afternoon. People should have been around, coming out to see them, to find out why they were being bothered.

"It's a ghost town," Elijah whispered.

Sawyer's anxiety sky-rocketed. She stopped the SUV and they got out slowly. She pulled a dagger, as soldiers raised their weapons as well. Everyone was on edge. This wasn't right.

She and Vincent walked together to a shed that some would call a house together.

The smell hit her five feet away.

Vincent gagged.

"Oh god," she mumbled, covering her mouth.

"They're all dead," he whispered. "Everyone who lived here."

Sawyer didn't answer, only kept moving forward to the home. She peeked in slowly and closed her eyes to the sight. "Four bodies," she whispered to him. "In here."

"We have bodies in this house," a soldier called out.

"Bodies here too!"

"These look fucking eaten on!" Another soldier.

"Quinn?" Vincent called out.

Sawyer moved away from the hut and back to the SUV. Her stomach rolled. The drive had taken a toll on her. She hadn't been ready for this. A hand touched her shoulder softly and she looked to see Quinn giving her a sad expression.

"Are you okay?"

"Fine. Just the smell hit me hard."

"It does that," he agreed.

She straightened up as she watched him move away. Surrounded by the death, he was different. Something about his walk was confident. Not in his normal defensive and tense way, but looser. He leaned down and grabbed a handful of soil, holding it close to his nose. She watched in confusion as he sniffed it, focusing on it. "She was here," he whispered.

Everyone went silent.

"Repeat that, Special Agent Quinn?" The colonel looked terrified and angry.

"She did this. Her magic is soaked into the soil. These people stood no chance. They've been rotting here since they dropped communication. I would suspect that some of the villagers won't be accounted for. There's no need..." Quinn dropped the soil. Sawyer watched him continue to walk and looked down. He wasn't leaving footprints behind him. He was using his earth manipulation to make them disappear.

She continued to look around, noticing that none of them were leaving footprints. She pushed her foot into the soil and pulled it back up. The soil reclaimed the spot immediately, wiping evidence of her away. She put that out of her mind and put her foot back down. She could ask Quinn about it later.

"Fertilizer for their land. Meat for their animals," Vincent whispered.

Sawyer's stomach rolled again. "Why?" she asked quietly.

"I think everyone is wondering that," Elijah mumbled, walking over. "Give me a cigarette."

Sawyer thought that sounded like a splendid idea. They all lit up and followed Quinn to the center of the village.

The colonel approached them quickly.

"What the fuck is this? Why would a Druid do this?" he demanded, and Sawyer only shrugged.

"We can only hope Quinn has some sort of answer," Vincent told him softly. "He doesn't give up his secrets without need, so we're a little blind too."

"God damn it," the colonel growled.

"Quinn?" Elijah called out his name. Sawyer could hear the concern in his voice and related.

Quinn turned to them and sighed. "I'm going to bury the bodies," he told them simply. "Then we'll talk."

"All right, buddy," Elijah called out.

"Do you need help?" a soldier asked, walking to Quinn. "We have the manpower to get it done in a few hours."

"I don't need it," he answered.

The ground beneath them rumbled. Sawyer had felt power like this before, when she'd gone and pissed him off with the books. This didn't feel unleashed though, or aggressive. This was calm. Someone yelled, and Sawyer looked in the direction of it with Vincent. She watched as a body sank beneath the earth.

He was burying them all without their help.

It ended in a minute. "There," Quinn whispered.

Sawyer walked to him and touched his shoulder gently. "Are *you* okay?"

"No. We can't leave now," he answered. "Everyone, attention on me!" he yelled out. Everyone was already paying attention to him. "The Druid that did this will do it again. We need to hunt her down and end it. We're camping here for the night and we'll leave at dawn. Keep a watch rotation at all times. She will notice we're in her territory. We need to hope she doesn't come for us before we go to her."

Sawyer's heart dropped.

"The second village?" Colonel Fischer asked, his arms crossed.

"Is probably just like this. It would be a waste of time to go north, find it and then start the hunt for the Druid that did this. Both villages are in this Druid's territory. That we know. Now, others could live here, but I'm hoping it's only the one who did this."

"Why would she do this?" the colonel continued his questioning.

Quinn sighed. Sawyer didn't like it. It seemed tired and the mission had just gotten off to a brutal start.

"Druids have a tendency to go mad," he began softly. The team already knew some of this. Sawyer crossed her arms in a protective fashion. She felt uncomfortable. Something about the way he was talking made her uncomfortable. "The area has been totally invaded by humans, who cut down the trees, poach the animals. Sometimes...sometimes Druids get angry about it, sometimes they disconnect with humanity and fight back against invaders. This is the result."

Sawyer didn't like that he made it sound unavoidable. As if they always went crazy and killed dozens of people.

"*If* there is a diplomatic solution, it will have to be one to stop us from driving Druids to this point." Quinn waved his hands around to point out the village. Sawyer felt it was unneeded. They all caught his meaning. "But right now, the best course of action is to go out and put this Druid down. Probably the second one too."

"How do we tell one Druid from the next?" another soldier called out. Sawyer thought that was a very good question.

"We won't, or at least not very well," Quinn called back, just as loud. "Their magic all feels the same. It's not unique among them, not like one of us. We all feel distinct to each other. There are some differences in the Druids, but they are very minor. Calmer Druids will have a calmer feeling over all, while wilder Druids will feel wilder. This one? She feels wild."

"How do you feel it?"

"I'm strong enough to, and I know what to look for," Quinn answered. "As we grow closer to her home, where she lives constantly, you'll start to as well. It'll feel like magic just hanging in the air, and it will grow more concentrated. As you start to feel, we'll know we're nearly on top of her home."

"How do we know when she's close?" Sawyer asked.

"I'll let you know," he told her. "I can't feel her right now. She's not close enough to us. If she were to use more of her power, I would. I will. That will be how we track her. Eventually, sometime over this night and tomorrow, she'll use her magic for something and we'll move in that direction. I'll be able to give everyone here a warning if she's close as well. No worries."

"Hence why we follow your rare orders," she muttered. "Okay."

"You heard him, war dogs," the colonel called out. "Set up camp!"

"Yes sir!" they all answered.

Sawyer winced at the volume. Too fucking loud for the middle of the goddamned jungle. "We're sleeping in the vehicles," she bit out, walking back to the SUV. She looked at the cigarette she was holding. She'd stopped smoking it and it had burned out. She pocketed the butt and lit another. She was taking a long drag when Zander leaned on her side.

"You don't have to stop. I just needed to be near something normal," he whispered.

"Okay," she replied, taking another puff. Jasper ended up on her other side. Quinn watched them all, while Elijah talked to Vincent, both still smoking as well.

"All these people," Jasper despaired. "So many of them."

"I hope it was quick," Sawyer added.

"It was," Quinn told them. "Most were strangled by vines in their beds. Those who were unlucky enough to wake up and find out what was happening...they died to animals. Some were probably bit by snakes. Depends on what this Druid most associated with."

"What do you mean?" Zander asked.

"My mother associated with wolves. Another Druid had an affinity for foxes. Some love snakes, some have no favorites and deal with everything equally. They do have some personal preference and that changes how they work. Some let the animals around them work things out on their own and only deal with the land itself, the plant life."

"To think Druids are just Magi with some fucked up powers," Sawyer mumbled.

"Legends are like that." Jasper groaned. "You know what really gets me?"

"What?"

"Druids are born to regular people, other Magi normally, like everyone else. They just...got unlucky, or lucky depending on how you look at it. Their powers manifested, and they are Druids and that's it. Think about being their parents, too. Their daughters just run off into the woods. That's it, and there's no stopping it."

"Just like any other Magi," Zander said, sounding pissed. "They're the ones who decide to go live in the woods and forget they're fucking human. Not many Magi go out and do shit like this."

"Zander is right," Quinn declared. Sawyer didn't like the angry expression on his face. "It is their decision. Their powers manifest like all of us, in their teenage years, and they decide they are better than humanity. They choose to leave. They choose to cut themselves off and separate from the world. They choose to be monsters like this. If this bitch hadn't killed off this town, I wouldn't hunt her down. I was hoping she didn't. I don't care about farmland. Humans need to just accept their losses sometimes, but this is too far. These people were mostly non-Magi and innocent. Too bad this bitch probably thinks she's a god."

Sawyer raised her eyebrows at the sudden hostility. It shouldn't have surprised her, but it was still a little shocking. He'd been calm and patient when they arrived, and now he was furious.

"God?" the colonel seemed shocked by Quinn's hostility as well.

Quinn snarled. "I won't say every Druid considers themselves that way, but it's my experience that they feel they can do as they please," he explained. "Everyone should get some good sleep tonight." He walked away from them all. Sawyer watched him go, hoping he would be okay.

She didn't notice Elijah walking to her with a bag until he spoke. "Food. Mostly snack type items for us to keep our energy up." He held it out and she reached in. She pulled out three granola bars and shoved two in a pocket, eating the third quickly.

"You okay?" she asked him softly. She felt like she was asking everyone that.

"Could be better," Elijah admitted. "Want to talk about anything?"

"Not really. Lots of people are dead here, and we're about to track down a Magi who has decided to use her... gifts to do it. Druid or not, this isn't acceptable. I'm worried, a little scared, but I'm glad we're here to do this." Sawyer took a deep breath. "Seeing this, I'm glad we're here."

"I almost agree with you," he agreed.

They spent the rest of the evening making sure they ate and they all had places to sleep comfortably. Elijah would be taking over the entire backseat of their SUV, Sawyer and Vincent deciding to take the front seats. The soldiers had tents, but the team weren't in the mood to do that and had the space in their vehicles. It earned them some teasing from the war dogs, though.

"Jasper," Zander called out.

In the dark, Sawyer chuckled. They both needed to get some sleep. She didn't know why they were still wandering around.

"What?" Jasper groaned loudly.

"Make sure to take your leg off. Sleeping with it on will give you a rash."

"I know, jackass," he snapped. Sawyer was in a fit over it. *Zander* was telling *Jasper* what to do? The planets must have aligned.

"Both of you just sleep," Quinn snarled. "You'll distract the patrol."

"You sleep too, Quinn," Elijah yelled out.

"Fine."

Sawyer heard doors slamming and was still chuckling ten minutes later. A small bit of humor in the horror of this mission. She liked to think that when the world was going to hell, a laugh was needed.

Vincent reached over and put a hand over her mouth.

"You, too," he whispered sleepily.

Sawyer was in another nightmare. The trees around her weren't the ones of the rainforest, but rather, the woods near one of Axel's homes. She was out there with several members of the Ghosts. She wore her mask to protect her appearance. They had no idea who the woman in all black was except that she was Axel's Shadow.

A body was dropped in a hole. Not one of hers. This was someone they killed, someone they had considered a friend. He'd tried to get out, and they had killed him for it. She was there because Axel wanted to remind her what running meant.

She walked silently back to the large house with Axel. The others just got in their own vehicles and left. She pulled her mask off, the liquid magic of it reforming into the solid mask.

He was in a bad mood and she knew it. Once they were alone, he decided to let it out.

The first blow took her by surprise. It sent her to the floor.

"Sawyer, fight back," Jasper called out.

She didn't need to be told twice. She swung up, connecting to a shield. It cracked. She swung again. It shattered. She jumped up and tackled Axel to the floor.

Then it was over.

DAWN WAS JUST COMING over the horizon. She could hear the slow, deep breathing of Elijah in the back. Vincent was also still asleep. She was glad she hadn't woken them.

She slipped out of the SUV without either of them noticing and went to the team's other ride. Jasper was already awake, watching her walk up. He opened his door and sat out the side. She could tell he wasn't wearing his prosthetic, the pant leg falling loose just below his knee. A stark reminder. It was easy to forget, honestly, since his prosthetic was so lifelike when he wore it. Enchantments made sure the leg acted as a normal one for walking and running, and Sawyer knew that they had worked on ways for Jasper to control it for climbing and jumping.

It was all much too complicated for her to really care about. It worked for him and that was all that mattered.

"You need to learn how to get lucid on your own, Sawyer," Jasper told her immediately. "But you fight back faster now. You don't take as long to listen to me, or second-guess yourself."

"So basically, I'm terrible at the most important part." She groaned, rolling her eyes at herself and her problem.

"Yeah, that sounds about right," Jasper whispered. "I need to get my leg on and we can go for a walk." He reached back and grabbed his leg. She watched him put it on, studying the straps and how snug his knee fit. She hadn't yet taken a long look at how he wore it.

When he was done, he kept the pant leg rolled up and she gave him a curious look.

"It's itchy first thing in the morning," he explained. "I like being able to scratch it. Also, I might need to readjust the tightness, and I don't want to need to pull my pants up ten times in the first thirty minutes of my day to do that."

"I never noticed," she commented plainly.

"I normally make sure everything is good before I leave my room." He shrugged as he said that. "So, nightmares still a problem, even out here."

"They were still a problem in Texas too, remember?" She crossed her arms as they walked. "It's one of the reasons we started doing this. So I could...take control of them. So I might get past them again."

"You were never really past them to begin with. They faded, but they always came back. We're working to give you control of it permanently." Jasper sighed. "I mean, this is just a band-aid. Eventually, you will need to open up enough to get therapy."

"No." Out of the question. She wasn't seeing a doctor.

"I know." Jasper shrugged. "We'll figure it out. I need to ask someone how I can teach you better. This isn't bad progress, but I feel like I'm screwing something up."

"Me or you. I think it's me. I get sucked in so easily."

Jasper didn't respond. He leaned down, tightened one of the straps for his prosthetic and they just kept walking.

They saw that the soldiers were already getting ready to break their makeshift camps. Some looked at Sawyer and Jasper, interested. "What happened?" one called out, pointing at Jasper's leg. "I know it's rude to ask."

"I had a building dropped on me," Jasper answered, smiling.

Sawyer chuckled. "Yeah, that's about the simplest explanation for it," she agreed.

"No fucking way." The soldier laughed, walking over. His name tag read Rodriguez. "Sorry. I'm one of the healers for this trip. I've never seen a prosthetic like that, so I got interested."

"My teammate, Elijah, the big one with the cowboy boots, got in touch with a company that makes them. He and Zander, our healer, did the enchantments for it." Jasper lifted his leg, bent it at the knee and rolled the foot around. It all seemed perfectly natural, except his leg was fashionably not real. "Special Agent Jasper Williams. Nice to meet you..."

"Sergeant Rodriguez. Most call me Doc."

"Of course," Jasper chuckled. Sawyer watched them shake hands and stayed quiet. She didn't want to interrupt the male bonding. Jasper ruined it, though. "This is Sawyer, our probationary agent. Uh..." He looked at her and she shrugged.

"Shadow. Yeah, I've heard." Rodriguez bravely stuck his hand out to her too. She decided to shake with him and held his hand tightly when she felt his magic. It was calming and strange. She'd been riled up still from the nightmare, which was why she agreed to the walk. She wasn't any longer.

"Don't try to manipulate my emotions," she whispered to him. "Empaths feel emotions, but you have emotional manipulation. Don't do that to me." She let go of him. The moment the contact ended, her own anger pushed through his magically-induced calm.

"Sorry. I noticed you were uptight and wanted to help a little." He seemed thoroughly chastised. "I'm not empathetic without touch. It's one of the quirks of emotional manipulation. Touch is needed to both feel and change the emotions."

"Yeah, I know how your damn abilities work," she snapped. She turned away and kept walking away.

Jasper moved with her. "Sorry. He didn't try anything on me or I would have cautioned against it."

"He was just being a damn healer. I'm mad because I don't normally shake hands until I know what abilities someone has. I made a mistake." Sawyer was more pissed at herself.

"Not a mistake. You're trusting people more easily. He wasn't trying to burn you for it. You got it right, he was just trying to be a healer." Jasper was trying to play voice of reason. "It's not a bad thing. He should have asked first, though."

"Mistakes all around then," she scoffed.

He just chuckled at her. "You ready for what's about to come?"

The mood immediately soured.

"Is there any way to be ready?" she asked back.

"I don't think so," he conceded. "We're probably going to head out in about an hour. I'm not sure I've really wrapped my head around this yet. Just a couple of days ago, we were thinking about a full three-month vacation."

"You're telling me," Sawyer groaned. "Let's go wake up everyone and get them moving."

17

SAWYER

Three days in the rainforest, and Sawyer was already ready to leave. It was hot and humid, the insects were awful, and she wasn't getting any sleep. The rain was even worse - not heavy enough to be the rainy season, but enough to get them all fairly wet. Some soldiers were beginning to complain about their feet.

They left their vehicles in the village, since the road had ended and the brush was too thick to drive or forge a path. Sawyer's legs cramped at the end of the second day as she collapsed next to Jasper, who wasn't doing so hot either. "This fucking blows," she complained. She rubbed her thighs slowly, hoping to work out the tight muscles.

"I won't disagree." Jasper groaned and leaned against the tree.

She flicked away a spider that was crawling next to her. She wasn't in the mood for the creepy crawlies that were around.

"Hey, we need to get tents up," Elijah told them as he walked by.

"Fuck," Sawyer snapped. She got back up, groaning.

"Make sure to get some rest tonight. Tomorrow, we've decided to move double time," Petrov commented blandly as she walked past as well, along with the other higher-ranking enlisted soldiers.

God. Two days of her and Sawyer wanted to strangle the soldier. Sergeant Petrov was a tough bitch, that was for sure. When soldiers were out of line, making jokes or comments, she was normally the first on their asses for it. Sawyer respected it, but she couldn't stand Petrov's uptight attitude about fucking everything. Snack on the walk? Not allowed. Talking in the ranks? Not allowed. A fucking stickler, including with the team.

The only thing Petrov did, or rather, *didn't* do that Sawyer liked was talk about the team like everyone else. A lot of the soldiers across the board were rude to the team for not being set up for this sort of work. The upper chain of command just made small remarks about the differences between the IMAS and the IMPO, but some lower ranking soldiers openly taunted them. The team just wasn't built for this sort of work. There was a reason this was an IMAS mission and not the IMPO's.

Vincent was exhausted. Elijah was getting cranky, but he knew how to camp and was used to roughing it a little. Zander was on another level of pissed off, since he kept needing to heal scratches, bruises, and bug bites. Sawyer and Jasper, they were both just fucking tired.

Only Quinn seemed completely at ease with the whole 'hang out and trek through the jungle' shit.

"Sawyer," Quinn called out to her. *Speak of the fucking devil.*

"Yeah?"

"Come help me," he ordered.

She looked to Jasper, who shrugged, standing up. She

got up next, steadying Jasper when he stumbled with a groan. "Get off your feet for the rest of the night," she commanded. "Take the leg off and relax."

"Will do," Jasper promised.

"Yeah, pirate, go relax," a soldier called out.

Sawyer glared at Petrov, who turned away to reprimand the soldier. The big-ass bear just followed and growled at the soldier once Petrov was done telling him to keep his mouth shut.

"I hate them," Jasper mumbled. "All of them. They like their nicknames. Hazing is also a serious problem. They like making life difficult for people until they prove they fit in."

"Oh great," she replied. They both walked to Quinn, who was setting up a tent. He pulled up earth to make a pedestal of sorts with no vegetation on it for the tent to sit on. Sawyer knew he would do it for every tent in their camp so that no one was down in the gross vegetation with the bugs.

Sawyer helped him finish the tent and then watched him walk off. "He's been so quiet," she mentioned to Jasper.

"He's focused on the task. He's probably overloaded too."

"What?" Sawyer frowned, pulling out a small folding chair from the inside of the tent. They had two tents, each fitting three people on the team. Each tent had a few small chairs, made of canvas. She was bunking with Jasper and Zander. Shade slept at their feet, Quinn wanting each tent to have a wolf to handle any threats like snakes while they slept.

"He has naturalism for an ability, remember? And he's in a new environment. He's probably being overloaded by all the information. He needs time to process what he's learning. Every time he brushes up against a new plant or runs across a new insect or something, he learns about them." Jasper sighed. "It's just the ability magnified by his power."

"I forgot about all of that. Hadn't even considered it." Sawyer shook her head at herself. "Fuck, the heat must be frying my brain. I actually miss Texas - it wasn't this fucking humid."

"I never thought I would ever hear that from you." Jasper chuckled, sitting down in one of their fold-out chairs. She sat next to him, watching Elijah and Vincent get their tent up, then sit down with them.

A thing fell in her lap and she looked down to see Jasper's leg.

"You can hold on to that," he said.

"Fine." Sawyer just left it there in her lap and ignored it.

Elijah pulled out the rest of the chairs. She chuckled at the way Vincent collapsed and nearly fell down with the chair since he hit it too hard. Elijah was laughing as he tossed MREs at them.

She gagged. The military rations sucked.

He was kind enough to throw her a couple of granola bars as well. "We're running low on those, so you need to cut back," he teased, sitting on her other side.

"Look. They're keeping me alive, all right?" Sawyer opened one of the bars and shoved it into her mouth. She was going to ignore the MRE for as long as possible. Processed, dehydrated, disgusting shit. For her, it just wasn't going to cut it. She had some standards. She swallowed the food in her mouth before continuing. "I mean, I'm already playing in the fucking dirt. I should at least eat something I can stomach."

"When you're out of them, don't whine to me," Elijah sternly told her, sitting down.

They relaxed for a good portion of the evening. It was

near dark when Sawyer could hear some soldiers get a little rowdy. "The chick is a fucking assassin. No joke. The fucking Shadow. You know, the crime lord's bitch. You know the rumors."

Sawyer knew she was camp gossip. It was unavoidable. Once it got out, there was no stopping it. She didn't blame Elijah for saying anything, since someone was going to slip eventually - like the colonel, who definitely had known before the mission began.

"Want me to say something?" Jasper asked her quietly.

"No," she groaned. She dropped his prosthetic in his lap. "I'm going to use the bathroom, then lie down, though."

"Be safe," Vincent called after her when she stood up, grabbed their roll of toilet paper, and walked off.

She passed Quinn on the way out. "I'll keep watch," he said, turning to follow her.

"I don't really need that, but fine," she replied.

After her business was taken care of, Quinn grabbed her arm. "Come on a quick patrol with me. It'll be slow. Stretch your legs a little without overworking them."

"Quinn," she groaned. "I just really want to get some sleep."

"Please?" he asked, refusing to let go of her.

"Sure," she whispered. He let go of her arm and she fell in beside him, the dark beginning to claim the jungle. "Can you see?"

"Well enough," he responded.

She watched him as they walked and again noted that he was quieter than normal, but oddly at ease. Something seemed free about him, and that struck her as strange. "What's going on with you?" she asked softly.

"What do you mean?" He frowned at her, and she shrugged.

"Even back at the village, you seemed...strangely comfortable. You've been different." She didn't know how to explain it.

"I like it here," he admitted quietly. "I like the space. I like knowing that if I wanted to disappear out here, I can. It's different from home and there's a lot of danger here, but..."

"I'm listening," she told him, looping her arm around his.

"I can use my magic out here and no one would question it. No one would call me a freak or feral. It's not like the overcrowded cities, or even the tiny plot of land I have at our home. This is free. I wish the circumstances were different, because I've enjoyed being here. I just haven't enjoyed knowing we're living under the shadow of finding and killing a Druid."

"We can come back one day," she promised him. "You can teach me how to enjoy this. Something fun to do in the rainforest."

"I can think of a few things," he whispered down into her ear. Sawyer could hear the innuendo. There was something raw and passionate about the way he said it that sent shivers down her spine.

"Are you flirting with me?" she asked him incredulously, trying to keep her voice down in case they had eavesdroppers. She was shocked.

"Do you mind?" He held her arm looped in his.

"Um. No? It's just a very Elijah way to flirt with someone," she explained, shaking her head at the weird situation.

Quinn flirting with her? *What?*

"I've never flirted and decided to try. I see him flirt all the time." He growled after that, shaking his own head. He tried to pull away from her and she kept her arm firmly wrapped around his. "I won't do it again. I just…"

"Quinn. Be yourself. People like that." She put her free hand on his chest, patting it a couple of times.

"People don't like me being myself. It's too different from them. I wanted to try to be more like everyone else."

"Being different makes you interesting. It makes you something new. If they aren't up for the differences, they aren't worthy of you." She shrugged. She liked him for who he was. Once she'd gotten used to it, she adored it, really. "People should be willing to put the work in to making something work if it means something to them. Not everything comes easy. Friendships, relationships, life. If they won't put the work in, then you should cut them loose. Like Zander and me? We both feel for each other and it's a pain, but we both want it, so we'll keep trying. We'll keep fighting *with* each other and *for* each other."

"Yes. You're right."

She didn't realize he'd stopped walking and jerked to a hard stop, still hooked to him by their arms. He pulled her back slowly and she raised her eyebrows when their chests met. Her pulse sky-rocketed under his ice-blue gaze. They stood out in the dark against his earth-toned skin.

Why did her wild friend have to be gorgeous and far out of her reach?

He flirted with her just to try something new. Her heart twisted. He was probably trying to learn for himself, which was good, but she selfishly wanted him to flirt with her because it was her.

It felt like a childish want.

"I know you don't like it out here, but really, thank you for being here."

"You keep saying thank you. Stop. Being here for you is

what friends do," she reminded him. She tried to pull away, but he just wrapped his arms around her in a hug. She hugged him back and reveled in it. It lasted much longer than the awkward one-armed hug in New York.

"Let's get back to camp," he ordered, pulling away. "I don't like us being out here alone for too much longer."

She followed him back, seeing how they were on the other side of camp at this point. They had to walk through the soldiers to get back to the team.

"Tarzan and the criminal," one soldier teased as they walked by.

"Hey. They say you can fight, Shadow. Want to prove it?" another yelled out.

Quinn snarled and began to turn to the camo-wearing soldier. Sawyer grabbed his arm and stopped his movement. He looked back at her and she just shook her head.

"Leave them. Not worth our time," she whispered.

"Scared? Don't want to fight anyone face to face?" the soldier taunted. "Or do you only stab people in the back? You one of those types of cowards, or is everyone in the IMPO a bunch of pussies?"

That got to her. She released Quinn and pulled a dagger from its sheath. She blinked into the face of the soldier, her dagger poised and poking his neck. She grabbed his shirt to keep him from backing away from her. A few of the people around scrambled away, shocked by her sudden move.

It had all happened in the blink of an eye.

"I'll recommend you don't call people cowards or pussies when they could very well and easily kill you," she murmured to him. "I'm out of patience with this mission. I'm running on fumes. My legs hurt and I'm cranky. I won't be taunted and teased, and I damn sure won't allow you to insult my team. Keep your thoughts to yourself." She glanced at his name badge and his rank patch. "Lance Corporal Todd."

"Let him go," a strong male voice came out. She turned slowly to see one of the master sergeants, Master Sergeant Coore. The highest rank of the enlisted soldiers, she knew this one would be able to make her life hard.

"Certainly." She let the lance corporal go and he collapsed. He'd been on the verge of fainting the entire time. "Just thought he deserved a lesson in competently judging a possible opponent. Maybe next time he'll know not to taunt the wrong person. Others might not be as forgiving as I am."

She stepped around the master sergeant and back to Quinn, who was giving her a small smile. It was impressed and maybe even a little turned on. That got her pulse going again. Had he liked that display of temper from her? That's what it was. She had lost her temper for a moment.

"Let's get back to the team," she said, walking past him.

She went straight into her tent, ignoring the team. Exhaustion weighed on her, but it did nothing to stop the thoughts of that smile Quinn had worn. She had enough men in her life. He had expressed absolutely no real interest in her. He was the safe one. She was imagining things.

Zander and Jasper both laid down and passed out long before she was able to.

Somehow, she'd ended up between them and they had pinned her in. She hadn't gone to sleep between them, that was certain, but she didn't honestly care too much. She was madder that she couldn't get up and leave because of the new positioning.

"Jasper," she whispered harshly. "Let me fucking up."

"Hm?" He blinked several times and also realized what happened. "Zander moved."

"Yes. I can tell. I don't want to wake up his cranky ass, though. Move, so I can get up."

"Sorry," he groaned, rolling away from her.

The sun wasn't completely up yet, but there was enough light for her to get out and do her thing. Alone in the jungle, she felt something brush her mind. It was similar to how Vincent or Zander felt when they used their telepathy, but nothing was said. It also felt very personal. She didn't understand, but something about it made her anxious and worried. It pricked at a memory that Sawyer didn't understand. She couldn't put her finger on it.

Back in camp, she saw Jasper searching through all their things. She shook off the weird sensation and decided to figure out what he was doing.

"Do you know where I put my damn leg?" he asked immediately. "I thought I put it in the tent bag but it's not there. Like, the entire bag is gone."

Sawyer groaned. She went to the second tent and pulled open their flap. "Guys, Jasper's fucking leg. You bring it in here?"

"No," Elijah grumbled. "Tent bag, outside the door to your tent."

"Not there. Bag is gone," she told him. She had never seen Elijah move so fast.

"It's not there? What, did a fucking monkey steal it?"

"What?" Vincent yawned as Elijah nearly barreled over her to get out of the tent.

"Jasper's leg is missing. Where's Quinn?"

"He always leaves before dawn with the wolves to check the camp perimeter," Vincent explained, moving out of the tent as well. He gave Sawyer a chance to move out of the way. "Jasper's leg is missing?"

"Yeah."

"Why wasn't it kept in the tent?" Vincent asked, frustrated.

"I don't know," Sawyer answered honestly. She realized the idiocy of it. She couldn't miss it. It had been right outside the tent, so she wanted to know more about how someone, or something, silently moved it.

"I hope it was just misplaced," Vincent snapped. "Great way to start day four in the goddamned jungle."

Sawyer just let him get mad. He had reason to be. Now they would either be slowed down by a severely handicapped Jasper or slowed down looking for the leg.

He went silent and sighed after a moment.

"Quinn should be on his way back to help find it," Vincent told her and walked over to Jasper and Elijah. Sawyer followed slowly. They were going through everything in their portion of the camp. Some soldiers nearby watched as they broke down their own tents, ready to get moving.

Shade and Scout were there first and began sniffing around. Sawyer watched as Scout's head shot up and he looked at her. She sighed. The wolf wanted her to follow.

Both wolves began to walk back out of their area of the camp, following a scent. "Let's follow," Sawyer declared. "Except you." She pointed at Jasper, who glared at her.

"Yes. I've realized," he retorted.

"It was stolen by a soldier, I guarantee it," Zander harshly snapped. "They love stupid fucking games like this."

"Jasper said they like hazing?" Sawyer asked him as they followed the wolves through the camp.

"Yeah. I'm going to beat the fucking ass of whoever did this." His temper was lit, and she grabbed his arm.

"We can't have fights," she reminded him. "We can push and argue, but we can't get into brawls. We have more important shit to worry about in this jungle."

"Says the woman who held one of them at knifepoint last night," Vincent noted. She turned a glare on him. "You were just trying to scare him a little, yes, I know. Quinn explained."

"Good," she bit out.

They were all cranky and this just made it worse.

"Let's just find the fucking leg," Elijah snapped. He stomped past them. Only Quinn wasn't in a completely bad mood, but she wasn't going to test it.

She spotted the leg first. The wolves were leading them through a particularly crowded area of the camp, and she caught a reflective glint that made her interested. It was propped up on a tree next to one of the soldier's tents. Sawyer walked directly for it, not bothering to call everyone over yet. She would grab it and go. No harm, no foul.

"What? He didn't want to come get it himself?" a soldier asked, grinning. A few laughed, finding the entire thing much too funny for her taste. She turned to glare at them as she lifted the prosthetic.

"Do it again and I'll just stab you," she warned softly. "This shit isn't acceptable. Not on a mission, not in the fucking real world."

"It's a joke. We were going to give it back to him, help him put it on," the first one explained. Sawyer didn't like his grin.

"Yeah, after he hobbled over here," another said, snickering.

She turned to leave. She would point them out to one of the higher-ranking soldiers before they broke camp.

"Guys!" she called out. Quinn looked over to her. The wolves were milling around. Sawyer guessed they must have lost the trail in the large area with so many other people going through it. "Got it!"

"Thank fuck," Elijah growled. He stomped over to her and snatched it away. "I hope they didn't sabotage it. They could get him killed."

Sawyer watched him walk away back to their area.

"I'll talk to the colonel. He'll pass a message along for them to not take our things. Can you point out who did it?" Vincent stopped at her side.

"Yeah," she answered. "Let's do that now."

"Okay. Zander, Quinn, you guys help Elijah break down the tents."

"Sure," Zander snarled. Quinn just nodded and followed Zander away, with Shade and Scout on their heels.

"It was just a few young guys. They had wanted to get a laugh out of Jasper hobbling around to look for it." Sawyer was pissed but she knew she couldn't go pick a fight. She wanted to. She really did, but it wouldn't do them any good.

"Come on," Vincent sighed. She walked with him to the largest tent where the colonel was having a talk over a map with his captain and the master sergeants. Vincent came to these talks, but Sawyer didn't. It was considered too sensitive for her to know. "Colonel, we need to have a talk."

"What about?" the colonel asked, straightening up. His eyes narrowed at her, and Sawyer grinned.

"Some of your soldiers, enlisted boys, decided they wanted to have a bit of fun. They stole something that belonged to one of my team. I want them reprimanded."

"What did they steal?" the Captain asked, frowning.

"Special Agent William's prosthetic," Vincent answered. "Sawyer can point them out. She found it with them."

"How did you find it?" Master Sergeant Coore, the one from the night before, asked cautiously.

"It was just sitting out against a tree. They weren't trying to hide it," Sawyer scoffed. "They wanted a laugh. They better hope they didn't fucking break it or ruin the enchantments. Shit will get ugly then."

"Roger that," the master sergeant answered. "I'll go with you. You point them out and I'll handle it. Colonel?"

"Go. Spread the word that we won't tolerate this."

"Yes sir." The master sergeant popped a salute and let Sawyer lead him and Vincent to the group that had stolen the prosthetic.

"That bunch." She pointed. 'That bunch' saw her and some even glared. Sawyer grinned at them too. Idiots thought that she was going to let it slide? Stupid.

"I'll take it from here," he told her and Vincent. "Thank you for bringing this to us."

"No problem," Vincent replied.

They went back to their own camp, everyone able to hear the Master Sergeant lay into the group of soldiers who thought they were funny. The team took its time getting ready, annoyed and wanting to be assholes to the soldiers who were all waiting on them.

"Let's hope this shit doesn't keep up with them," Sawyer said as she pulled her main bag over her shoulder. She was armed and ready for any fight the jungle could throw at her.

"I think we pissed them all off," Zander whispered in a mischievous tone. "Making them wait an hour on us."

"Fuck em," Elijah growled.

"Amen," Jasper huffed.

"I never asked the guys how they did it." Sawyer realized

that with a bit of regret. She wasn't going to ask them now since they had gotten reprimanded because of her.

"Does it matter?" Vincent asked, ready to get moving.

"Maybe?" She shrugged and forgot about it by the time the group began to move even deeper into the sweltering jungle.

18

SAWYER

For two more days, they hiked. Through the underbrush of the rainforest, through a stream that was deceptively deep, through a hot, humid hell that was driving Sawyer insane.

One thing was certain to her though. They were getting closer.

"Do you feel that?" Zander asked her towards the end of their fifth day. She knew what he was talking about.

"Yes."

The magic in the air clung to them and everything around them. It vibrated like Quinn's magic, unrestrained, a little feral, but it was *everywhere*. It had gotten stronger, much stronger, throughout the day. It had started like an itch to Sawyer in the morning. As the day progressed, it began to weigh in on them, suffocating their own magic. Even the weakest of the soldiers around them were noticing the power in the world around them.

"Quinn," Jasper called out. "Have any idea how close we are?"

"I would guess another couple of days," Quinn

answered, stopping to look back at them. Sawyer admired the courage from him. He'd been leading them for days, always in the front, directing their progress. It meant if they stumbled on the enemy, he would be the first in the fight. "We're coming towards the center of her territory. She might not be there, but the magic in the area is too rich for me to feel her specifically.

"You saying we're flying a little blind?" the colonel asked, walking through the ranks to him.

"We've been flying blind since we landed in Brasilia, Colonel," Quinn growled. "I warned you this would be dangerous."

"You did," he agreed. "Are we going to keep moving?"

"I think we can do another couple of miles today." Quinn looked away from the group. "If we find a place to stop before then, we will."

Sawyer groaned and kept walking, Zander and Jasper flanking her.

"I don't like how long this has been taking," Jasper commented after another twenty minutes. "I don't like that we're just stomping out in the jungle with only Quinn's direction to a fight we might not win."

"We'll win," Zander promised. "We'll fucking win. I hate being around all these soldiers though. They are idiots. Damn Cavalry."

"Cavalry?" Sawyer hadn't yet learned all the nuances of the IMAS.

"You'll notice many of them have animal bonds. Cavalry, like people who used to ride on horses. For the IMAS, it's having an animal bond. A specialized group, sure, but nothing too special. If you have an animal that could have strategic value, you can apply to Cavalry. You'll probably get accepted, since the IMAS is at an all time low for their numbers. They haven't done a good job at recruiting in the last decade or so," Jasper explained in his rambling, never-ending way.

Sawyer could hear younger guys in the back having a good time as they walked and rolled her eyes. "Do they take nothing seriously?" she asked, looking back for a moment and seeing a soldier grin at her.

"No," Jasper replied curtly. "They don't. They're young, and they have no idea what kind of power is waiting for us out here. The IMAS instills this belief that their soldiers are unstoppable. The younger guys live like that, really do believe it. Nothing scares them the way it should."

"Then they start dying," Zander mumbled angrily. "The survivors learn pretty quickly if they want to continue surviving."

"Zander," Jasper chastised him.

Sawyer raised her eyebrows. She didn't know much about her guys' times in the IMAS. It sounded like there was a story there.

"Yeah, yeah," Zander scoffed. He stomped ahead of them and she watched him fall in next to Vincent and Elijah.

"What's up?" she asked in a hushed tone, hoping Zander couldn't hear her.

"Zander and I were lucky enough to get in the same unit when we joined, but we got split up when another unit needed a healer. It was temporary. They had a thing in Saudi Arabia. People died. Zander couldn't heal them all, and he fought with their command about the decisions made that led to it. He was busted back a rank for it. He came back angrier. He hated the IMAS after that. Vincent found us three months later and Zander thrived in the IMPO and I thought it was better. I didn't realize how angry he was going to be on a mission with the IMAS."

"A hot-tempered, reckless man hates reckless decisions?" Sawyer crossed her arms and gave Jasper a look. She didn't believe him.

"Zander will do something that gets himself killed or gives him a chance to heal someone else. He's not out to get other people killed. He draws a line," he reminded her. "A lot like you."

"I'm not reckless."

"No, you think something through then you do something dangerous," he teased softly. "Not reckless, just confident in the idea that you have it all figured out."

She chuckled quietly, nodding.

When Jasper stumbled and cursed, she was laughing harder. "Are you okay?" she asked through the laughter, grabbing his arm.

"I'm fine..." Jasper sounded concerned and Sawyer felt her humor fall away.

"What? You stumbled, it was funny." She frowned as Jasper stopped. He looked down to his prosthetic and she watched him rotate the ankle, bend his knee. It was all working just fine. "Jasper?"

"It...pulled back and caused my step to go wrong," he told her. "I'm not sure what happened."

"That's weird," she agreed. "We'll have Elijah and Zander check the enchantments on it. Is this the first time?"

"Yeah," Jasper confirmed, nodding. "I've never had it do something like that before. I've had it for over a month and it's worked completely fine."

"You adjusted quickly, but this might just be a kink Elijah needs to work out. It's being put through its paces right now. We haven't stressed it this much." She tried to sound reassuring, but there was no way to do that. This was a very bad time for his prosthetic and the magic in it to go wrong.

"I'll have him look at it when we stop," Jasper said, walking away from her and catching up to Zander with the rest of the team.

She sighed and followed. This entire mission was hell.

Sawyer listened to Jasper explain what happened to Elijah as they walked, but she couldn't pay attention. The heat was bothering her. Texas had been dry. This was humid, even more so than the southeast United States. She was practically dripping with sweat, which only added to her general displeasure with the soft rain that was constantly coming down on them. She looked down and watched her boots trudge through mud and decaying plant life.

This all sucked.

"Sawyer?"

She looked up and nearly walked into Vincent.

"Sorry," she murmured, grabbing his arm to steady herself. "I wasn't watching."

"We're stopping," he told her. "Quinn is going to clear an area for us to stop. With Jasper's leg acting up, he doesn't want to accidentally stumble on the Druid if Jasper isn't ready."

"All right."

They could all feel Quinn's magic radiate off him. Sawyer watched the leaves disappear, fresh earth moving up to take it and leave barren land for them to stop and camp on.

"I'm so glad we have him," Sawyer said plainly, making Vincent chuckle.

"Me too," he agreed. "He has been making this a little easier on us."

"Thank the gods for that." Sawyer walked past him and went to Zander, who was already finding a spot for their tent.

It took time, but the entire hunting party did get set up for the night.

"Jasper, there's nothing wrong with it," Elijah declared, still looking over the prosthetic. He held it out to Jasper when he was done, shrugging. "The enchantments are still holding just fine. There's nothing that should cause what you described."

"Are you sure?" Jasper sounded worried, and Sawyer looped her arm through his to offer some reassurance.

"Trust Elijah," she whispered to him. "He knows his shit."

"I know," he mumbled, grabbing the leg back and dropping it into his lap.

"I'm positive," Elijah agreed with her. "I don't know what's going on but it's not my magic or Zander's."

"With that, Sawyer and Jasper, you two can do a patrol with me," Quinn announced. "If the incident doesn't repeat itself, then everything should be okay."

Sawyer looked over to Quinn. She really enjoyed this fearless, decisive leader version of him. He was commanding and ever-present. He left no place for argument, and he had shrugged off the uncomfortable nature he'd carried for as long as she'd known him. Every day it became more apparent as he stepped up and took charge of them all. Even the soldiers were asking *him* for help now, including the officers.

"Can do." Sawyer jumped up from her small fold-out chair and helped Jasper up once he put his leg back on. He stood up close to her and she felt the need to kiss him, reassure him that it was all going to be okay. She didn't, though, stepping back before the need became reality.

She hadn't touched any of them intimately since the mission started. Just like in New York, to everyone else they were just teammates. They didn't know if the soldiers were keeping tabs on them, looking for something to report back to their superiors. She hoped that politics didn't follow them into the jungle, but she didn't trust them. She didn't know the soldiers, and they hadn't endeared themselves to her yet or any of the team.

Jasper noticed the step and nodded minutely. She knew he agreed with her. They would get through this, shove it up the ass of Councilwoman D'Angelo, and then spend some blissful time together at home where no one could bother them.

"Go get the patrol done so we can have dinner," Zander spoke up.

No one could bother them except each other, Sawyer reminded herself, looking over to Zander with a glare. He just grinned at her, leaning back in his seat and kicking his legs out. She flipped him off and began to follow Quinn away from the camp, Jasper close behind.

They went in silence. Sawyer didn't know what to talk about. They were in the jungle, they were on a mission, they were hoping Jasper's leg wasn't fucked up, and none of them wanted to die, which could be any day.

Quinn forced Jasper to walk ahead of him and she realized that the feral Magi was watching his leg carefully. She didn't see anything wrong with it and she had missed what happened the first time, only seeing him stumble. She hadn't been paying attention to his leg.

"How long are we going to do this?" Jasper asked, nearly thirty minutes later.

"Until I'm positive you will be okay," Quinn answered. "I won't let you get hurt."

"People are going to get hurt, Quinn," Sawyer reminded him gently.

"Not my pack," he snapped back at her. She jerked back from him, eyes going wide. "You, and Jasper, and the others. *Our* pack. None of you will get hurt. The soldiers can get themselves killed, but I won't allow my pack to get hurt. I'm going to make sure that Jasper is okay with continuing the journey, then we're going to rest. This could come on us at any time, so you all must be ready and able."

"Jesus," Jasper mumbled, also watching Quinn intently. "We'll keep walking. No problem."

Sawyer's pulse was racing, and she didn't know why. Something about the ferocity of Quinn's small speech had scared her a little, but also inspired her. He was always so intense, and that turned into dedication to those he cared about.

Our pack. He put her in it.

"Our pack will not get hurt," she agreed, looping her arm through Quinn's. She got Jasper with her other arm and walked with them for another twenty minutes.

"Let's head back," Jasper groaned. "Nothing has happened with it."

"Okay," Quinn said. He pried himself loose of Sawyer and led them back to the camp. They hadn't gone far, having looped around the camp a few times.

"He's so different out here," Jasper commented as they followed behind him.

"He is," Sawyer said, with a wistfulness that she hadn't expected or been thinking would happen. "I like it."

Jasper didn't say anything to her comment.

Before they made it to camp, Sawyer felt something

brush against her mind again and stopped, her eyes searching for the cause. "Did you feel that?"

"Feel what?" Jasper frowned at her, his head tilting minutely. "What did you feel?"

"I don't know," she whispered, staring off into the dark jungle. Night was falling upon them quickly.

Between that and the unusual feeling, she was wildly uncomfortable. This had been happening a few times every day since the first time, the morning Jasper's leg had gone missing. She didn't like it. She didn't trust it. It was too similar to a feeling she remembered that she hated. She wanted it to stop but didn't know how to make it stop.

"We should get some rest," he said, pulling her along. She nodded and let him move them into the camp.

Quinn was farther ahead of them in the camp when Jasper finally stumbled, cursing as he went all the way down.

"Fuck," she hissed out, kneeling next to him. "You okay?

She ignored the soldiers around them laughing hysterically at the fall. She kept focused on Jasper as he pushed himself upright, still cursing silently to himself. "There's something fucking wrong with this leg, I swear. This is not fucking normal."

"We'll tell Elijah. We'll figure it out," Sawyer promised him, helping him stand again. "Come on, let's get you sitting down."

"I wish I knew what the fuck was going on," he snarled out, jerking away from her. "I hate this. I thought everything would be fine with this prosthetic, but it's becoming more of a pain in the ass than my fucking real leg had been."

"Stop," she commanded fiercely, continuing to ignore the laughing soldiers around them. Jasper had gone down hard in front of over a dozen of them. "Don't start getting fatalistic with me. It's only happened twice. We're in a shitty place, in a shitty situation. These things take time to work out. We were jumping the gun thinking this was going to be easy going forever."

"I'm sorry," Jasper quickly said, shaking his head. "I'm just in a bad mood."

"It's fucking hot. Everyone is in a bad mood." Sawyer pulled him along, back to the team where they could talk more quietly. Away from the nosy, laughing soldiers all kicking back around their own fires.

"Elijah, it fucked up again in camp," Sawyer said immediately once they got back to the team. Jasper collapsed in his chair and pulled it off, throwing it at their cowboy.

Elijah caught it, glaring back. "There's nothing fucking wrong with it," he snapped. Sawyer knew he would. Everyone was getting snappy and short tempered. "Don't fucking get pissy with me. Maybe you fucking tripped."

"There's something fucking wrong and it needs to get fixed," Jasper growled back. "I can't be of any use if it's fucking knocking me down all the time."

Sawyer shook her head. She couldn't get into this. Everything about this was a pain in the ass. Jasper's leg, the heat, the rain, the soldiers. She almost wished the damn Druid would show up and hash this out with them sooner rather than later because she was losing her damn patience.

She sat next to Vincent and leaned on him.

"I know it's slow going, but we'll get through this," he whispered.

"Quinn promised none of us would get hurt," she told him.

"Do you believe him?"

"I want to," she admitted quietly. She and Vincent

watched the fire, while Elijah and Zander redid all of the enchantments on Jasper's prosthetic. Sawyer didn't like that their healer was burning his magic to do it, or Elijah. She didn't even understand how they were doing it, but she really didn't want Zander low when the fight broke out and the work of redoing the enchantments seemed intensive.

The rain slowed and stopped after an hour and Sawyer closed her eyes, blissfully happy to not be getting pummeled by rain anymore. Vincent pointed her to his and Elijah's tent for sleep that night and she went without complaint.

THE NEXT MORNING, Sawyer was up last. Vincent had let her sleep until the last possible moment, something she was thankful for. One good thing had happened in the rainforest. There was so much going on that she wasn't having dreams or nightmares. She was sleeping so deeply that nothing was coming to her, haunting her. Exhaustion took her past that point.

"No missing leg today? Nothing?" She grinned, feeling a little lighter.

Elijah handed her a granola bar. "Nothing crazy this morning," he answered. "Except that's the last one of those."

"Fuck," Sawyer groaned, opening it and taking a slow, sad bite. She was going to miss these bars so much. She moaned at the taste. It was mostly honey-flavored and she loved it. Just a little bit of sugar sweet to give her some pleasure without making it too terribly unhealthy.

"We're moving out once all the tents come down," he explained to her quickly.

"Okay, Cowboy." She gave him a thumbs-up and shoved

the rest of the bar into her mouth. She moved to Vincent, who was already pulling the tent down.

They were moving only thirty minutes later, once everyone did their business and shoved food in their faces.

Sawyer wasn't looking forward to another day of slow trekking. They really weren't making that much distance each day due to the size of their party. To Sawyer, it felt like a crawl, a slow crawl to their deaths.

"This fucking blows," Zander groaned an hour in.

"Yeah it does," Jasper agreed, stomping.

"How's the leg today?" she asked, pointing down to it.

"No issues yet," he answered, shrugging.

As they walked, she fell back and just watched. She wanted to see it if it happened again.

It took three hours, but her diligence paid off. He was taking a step with his real leg and the prosthetic seemed to get pulled out from behind, causing him to stumble hard into Zander.

As Zander and Jasper cursed over it, Sawyer just narrowed her eyes, still watching the prosthetic. Soldiers were laughing, having a good time over the clumsy cripple of an IMPO Special Agent.

That hadn't been natural, though, and that bothered her. Jasper hadn't been caught on a root or anything of the sort. His prosthetic just got pulled back and out from underneath him. Having seen it, she had a sneaking suspicion. She eyed the soldiers chuckling and recognized a few from the time his leg had been taken as a joke.

Telekinesis or magnetic manipulation were two options. Telekinesis could be anyone. It was a common ability that popped up in one out of every two Magi. Magnetic manipulation was rarer. She could cross that one off the list first. It gave her some sort of starting point.

Soldiers continued to chuckle long after Jasper's stumble, as if they had some private joke. She stopped walking, letting them pass by her until she saw the one she wanted. "Doc." She waved Sergeant Rodriguez down, who gave her a confused look. "I have a couple questions."

"Sure," he moved closer to her and they fell into step next to each other, following the crowd. Sawyer could still barely see her team, but that was going to work. She had questions.

"Do you know who here has what abilities?"

"Of course I do, but I'm not sure I'm comfortable sharing with a stranger," Doc answered honestly. "These guys trust me, ya know? We don't tell outsiders those sorts of things, like most Magi."

"I want to know who has magnetic manipulation." She ignored his comments. She figured he had the information she wanted.

"Why?" Doc was smartly cautious of her.

She smiled a little. "Strategy stuff." The lie came easily, and she knew it wasn't going to land. Doc scoffed at her, shaking his head.

"Then you need to talk to Colonel," Doc told her. "How's Jasper doing? Something wrong with his..." Comprehension bloomed on his face.

"Now you understand," Sawyer whispered, almost purred, at him after he trailed off. "When I find out who's fucking with him, things are going to get messy. Spread that around, will you? I'm going to start hurting people if they keep fucking with my guys."

"Roger that."

Sawyer didn't miss the healthy amount of fear in his voice. Something about it made her insanely happy. If he was scared of her, the healer, then his guys should listen as well. Of course, she could probably kill someone faster than he could heal them. He had a good reason to fear her making this mission messier than planned.

"This shit is dangerous enough, and I know you would agree. We don't need a full brawl between my team and yours. I would rather not take this to the guys in charge, who will make a scene. I'm going to trust you to get out there and handle it since they all trust and respect their healer."

"Roger that," Doc repeated, nodding.

Sawyer nodded and sped up, moving back up through the ranks to her team. Sergeant Petrov fell in next to her, causing Sawyer to raise an eyebrow.

"What?" she snapped at the female soldier.

"What did you need my healer for?" she demanded.

"To spread word on something that has nothing to do with you," Sawyer answered, glaring at the blonde.

"I'm just trying to look out for my soldiers. You need anything from them, you come to me or my superiors and we'll handle it."

"Sorry, but I'm looking out for my team and I like my way better." Sawyer shrugged. "Forgive me for not wanting to deal with the stick up your ass."

"Look, Matthews," Petrov growled. "I get that the IMPO do things differently, but my ass is on the line if you fuck with my men. I won't allow it. Tell me why you needed my healer."

"So he can tell your soldiers that if they keep fucking with my team, I'll fucking kill them," Sawyer snarled towards the end, her anger over it pushing to the surface. She didn't have the patience for this chick's shit. She was already trying to control her temper since she found out that it was probably magic causing the problem.

"Fucking with your team?" Sergeant Petrov looked at Sawyer like she'd grown a second head.

"One of the assholes here has magnetic manipulation or telekinesis and is jerking around Jasper's leg, literally. I don't know who, but if I find out, I'm fucking handling it. I told your healer to use his place of trust to pass the word along. I think you higher-ups will just get someone in trouble and make this shit worse than it already is. Cause blowback we don't need." Sawyer explained it quickly and quietly, hoping the blonde got her point. "Stay out of it."

"You don't give me orders. I'll find out who it is and make it stop. You need to stay in your lane," Petrov answered, stepping ahead of Sawyer. Sawyer groaned, shaking her head.

"Fuck," she snapped under her breath. She caught up to the guys and stopped next to Vincent. The first words out of her mouth? "I'm sorry."

"Why?" Vincent gave her such a look of confusion that she nearly laughed. Instead, she groaned, knowing this could get uglier.

"I think I know what's going on with Jasper's leg. One of the soldiers is messing with him. I asked one of their healers to let them all know to cut it out, but Petrov wanted to get more involved."

"We'll deal with it as it comes," he said casually. "If it stops, then great. If it doesn't, then I'll get more involved. Thank you for taking the initiative to talk to someone, though, and trying to work it out."

"That's very reasonable of you," Sawyer noted. She'd expected him to say she should have gone to him first with her suspicions. Instead, she was getting a chill Vincent who seemed unconcerned.

"I'm not in the mood to be mad and you did what you

thought was necessary. I would have taken it to the master sergeants or Colonel Fischer, and your instinct on it is probably right. We can hope that whoever is having a good time just stops though."

"I guess we'll find out tonight when we camp." She didn't have a good feeling.

Jasper stumbled three times before they made camp at the end of the day. She was getting pissed off as she eyed the soldiers who were laughing the loudest.

19

VINCENT

Vincent, at camp that evening, had an uneasy feeling. He didn't know if it was the situation with the IMAS soldiers, the mission itself, or the magic that clung to the air and everything around them. For all he knew, it was all of the above.

Six days in the Amazon Rainforest and they had no idea when the action was going to get started. He was only getting three to four hours sleep, his anxiety over the entire situation making it nearly impossible. He was used to planning, being in charge, and he was flying blind, letting Quinn guide them.

He trusted Quinn with his life.

He looked around at his teammates. Zander and Jasper were arguing over the leg. He hadn't told them what Sawyer brought to him yet, and neither had she. He should, but he knew those two would go pick a fight with the soldiers in a heartbeat. They wouldn't tolerate being bullied by those who never respected them to begin with. They had hated their lives in the IMAS.

Elijah sketched, looking lonely. Quinn was preoccupied

with one of his nightly patrols, and the wolves were off with him. Sawyer was sitting next to Vincent. Elijah was alone. Vincent felt sorry for his normally happy friend for a moment. He was half in love with Sawyer and she was completely blind to it.

He finally turned and eyed her. Sawyer Cambrie Matthews. He loved her name, even though he found it a little odd. It suited her in its weirdness.

He trusted Quinn with all their lives.

And he knew better than to think Quinn would actually be able to save them all. He wondered which of them he was going to lose on this mission, if it wasn't him. He hoped he would go down before any of them.

"Stop arguing," Vincent snapped at the fools with the prosthetic. "Deal with it in the morning if you can't stop getting hot-headed over it tonight."

"But-" Jasper began, but Vincent wasn't having it. He was seconds away from hunting down Colonel Fischer to give over the names of anyone with the powers to mess with Jasper. He was fucking tired of the bickering. It was too hot, too wet, and the days were too long to listen to this when they were supposed to be getting a moment of respite.

"Shut. Up." Vincent stood up and looked down at Sawyer. "Take Jasper out and roam around near camp. Maybe it'll cool his temper."

"And Zander?" she asked.

He scoffed, rolling his eyes up. "His temper never cools, you know that."

"I was just making sure you did," she teased, and he knew she was trying her hardest to lighten the situation. She stood up next to him and for a moment, he thought she was going to kiss him. Then she didn't. He knew why: the mission and the soldiers. He'd talked to the guys, all of them, privately before they left the house for the mission. He knew she'd be on her guard around all the strangers with the politics going on in New York. He wanted to make sure the guys understood as well. None of them had argued, so they all let her keep her physical distance from them.

He agreed with her, but he still was sorry for not getting that kiss.

"Be safe. Check in with Quinn," he ordered her quietly. He didn't like when any of them were out of his line of sight. Not here. He didn't know what could happen or when. It was why he'd convinced her to stay last night in his tent.

She nodded and held out a hand to pull Jasper up. "Come on, my friend. Let's do a walk while the temperature cools off."

"Cools off? Maybe like five degrees," Jasper muttered, annoyed.

Vincent sighed and shook his head, watching them walk away. *"Tell him out there what you think is going on. I'm going to annoy Colonel Fischer about who it could be. I'll try not to let it become a scene."*

A wave back from her told him she heard and understood. Good.

He left Elijah and Zander, both lost in their own thoughts. Elijah, who watched Sawyer walk away with a look of longing that he probably didn't realize he had, and Zander, who was definitely staring at her ass.

They were all fools for her. Vincent was too.

They needed the vacation.

They needed to survive this.

He wasn't arrogant enough to think they all would.

"Colonel," Vincent called out as he neared the IMAS main tent, a huge structure they propped up every night to talk about their plans. He hated going to it. Colonel Fischer knew who he was. Knew he was the son of a criminal family. Knew he was the brother of a criminal mastermind.

Vincent stopped walking and thought about that for a minute.

He couldn't really call Axel a criminal mastermind anymore. His own madness and obsession for perfection had led him to obsess over Sawyer and her ability to just stay alive when he wanted her dead. It had been his downfall.

The rainforest was making Vincent thoughtful. The long hours in the heat sapped his energy to hold conversation.

"I need to get out of my head," he muttered to himself. "Or I'll end up like him." He pushed into the tent and waved the colonel down. "Colonel Fischer, I wanted to speak to you about something."

"Shoot, kid," the colonel answered.

Vincent lost his impassive expression and glared at the older man. Fischer was professional to a point in front of his troops, but he was rude to Vincent in private. He was getting annoyed with it. They were practically of equal rank.

"I have a suspicion that one of my team is getting hazed by one or more of your soldiers," Vincent explained, closing the flap of the tent behind him to keep the conversation as private as possible. "I would like to discover who it is. If you don't want me to know who it may be, then you need to make it stop."

"Sergeant Petrov brought this to me. Said Shadow threatened one of my healers," Fischer responded, sitting down. "Petrov also talked to the most likely candidate for the teasing."

Vincent hoped Petrov and the IMAS healer got the message across to the idiot who was 'having a bit of fun.' He knew Sawyer was possessive as hell over them and messing with Jasper, who had lost that leg in the fight to save her, was a recipe for someone not making it home. She would slide a dagger between the soldier's ribs.

"Sawyer," Vincent corrected after a moment. "Sawyer wouldn't threaten a healer, by the way. She will, however, hurt the person who is jerking around Jasper's leg while we're moving. I'll even let her, since it undermines the trust and security he needs with the prosthetic to perform at his peak."

"Look at you," Fischer said, chuckling. "Don't like a few soldiers just trying to have a good time?"

"Not at the expense and safety of my team." Vincent took another one of the seats in the tent and leaned back. "Between Quinn and Sawyer alone, my team beats your soldiers, let's be honest. Do you really want to see them both lose their temper by fucking with someone they consider theirs? Sawyer is the only person on the team besides me that has this suspicion, though I'm having her tell Jasper himself right now. If Quinn finds out, he'll be distracted from helping us find this Druid and focused on punishing the fool who is messing with one of his 'pack.' None of us can stop Quinn when he's angry. I would say Sawyer and I have the best chance, but it's not certain, and she would be on his side."

"Are you saying that if my soldiers continue to have some fun, people will get hurt? And you won't stop them or even be able to?"

"Yes." Vincent didn't even feel bad for it. He refused to feel bad for his strongest team members defending the others. Sawyer with her cold ruthlessness and quick temper. Quinn with his sheer power and loyalty. "Now, I don't want you to make a scene over this, because I don't want retaliation from your soldiers because I've gotten them in trouble. You need to handle this quietly and quickly. I'm out of patience in this fucking rainforest, Colonel. We have bigger fucking problems than this, and your soldiers need to realize how dangerous this is and cut the shit."

They stared each other down for a long time. Colonel Fischer stood up and poured himself a drink, handing one to Vincent as well. He didn't drink any of the whiskey, but he took it, knowing it was a peace offering.

"I had only wanted your one agent because of the strength and knowledge he has. I didn't expect to get all of you," Colonel Fischer informed him. Vincent gave the older man a small smile. "I wasn't prepared to make sure I had soldiers that would be the most professional. I just brought my best."

"People continue to learn that blackmailing my team is ineffective. Let's not lie to ourselves or each other. You, your General, and Councilwoman D'Angelo blackmailed Quinn into coming on this mission by threatening Sawyer's safety and security. D'Angelo had hoped she would screw Sawyer in the process. *Politics.* We weren't going to let him come down here and die for you on his own. Which means you got more than you asked for. I'm not going to feel sorry for it." Vincent rotated his wrist slowly, watching the whiskey swirl in the glass. Colonel Fischer was in here drinking whiskey, and everyone else in camp ate MREs and were running low on clean water. Sawyer was out of granola bars.

But this motherfucker had whiskey.

"I'll talk to the war dogs," Fischer finally told him. "You're right that we need to make this work. If he were still in IMAS, he would have been discharged for losing a leg, but you're an IMPO team, a well-known one at that, and I need to make do with that."

"You do," Vincent whispered.

"Fight!" a male voice screamed across the camp.

"You might be too late." Vincent slowly got out of his seat, placing the whiskey on the room's center table.

"God damn it," Colonel Fischer growled. "Who do you think it is?"

Vincent had his suspicions. He walked out of the tent quickly, his anxiety climbing back up. If the fight had already started, then there was nothing he could do to stop it. He had hoped he would get the evening to handle this.

A group of soldiers were beginning to congregate. He pushed through, Fischer following him. They ran into a shield around Sawyer and a handful of soldiers. He saw her first, black hair flying free from her standard, curly ponytail as she deflected an amateur punch and hit the soldier in the gut.

"You think you're fucking funny?" Sawyer snapped out the question, violence saturating the words, and Vincent could only see rage in her eyes. Even under the weight of the Druid's magic in the area, he could feel a creeping cold radiating out from her. It was buried, muted, but it was there.

"Fuck, bitch. We were just having some fun, and you had to get all pissy about it with our sergeant." The soldier coughed when he was done, holding his gut. Vincent's eyebrows shot up as he saw another soldier try to jump Sawyer, who sublimated out of his way and reformed to grab him. Vincent watched her deliver a swift knee to the young man's balls and toss him to the ground.

"Sawyer!" he roared, hoping to snap her out of the anger.

She ignored him, getting back to the fist fight with the offender that she started with. When he went down, Sawyer pulled a dagger, but the shield covered the entire fighting area. Vincent couldn't get in. He knew whose magic it was.

"The asshole deserves it," Zander's voice cut in. He was beside Vincent now.

He turned and glared at the red-headed healer. Their damn healer was going to let Sawyer kill a guy. "What happened?" Vincent demanded.

"That shit got in trouble and sent Jasper down hard for it. Jasper almost broke his wrist in the fall. The little fuck gave himself away by taunting Sawyer. She's fucking furious. Jasper is fine, by the way. I healed him up, no problem."

"Drop the shield," Vincent ordered.

"No. Fucker deserves it."

"Sawyer doesn't," Vincent snapped, grabbing Zander's shirt. The hothead didn't get it. "I get that you two want to fight the fucking world, but this is murder. She'll fucking carry this for the rest of her life. Drop the fucking shield." He wasn't going to let her carry around another death on her soul. Not another one.

It was too late for that.

The shield shattered as a bear slammed into it.

Vincent and Zander were both blown back by the magic that was released from the hit. When Vincent was able to get up, he saw everyone was dazed at the hit. The bear roared, and Vincent saw Petrov blink into Sawyer's face and land a hit directly on his assassin's chin. It sent Sawyer back a few feet, looking dazed. When she realized what had happened, she dove for Petrov, sublimating and flying around behind her for a better angle.

The fight was on.

"Do you have anyone else who can blink?" Vincent asked the colonel, watching Sawyer and Petrov, trying to find the best option to break the fight up.

"No. She's Spec Ops quality. She's the best soldier here, but don't tell the General that. I'm going to have to reprimand her for this." Fischer rubbed his face. "Do we just let them fight it out?"

Vincent just watched for a moment longer. He saw Sawyer's face clearer once and saw blood pouring from her nose. Sergeant Petrov had an eye that was going to turn black. He winced as Sawyer took another hit before blinking off, Petrov's arm wrapped around her neck. He winced again as Sawyer slammed back into a tree, Petrov hitting it hard enough to release her.

There was absolutely nothing anyone in the camp could do to stop the blinking battle. Both of the woman were obviously experts in their abilities, turning a simple brawl in a duel across the camp as they teleported around, trying to get grabs and keep them.

Everyone just watched in a moment of dazed silence. The two best fighters in the camp were women who didn't play games or toy around. They were going for blood.

"No," Vincent sighed. He knew who to get. *"Quinn. Camp. We have a fight that needs breaking up."*

He felt the earth shake. Then, the moment Sawyer and Petrov were stopped for a second to throw punches, he watched the ground open up underneath them and pull them down by their ankles. And close up. The land smoothed as if they had never been there.

"Are they dead?" Fischer sounded horrified.

"No," Quinn answered, walking into camp. "They can continue their fight down there or stop. I'll let them up when they are done."

"Do they have air?" Vincent asked cautiously. He'd never seen Quinn do something like that.

"Yes." He didn't look angry, just annoyed. "Why was there a fight?"

"I'll explain by our tents," Vincent told him quickly. He

didn't need Quinn losing his temper at that moment. Not in front of the tense soldiers.

"Everyone, get back to work," Fischer roared, causing soldiers to jump to action and move away. "Except you three." He pointed to the few young men that had tried to fight Sawyer, one of whom had been the one messing with Jasper. "You'll report to my tent immediately. Move it."

Vincent watched the crowd disperse and walked with Quinn and Zander to their area. Jasper was rubbing his wrist, his leg off so Elijah could look it over.

"Any damage?" Vincent asked immediately.

"No. Thank God." Elijah was short with him, and Vincent knew the entire team was riding short tempers.

"What do I not know?" Quinn asked, sitting down next to the cowboy.

"One of the soldiers was yanking around on Jasper's prosthetic, causing him to stumble and then fall." Vincent sighed heavily and looked back to the spot where Petrov and Sawyer were buried beneath the earth.

"They are fine. They stopped fighting. Was she one of them?" Quinn's question was innocently asked. Vincent knew it wasn't an innocent question. He was asking if he needed to kill the woman underneath with Sawyer.

"No. She had reprimanded the soldier already for it," Vincent explained. "Let them out soon."

"Well, he was pretty pissed for getting in trouble, because he yanked me down fucking hard and I landed bad. Zander had to heal my wrist."

The earth rumbled. Vincent took a deep, shaky breath. He'd known Quinn would be pissed off.

He didn't have the energy for this.

"He's still alive?"

"Yes, Quinn, the guy who did this is still alive. We can't

have Sawyer killing people. She would hate herself for it, and the WMC would take her from us no matter what." Vincent rubbed his temples and pulled out his pack of cigarettes. He lit one and took a long inhale. "I'm assuming Petrov jumped in since Sawyer pulled the dagger." He pointed at Zander. "Next time I give an order, I don't fucking care what you think, you follow it. Do you understand me? I'm not the leader of this team without a reason. I actually think about how our actions will impact our jobs and Sawyer's future. Don't disobey me again."

"Fine," Zander growled, crossing his arms and leaning back in his chair.

Vincent shook his head slowly. He started to walk away from the team, needing a moment to be alone and breath. This was a disaster of a mission.

He made it thirty feet from camp before Kaar landed on him. "Hey, Kaar," he whispered to his raven. He felt a wave of concern and love from the raven and chuckled. "Thanks. We'll make it out of this and go home soon."

The raven ruffled, shaking a couple of loose feathers out, and snapped at his hair. Vincent waved a hand, trying to get Kaar to stop. The humor coming off the bird as he messed around made him chuckle more.

"Stop that, you shit," he ordered. Kaar hopped and made him sway to the side. "You're getting fat out here. How does that happen? You're flying around all day and you're still getting fat."

Indignant anger coursed through him and Kaar cawed loudly in his ear.

"Asshole," he mumbled. "I'm just saying, lay off the snacks. What have you been doing? You are supposed to be keeping an eye out for us and staying out of trouble. Are you eating all the time?"

Kaar sent an image to Vincent that made him frown. He'd followed Shade and Scout somewhere during the day. They had been following a trail far from the group, searching the rainforest for something.

They had found it.

Vincent couldn't identify the object, but Shade and Scout hadn't been aggressive towards it, and Kaar seemed happy about the find but didn't offer more information. He didn't understand the undercurrents of emotion from the raven.

He took a drag on his cigarette.

What was Quinn having his wolves do? He understood the messages he got from them better than Vincent and Kaar. Vincent had a typical relationship with his animal bond. They were partners, but Vincent didn't speak bird, just like Sawyer probably couldn't understand the nuances she must have gotten from Midnight.

"Why didn't you tell me?"

He groaned at the question and looked back at Quinn. "Because I trust you with our lives, but I need you focused on the important stuff, not the petty drama between our team and the soldiers."

"Okay."

"That's it? You won't get mad at me?" He took another drag on his cigarette.

"No. I trust your judgement. You're right. If I had known, I would have been focusing on the group and not what's out there." Quinn pointed out to the darkness of the rainforest.

"What did Shade and Scout find?" Vincent asked carefully.

"Something I hadn't been expecting. But she's not ready yet."

"What?" He coughed as he tried to exhale. Quinn was

getting cryptic on him again. Vincent knew how people worked. He knew how Quinn worked on the surface. But sometimes, Quinn threw him for a loop. He went somewhere that Vincent couldn't follow. He knew that the mind of his wild teammate and friend was full of things he couldn't begin to understand. Quinn just showed him a tiny piece and he couldn't unravel it. He could at least cross off a Druid. Quinn wouldn't have been calm if it was one of those.

"You'll see. I'm going back on patrol. I've let the females out." A pause. "Women. I let Sawyer and the other woman out."

"Make sure you get some sleep tonight," Vincent told him, hoping he listened. He had no idea when the last time Quinn had slept was. A couple of days?

"I will," he answered, and Vincent heard a creeping note of exhaustion in his voice. "It took too much energy to pull them both down like that. Energy I didn't want to expend." With that, Quinn disappeared into the night.

This mission was going to drive him mad. Hazing, fights, Druids in the night, Quinn with secrets. The heat, the rain. Vincent just wanted it over with. He wanted to go back to a place where he had any sort of control over the situation. He didn't in the Amazon. He didn't have a single shred of control.

It terrified him.

20

SAWYER

The earth was dark and cold. Sawyer hit it hard, ignoring the pale blonde in the hole with her. She was pissed. She couldn't believe Quinn would toss her down here and lock her up. Couldn't fucking believe it.

"Quinn!" she roared. "Let me out, you ass!"

She knew he could hear her. She knew he was keeping an eye on them. He wouldn't throw them in a hole without knowing exactly what was going on in it. She wasn't stupid enough to try and phase out. He would just pull her back in if she could, and she didn't know how deep they were, so she probably couldn't.

"Does he always do this?" Petrov asked, wrapping her arms around herself.

"No. I've never seen this before." Sawyer growled. She looked over to the sergeant and noted she had really done a number on the woman's face. There was just enough light to see her. Sawyer looked down and saw that Petrov had a small flashlight.

"I'm not sorry for any of that." She pointed at the woman's face as she spoke.

Sawyer was still riding her temper from the fight. Well, the temper from Jasper getting hurt. That little fucking prick of a soldier thought he could fuck with her team. He got Jasper *hurt*, that motherfucker. The need to hurt him back was like the need to breath for her at that moment.

"It's fine. We have healers, and I jumped in knowing it would be a hard fight." Sawyer noted the healthy amount of respect in the soldier's voice. "I wasn't planning to break up the fight," Petrov told her. Sawyer raised an eyebrow. "I had reprimanded him. Told him to knock it off, and that if he did it again and you caught him, I wasn't going to save him. Hazing is against the IMAS Code. He knew better. He knew I would bust his ass back a rank if it kept up."

"But?" Sawyer crossed her own arms and leaned against an earthy wall of their tomb. She wanted to know why this bitch jumped into her fight.

"You pulled a dagger. He fucked with you and I expected you to fuck with him. I wasn't going to let you kill him. He's one of my soldiers, and I take that seriously."

Sawyer nodded slowly. The temper drained. The anger faded, only a little, but it left just enough for her to really consider what she had been about to do.

She couldn't kill a guy for that. It would get her taken away from the team.

"Thank you," she told the blonde.

"What?" Petrov sounded confused and wary.

"Thanks. For stopping me." Sawyer shrugged, looking away. She ran a hand over her face and could feel the hot blood trickling out of her nose. The chick had done a number on her too. Her nose and one of her cheeks ached with a pulsing pain that told Sawyer something might be fractured. "I...I don't like killing people."

"Then why did you?" Petrov sounded purely curious. No

disdain. No disgust. Just professional curiosity. It made Sawyer curious in return, and her anger faded a little more. It hadn't been a reaction she expected.

"That's a long story," Sawyer said. "This time? I lost my temper. I needed to beat on him for fucking with Jasper. Jasper lost that leg for me. I won't...I won't have someone consider him less than perfect because of it. He got hurt for me. That set me off pretty hard."

"I'm sorry. I had hoped you would be wrong about them getting retaliation. That my men would listen to me without finding it insulting - but I overestimated their respect for the rank on my arm."

"Why do you say that?"

"I'm a woman in IMAS." Petrov laughed bitterly. "It's a man's world. No matter how high I climb or how hard I fight, I'll always be not good enough. I should have known they would take being reprimanded by me as an insult. I laid into him hard for hazing your agent when we were making camp."

"I had no idea it was like that," Sawyer replied. "I was told something about you passing the trials or something? I thought that meant something."

"It does. I've passed the trials every six months for three years to join Spec Ops. Our version of Special Agents, I guess. Advanced, highly trained teams. Missions in hostile countries, or against hostile organizations. Basically, you, the IMPO, finds the bad guy, but Spec Ops is normally called in to clean up, with backup teams of Cavalry and general foot soldiers."

"Good to know. Why aren't you Spec Ops? Why in Cavalry?"

"I'm a woman," Petrov bitterly answered.

Sawyer frowned. There was a surety to the answer that

made her a little pissed off. "Seriously?" She furrowed her brow.

"Yes."

"Wow." Sawyer huffed and slid down to sit in their hole. "So, Petrov, any other cool things I should know?"

"My name is Varya," she answered. "Use that. Nothing cool about me. I joined the IMAS at eighteen."

"Why not the IMPO? From what I've seen, women aren't hated on. Well, I am, but I'm also the very thing they want to catch."

"The IMAS took me out of Russia," Varya answered softly. Sawyer knew the importance of that. Russia was a bad place to be a Magi. "I idolized them. Joined the moment I could, then got a reality check. But I am good at my job and I follow the rules. They have no reason to force me out, but they have no reason to help me advance into better positions either. They just rank me up when they are required to, because they can't argue against it." Varya sighed, shaking her head. "How does an assassin join the organization that would see her hang?"

"Just say it. How does an assassin become an imp?" Sawyer chuckled. "Long story. There's a lot of dead people in it. It's a mess and it's complicated, but here I am. In the fucking rainforest with a team I would die for."

"That doesn't explain anything," Varya replied. "How does a criminal turn into a good guy?"

Sawyer thought about that, watching Varya sit opposite of her. They maintained eye contact.

"I never wanted to be the bad guy," Sawyer admitted to her. "I never wanted to be the monster."

"How did it happen?" Varya's curiosity should have pissed her off, but down in the dark hole that Quinn dropped them in, Sawyer couldn't summon the energy to get angry. There was no reason to not tell Varya.

"I fell in love with a madman."

"So you survived by killing for him until you could get out," Varya guessed.

"You are nearly entirely right. I couldn't save those I killed for, not really. He blackmailed me into it by threatening the lives of my animal bond...then his own son."

"You have an animal bond? I haven't..."

"I don't have an animal bond anymore."

"Oh." Varya paled in the dark. Sawyer knew where the soldier's mind went. She was imagining losing her bear. The big thing called Anya. "You must be strong to have survived the loss of that bond."

"That's what I've been told."

"We're both survivors then. I'm sorry for disliking you," Varya whispered in the dark. She flicked the flashlight off. "I want to conserve the battery."

"What did you survive?" Sawyer was getting curious in return.

"Russia."

"The burnings or the labs?" Sawyer had heard what Russia was like. The WMC didn't have political relations with them. Some countries would never accept Magi. Most of their kind were pulled out, protected in other countries, but there were always some that couldn't be saved. Some places, like Iran, only burned them. Other places, like Russia, worked with awful companies and scientists to study them. Sawyer didn't know much past that.

"The labs. I survived the labs from age five to age ten. I lived the longest of any of the children there. Spec Ops raided one night and took me out. Spent the rest of my youth in America, under the watchful eye of an adoptive family. Learned English and joined the IMAS as fast as I could."

"You know what? I'm sorry for disliking you too," Sawyer told her. She leaned over and extended a hand to the blonde. Varya looked down at it and nodded slowly. They shook. "You need someone dead, come find me."

"You need someone to put you in your place, likewise," Varya responded. It caused them both to laugh until Varya groaned. "Oh, my face hurts."

"Sorry. Mine kind of does too." Sawyer gently touched her nose and winced. Yeah, that might be broken. "Thank god for healers."

"Are we good?"

"We're good. Well, you know, we were never bad. You just rub me the wrong way. You're a stick in the mud that is always throwing the rulebook at people."

"And you have no respect for authority or the rulebook, which I'm sure you would set on fire," Varya retorted.

"I'll give you that." Sawyer couldn't find a way to argue with it. "We'll just stay out of each other's ways."

"Good plan."

Sawyer still didn't want to like the blonde, but she respected her now. Understood her a little more.

As if on cue, the earth above them opened and they were pushed to the surface.

"That ass," Sawyer groaned.

"What?" Varya frowned at her.

"Nothing," she mumbled. Quinn had let her out because she and Varya had worked things out and cooled off. He had been listening.

Sawyer stood up slowly and growled at soldiers staring, wide-eyed, at her and Varya. Most went back to what they were doing, and those that didn't got yelled at by the

Russian. Sawyer even got a chuckle out of it. She limped back to her guys, where most of them were huddled in chairs, talking.

"She did a number on you," Zander pointed out immediately. Jasper and Elijah were both staring at her as well, but were smart enough not to say anything.

"Fix it, please," Sawyer pleaded, sitting next to him. She pulled out a cigarette but didn't light it as Zander gently took her face in his hands. She felt them grow hot and hissed in pain as everything healed. Bones were moving. That wasn't comfortable.

"Done. You'll have some light bruising. I can't fix everything, but that should make sure you have no permanent damage." Zander pulled his hands away. "Does she need someone?"

"She'd going to their healers," Sawyer informed him, standing back up. "Vincent is..."

"That way, having a cigarette too," Elijah told her, pointing off into the dark jungle.

"Thanks," she said quietly, walking off to go apologize. She had to. He'd wanted to take care of things, and while he probably thought she was justified in the fight with the soldiers, she'd heard him screaming to not kill the guy. She'd been about to anyway.

"Vincent?" she called out, walking further out. She saw his back and sighed. "Vin-"

"You're sorry. I know. Come smoke. You've probably already figured out my feelings, and I've probably figured out yours."

She walked beside him and reached to run her hands through his dark curls. He looked over to her and she didn't like how exhausted his dark olive-green eyes were.

"He hurt Jasper," she whispered.

"I know. I don't blame you. I just didn't want you carrying around a kill you did in temper."

"They would have taken me away from you guys if I had gone through with it. I'd be in a cell the moment we got home."

"Yes. That too." Vincent nodded slowly.

They smoked in silence after that. He surprised her by sneaking in a kiss, a long one, before they went back to camp. It had been desperate and tired, needy and wanting.

For both of them.

She wanted to go home with them. She was tired of the jungle.

21

QUINN

It was close to midnight when Quinn decided to leave his patrol. It was another peaceful night, another peaceful day - discounting the fight in camp.

He didn't have the focus to deal with that. He knew the team would manage it. He'd broken up the fight because no one else could, but he wasn't going to get more involved. He couldn't. Vincent's point about Sawyer killing the soldiers was valid. Past that, Quinn needed them all, needed as many Magi as he could get for this.

He needed to sleep, he knew, as he rubbed his face, hoping to stop the exhaustion. His body was physically tired, which made his magic harder to use and control. He still had plenty of energy, but he needed to be able to focus, or he would hurt teammates if a fight broke out.

"Quinn, right?" a soldier on patrol asked. Quinn looked over at the pair. They were required to stay together, only leaving camp for patrols in pairs or more. They knew why, since he had told them. One of them would probably die, but the other could get word back to camp.

"Yes." He didn't know why it was a question. He frowned at the soldier, Lance Corporal Peters.

"Just wanted to say hi. You seem lonely," he explained, smiling. "You're always out here. Why don't you hang out with your team and take a break? Get some sleep?"

"Leave him alone," the other whispered. "He probably doesn't want us bothering him."

"You're fine," Quinn interrupted the second one. "I'm not..." He growled, looking for the words. He was fine having a conversation with some of the lower soldiers, those that didn't whisper about him. Some were good males and these two were ones he included in that. "I'm fine talking for a moment. I'm actually headed back to camp right now to get some rest before we begin travelling again."

"Good, you work too hard," Peters told him, grinning. "This mission fucking blows, ya know? No reason for you to run yourself ragged. We have watch."

"Thank you," Quinn murmured honestly. In another life, Peters, a young dark-skinned man probably Sawyer's age, would be someone Quinn liked. "Be safe. If anything happens, you know what to do."

"Of course." Peters nodded. "We got this."

"I trust you." Quinn couldn't resist giving the young man a smile. Something about him was good.

He left them to their watch and went to his shared tent with Vincent and Elijah. Elijah wasn't in there, but Sawyer was, curled in a ball on the opposite side of Vincent, leaving a space for him in the middle. He saw Shade laying near her head and Scout by her feet.

Protecting her, like he'd told them to. She had to live through this. She was priority, then the team, then himself. The soldiers, Quinn would try to save, but he couldn't protect everyone. His pack came first, starting with the female that had to survive.

He felt momentarily bad for Peters. He'd been kind. Most didn't approach Quinn like that. He felt guilty that the soldier was his lowest priority. Him and his brothers, the others. None of them mattered like her. None of them, not even himself.

He slid between her and Vincent and closed his eyes. Shade sent him images and feelings from the time when they had been separated. Just her, sleeping after being healed by Zander. Just his team being short-tempered and annoyed with each other. He couldn't blame them. This was not their environment or their home.

This place was calling to him, though, and he couldn't bring himself to get angry with it. He felt an undying need to just walk away from the camp and never come back. Leave them to the mission and go find a place where none of the Druids had claimed and live away from it all. Away from the metal cities, overcrowded streets, and dirty air. The people who acted in ways that he didn't understand.

He was tired, but he also loved it. So far from everything. So deep in nature that if he wanted, he could leave, and no one would find him.

The earth beneath them was clean. The life around them was untouched.

Pure. It was all so pure.

Sawyer stirred next him, and he held his breath as she rolled onto her back. He saw her hair fall over her face, beautiful even with the sweat causing it to stick to her forehead.

Would she stay with him if he wanted? She could survive in these wilds. She was strong enough.

No, he knew she hated this sort of area. She hated

'playing in the dirt,' as she called it. She would want to go home. To her metal cities and crowded streets.

Quinn wondered if that was why she wasn't ready.

He reached out and touched the assassin's face. So strong and resilient. She'd changed so much about them and she continued to change them, to change him. She opened her mouth and he listened, for she always had some wisdom he didn't know or understand. Elijah had probably told him some of these things before, or Vincent, Zander, or Jasper, but something, when she spoke, made him listen and made him think.

He shifted closer to her. He enjoyed sleeping next to her. He'd discovered it in Texas, but hadn't done it since. Closer, he gently touched her cheek and stopped as her eyes flew open.

"Quinn," she whispered airily.

He listened to her breathing speed up, shallow. He could practically feel her pulse jump. He'd scared her. Anger at himself flooded her. He knew better. He knew he was too powerful for her to want, to be comfortable with. He was strong enough to do worse things than Axel ever had, even if he'd never do it to her. He didn't blame her instincts for being scared of him. Survival was for those smart enough to recognize threats and avoid them. Sawyer was a survivor.

"I'm sorry. Go back to sleep. I'll move."

"You're fine," she said quickly. "What were you doing?"

"Nothing." He rolled over and put his back to her, staring at a sleeping Vincent instead. He tensed when a hand touched his back softly.

"Good night, Quinn," she whispered.

"Good night."

He didn't sleep, just waited for her to go back to her dreams. He hoped they were good ones.

His own eyelids were beginning to drop when he felt it. A small pulse of power.

"Everyone, get up," he snarled, hitting Vincent's shoulder and making him jump up. Sawyer was up immediately after, on her own. He left the tent the moment he knew both were conscious. He yanked open the other tent. "Up now!"

Another pulse of power.

Elijah and Zander were up fast. Jasper grabbed his prosthetic and began to put it on. Quinn didn't have time.

A scream tore through the night.

He ran through the camp. "Everyone up!" he roared out. Soldiers jumped into action. "She's here!"

Another scream.

Quinn ran for the source, soldiers behind him.

He saw Peters first, pale and trapped in vines. He was still screaming.

"Peters," a soldier gasped. "Where's the other-"

Quinn knew Peters couldn't be saved. He looked down to the man's legs and resisted the urge to vomit.

Ants were crawling up, biting over and over.

Eating him alive.

Quinn did the one thing he could. He used the earth to pull the man into his grave and crushed him with the ants that were feasting.

"What the fuck?" a soldier groaned. "That's it?"

"No, that was the warning," Quinn whispered.

Screaming broke out in the camp. Expletives and yelling.

More terrified screams.

Gunfire started, lighting up the world with flashes.

"Watch out for the snakes!" someone screamed in camp.

Quinn cursed. "Go, help them. I'm going to hunt her

down." When the soldiers didn't move, he snarled, nearly shifting as his jaw elongated and his canines grew. "GO!"

As they ran back for camp, he looked back out into the darkness. Where was she?

Shade and Scout ran out past him and he saw a dark shadow creeping towards camp. He nearly reached out to grab it, to stop it on whatever mission it was on. Shade immediately told him that it wasn't a threat and Quinn dropped it.

The wolves searched for the scent while he felt for her magic, running deeper into the woods. She had to be close. He had to trust the soldiers and his team to stay alive. It was too dark and too sudden for him to get any of them to help. More of them would die being away from the main group.

"Rogue Wolf. You knew better than to come to my home. Did you think you would be welcome here?"

Quinn stopped running and turned to the sultry voice. "You know my name - what's yours?" he asked softly, looking at the young Druid in the moonlight.

"I was called Camila, before I came here," she answered in Spanish.

He swallowed as she walked closer. He pulled up earth walls slowly, stopping vines from creeping to him, deterring snakes from using those vines as cover. "Stop this," he ordered, continuing to use English since she obviously understood it. "There's no reason for more people to die."

"You're here to kill me," she reminded him.

"Because you kill innocent people. You know the law. You murdered them, innocent non-Magi people."

"None of them are innocent!" she screamed, her sultry voice becoming shrill. Quinn stepped back. "They destroy the land! They kill my family!"

Quinn didn't have time for the madness. He raised the

earth over her feet, hoping to just pull her down quick and crush her, only to get surprised by a large animal barreling into him. Claws tore down his chest. He tried to shove away the jaws trying to take his throat. Vines wrapped around his legs and his torso.

"You'll die here. But first, I'm going to kill all the humans you brought here." Camila sneered. "You killed that Druid while she wasn't paying attention. I'm not so stupid. My baby will hold you while I clear this infestation you brought here." She began to laugh and stopped. "Tell your wolves I'm sorry they were foolish enough to bond to you."

Quinn heard another growl and then another, the rainforest alive with the sound of violence. He felt the pain lance through him and Shade and Scout began fighting off their own attackers.

22

SAWYER

Sawyer waited for any sign of activity after Quinn told them to get up. He'd run off into the woods, a few soldiers following him, but Vincent had stopped her or anyone else from following.

"We can't go out into the dark. We'll be helpless. He can hold his own," he reminded her.

"I know," she whispered, uneasy with the screaming she heard out there.

"It could just be a snake bite, an accident," Elijah offered. "But until he knows, we need to stick together."

"I know," she snapped harder. She understood the reasoning, but she hated it.

The screaming stopped.

"What the hell are we awake for? What is going on?" The captain stormed over to them, followed by others.

Sawyer raised an eyebrow. Where was Colonel Fischer?

"Screaming. Quinn wanted us all up. He and a few of your men went out to see what happened," Vincent explained quickly.

"Where's Fischer?" Sawyer asked, too curious about his absence.

"Probably getting dressed," the captain answered, shaking his head. "I don't like your fucking wild man ordering us all to be awake for some guy out there spraining a goddamned ankle."

"We don't know-"

The next scream came from in the camp.

Sawyer spun to the soldiers, getting ready. They were all looking up and none were screaming. Her eyes slowly drifted the same direction.

A soldier was being strangled by vines above them.

"Oh shit," she whispered.

"Get him down!" the captain roared out.

Sawyer sublimated and flew up. Once at the level of the soldier, she reformed and grabbed the vine, but she didn't have time to pull a dagger as other vines began to grab her.

"Fuck!" She sublimated again, falling back to the ground in her smoke form. When she looked back up, the soldier was dead. He wasn't screaming anymore.

Terror pulsed through her. She couldn't fight the fucking trees.

All hell broke loose.

Sawyer watched another soldier get entangled in the underbrush and pulled down. She lost sight of him. Another was jumped by an animal, a large jaguar.

Then the snakes came, silent, all over the ground, moving into the camp.

People started shooting.

Sawyer was frozen.

"Watch out for the snakes!" someone screamed in camp.

"Fischer is already dead!"

"RUN!"

Sawyer unsheathed her kukri, snapping out of the horror for a moment, and began to slash down at snakes coming towards her in any way she could. She sublimated and moved quickly to her guys, Elijah holding a ring of fire around them until she got inside.

Then Zander slammed a shield over them.

"Walk and I'll hold!" he screamed to them.

They began to move, watching the world around them fall apart. Elijah kept fireballs on his hands while, she, Vincent, and Jasper just kept their eyes open for anything that could break Zander's shield.

Sawyer didn't like that they were missing someone. Where was Quinn? Why wasn't he with them? Was he fighting the Druid somewhere else alone?

Dread filled her.

Was he already dead?

Other soldiers began to see what they were doing. Shields began to appear.

"Keep moving," Vincent ordered.

As they moved, Sawyer saw Anya, the bear, fight off a pair of jaguars, Varya trying to help. The bear was already bleeding, dark patches of blood forming all over it. She could see the pain on Varya's face.

Sawyer knew she couldn't let it happen. Not to someone else. No one deserved to lose that bond.

"Let me out," she commanded. Zander didn't give her a space to leave, shaking his head. "NOW!"

"Do it," Vincent joined in. Then he looked at her. "Stay alive."

"Of course."

She ran out of the space Zander made and felt the force of him closing it behind her. She blinked closer and drove the kukri into a jaguar on the bear's back. Varya gasped, weaponless.

"Here," Sawyer told her, pulling one of her twelve-inch daggers from its sheath. Varya didn't take it. "You need something!"

Varya took the hilt quickly and slashed at a snake coming near, as Sawyer went for the other jaguar jumping towards them. Their impact knocked the air out of Sawyer, but she couldn't let the jaguar tear out her throat. She buried the kukri in its gut after it took her to the ground and kicked it off. She turned to Varya and Anya, waving them on.

"Go to my team. They will let you in!" Sawyer pointed off to the guys, who were making steady moves towards them.

"And you?"

"I have to find someone," Sawyer answered honestly.

Quinn wasn't in camp with them. He'd gone off on his own.

A brush on her mind, calling her deeper into the darkness.

She looked at her team, all of them watching her. She trusted them to stay alive together. Then she turned and followed whatever was calling her, running into the darkness, having no idea what she would find.

She hoped it would be her last friend.

23

ZANDER

Zander watched Sawyer run into the dark. Why? He wasn't the only person wondering.

"Vincent, what the hell?" Jasper screamed.

"She's going after Quinn," he answered harshly. "It's not in her nature to huddle down and wait and protect herself. Let the bear and the Russian in."

"Fine," Zander pulled back a section of his shield and pushed it out wider. He closed it the moment he knew Petrov and her bear would fit.

He ignored the screams of others. They all did. There was nothing they could do except hope the Druid died soon.

Zander was scared. He didn't know how long he could hold the shield as they moved away from the war zone that the camp had become. Still, soldiers were being dragged away by vines. Others just ran, back in the direction they had originally come.

"Are we going to help?" Elijah asked, angry.

"I don't know if we can," Vincent answered.

"I think Elijah can burn the forest down," Jasper cut in.

"I can push it out. It'll be destructive, but it'll give us something."

"Shit." Vincent nodded. "Elijah, it's pretty wet here."

"That won't be a problem," Elijah replied, chuckling darkly.

Zander pulled the shield down. That's all he needed to hear.

"What?" Varya gasped, holding a dagger. Zander looked down at it for a second. It was one of Sawyer's. It irked him a little.

"Zander, pull the water to us, so it'll be easier for me to burn this place to the ground," Elijah said, the fireballs on his hands growing to consume his arms.

He did as he was asked, but it was a lot of water - in the very earth, in the decay of the undergrowth. While he worked, Elijah threw out a fiery circle around them. It evaporated the water Zander drew forth and Jasper used his control over the air to keep them free of smoke and able to breathe.

Next, Elijah threw out several balls of fire, lighting up trees.

"Burn the vines grabbing people," Vincent yelled out.

Zander watched soldiers struggle, then watched the fire cut through the thick vines that were dragging them away. He could also see them bleeding out.

"I'm going to help," Zander yelled, and jumped through the fire Elijah had around them. He shielded himself, skin-tight, and ran for a fallen soldier.

Dead.

He moved to the next one.

Dead.

A snake tried to bite through his shield and he slammed

a boot on its head. He didn't have time for them to try and kill him. He had people to help.

He found another body, hoping the young man even had a faint pulse.

Dead.

"I have wounded here! Leave the bodies, I already checked!"

Zander's head snapped up and he saw one of the soldiers' healers in a shield as well, tending to some he could drag in.

He ran for them, watching fire burn a circle out from them. It rose into the trees above them. Branches in flames began to fall. Zander threw a shield over him to stop one from knocking him unconscious but its impact to his shield still was too much. It shattered the shield and Zander jumped out of the way, barely given enough time to move.

He was let into the other shielded area and ran to the first wounded soldier.

"Where?" he demanded.

"I got bit three times on my legs," the female soldier cried. "Oh god."

Zander grabbed her, his hands on her skin, and focused. The venom was quickly necrotizing the tissue around it. Muscles were dying. He concentrated hard on the area and poured magic in and used his control over water to push venom out. It wouldn't be perfect. They were too far away for more help and he couldn't get everything. Her right calf, with two bites, would be permanently damaged.

"Tourniquet both," he ordered. It would slow the spread of venom to other parts of the body. She nodded, tears still on her cheeks. He didn't blame her. Even a lot of the guys, injured, were crying out in pain.

He looked around and did a count. There were fifteen

soldiers in the shield. He added his own on the outside of theirs, creating another layer of protection.

"Oh my God," one whispered, pointing out.

Zander followed the gesture.

He wished he hadn't.

A soldier, very dead, was still being constricted by the massive anaconda that had him. Bodies were hanging from the trees.

"Ignore the dead," he choked out. "We can't save them now."

"We need to get the fuck out of this place," one screamed out. "We need to fucking go."

"I know," Zander agreed. He tried not to sound worried or angry. He needed to be a healer. He had to save these soldiers around him.

He went to the next and nearly broke. His back was broken. Zander didn't know how he was even still alive. He couldn't fix the damage to the man's back.

He grabbed the guy's face and began to heal what he could. The cuts and bruises. He wouldn't bleed out at least. He would never walk again, but he wasn't dead yet.

"Where is everyone else?" Zander asked as he moved to another soldier. More snake bites, five on the legs. At least they were all far from the heart.

"I think your guys and us are all that's left," the other healer answered. "Call me Doc, or Rodriguez-"

"I've heard about you," Zander cut him off. Jasper had told him about the cool healer who had tried to do something nice for Sawyer, but he didn't have time to make introductions. "How many more injured?"

"We all are," Doc answered. "I got a bite while trying to grab someone to get them to safety."

"Fuck," Zander snapped.

He looked back to his team and reached out to talk to Vincent.

"Everyone here is injured, most with snakebites, others with broken bones, scrapes and bruises. We can't stay. We need to get them out of this fucking jungle."

"Elijah just got bit," Vincent replied. *"One was in the ring of flame - dropped from the trees, and we missed it."*

Zander filled with more dread, his hope at saving the few of them left fading into obscurity.

Not Elijah. Not one of the team. Not one of his brothers.

"We can't wait on Sawyer and Quinn," Vincent whispered into his mind. *"We need to get this moving. Maybe with distance, they will lay off, especially with the fire."*

Zander's heart broke. He knew Vincent's was too, could hear it in his mental voice.

Save many and leave the love of his life, or doom everyone to die.

She would kill him if he saved her, kill him if all of these people died so he could stay for her. She would never forgive him for it.

"Get here and we'll all move under the same shields. I can't move the wounded to you and I'll need hands to help carry some."

24

SAWYER

Sawyer ran into the darkness, following the irresistible pull. She could hear snarling and fighting in the bushes close by.

She broke into a clearing and saw Shade and Scout fending off jaguars. They were outnumbered.

Before she could move, one of the cats jumped for the wolves, who couldn't keep an eye on all of them.

A black blur slammed into the jaguar. Sawyer blinked forward to Scout, injured and whimpering. As she checked him, hoping he wasn't bleeding out, another cat jumped for them and she threw her body over the wolf, holding him as Shade went for the jaguar.

"Lay down, boy. I've got you now," she whispered to the small wolf. "I've got you. Where's Quinn?"

A whimper. Shade limped to her and she looked around. The cats were gone.

"Where's Quinn?" she asked him. The dark shadow of a wolf turned, his head pointing to a mass of vines. Sawyer swallowed. Quinn was in them.

She scrambled for the mass and began to cut it away. Dread filled her. What would she find?

"What are you doing?" a sneering, angry feminine voice asked from the dark. "He's mine until I say he isn't. He's to stay alive until all of his precious humans are dead. I'm almost done."

"Sorry, you can't take something that belongs to someone else. It's stealing," Sawyer retorted. She pushed the kukri deep into the vines and tore them open, finding Quinn's face. His eyes were open, and she wanted to weep.

"You do know I'm going to kill you and every other dirty human in my rainforest, but fine, look at your mate's face one more time," the Druid taunted.

Sawyer felt vines take her ankles. They didn't concern her. She only touched Quinn's cheek gently and felt blood. His eyes closed.

Dread had been replaced by relief that Quinn was alive. Her relief was being replaced with fury. Cold, dark fury.

"Time to die, little human," the Druid hissed in the dark. Sawyer sublimated out of the vines and went back towards the clearing.

"Sure." Sawyer spun the hilt of her kukri in her hand.

She needed to find the woman, the mad Magi Druid, before she decided to just kill Quinn instead. Sawyer wasn't losing him. He was the reason she was there, so that he wouldn't come down here and die without those who cared for him. She wouldn't leave him to this.

Something connected in her mind, a click, an anchor, a hook. Sawyer knew the sensation and couldn't question it. Not yet. She would worry about it when they all survived the night. They just had to survive.

An image floated into Sawyer's mind, and she didn't question its origin. Now wasn't the time to wonder.

The woman was behind her.

She wasted no time. With the image in her mind, she didn't need to turn to look to the spot. She blinked to it and the Druid screamed as Sawyer struck.

A force slammed into her back and she went to the earth, not prepared to get hit. Claws tore into her back then were wrenched away, making her scream in pain.

Blood poured out of a cut on the Druid, but Sawyer couldn't land another blow as a vine wrapped around her waist and yanked.

Sawyer sublimated out of the hold and went after the Druid, who was pulling vines around herself. She hacked at them, hoping to break through and kill the bitch who had slaughtered everyone.

A sharp pain on her leg stopped her, and she looked down to see a viper pumping venom into her calf. She swung her kukri down and cut its head off. Vines grabbed her legs and she sublimated again, flowing through the vines, but she found no space around the Druid to reform and attack.

When she reformed, ignoring the snarls and fights breaking out around her again, she tried to just stab into the mass and heard the scream from the Druid.

Something hit her again and she fell hard, her kukri falling from her grasp. She screamed as teeth sank into her left shoulder. The pain took over her mind, and she couldn't concentrate on using her magic. She would need to get out the hard way.

She punched the cat's head as it shook her shoulder, tearing open the wounds wider. She reached down with her other hand and found another of her blades, one of her throwing knives.

She brought it up and buried it into the soft tissue of the

cat's head, killing it instantly. Pushing the body off her, Sawyer stood up, grabbing her kukri. She looked around quickly.

The Druid was gone. The fighting was continuing, but a snarl and a feline screech ended it. She swayed, hoping it was over. She hoped that bitch was bleeding to death somewhere, but Sawyer had no idea if she'd succeeded. She could only hope.

A whimper had her limping back to Quinn. The vines were reaching over him again. Sawyer saw Shade trying to pull them open. She cut the vines open again, hoping to find those blue eyes watching her. When she revealed his face again, she just kept pulling it open. She couldn't stop, or she would lose progress.

Scout laid by her side while the black blur, the black jaguar that had joined them, helped rip back the bonds holding him. Sawyer didn't spare the cat a glance and ignored the onslaught of emotions rushing through her, unsure who they belonged to.

She wasn't ready for what it meant. None of it.

"Quinn," Sawyer gasped, finally able to pull him out. "Oh, baby." She dragged him away from the mass that had held him and looked over the damage.

Large gashes covered his chest and gut. He was bleeding heavily, or had been. He'd passed out from the blood loss.

"We'll get help," she told him, knowing he probably couldn't hear her. She tried to lift him and grunted from the exertion of it. Quinn didn't look heavy, but she'd never thought she'd be pulling him around the jungle unconscious. "I have to get you to the team, Quinn. We're not going to die out here."

She had to do it fast. She had no idea if the Druid was going to come back and finish them off. Sawyer didn't know when the jungle would start coming after their lives again.

"One of you show me to the team," Sawyer ordered. She had no idea where she was in the jungle, no idea how to get back to the guys. It was too dark, and the magic around them was too much for her to just feel anyone else.

The jaguar began to tug on the bond, pulling her. Sawyer resisted growling at the feeling. She should have been happy, but something about having a new animal bond pissed her off. It felt like an invasion. Sawyer had had her own mind for years, and now she was sharing again with an animal that wasn't the one she'd lost.

This cat wasn't her Midnight.

Having a new animal bond meant Midnight was really gone.

Shade and Scout limped after the jaguar, though, and Sawyer pulled Quinn, hoping she wasn't causing his injuries to get worse. Her own left shoulder was revolting against any sort of movement she asked it for. Her left arm wasn't completely useless, but it wasn't much of a help either.

"I need to make a litter," she decided after twenty feet. "I can't carry him."

She knew the lesson he'd taught her: large leaves, a couple of sturdy branches and some rope or vines to tie it all together. It was surprisingly fast and easy, but she was slowed down by her own injuries. Shade and Scout brought her things to use when they realized what she was doing.

She rolled him on the litter gently, all the animals watching her. She looked up at the black jaguar and glared at the gold eyes.

She hurt too much to deal with those gold eyes.

"One of you want to pull?" She showed them the vine ropes she'd made to yank the litter along.

The jaguar just headbutted her leg and she cursed, pain racing through her like a lightning strike. She looked down to see the snakebite and cursed.

She reached for more of the ropey vines and fashioned herself a tourniquet. Sitting down, she considered what else she could do. She had nothing else to stop the bleeding on Quinn, nothing to stop the bleeding on her back and shoulder.

They were probably going to die, but Sawyer was going to try to her damnedest to make sure they went down fighting. She pulled off her shirt, biting back a whimper at the pain and used it cover the rips over Quinn's torso.

It was all she could do.

Shade grabbed the ropes she'd shown them and began to pull. Scout nudged Quinn's face, but her feral friend didn't respond.

Tears were in her eyes as the jaguar nudged her. She looked at it, big, muscular, and nearly perfectly black. She could still see the faint pattern of spots. She wanted to hate how beautiful the animal was.

Another nudge and Sawyer realized the jaguar wanted her to get moving. Help. They needed to get to help.

"I'm going," Sawyer muttered, standing up. She limped after the wolves with Quinn, and the jaguar trotted past her to lead the group. "I shouldn't be surprised you aren't injured," she mumbled, feeling petulant. Of course the jaguar wasn't hurt. It was from the area. It knew how to fight the things here. "You have a name? Do I need to name you? You'll need to give me a few days, or I'll give you a shit name like Shithead. You don't want that."

Humor, a sad humor radiated back to her. She snorted. Midnight had given her the same feeling when Sawyer tried to make jokes when she was in pain.

That pissed her off, but she locked it down. The jaguar didn't know that she was hurting Sawyer by existing, and she hurt too much physically to handle the emotional load that was waiting to crash into her.

Dawn was beginning to come, a faint light breaking through the trees.

Over the course of what felt like hours, Sawyer realized they weren't headed back to the team or the campsite. "Where are we going?" she demanded.

The jaguar sent her annoyance and impatience. Follow her. Trust her.

Sawyer growled at the cat and the cat snarled back.

Trust her.

Sawyer swallowed her anger. They had nothing else they could do. She checked Quinn's pulse. Weak, but steady and there. The bleeding had stopped thanks to her shirt and time. She needed to make sure nothing got infected, but she had nothing to help in that cause.

Follow her.

The cat's pull on their bond was irresistible and stubborn.

Sawyer continued to walk after the cat deeper into the jungle, further away from the team.

Trust her.

25

JASPER

They never stopped moving.

Once they were together, the few of them alive didn't stop moving. Those who were relatively uninjured helped pull along those who needed help.

By midday after the night of hell, the world quieted again. Rain put the fires out and the animals stopped bothering them.

During the hike, four died. They took the dog tags and left the bodies. They couldn't keep the dead weight.

They never stopped moving. Jasper's heart broke every step.

Further away from their missing teammates, their missing family. Sawyer and Quinn were still out there, alive or dead. He felt like he'd failed them. He felt like the team had failed.

"Fuck," Elijah stumbled, looking down. Jasper grabbed him and didn't let him fall.

"We can make it," Jasper whispered to him. "We have to make it, my man. Don't stop."

"Why not?" he asked. "Why not just leave me?"

"Why the fuck would we do that?" Zander demanded, snarling as he stormed to Jasper and Elijah. Vincent looked over to them and the soldiers kept quiet. Jasper knew they were all dealing with the same issues.

"You can move faster without me," Elijah answered.

"Stop," he snapped. "If I can get out of here on one fucking leg, you can too."

"I can't leave them," Elijah's voice broke. His country accent grew thick with despair.

"If anyone can survive out there without help, it's them. It's Quinn and we have to hope Sawyer is with him," Vincent reminded him.

This wasn't the first time they had the conversation. Elijah was the most vocal about going back out and finding them. But Jasper saw Vincent's and Zander's points as well. Sawyer and Quinn would never forgive them for leaving the soldiers to die or getting themselves killed to find their two most capable teammates. It would be a waste of life for two people who were strong enough to figure themselves out. Sawyer would just hate them for it.

"I can't..."

Jasper hated the tears in Elijah's eyes. They brought his own. He pulled Elijah to keep walking, and the cowboy moved without a fight.

On day three, only an hour after Elijah's outburst, they made it back to the village where their vehicles waited, safe.

"Oh thank god," Vincent whispered reverently.

Jasper saw the extra vehicles. So did some of the soldiers, all confused.

"Halt!" someone yelled.

Jasper frowned at the soldiers that came out from cover and walked over to them, their weapons raised.

"Wait, we're Cavalry Unit 08," Varya yelled out. She'd

told the team her name during their long walk back. "We're survivors. We have several severely injured."

"We're Team Ares and Team Mars, IMAS Spec Ops. When no one called in three days ago, we were asked to come out and find out what happened. We found your vehicles yesterday." A soldier in all black, with black paint over his face, walked through the ones with the weapons raised. He waved, and the weapons went down; the Spec Ops soldiers relaxed. "I'm Master Sergeant Lewis. We'll get you out of here."

Elijah went limp and Jasper cursed as the massive cowboy nearly took them both down.

It happened in a blur. Some of the new soldiers grabbed Elijah away from him. Others took the rest of the wounded. Zander and Doc talked loudly to the Spec Ops healers, explaining the different injuries, who needed what help.

They were loaded up. Jasper was nearly thrown in next to Vincent in a Humvee. Kaar swooped in and joined them. Jasper was exceedingly happy to see the bird alive. He hadn't seen the raven in days.

"Wait!" Vincent called out, grabbing a soldier before he could leave them there to drive away.

"What?"

"I have two agents still out there. They were alive last we saw them. Quinn Judge and Sawyer Matthews. My raven was on the lookout for them but never saw anything, and I'm not willing to leave him here with you."

"I know the names. We...we were asked to report on the status of both of them specifically if we found you all. Team Mars is going to get you to the closest hospital. I'm on Team Ares. We're going to go in and find any other survivors and report the dead, maybe even handle the Druid if she hasn't been."

"It took us three days of non-stop hiking to get back here," Jasper added. "Seven days to get out there originally."

"Roger that," the Spec Ops soldier replied.

"God speed," Vincent whispered.

"You as well."

The door was slammed shut. Jasper's eyes were heavy. He leaned back and slid onto Vincent's shoulder.

"We're getting these men home safe," Vincent told him.

"Sawyer and Quinn are out there," he choked out, the exhaustion and despair reclaiming him. Tears filled his eyes. He didn't have the energy to cry, though. They just fell down his cheeks. He wasn't the only one. He knew everyone in the Humvee was crying or passing out.

Hell. Bodies hanging from trees. Others carelessly scattered over the earth. The world itself had tried to kill them.

"I'm going to have nightmares," Jasper whispered.

"Me too," Vincent answered. "We should sleep. I'm sure their healers are working on Elijah, and I have no idea where the closest hospital is."

"Sleep sounds good," he mumbled, nearly unable to get the words out. Vincent stretched an arm over his shoulder. All around the Humvee, soldiers they had gone on this hell-mission with were curling together, trying to find some solace that they were getting out.

"Did you know that Spec Ops teams are all named after gods of war?" he mumbled, so exhausted, but desperate to stay awake for some reason.

"Yes," Vincent whispered. "Sleep, my friend. Just get to sleep. We can't do anything now."

As Jasper and Vincent fell asleep, he knew they were both thinking about their family still out in the wilds.

26

ELIJAH

Machines beeped. Elijah hated them. Healers hovered over him. He hated them too.

He would keep his leg. Zander and Doc's work on the walk back to the village had seen to that. The antivenom and the healers at the hospital did the rest. It wasn't perfect. He knew he had a golf ball-sized hole in his left calf, where Zander had forced the venom to stay. It had killed all the flesh there, all the tissue.

He didn't care. He could have been an amputee like Jasper. He would have been fine with it.

"Elijah, talk to me," Vincent begged.

"Go to hell," Elijah growled, tired of his *friend* bothering him.

Vincent walked out of the room and didn't come back.

He didn't care. Vincent and Zander had made a decision he hated them for. They left Sawyer and Quinn out there. For what? To save his fucking leg? His friends could all rot. If Sawyer and Quinn didn't come out of that fucking rainforest, he was quitting the team and disappearing. He was never going to speak to them again.

Hours later, Vincent was back with Zander and Jasper.

Elijah glared at them but didn't speak.

"Elijah, only another day or so and then we can ship you home to recuperate," Zander told him, pulling up the charts at the end of his bed.

Elijah ignored him. Twenty-four hours in the hospital, and he was plotting.

He wasn't leaving this fucking country until he found them or their bodies. God have mercy on their souls if he found bodies. He would kill Vincent if those two had died because of them. He would kill all three of them.

"Elijah," Vincent tried again.

"Go. To. Hell," Elijah snarled.

"You need-"

"You left them to die!" he roared.

Something hit him hard across the face, as something else hit him in the chest hard enough to force air from his lungs.

"Fuck, Kaar. You can't fucking do that," Vincent snapped, grabbing his raven roughly and lifting it off Elijah's chest. "Sorry. He clipped you with his wing while landing."

Elijah glared at the bird. Damn thing was actually why Elijah couldn't kill Vincent. Quinn wouldn't want Kaar to suffer for the human he was bonded to.

Fucking shit. He could kill Zander and Jasper, then.

"Sawyer and Quinn would have wanted it," Zander reminded him.

"I don't fucking care," Elijah angrily spat out at the healer. "I don't give a shit. Of all the damn people who should be on my goddamned side. You really proved your love for her this time." Elijah ended that on a snarl.

"Don't." Vincent ordered before Zander could retort. "Quinn would have my hide if I let you die. Sawyer would have Zander's head if he let those soldiers die. She would hate you for hurting yourself. Quinn would just think you're a goddamned idiot, because you are right now." Vincent released Kaar, and the raven landed on Elijah's chest again. "Kaar thinks they are fine. I'm going to let him beat on you until you get your head out of your ass."

"Fuck you and your bird," Elijah growled, pulling his head back to dodge a wing reaching out to whack him again. The raven jumped on his chest, making Elijah groan.

Zander and Jasper left, both angry at him, leaving Vincent to watch his raven harass Elijah.

"Elijah, we need to talk," Vincent told him sadly, after twenty minutes of Elijah trying to push the asshole raven away.

"We left them to die," he growled. "We left them out there in hell. We did that. If they don't come back, it's on us, and I..."

"You think you're the only one who is hurting?" Vincent asked, exasperated. "Elijah, we've been friends for years. Years. You know I do nothing lightly. And them? Quinn is the most genuine person I've ever known. He might not know how to handle his emotions, but he's always honest with them. And her...Sawyer is..."

"Everything," Elijah whispered.

"Yeah," Vincent agreed softly.

"I never got the chance to tell her," he admitted. "I've been holding off. She has so much going on, and Quinn is so madly in love with her and doesn't realize it, and I want him to be happy. I wanted to stay back until they figured it out. We're in a weird fucking situation. We could have never known she would be...everything."

"She has no idea how you feel?" Vincent frowned at him.

"No. I've kept it all innocent. Well, as innocent as I can

get. I just..." Elijah swallowed a frog in his throat. "And Quinn..." Elijah had never wanted to admit he loved that boy more than he already did. It wasn't love that would burn for ages, but he loved him for what they had. Friendship, brotherhood, understanding that they received nowhere else.

It was changing with Sawyer around. Quinn had once told him she did that, she changed everything, and that he knew the moment he saw her that she would.

Quinn had been right. They wanted each other less and less, and instead sat and pined over her.

Elijah closed his eyes, hoping the tears didn't come. His two favorite people were out there without him.

"Talk to me, Elijah," Vincent commanded gently, sitting on the edge of the hospital bed.

"I'm in love with her." Elijah sighed. "I was too much of a coward to ever tell her, and she has no idea. Quinn is out there, surrounded by things that want him dead, and I'm not there for him."

"What can I do to make this easier?" he asked, reaching out.

"Let me stay," Elijah told him. "Don't send me back to New York or Georgia, not without knowing where they are, if they might be okay. Don't make me leave until we know."

"Okay. When you're discharged, I'm going to put you on light duty. You'll work with local governments to see the areas the Druid claimed. Talk to families who escaped their lands. See what can be done to stop this from happening again."

"Thank you," Elijah whispered. It would keep him close, so he could know early. It would keep him here to see them if they made it out. "I know you were right, by the way. I just hate it."

"We all do," Vincent said. "We all hate it. The good news? There's finally a team out there with the training that should have been on the mission originally. Team Ares is the top-rated Spec Ops team in IMAS. They are fucking good at their jobs."

"Yeah and Team Mars is number two. I know," he mumbled.

They sat in silence for a long time and Elijah reached out to pet the raven. Kaar fluffed and shook his feathers, then bounced up his chest for a cuddle.

"He never wants to cuddle with me, but he'll cuddle with you. Fucking shit bird."

Elijah couldn't resist a weak chuckle. It was half-hearted, since his heart was out in the jungle, but Vincent had pulled one out of him nonetheless.

27

SAWYER

S awyer didn't know how long she followed the jaguar. She just knew that at some point, she couldn't continue and had collapsed. Something grabbed onto her bra and pulled her, dragging her over the earth, slowly but surely.

SOMEONE SPOKE, but Sawyer didn't understand the language. It was harried and worried. Frantic and distraught. Feminine.

Other voices joined in. Growls erupted. A snarl silenced the growls.

A wave of relief went through her.

Hands grabbed her and lifted her from the earth.

Voices continued in the language she didn't know.

The hands were rough and calloused, but gentle with her.

They were moving fast. She could feel the air on her face.

She was placed on something that felt like furs.

"You will live," whispered a heavily-accented female voice. "Do not give up yet."

Burning hot hands touched her and she screamed.

❧

Sawyer woke up with a start, reaching around for anything. She didn't know where she was. Disoriented and scared, she fell out of the mat of skins and furs she was laying on and crawled around, trying to stand.

Her legs shook with exertion, but she succeeded. Her eyes searched frantically around the...

She slowed.

The hut was grass, it seemed. Grass and mud compacted into walls, in a tent-like shape.

A male voice began to say something, and Sawyer snapped her eyes in his direction, reaching to pull a weapon.

There was nothing she could arm herself with, because she was completely nude. She stepped back, wondering if there was going to be a fight with the tribal man in the doorway. He was dark-skinned, just a few shades darker than her and Quinn. He had red painted over parts of his body. He didn't seem threatening, since he carried no weapons. Only dressed in a simple loin cloth, he was nearly as nude as she was.

If he wasn't a Magi, she wouldn't have been worried at all.

But he was.

And as powerful as Quinn, if she could even begin to guess power at that magnitude. His had the same wild feeling as Quinn's, but less angrily feral. Just wild, just like the deep jungle, but not angry.

She continued to look over her possible opponent, who said nothing. Older than her, but she couldn't be certain.

She had a feeling that life expectancy in these parts was low.

A female voice, in the same foreign language, called out, and he turned. Sawyer ignored the ass that entered her vision. She was thankful he'd been covering the front, but it was all he'd been covering.

The man left the door, walking away towards the woman's voice.

Sawyer took the chance to look around for anything to wear.

"Here," a voice whispered into the hut. Heavily accented, but Sawyer recognized it. It had whispered to her that she would live.

Sawyer looked back at the door and saw a woman this time. She was more dressed than the man. Her hair was much like Sawyer's - wildly curly, long, and frizzing from the humidity.

"Clothing. I had your pants cleaned, and I still have plenty of modern clothing that should suit you. And a towel. I will show you where we bathe." The woman held out the bundle and Sawyer reached forward, taking it slowly.

She knew what this woman was.

"You're a Druid," Sawyer whispered, wondering if the fight would recontinue. This wasn't the one that attacked them.

"Yes. I live with this tribe, and protect them as well. One of them is my husband, my mate." The Druid sighed sadly. "I'm not going to hurt you."

"Really?" Sawyer swallowed. She didn't have any energy. She hadn't even looked over her injuries.

"No. I believe in remembering that I'm human, and humans can be educated, so that's my approach to keeping my territory healthy and safe. You met..." The Druid shook her head, not finishing the sentence. "We're not all like that."

"Not what I've heard," Sawyer retorted, still cautious. "Or experienced."

"There's a reason most Druids are considered peaceful," the Druid replied. "Because we are."

"If we don't step on your toes," Sawyer hissed.

"No, if you don't destroy our homes and kill our families."

Sawyer let that soak in. She couldn't blame the Druid for that. "Okay."

"Would you like to know who healed you?"

Sawyer dropped the bundle on the cot and touched her shoulder. Scars. She looked down to her leg. There was a small hole where tissue must have died, but nothing more.

"Yes, and how long was I asleep?"

"Two days, and the man who came in is who healed you. He doesn't speak English, but if you know Portuguese, he has some passing ability. He's been trying to learn for me, just as I know his tribe's language for him."

"I speak Spanish. We should be able to cobble together some communication." Sawyer had to do it before. The languages were different, but the similarities made it possible to understand some things, get general ideas across. "Husband?" Sawyer guessed, pulling out a bright blue t-shirt. She resisted the urge to wince at the color, but she pulled it on without saying anything. Next, she found her pants. Holes were sewn up, and she slid them on next. The Druid held out one more item. Sawyer took her ring and slid it back on. She was amazed the damn thing had survived the trip so far.

"Yes. I knew you would understand." The Druid

extended a hand to shake. "Come. My name is Yasmin. Be welcome here."

Sawyer took the offered hand and they shook, but the Druid didn't release her, pulling her out of the hut before she could stop it.

"Where's Quinn? The guy. He should have been with me?" Sawyer looked around the tiny village of grass and mud huts in a small clearing of the jungle.

"Still asleep. He lost a lot of blood, and my husband knows his own when he meets them and wanted you awake before we woke your friend."

"His own?" She didn't like that. She didn't know what it meant.

"Children of Druids are always a bit different. More magical than others. There's no one quite like them and you are with Rogue Wolf. He's...trouble for Druids, and my husband wants us to be safe," Yasmin explained. "My husband is the son of the Druid who ran this territory before me. She passed away only a couple of years ago. She had accepted me when my powers manifested and I ran out here as a teenager. He and I grew up together."

"Rogue Wolf?" Sawyer frowned, following Yasmin as she led them somewhere.

"You...you called him Quinn," Yasmin said, nodding. "The name by which we Druids know him is Rogue Wolf, the name his mother gave him."

"How?" Sawyer crossed her arms, stopping. "How..."

"There isn't a Druid on the earth who doesn't know the story of the rogue," Yasmin whispered. "But I feel like he must tell you his story, since you are his mate. It's not my place."

Sawyer didn't answer. Mate? She would correct that later. Not like she didn't wish someone as sexy as Quinn would want her, but that just wasn't in their cards, she thought. She just followed the Druid in silence to a pool, and Sawyer sucked in a breath at how beautiful the area was. Waterfalls cascaded into the pool, which led to another waterfall on the other side.

"The water is clean and safe for you to bathe. We have drinking water in the village," Yasmin told her. "You will get clean and we will talk more before waking up your Quinn."

Her Quinn.

She could agree with that. Not all hers, but part of hers.

Sawyer stripped back down, placing her towel and her clothing on a rock, following Yasmin into the clear, clean water.

It was like she'd never been clean before. It was refreshing and the best bath she'd ever had. The world smelled like flowers, and Yasmin sang softly, wading closer to the waterfall.

"You said children of Druids are also different. Are they Legends?"

"No," Yasmin answered. "They are Magi. We all are, just humans with magic. But, think about it. We Druids have a lot of power, so of course, our children would as well. It fades as they get further from the Druid, but immediate children are always so strong. My husband is very powerful, but he can only heal. Rogue...Quinn is exceptional. His natural abilities match ours to some extent. I can't control the earth itself, only the things that grow and live on it."

Sawyer considered that, nodding slowly as she dipped lower into the water. She bathed in silence, unsure what else to ask. She felt a tug in her mind and flood of worry. She looked up to see the black jaguar.

"Yes, Sombra. She is well," Yasmin called out softly.

"Sombra," Sawyer whispered. The jaguar turned to her.

She knew what that word meant in Spanish. Yasmin had called her new animal bond Shadow.

Sawyer was bitter at the cosmic irony of it. She wanted to laugh and cry at the name.

"She has waited a long time for you," Yasmin continued. "I named her Sombra when she was born. Her mother is one of my bonds, but Sombra didn't want me. She knew she was born from the death of another and was destined for someone."

She swallowed on a lump in her throat. Too much emotion filled her. A wave of uneasiness hit her that didn't belong to her, as if Sombra was worried about Sawyer's opinion of her.

"She's beautiful," she mumbled honestly, looking away.

"What's wrong?" the Druid asked gently, wading closer. "She is your bond. Your lifelong companion."

"She's a replacement," Sawyer muttered. "I'm not sure... I'm not sure how to handle that."

"Do you want to know what we Druids think? We go through animal bonds, you know. Certainly, if they are strong, they can live for as long as we do, like any animal bond, but they are still wild like we are, can be injured, hunted, and die." Yasmin touched Sawyer's shoulder. "She is not a replacement. She is the same bond you once had, just come back. She knew her duty wasn't over. She might not have those memories, but she has that magic. You grew and changed...so she did, born into a body that befitted the power you have, so that she could continue to be the companion you needed."

"Reincarnation isn't real," she said, feeling snappy and agitated. Sombra wasn't Midnight. Not even the strange similarities of their feelings and looks could convince her. This massive black jaguar was not her tiny black housecat.

"There was a time when people didn't believe in magic," Yasmin reminded her.

Sawyer felt a flood of tears hit her behind her eyes. That feeling that the dam was about to break. She didn't let it, but she couldn't deny that Yasmin was right. There was once a time when the world didn't believe in magic. Who was to say she wasn't wrong about their bonds?

"Why did you name her Sombra?"

"Because she is a shadow. She's elusive and dangerous, holding secrets from me even though she is a part of my family and lives in my territory. I mean, look at her. The name fit." Yasmin made it sound so simple. The name did fit. In so many ways.

"Do you know who I am?" Sawyer looked up to Yasmin and met the dark, endless-looking eyes.

"No. Do I need to? There must be a reason a cat like her would wait for a woman like you. That's all I need to know. She brought you and Rogue Wolf here to be helped, and I trust her judgement."

Sawyer cried then, covering her face. Yasmin backed away, leaving her to her tears. She sank to her knees in the water and nearly went under.

A splash, and suddenly Sawyer had a large wet cat next to her, rubbing across her side. Sawyer wrapped her arms around Sombra and pulled her close, crying into wet fur. A hole was filled. A piece of her soul was returned to her, and Sawyer had never imagined she could feel that way again. Complete.

Love filled her from the feline. Such a pure, but also mildly annoyed, love. She wanted to get out of the water. She wanted her Magi to be strong and stop crying. Human tears confused her and made her uncomfortable.

Sawyer pulled back and glared into gold eyes. It was going to be like that?

The jaguar just huffed, causing water to fly off her nose into Sawyer's face.

"Let's get dry," she told her cat, sighing. Then she laughed. She laughed harder than she had in a long time, still holding the jaguar. "Then we'll get Quinn and find out how to go home...well, my home. I hope you'll like it."

Sombra seemed unconcerned, moving towards the shore. Sawyer followed and dried off, trying to not watch Yasmin do the same.

"Why did you help us?" she asked once they were dressed and on the way back to the village.

"Sombra brought you here." Yasmin shrugged. "There's no reason to waste life in such a way, and...if you die, so does she. If your Quinn dies, so do his wolves. Wasteful murder by a young woman who knows better."

"Not survival of the fittest?" She was confused. Wasn't this supposed to be a woman who thought that's just the way the world worked? Like Quinn?

Yasmin not only disagreed, she did so strongly. Sawyer didn't know where the Druid's physical strength came from, but the Druid grabbed her shirt and yanked her close.

"Murder is a perversion. It's not the natural order. It is not *survival of the fittest*. If you had been bitten by a snake while looking for food, I would say you made your own mistake." Yasmin stopped, just holding Sawyer in place. She shook her head. "Forgive me. My husband and I have argued for months about the situation. He thinks I should just let it happen and step in if she comes for us here. I want to help all those in this place, not just those in my territory."

"I'm sorry," Sawyer mumbled. She didn't know why she was sorry. "And, um, thank you."

"Don't thank me yet. We must wake Rogue Wolf, and he will not be happy to be here."

Sawyer didn't believe that. He would see how they helped him and her. This Druid was more in line with what she'd always thought about Druids. It wasn't until she met Quinn and then this mission that she'd learned otherwise. They weren't just peaceful, weird hippie Magi with too much power. They could also be the stuff of nightmares.

Sombra followed them to a hut near the outskirts of the village. People ignored her. Strange. She'd thought they would watch her. She was an outsider and she was used to standing out, being watched.

"My husband is waiting for us. Everyone else will clear the area just in case," Yasmin spoke as they neared the last hut.

"What's his name?"

"You should just call him Tez. You wouldn't be able to pronounce his full name."

"I'll trust you on that," Sawyer agreed softly. She raised a hand when they saw him come into view. "Hi, Tez." She said it in Spanish, hoping he would understand the words. Close enough to Portuguese.

He grinned, nodding. He even raised a hand to wave back.

"He's not a talkative man, my husband. Not with newcomers, anyway," Yasmin whispered to her, then launched a diatribe at him in the language that Sawyer didn't understand. She couldn't even recognize it.

Tez replied, just as fast and passionate about something. His hands moved as he spoke, animated.

"He says Quinn's injuries are completely healed. We've kept him in a healing sleep and he will be very disoriented when he awakes. Tez thinks you should stir him and we should wait outside." Yasmin motioned to the hut and Sawyer nodded slowly.

She went in alone. It was the exact same as the hut she had been in. A cot covered in furs was the only thing inside.

He looked so peaceful asleep, her feral, wild friend. Shade lifted his head and whimpered softly. Scout trotted to her and bumped his head to her thigh. She scratched both behind their ears and went to Quinn. Sombra didn't follow her into the hut, and Sawyer wondered why that was.

Sombra replied with a wave of 'hurry the fuck up' and she rolled her eyes. Of course she got a cat full of attitude.

"Quinn," she whispered.

She wondered when she fell in love with him. What had Elijah said? She gave away pieces of her heart like candy on Halloween? It made her want to laugh and cry. She really did.

Tears filled her eyes as she went to her knees next to him and touched his face gently.

His eyes flew open at the contact. He moved faster than she could. She hadn't thought he would be so fast to wake up. She definitely hadn't been expecting the takedown.

One moment she'd been kneeling next to his cot, the next she was underneath him in the furs on the cot. He growled down at her. She wasn't scared of him killing her, or even hurting her.

She yanked his face down to hers and kissed him, hard. It was like kissing a wall, completely unreciprocated, but he didn't stop it either.

She just needed to do it. He was alive.

She let his cheeks go and he pulled his head away from hers, looking confused.

Silence fell on them.

Time passed slowly.

Still, he said absolutely nothing.

"Quinn," she plainly said, staring into his eyes. She decided they were just going to pretend the kiss never happened.

"We're alive." He didn't release her.

"We are, but the situation is a little complicated."

"Explain." Someone was cranky. She didn't miss the growl in the word.

"Let me up and I will." Sawyer wiggled her fingers, trying to remind him that he had her wrists. She didn't think this was a conversation to have with his body pressed to hers. He was nude. She figured he would be, and she'd seen it all before, but she hadn't been expecting to be pressed up to the nude form of Quinn Judge.

"No."

"We're not with the team. A tribe saved us and-"

"Druid," he snarled, his head spinning to the opening of the hut. The earth rumbled.

"She saved our lives. She's not the same one," Sawyer told him quickly, yanking her wrists free. She grabbed his head and forced him to look back at her.

"Why?"

"Apparently she raised my new animal bond."

"Ah," Quinn sighed. "You've met her."

"You knew?" she asked, narrowing her eyes on his.

"Shade and Scout found her. You weren't ready for her yet, she thought, but I guess she didn't want to fight alone." Quinn relaxed, but only minutely. "Her name?"

"Sombra," Sawyer whispered, relaxing as well.

"Good name," he murmured.

"Can we get up?"

"No. You'll stay here until I know it's safe."

"They can hear us," Sawyer drolly replied. "And I've

already been out there with them. I got to get clean before coming to wake you up."

"You didn't wake me up immediately?"

"They told me no, plus I wanted to be able to give you the information I could get so you didn't worry about it." Sawyer watched him war with himself. She knew he wanted to trust no one, but so far, none of the innocent people in the village or Yasmin had given her a reason to be wary. She knew Quinn was realizing that. "Don't hurt them. They raised Sombra. They saved us when she brought us here, trusting her judgement about us."

"Okay," Quinn growled.

When he still didn't let her up, she grew worried. "Quinn. Up. Off the cot. Let's move."

"I'm sorry," he mumbled, jumping off her. She sighed happily to see him moving as she sat up and watched him check his wolves. New scars covered his body, just like they did her. The long tears to his chest and abdomen were now scars, looking long healed and faded, thinner than she would have expected. He turned his back to her and she gasped. He spun back around. "What?"

"Let me see your back," she demanded. He turned slowly, and she stood up. She reached out and touched him. For as long as she'd known him, his back was a mass of crisscross scarring that stood out. White bold lines, thin ones.

They weren't gone but they were barely there. They were no longer so apparent. From a distance, she wondered if people would even notice them.

"A healing from my husband tends to be full body. Scars will never truly fade, but he can lessen them," Yasmin called in. Sawyer saw her standing in the door, Tez at her side.

"You are the Druid that saved us?" Quinn asked, frowning at her.

"Who else would I be?" Yasmin teased, smiling. "Well met, Quinn Judge."

"You know my name, don't play coy," Quinn snarled.

"She calls you Quinn, so I feel that must be the name you like more. But, if you wish to always be Rogue Wolf, so be it."

"Quinn is fine," he said quickly. Then Sawyer watched him look at Tez, who grinned. Quinn's eyes went wide. "You're…"

"His mother was a Druid in the area once," Sawyer whispered to him. "He's like you, but he can only heal. Though…healing at a power like you and him obviously is some impressive shit."

"We must talk," Quinn told Tez. Tez tilted his head, not understanding and Yasmin translated. Quinn snapped his fingers and started off in the language Sawyer didn't know, leaving her out of the conversation completely.

Something harsh was said and Yasmin left, her hands raised in peace. Quinn relaxed more when she was gone, but Tez made an angry comment after that.

Sawyer crossed her arms and walked out. She rolled her eyes and found Sombra laying in the sun.

Shadow in the light.

Sawyer didn't miss the metaphor or the humor coming from the cat.

"You don't know anything about me," Sawyer mumbled. "That'll change."

The cat didn't care about anything from before she met Sawyer, which irked her.

"You should know who came before you."

That got Sombra's attention, her eyes opening. Her head came up and bobbed.

"Let's go and I'll tell you about Midnight," Sawyer whispered to her jaguar. Sombra stood up and walked away. She didn't follow until Sombra looked back, a wave of annoyance hitting the bond. "I'm coming."

She glanced back at Quinn, deep in conversation with Tez. He looked upset, but she waited until his eyes met hers. A blush, her first in a long time, crept over her face, heating it.

His face softened, and he smiled.

Her heart skipped several beats and she went to follow her new animal bond, trying to ignore how he made her feel. She had enough problems. She loved Zander, Jasper, and Vincent. Was she really so greedy to want Quinn too?

Yes. She was. Her heart was greedy enough to take anything it could get.

28

QUINN

Quinn wanted to hate Yasmin. The Druid that saved him and Sawyer was just that: a Druid.

He didn't want to trust her.

He didn't want to eat with her or see her.

He was allowed none of those things.

Quinn and Tez had argued that first hour. Quinn wasn't foolish enough to attack the male's mate, Druid or not. He'd just lost a fight with a Druid and wasn't keen on losing a second with one who had a powerful healer for a mate. Husband. They had used husband. Married, bound together.

Quinn had never heard of a Druid doing such a human thing. Marriage. His mother never had. Other Druids he knew never had. He'd also never met a Druid that lived with other people like this. He'd grown up in a region where the closest other humans were miles away, unwilling to go so far north to see the Druids unless it was short summer months.

Sawyer liked her too, this Yasmin, the married Druid.

Now, he was watching her play with the black jaguar. Sombra. A good name for the feline. Sawyer and the jaguar were wrestling, and the cat slowly swatted at Sawyer's head, in a very non-threatening way.

He forgot about the Druid and just watched his female play with the missing piece of her soul, entranced by the sight.

His.

He touched his lips and pondered what had happened. He knew what a kiss was - that wasn't what had him shocked.

It was his first one. No one had ever given him one before. It was too intimate a gesture for him and Elijah. His previous encounters with lovers had never been close.

She'd kissed him, though, which meant she had feelings for him. Which meant he needed to decide what to do about her. Did he offer himself? He wasn't sure. Elijah was easy. Get him turned on and that was all that was needed. It wasn't tied up in other problems.

So Quinn just stood there, watching the sun go down, and her play with Sombra. Shade and Scout stayed close to him, also observing. They liked Sombra. They had found her three days into their trip into the jungle and she had taught them different things about the area behind his and Sawyer's backs. It also had widened the search area for the Druid.

Not like that had mattered. The bitch had still taken them by surprise.

His pack. Only he and Sawyer were here.

"Sawyer," he called out. "We need to talk."

"I know," she called back. "But we're not allowed to leave for at least another day, Quinn. Yasmin and Tez made it clear."

He growled at her and she bared her teeth, which made Sombra snarl at him. Quinn didn't react, but he wasn't going to pick a fight with the jaguar either, so he dropped his gaze respectfully. He'd win, but the scars over his chest were a stark reminder of what a jaguar could do to him in the meantime.

He knew Sawyer was right. When they ate lunch, Tez had explained that he had healed them, but they wouldn't be ready to travel for a day, at least. He wanted to make sure the snake bite on Sawyer's leg wasn't going to lead to more problems. He wanted to know Quinn as well. He'd met others like them, children of Druids. They were apparently common in the uncontacted tribes of the Amazon.

Quinn stomped down to Sawyer and looked down at her laying on the earth with Sombra to her side. "We should still talk."

"I'm not ready," she answered.

"What?" Quinn frowned at her.

"I left them to find you. They could be dead. I don't know and I'm not ready for it." He heard the tiny shake in her voice, one she was nearly perfect at hiding.

He nodded slowly and sat down next to her. "I'm worried too," he admitted.

"God," Sawyer groaned. He watched her run a hand through her thick hair. "I left them together, at least, but...I asked Sombra to get us back to them and she brought us here. Blame her."

He looked at the jaguar, who just rolled on her back in the sun, ignoring him.

"Quinn, I just want to pretend for a moment that it didn't happen," she whispered it like a secret. "That we didn't see what hell on earth looked like. That I didn't fail in saving some poor fucking soldier who got hung from the trees. That I didn't see you dying under those vines, waiting for her to finish the job."

"Camp was that bad?" he asked softly, laying back to get next to her.

"It was horrifying. Snakes fucking everywhere. Vines were pulling people away. I'm sure there was more. I helped Varya save her bear from some jaguars."

"I met a soldier on watch that night. Young man named Peters," Quinn told her. "He was nice to me. I liked him. He wanted me to get some rest. He was the one screaming first, when I ran out of camp."

Quinn closed his eyes and saw the scene he'd found. The good soldier being eaten alive. He had done the only thing he could and killed him faster. Mercy.

"Fuck."

He heard Sawyer's voice catch and pulled her to him. Her shoulders were shaking, and he just let her cry silently on his chest. He didn't blame her. It didn't make her weak.

They had survived hell and there was a very real chance they were the only ones. He didn't blame her for not being ready.

When she stopped, he lifted his head and kissed her forehead. He'd never done something like that.

"Quinn?" She looked up at him and he knew what the awful clenching of his heart was. He was an idiot and he was in love with her.

"Yes?"

"I learned something, and I hope...you're willing to share." The hesitancy in her voice meant it was about him.

"What did Yasmin tell you?" He wouldn't be angry. Yasmin didn't know that Sawyer knew nothing. Something had to have slipped.

"Rogue Wolf," she whispered. "What's his story?"

Was he ready to tell her that? Quinn pondered the question for a long time. They were out in the Amazon because of his past, because of what he was known for. Something that only Druids should have known, until his mother let that bitch know and got him roped into this.

Would she still want to kiss him if he told her?

He had a feeling the fears were for nothing. Sawyer, assassin, a woman who had fought harder battles than even his own. She would understand exactly why he'd done what he had.

"Do you want to know who named me Quinn? Elijah and Vincent. They thought it fit and I didn't care. Judge? I never had a surname before it. We were in a courtroom. I wanted to know the title of the most powerful man in the room. Vincent told me he was a judge and he meted out justice on those caught for crimes." Quinn took a deep breath. "I liked it. So, I became Quinn Judge. Rogue Wolf is the name my mother gave me when my abilities manifested."

"You had to be a teenager when that happened, so what were you before that?"

"Boy. I had no name because she thought I wasn't worthy of one." The memory of her telling him that over and over still made him a little bitter.

"I'm sorry."

"It was years ago."

"Really?" Sawyer frowned, confused with him.

"I'm infamous because at sixteen, I mated with a Druid and left my mother's home to live with her. I was the Tez to a Yasmin, but not husband."

"You were in a relationship?"

The shock that radiated off his favorite female almost made him chuckle, but the answer he was going to give her wasn't one that was humorous. "No. Mate, and that was all she wanted from me." Quinn could remember it. He'd been excited to be with this Druid closer to his age, away from his mother.

She'd never kissed him, not like Sawyer had. She'd never really cared about him. He was a strong, young, healthy male willing to help her have children and raised to listen to the Druids around him, having had it beaten into him by his mother.

"Oh."

"Yes," Quinn sighed. "I did my job well."

Sawyer coughed and tried to sit up, but Quinn just pulled her back down on his chest. He wasn't ready to lose the contact.

"You're a dad?"

"I was." His voice cracked minutely.

"No," Sawyer gasped, soft. He could feel her pulse begin to race. "Oh, baby, I'm..."

"I didn't know I couldn't trust her with our one-week old son." Quinn stared at the canopy above as he remembered. "Females in the wild have the right not to raise young that won't survive. Natural. Acceptable. It carries on healthy genetics and keeps the population healthy. No lost resources."

"Quinn..."

"He'd had a...I think it's called a cleft palate. I did research on it later. He hadn't been perfect, but he'd been mine. When I found out, she didn't think I would find it a problem, having been raised by Druids. I would fall in line with her decision and give her another child, try again. One that was...perfect." Quinn pulled Sawyer higher up against him, so their eyes met. "She was tending the fire. I walked up behind her, broke her neck, and began a long trip south. I stumbled on some people, killed them too, then Vincent and Elijah found me. They convinced me not to kill them."

"She…"

"My Druid mate killed our son because it wasn't perfectly healthy and she didn't want to try and find modern human help. She didn't even give me an option to have him and leave, try on my own to raise him. Who was going to tell her she couldn't? Druids can't be trusted, Sawyer. You like Yasmin, but in the end, they're *all* mad."

He pushed her off gently and sat up. He got to his feet, brushing off the dirt and twigs. He didn't look at her as he began to walk away. Scout whimpered, following him. Shade howled up at the sky. They were the ones who had witnessed it, had found the buried beautiful body of his child.

He thought he'd been a strong male who could have strong children. The whore had only wanted girls, in hopes they could be like her.

He stumbled on his path and Tez was there. "You need more healing," Tez told him roughly. "Come."

"I'm fine," he growled. His body was fine. He didn't need to be healed.

"Come." Tez grabbed his arm and pulled. Quinn followed. He could defeat the healer, but he wouldn't. They were the same, but different. Both children of monstrous women.

They were going back towards the tribe's village when Tez diverted them down a trail.

"Our home," Tez said, pointing to a set of huts away from the others. "Watch."

Tez whistled and Quinn waited.

Two young children ran out of one of the huts, laughing. Tez grabbed the younger one, a small boy, and swung him for a moment. Quinn's heart ached at the smile on his face. The older one was a little girl that looked like the Druid. She smiled brightly at him, and he looked away.

"Mine, with my heart, Yasmin," Tez informed him.

"What are you trying to say, Tez?" Quinn was tired of mystery.

"Not all humans out there destroy nature and our homes, or poach animals. Not all animals are venomous. Not all Druids go mad. Some are just women, doomed to have powers that make others misunderstand them. It drives them to run from their lives and their families. Some can't handle that and get twisted along the way, others just want to reclaim what their own magic drove them to lose. Family, home, friends, a life. Druids here are wilder, but they are not insane because of it. They just are." Tez put his son down. He tapped Quinn's chest. "Your body doesn't need to be healed, Wolf. Your heart does. That is why I will not let you leave. I will not see you leave my home carrying the poison the Druids you once knew put there. I will not see you feel the urge to kill the next one on sight just because she was born. You must heal."

Quinn shoved the hand away and stormed back down the path. He didn't know what to think, but Tez's life made him curious.

He passed Yasmin on the way. Instead of growling at her like he had before, he stepped out of her way on the path and lowered his gaze.

"I don't like that. I'm not a goddess. Stop it," Yasmin snapped. He flinched. "I'm sorry." Her voice was softer, saying that. "I'm just...I wish Druids like Camila and your mother didn't exist. Your mate was a...monster. I love my children with everything I am, yet you look at me like I'm a threat to them. We Druids...they say we don't have it in our nature to be anything but peaceful. We do. We're as fierce as the animals around us, but we are also just human. Just human. We're susceptible to the same problems, the flaws. I wish people remembered that too."

Quinn didn't say anything. Yasmin must have realized he wasn't going to say anything, since she just continued the walk to her home.

Her home with her *husband* and her *children*. A boy and girl.

Shade and Scout met him back where he had left Sawyer. Shade sent him an image of her leaving, wiping her face. They thought she had gone to the bathing pool.

Quinn went to find her. He needed her. He needed her in that moment more than he needed breath.

29

SAWYER

Sawyer stripped her body to match the feeling in her heart. Stripped. She was raw.

Quinn had been a father and his newborn son had been murdered. The story echoed in her head, refusing to let up.

Then he'd stormed away from her, leaving her reeling. She had wanted to hold him, comfort him. Tell him that it was all going to be okay, but it wasn't. She knew what it felt like to be comforted when the comfort changed nothing.

Nothing would bring Henry or Midnight back. Nothing would bring back his son.

She'd always wondered why he seemed so passionate about Henry. She'd thought it had just been Midnight, but looking back on that day in the bank with her lockbox, before she told them her story...

He'd been asking about both. He probably saw Henry and thought she killed him or something.

She waded into the water and sank. Sombra was leaving her to this, to process.

She rubbed her temples and forehead, wondering what

in the hell she was supposed to say or do. How does someone comfort a friend who lost something so dear? She knew from experience the comfort just didn't help. Nothing would ever make a senseless act of violence seem like less of a nightmare. Nothing would lessen the pain except time and distance, and those were both band-aids. They were temporary. Anything could rip the wound back open.

She traced her new scars while she soaked in the pool. Her shoulder had been torn open. She hadn't realized it was so bad, but the places where that jaguar had sunk its fangs were telling.

"I'm sorry for running off," Quinn called out softly from behind her. "I shouldn't have. We were talking about something."

"I understand the need to run from a discussion like that," she replied, not turning to look at him. She decided on a lighter topic. "I have a myriad of new scars, it seems."

Water splashed behind her. When he didn't respond, she turned around. He was within a foot of her, so close. She tapped the sore scars on her shoulder.

"You have claw scars on your back as well," he told her, stepping closer. Sure enough, his arm went around her and traced those new ones on her back.

"We'll match," she teased softly, tracing one of his new ones over his abs. The jaguars had nearly gutted him.

"The ones on my back..." She watched something uncomfortable flash over his face.

"Are similar to the one on my face?" She posed it like a question, but she had always known what scars like his meant. He'd been beaten or tortured, probably both.

"My mother wanted a strong child. She wanted a disciplined child. When I failed in a task, I was disciplined for it."

"Why?"

"Because the strongest survive," he answered softly.

"Why..." Sawyer looked for the question. "You hate Druids because they've treated you badly, and I completely understand that, but then what is Yasmin? Or the Druids that are famous in Yellowstone National Park? They live peacefully with others."

"I don't know," he admitted. "I don't. It seems, for an expert on them like me, I can be very wrong."

"I would kill them for you if I could," she murmured to him. "I would hunt them down and make them pay for what they did to you. So would Elijah, and the guys." The team. She desperately hoped they were alive.

"I know."

She blinked, trying to hold back more tears. She was crying a lot now and she was beginning to hate it. She was tired, confused, and desperate. Lost in the jungle with a tribe most people probably didn't know existed, with a man who confused her and broke her heart. The one she was on this mission to protect - and she'd failed to protect any of them.

"Sawyer?" Quinn leaned down slightly to look in her eyes. She waved a hand and began to turn away from him. He grabbed her, and she stopped, breathing at the contact. His hand on her hip, holding her to look at him. Too close. She was too emotional for this. She pulled away. "Are you scared of me?"

The desperation in the question made Sawyer jerk to a stop. She shook her head, trying to figure out where that came from. "No. Quinn, your power is both fear-inspiring and awe-inspiring. There was a time when I was scared of you. But not anymore. You *power* is fear-inspiring, but you're just what the world made you and it's beautifully unique."

She shrugged. "Once I figured out what you and I could be, friends and teammates, I stopped being scared of *you*. Why would you think that I am?"

"You pulled away from me," he whispered. She saw sadness in those blue eyes she would have never expected.

"I pulled away because I'm feeling emotionally raw and vulnerable. This was very heavy and I'm tired." She wiped her face. "What else do you want to talk about?"

"Nothing," he answered. He reached out for her again. "If you aren't scared of me, I don't feel bad for doing this and I need to do this."

"Excus-"

He yanked her back to him and the rough, unpracticed kiss he gave her left her shocked and dazed. It was possessive. It was needy. It was desperate. One of his arms wrapped around her waist and held her against him. She could feel his cock hard against her lower abdomen.

"Quinn," Sawyer gasped, pulling her mouth from his. "What?"

"You kissed me earlier," he reminded her softly. "Did you know it was my first one? I was too shocked to keep going, too shocked to respond."

"Oh." She couldn't breathe anymore. She'd been his first kiss? She'd figured...

She didn't know what she figured but it wasn't that.

"I want you," he growled softly. "I've wanted you for a long time."

She could tell.

"I had..." Sawyer shook her head. "No idea..."

"I thought it was just physical. I thought it was the normal attraction a male should have to a female. But..." Quinn placed his lips to her neck, still holding her against his body. She could feel her pulse race, erratic and wild. "I think it's more than that."

Sawyer's mind raced. There was something she needed to remember, to make sure of. Her brain was not cooperating though.

"I know about the deal. I would never compete with my brothers for you." His eyes met hers again. That was it. That was the thing she'd forgotten about for a moment. "Strong females deserve their choice in strong males."

"Oh," she sighed, giving up. She pulled him back down for another rough kiss, delighting in the growl that erupted from his chest. Possessive and dangerous.

Hers.

She was just as possessive as he was, and he was *hers*.

He lifted her, and she threw her legs around his waist. She was glad there was no clothing in the way.

"Where are we going?" she asked as he moved them. She figured it out as they went under the waterfall and laughed. "Romantic much? I wasn't expecting that."

"I know a couple of things," he told her. "Now...let me do this for you. We have the time, trapped here until they feel we can leave."

That sent shivers down her spine. He laid her on some rocks just behind the curtain of water. She felt like a meal from the way he looked her over. She was finally the hare that had been caught by the wolf.

"A good male knows that his female's pleasure is the most important," he began softly, leaning down to nip her right nipple. It sent fire through her.

His long hair fell over her chest and stomach. It was beautiful, and she couldn't stop herself from running her hands through it for the first time. Soft, silken, a dark cascade.

Her back arched when he bit down harder on her nipple and swiped his tongue over it at the same time.

"Quinn," she moaned out as his surprisingly soft hands moved up her sides.

"Sh. Enjoy it. Let me do this," he told her again. "Let me prove myself."

"You don't need to..."

"A male should always prove himself," Quinn whispered huskily to her.

He rolled her over onto her stomach and she erupted in goosebumps as he ran his hands down her sides again and kneaded out tightness in her muscles. He was careful and gentle, picking up the pressure as he continued. She was aching for him, and he took his time.

She was spaced out when she heard him growl and felt him pull up her hips. She pushed herself to her hands and knees, enjoying the feeling of his hands holding her hips hard, the feeling of his erection against her ass.

"Sawyer?" Quinn growled in her ear, nuzzling his face to her hair.

"Yes," she whispered airily back to him.

He pulled back and slammed into her without a moment's hesitation. She cried out. She'd been ready, but damn she hadn't expected that. He leaned back over her, thrusting relentlessly. He braced on a hand while his other wrapped around her and rubbed one of her breasts.

She was hot and cold. Her body burned as he drove her further, but the water was cold, delivering a different sort of sensation. She didn't know whose dark hair was whose. It all just fell around her, blocking her vision of the world.

He pulled away again, grabbed both of her hips and yanked her back to him as he thrust more. That change left her reeling as he went deeper than before.

It was never-ending, and she couldn't resist the orgasm slamming into her. Her arms were shaking as her core muscles rippled. Quinn snarled behind her, continuing the hard pace. She went down to her elbows, unable to hold her body up any longer.

Her knees slipped next, leaving her on her stomach, but that didn't change anything either. Quinn was still in her, having just moved as she slipped down.

"We're not done," he growled down at her. It wasn't threatening, but a sensual growl that made her concerned whether she'd be able to walk after this.

"Oh fuck," she moaned, her forehead on the stone. She couldn't stop him from pulling her back up. He kept an arm wrapped around her torso and held her to continue.

His hand slid down her stomach as he thrust. She screamed out in pleasure as his finger found her clit and rubbed hard. It was like she'd been struck by lightning. Overly sensitive, she jerked at the touch. He didn't let her move away.

The second orgasm came harder. His name flew out of her mouth like a prayer and a plea. He pulled his finger from her clit and his hand went up and wrapped around the base of her neck. It wasn't tight. His thumb, as her orgasm continued to roll through her, pushed her jaw to turn her head. He leaned back over her and kissed her, burying himself one final time. The growl he gave as they kissed punctuated the orgasm she knew he was having.

They were panting like animals afterwards. He finally pulled out of her and she collapsed, sinking down onto the rock.

"Oh gods," she panted out like a fool.

"I take it I performed well?" he asked, some humor in his question.

"Arrogance doesn't become you," she moaned. At his soft laughter, she smiled. "I would almost say you're becoming cocksure on me."

"I get that play on words," he told her, smiling. She sighed happily. He had such a beautiful smile.

"Are you sure you're okay with...this? Us. Them." She tried to find the words. "We have to go find them."

"We're going to leave tomorrow. Yes. I'm fine. I couldn't... I couldn't be with you alone. Without them...Sawyer, I'm positive I would have killed you a long time ago. Before you, I didn't think there was a female on this earth I could trust, that I could like." Quinn laid next to her and pulled her close. "You changed...everything for me. You confronted my insecurities with courage, helped me overcome them, and you make me feel less wrong. The world makes me feel like a freak, but you just make me feel like a man who is just different. Someone who just needs to find his place."

"Where is your place?" she asked him softly.

"With the team...and you. They are *our* place. We'll find them. They are strong. Trust them and we will get back to them." Quinn placed his lips to her forehead. "Then we'll go home."

"Home sounds good." Home sounded so far away.

"It's the only one I've ever known. A real home, anyway."

"I'm glad we share it," she whispered into his chest.

"I am too. I am also...relieved that I shared this with you. It feels like my chest is lighter. I had never told...anyone what happened. My son. I never..."

"Thank you for choosing to share with me." Her heart broke for him again. "I know the pain."

"It's why I chose to share with you. You understand the loss. The anger. The hurt." She felt his chest rise with a deep breath. "We should get out of the water."

"We should," she agreed, nodding. He got up first and helped her up with a hand.

Together, they made their way to their clothing, finding towels placed out for them. Sawyer raised an eyebrow.

"Tez came to check on us."

"How do they have towels though?" Sawyer knew one of them had snuck up and placed them, but this village was completely devoid of anything from the civilized world.

"Probably Yasmin. This might be her home village, but if she interacts this much with other humans, then she might have contacts with others and have certain items she grew up with brought in." Quinn shrugged. "It's not a big deal."

"It's still weird." She frowned at him, hoping he would agree.

"I knew a Druid with a cellphone once. She never let me see and I didn't understand. I saw Vincent with one and Jasper explained what it was years later."

She rolled her eyes in light exasperation. He not only didn't agree with her, he introduced a weirder situation. But it gave her an idea.

"Maybe they have a satellite phone," Sawyer gasped. "We can call for help."

"Good plan," Quinn agreed. Once they were dressed, he offered his arm tentatively and she took it. They walked back to the village side by side, like they had walked before. A unit, comforting and friendly. He held her closer than before, though. It was the only change.

Once they arrived in the village, Yasmin stood waiting for them, smiling.

"Mates are a beautiful thing," she told Sawyer. She nodded slowly, feeling Quinn tense. "Come. Food is ready. We'll eat and talk about your situation now that you both have worked out whatever was between you." Her eyes fell on Quinn. "Less angry now, I hope? Healing? Tez won't let me let you leave until you show any progress."

Quinn only growled back at her. Sawyer swatted his stomach gently. He looked over to her and frowned.

"Be nice," she told him. "She's helping us, remember?"

He took a deep breath and nodded. She wasn't going to get in on whatever was happening between them, but she wasn't going to let him treat Yasmin badly. Yasmin was unfortunate enough to be in similar company of the women who'd hurt him. She didn't want to see Quinn continue the habit of judging someone not on their actions, but how they were born.

"I'm sorry," he said. "I will never forget the kindness you've shown my mate and I here."

"Then we will talk." Yasmin continued to smile and led them to a large hut. Sawyer had passed it before. It seemed like a community building of sorts.

Once inside, Sawyer decided to start asking questions. "I was wondering if you may have a satellite phone or-"

"We have no technology here because we can't make it. I'm sorry." Yasmin raised her hands. She sat down slowly on a mat.

"You have towels." Sawyer was confused. She needed to know what she was working with. "You don't make those."

"I receive things from hunters who know me passing through. They bring me pieces of the outside world, new textiles and the sort, and I give them some information about their hunt. It's a common occurrence. I know they aren't poachers and they know I won't come after them if they are in my territory." Yasmin sighed. "They offered me a cellphone once. Sadly, there's no use for it out here and my people here find technology uncomfortable. They don't want it."

"Where's the closest technologically capable village?" Quinn asked, leading Sawyer to sit with him across from Yasmin.

"Days away."

"Quinn, we can't just go find another village," Sawyer spoke out. "We have to go back to the camp."

"Why?" he asked.

"We need to make sure they aren't dead out there," Sawyer reminded him, closing her eyes. Their faces flashed in her mind. Part of her heart was secure, sitting right next to her, but the other pieces were out there.

"You're right. I was thinking we would find them, then lead them back. Don't worry."

"Quinn is a wolf. He's pack-oriented. If your pack is back where you fought Camila, then he will be unable to resist the urge to account for them," Yasmin added. "I didn't expect it from a feline though."

"I'm not a jaguar," Sawyer scoffed. "I'm a lot of things - a cat ain't one of them."

"Druids tend to equate someone's animal bond as a judge of their personality," Quinn explained. "I think a feline suits you...remember?"

"Okay, moving on," Sawyer said in a decided tone. "How many days back to the camp?" A small growl and Sawyer turned to see her jaguar walk in with Shade and Scout. Images flashed in her mind. Sawyer walking. Two dawns, one night. Fell. Dragged until another night. "Two days."

"Three," Yasmin corrected. "I went out when I felt Sombra coming back into my territory. She was dragging you. Another day to get here."

"And we slept for the day of travel here."

"And another day here, yes," Yasmin confirmed. "There's one problem."

"I don't like problems," Sawyer mumbled.

"Camila is waiting on the border. She wants your heads."

Sawyer felt like ice water had been thrown over her. "The way back to our teammates, to make sure they lived or died...is through the Druid we were sent here to kill." She considered that, grinding her teeth in some mix of frustration, dread, and general annoyance. She'd been hoping she stabbed the bitch hard enough to kill her.

"She's injured, if that helps. Apparently, someone got a couple good hits on her," Yasmin commented lightly.

"Damn right I did," Sawyer growled.

"What?" Quinn blinked several times, turning to look at her.

"You think I snuck you out from under her nose. Fuck no. I stabbed her," she told him, glaring. "I'm pissed off she's not dead, though."

"Well, a Druid's knowledge of local plants and resources makes us capable of handling wounds. Healing salves and the like. Might not be perfect, like having a healer on hand, but we survive. Some Druids I've met have sold these things to their local villages or given them out in return for working together."

"Why can't Camila be nice like that?" Sawyer asked incredulously.

"Camila is a self-important little girl who feels too deeply and refuses to understand the balance of the world we live in," Yasmin answered. "She took over that area, demanding the villages fall in line but receive no benefits for working together. When poachers started going into her territory, added with the villages that refused to work with her..."

"She lashed out and decided to purge the area of

'invaders,'" Quinn finished. "Let me guess, one of her animal bonds died to poachers."

"Yes," Yasmin confirmed softly. "Instead of remembering and accepting what we taught her-"

"We?" Sawyer perked up at that.

"Tez's mother and I trained her when she arrived, running away from her home to find a place where she and her magic would feel at peace. Like all Druids do, remember?"

Sawyer did, nodding.

"You want us to kill her." Quinn groaned. "Haven't we done enough?"

"If you want to get where you want to go, you'll need to."

Sawyer just listened to them argue now. Quinn wanted to find any way around Camila, while Yasmin told him there was no way. The moment they stepped foot in her territory, she was going to hunt them down.

Sawyer pulled her legs up and wrapped her arms around her knees, considering. Thinking.

What would Vincent want? Jasper? Zander? Elijah? What would any of them want from this situation? What skills could she draw upon to not only live through getting back to them, but also deal with problems she hadn't yet wanted to consider?

Leaving the jungle wasn't just going home. The WMC and the Councilwoman D'Angelo were still a problem. The mission could still succeed. Vincent had offered trying to find diplomatic solutions.

Sawyer tuned out of the argument completely as Tez joined and moved into the language she didn't understand. Her eyes fell on Sombra. The jaguar only sent her a willingness to do anything. She would follow Sawyer anywhere and do whatever was needed of her.

"I can kill her, but I need help," Sawyer said, cutting them both off. Those were the skills she had. She could kill. She could finish the job she started, one she thought she had already succeeded at.

"Sawyer-" Quinn switched back to English, desperate-sounding.

"I can, Quinn. I can sublimate, get inside her defenses. I did before, but it was pitch black and I barely had any back up, from only Sombra. With proper back up and help, I can take her down." When he tried to cut her off, she waved him down and kept going. "You should have never tried to fight her alone."

"You were safer. You and the team were safer together, but someone had to try." He looked furious with her.

"Did you forget you have an assassin?" She raised her arms, questioning him, motioning to herself.

"Assassin?" Yasmin gasped, looking at her.

"They once called me Shadow," Sawyer told her, smiling. Yasmin's eyes went to the size of dinner plates. Sawyer was glad to finally have that out. Shadow and Sombra. Yasmin's eyes flicked between the two of them, understanding her name might not have been the most appropriate, but it was the most fitting.

"We help," Tez said in broken English.

Sawyer grinned as Quinn cursed.

"Sawyer..."

"Quinn." She crossed her arms. "And thank you, Tez." That made Quinn growl. "Speaking of you and Yasmin. We had another goal out here, not just killing Camila for what she did. Our team leader had offered the WMC the chance to search for diplomatic options to keep Druids and those around them happy."

"Meaning a Druid from the Amazon would need to go

meet the WMC," Yasmin guessed. "Because the problem lies here, because our problems are different from the problems of other Druids around the world."

"Yes." Sawyer shrugged. "The Druid of the Florida Everglades doesn't kill people." The Everglades also didn't have rampant poaching, deforestation, and corrupt human governments ignoring the pleas for those things to stop. She didn't say that out loud.

"I can't do that," Yasmin sighed. "There's a reason a Druid has never walked into the halls of the WMC. I might recognize them as the government of my people, of all Magi, but I can't go to New York."

"Someone needs to. It shouldn't be long. I feel like they might be very accommodating."

"I can't."

"Yasmin, please," Sawyer begged. She didn't need to do this. This was extra, but she felt like she'd be failing Vincent if she didn't convince Yasmin to go.

Yasmin looked considering, shaking her head with her eyes closed. Tez whispered something, but Sawyer didn't understand.

"I'll think on it. We'll help with Camila and then give you an answer," Yasmin promised. Sawyer nodded. That worked for her. "Sleep tonight. We'll leave in the morning."

Quinn cursed and growled at Sawyer again.

She snarled back, baring her teeth. "We're going to fight our way out of this jungle, Quinn. Deal with it."

"I'm allowed to be mad at you for wanting to get yourself hurt."

"Don't start treating me like a princess now," Sawyer ordered. "You haven't before. I'll remind you...I saved you this time."

She left the hut to go back to her own. Quinn and all

their animals followed. When she made it, she rolled her eyes at the new, bigger cot inside. Yasmin was sneaky. Her weapons were clean and laid out on the cot as well. Nothing was unaccounted for, except the dagger she had handed Varya. She hoped that dagger had kept the blonde alive.

"I'm sorry. You're correct," Quinn said as he walked in. He mumbled the next part. "I've been saying that a lot recently."

"It's dangerous, and I'm worried too - but it's really our only option. If they died in that camp, I need to...I need to see. If that means finishing this god-forsaken mission and killing Camila to do it, then so be it."

"Of course." He sat down on the cot next to her weapons. "I agree, but..."

"It's natural not to want to see someone you care about get hurt," she murmured, kissing his forehead. "I'm not angry with you. A little annoyed."

"No, I've seen you angry. I know you aren't that. We will eat dinner tonight and rest well. Then we go hunting."

"Then we go hunting," she agreed.

30

SAWYER

The next dawn, Sawyer was ready already. She'd woken up before most in the village, Quinn by her side. They had prepared quietly. Yasmin showed up and gave them some sort of bread to eat.

"Are you going to go to the WMC and New York with us?" Sawyer asked immediately, taking the bread.

"I haven't decided," the Druid answered quietly. "I will once we see who does and doesn't survive this. I'm sorry. It's a...hard decision to make. I'm scared to leave my children, scared of leaving my bonds, scared of going back to a world I haven't been in for...decades. Since I was a girl."

"I understand." Sawyer sighed, nodding. The answer would come soon.

Very little was said as they left. Yasmin and Tez led, back down the path that Sawyer guessed they had been brought in on. It was a fast pace. Tez and Yasmin knew the area well and Quinn was accustomed to the outdoors, able to keep up. Sawyer was the slow one, but she cheated. She phased through obstacles and blinked when she fell behind.

"Wasteful," Quinn teased her.

"You all move faster than me and I'll be fine. My Source is deep enough to handle it and we'll be resting at least one more time before we run into her."

"Those points are all valid," he agreed. She liked the small smile on his face. She was glad to see he wasn't getting dark on her, withdrawn as they left to fight this bitch one more time for all the marbles. He'd pulled away a little while they had hiked into this hot, humid hell. She enjoyed that he was smiling on their path out. Then he asked a question she hadn't wanted to answer yet. "Are you ready to kill again?"

"To keep my family together?" Sawyer chuckled darkly. She'd done it before and failed. "Always."

Sombra brushed against her mind, reminding her of the last time she'd failed. It should have been Midnight, but Sawyer was growing used to her new jaguar. She wanted a lifetime with her new cat, and her men.

This time, she wouldn't fail.

THEY MUST HAVE BEEN GOING MUCH FASTER than Sawyer originally had. Yasmin raised her hand on the evening of the second day to stop them.

"We'll reach the disputed area between Camila and I by nightfall. It's not that we fight over it, but our magic intermingles. It's about two miles that belong to both of us. It's a natural overlap, really."

"Where did you find me and Quinn?" Sawyer crossed her arms, leaning on a tree to relax.

"We passed that already. You made it through this area somehow. Sombra brought you into my territory. Camila was too injured herself to chase until you were in my space. She wouldn't dare cross into my home to do it."

"Why did we stop here?" Sawyer felt like she was out of the loop. Quinn wasn't saying anything and didn't seem confused in the slightest.

"Camila can reasonably begin attacking us once we enter the overlap," Yasmin answered. "She would wait until we enter her territory fully, if she was smart, but I think she's too angry for that. She's in the middle of the overlap, waiting."

Sawyer couldn't see this overlap. It all just looked like jungle to her. "You can feel her," she said plainly.

"Of course. The magic in the world might be too much for you, Quinn, and Tez, but we Druids are strong enough to know where our kind is, especially so close."

"So we stopped why?"

"Yasmin wants us to make sure we're ready for this. She'll be fighting with Camila for control of the jungle. Any of us could die."

"She knows Tez is a healer," Yasmin whispered into the wind. Sawyer watched her hold her husband's hand. "She'll have her target once she knows that we're in the fight and she probably already assumes we are. Are you ready?"

"You all need to stop asking me that." Sawyer huffed. "Let's do this."

She started walking again.

The Druid Camila stood between her and her home, her men, her new family. Sawyer could only do what she did best now. Kill her for it.

"I guess we're doing this now," Yasmin said with a sigh. "Well."

"I'm not sure if Sawyer has ever backed down from a fight," Quinn commented, following her.

Together they walked as the sun began to set. With each minute, the lowering of the sun brought out something in Sawyer she'd long put away. When the mission had started, she'd been cranky, distracted by politics, the consequences of everything she did.

Now, with no soldiers, and only one objective, she focused.

She hadn't felt like this in a very long time.

It was a clarity of sorts. The last few fights she'd been in had been hurried, fights for her life or the lives of others.

This one was like every assassination she'd ever done. It was a hunt, and it brought her a focus. To fail would mean the deaths of others in an abstract way; she had the time to be patient and consider her options.

Like every assassination, she thought of objective wins and losses possible. To lose, any or all of her group would need to be dead and Camila would still be alive. The only win condition that included a death was if she died, but so did Camila. Sawyer didn't acknowledge the idea of the deaths of others. She would need to kill Camila fast enough to keep herself the largest threat and Tez, Quinn, and Yasmin as secondary threats.

She could use her sublimation to avoid dangers. Phasing was too risky with how fast things would be moving. She couldn't risk having a vine or snake in her body if she accidentally screwed up, or the chance of losing a limb.

Blinking would get her close to the Druid and do it quickly. If she got line of sight, or Sombra did and gave her a clear image, Sawyer could get on top of the Druid before she knew how to defend herself.

For the first time in her life, and probably the only time she ever would, she sent a private thanks to Axel Castello for making her the monster. It was proving to be her strongest skill, her ability to detach and analyze.

Night was falling, the sun nearly gone, when Yasmin whispered they were entering the overlap. None of them responded to her as they came upon Camila.

Sawyer was glad for the night, the darkness of the jungle. Now, focused, it didn't hold surprises for her. It was just her domain.

"Camila," Yasmin called out in Spanish. "You wanted to see my new charges?"

"They invaded my territory and attacked me, Yasmin!" Camila screeched. "Hand them over and walk away."

"They were doing their jobs, Camila. I warned you that attacking, thinking you could eradicate humans, only brought trouble. We're Magi and we answer to the W-"

"I answer to nobody!" Camila screamed. "This is my territory! I rule! No one is as powerful as me, and it will be run my way!"

"Camila, they just want to go home, and you are between them and their home," Yasmin continued to try. "I am going to go with them and talk to the WMC."

Sawyer didn't know this was part of the plan, but she could imagine Yasmin wanted to find any way for this to work that didn't result in her husband getting killed.

"I don't care about the WMC. What can they do to me?" Camila gave a shrill, nearly maniacal laugh.

"Send more soldiers until they put you down, trample your home." Yasmin was trying so hard.

Sawyer felt a breeze and nearly sublimated to let it take her into the darkness but refrained. She needed other things to be happening, a distraction before she moved in on the Druid in front of her.

"They've tried that. After dealing with those two, I need

to go clear out a secondary infestation. I'll kill anyone they send here." Camila's face was filled with nothing but contempt. "A plague, that's all humans are. I won't let them poison my home any longer."

"You are human," Yasmin told her. "Camila, you are-"

"I am much more than a human," Camila snapped. "My time alone here has shown me that I am so much more. The animals bow to my will. Trees grow when I snap my fingers. I'm a Goddess and my bonds are my family."

"I'm so sorry," Yasmin whispered.

"Hand them over, Yasmin."

"No." Sawyer watched the chin of her new friend go higher. "I'm sorry, but I can't let you kill more people."

"You know they were sent here to kill me!" Camila screeched, turning to glare at Quinn. "They even sent Rogue Wolf to do it."

"We were sent to investigate the reason you were acting like a bitch," Sawyer called out. "And kill you if we had to. I would say slaughtering innocent people in their homes and then attacking us in the middle of the night is reason enough to kill you."

"Yasmin! Hand them over!" Camila screamed one more time. "Don't make me go through you."

"No. They're right," Yasmin answered.

Sawyer felt power ripple out from each Druid and the rainforest sprang into life. Sawyer took her chance and blinked forward focused on Camila.

"Not this time," Camila snarled. Sawyer was nearly done pulling her dagger when the jaguar jumped her.

She was knocked to the earth and sublimated the moment she could, ignoring the ripping sensation of claws in her skin again. She was used to that pain now; it didn't surprise her like it had before.

As she drifted from the jaguar, Sombra pounced on it. Sawyer reformed, smiling at her Sombra. *Good girl*, she pushed through the bond as her jaguar tumbled into the underbrush with the other one. Sombra outweighed the other, and Sawyer was confident in her cat.

"TEZ!" Yasmin's scream shook through the rainforest and a wave of power blasted. Sawyer watched Tez get pulled up and saw Camila already hiding in her defensive layer of vines.

It would take too long to kill Camila now. She sublimated and pushed up to Tez, who was trying to pull the vine from around his neck as it pulled him higher. She reformed and grabbed the vine before she could fall back down.

"Be ready for a hard landing," she yelled to him in Spanish. She hoped he got it.

Vines once again tried to grab her, but she held on to the rope with Tez. She phased her wrist through a vine that grabbed it. She'd always been hard to hold down, and now she was putting it to the test, sublimating to get through the ones around her torso.

She finished cutting through the rope and grabbed Tez's shoulder. Holding him, she focused on the earth and blinked, the fall turning from thirty feet to only five.

It still knocked the air out of her. Tez put his hand on her and a flash of burning from his hands made her dazed. Only for a second. She blinked, and he nodded to her, before running back to Yasmin. She looked around to see Quinn pulling up a wall of earth, only for roots of the trees to bust through.

Sawyer blinked to him. "Where is she?"

"Hiding. She pulled her cocoon up into the trees. Yasmin

can't bring her down, only keep stuff off me. Tez needs to stay by her, though. He got grabbed trying to heal me."

"Make me a jump," she ordered.

He nodded, and she felt the earth beneath her rumble. She shot up on a pillar at a speed she had not expected. She would need to remember how he was for the next fight. She was beginning to realize there would also be more fights.

She was reaching the canopy when the pillar started to crumble instead of growing. A glance down told her roots and vines were tearing into it. She jumped for a branch and pulled herself into the trees.

She sublimated when something tried to grab her, ignoring what it was. A snake lunged for her when she reformed higher in the trees. She cut its head off after it missed its strike. She climbed higher, trying to keep her eyes open for where Camila would be hiding.

"Come out, you bitch," Sawyer snarled out into the trees. "Fucking coward."

She sublimated when an animal hit her back, letting it fall through her and down. She reformed, squatting on a thick branch, and glared at the monkey - then her eyes went wide.

Monkeys lived in family groups. She looked up slowly. There were dozens of them and she was smack dab in the middle.

"Fuck me." She growled and sublimated again as more dove for her. They were fucking screaming, but thankfully, the world sounded slightly quieter in her smoke. She flew through the trees, wasting magic and getting away from the damn monkeys, screaming as they jumped around and through her.

Sawyer needed to find the damn Druid.

She reformed for only a second and screamed. "COWARD!"

She sublimated again before the monkeys jumped on her. She took a second to see Quinn pulling earth around the group down below. They were counting on her to find this bitch. Yasmin was overwhelmed, fighting her side of the jungle versus Camila's. Tez was only a healer and Quinn...

Beautiful Quinn looked ready to die in a blaze of glory, trying to defend them if they needed it.

Vines were beginning to wrap around them, but they didn't seem scared. Sawyer wondered if Yasmin was going to block attacks like Camila was.

Sawyer went higher in the trees. She was going to run out of magic soon. She got to a branch she could stop on, sheathed her twelve-inch dagger and pull out her kukri. She hacked at the monkeys as they jumped on her. She swung blindly, pulling them off her back when she needed to. She got bit and scratched.

Eventually, there weren't any more, but Sawyer looked at her arms and wondered if it was worth the cost to stop and deal with them. They had bit holes in her. She swayed and continued her search.

She climbed higher. She had a feeling that Camila would have gone as high as she could, letting anything she could stand in the way.

"COWARD!" Sawyer screamed again. This bitch.

At nearly the top of a nearby tree was a mass of vines. They were protecting Camila. Sawyer blinked closer, and gasped as she realized that was nearly it. She had nothing left. In the course of the fight, she went from full to empty, and being injured wasn't helping. If she needed magic now, she'd need to pull directly from her life force, something

Sawyer had refused to do since the night she died. It was the thing that had saved her that night.

"Camila! You little bitch. Show yourself!" Sawyer roared at the Druid in her cocoon.

Vines came for Sawyer and she had one option. Holding her kukri in one hand, she ran for the cocoon. She jumped and landed on it. The vines grabbed on to her and tried to pull her away.

She drove the kukri in and pulled it back out, angry when she didn't see blood. She touched her life force and pulled it for magic, sublimating to get free of the vines trying to pull her away.

It felt like ten years came off her life in a split second.

She moved to the other side and stabbed inside again. This one got a scream from inside, muffled and scared. She didn't pull it out, but instead, she yanked it down, ripping open vines to reveal a bleeding Camila.

"Don't kill me," Camila begged, a bloody wound on her side. "I'll let you leave! Please!"

Sawyer considered it for one second. The vine creeping over her shoulder and around her neck made the decision though.

"There are no gods," Sawyer snapped, sinking her kukri into the Druid's chest before the vine could tighten further. It went limp.

All of it went limp and Sawyer, Camila's body, and her cocoon dropped like a stone through the air. Sawyer got her kill, and now she needed to not die when she hit the ground. They were nearly two hundred feet in the air. It was a long fall and Sawyer slammed into a branch. Pain bloomed through her body again. She knew there would be more if she didn't try her magic again.

She reached inside herself and pulled from her life force

again and felt the drag of her lifespan decreasing at a rapid rate again. She sublimated and slowed. The vines of Camila's cocoon were dragging down things with them, branches and the like. Sawyer moved out of the way and reformed on a safe branch. She sat down slowly on it. She still had a long climb down; watching Camila's body make the fall towards the group felt like ages. She groaned.

It was over.

They just needed to make the trek to the camp now, and hopefully not find the bodies of the people they cared about. She and Quinn couldn't do it without their team. They were both tied with a need to the other men. She needed them for her freedom and her heart. He needed them for his peace of mind and his heart. They were pack.

She slid off the branch onto the one below her. She could climb down just fine. No rush. She needed to make sure she didn't slip and she wasn't going to call her magic just to make the trip faster unnecessarily.

When she reached the bottom branch, she jumped and rolled to soften the fall. She didn't stand up immediately. She rested on her knees until Quinn walked over to her and pulled her up.

He touched her cheeks gently and pulled her into a kiss that felt like home. Really, it felt like their swimming hole. The woods. His fire pit and lean-to.

"Well, the assassin once called Shadow," Yasmin sounded impressed, a little hysterical, and tired. "You are now...the second person on earth to kill a Druid...that isn't a Druid."

"Quinn being the first?" she asked, pulling away from her feral lover. Lover. Such a good word in her mind.

"Yes, but you are most special. You beat her in combat." Yasmin sighed, smiling wearily.

"Oh, good for me," Sawyer replied with a healthy bit of sarcasm. She was only happy about one thing. She'd won so she could go home.

There was still so much to do though.

"We need to get to the campsite and see..." Quinn trailed off.

"Now's your chance to decide, Yasmin. Follow us and go back to New York...or turn around and go home."

"After that...I'm coming with you. Tez will stay with our children. I will take some of my animal bonds. They are already on their way. They will catch up before dawn." The Druid reached out to her and Sawyer closed the distance. She was surprised by Yasmin touching her cheek but was too tired to react in any real way.

"I see why Sombra waited so long for you," she whispered. "You are a fierce warrior, Sawyer Matthews."

"I try," Sawyer chuckled in exhaustion. "I'll be damned if some fucking bitch out in the woods stops me from going home."

"Of course," Yasmin said, smiling sadly. "Thank you, for being so brave and doing this."

"I didn't do it alone," she reminded the Druid, waving around at all of them. Then she swayed on her feet. Quinn caught her and held her up. Tez jogged to her and Sawyer watched the monkey bites form into tiny scars as his burning hot hands grabbed her forearms.

"Small. Easy to heal. Scars fade quickly," Tez said in that broken Portuguese.

"Thanks," she mumbled, tired.

"He can't replace your magic, of course. You will need to take things very easy for quite some time. You've completely burned out," Yasmin told her gently.

"Yeah. I pulled from my life force there at the end," she explained. "I know I'm burned out now."

"That was foolish," Quinn murmured in her ear, still holding her to his body.

"It was the right thing to do," she retorted, leaning on him. She wasn't bleeding anymore, but she still ached. Sombra, Shade, and Scout walked into view. Other animals did as well. "I killed a Druid," she giggled.

"I would recommend never going into any forests, jungles, or national parks for the rest of your life," Yasmin said pragmatically. "You might not be welcome."

"Can I visit you here?" She probably never would, but Sawyer felt the need to ask. Maybe one day she would revisit that waterfall with Quinn.

"Yes. If you come back to see us, I would always welcome you."

"Then let's get the fuck out of here," Sawyer ordered and began to walk, dragging Quinn with her.

She didn't make it very far. Her burned out Source and depleted life force dragged her into unconsciousness.

31

QUINN

Quinn grabbed her before she hit the dirt, knowing she wasn't going to make it very far.

"I've never met such a warrior," Yasmin commented. "We should rest until dawn."

"I can carry her," Quinn said, lifting Sawyer into his arms. "How long do we need to walk?"

"From here? *Maybe* only another day. We should be back at your camp by midday, I think." Yasmin shrugged slightly. "Tez will be staying here. I will be going with you."

Quinn looked at the other male. They were so similar and so different. Both marked by who their mothers had been, powerful because of it. But Tez had been raised with such a different outlook on life. A community built around him. Quinn had been raised alone by his mother, who could barely tolerate other humans unless they were other Druids. Quinn's childhood friends had been wolves, Tez's had been his village and his future wife.

He awkwardly extended a hand. Tez took it and they shook slowly.

"Thank you," Quinn told him in his native tongue. Tez smiled and clasped his hand with both of his own after that.

"Continue to heal and grow, Wolf. We will tell the world that you are no longer a rogue, but rather a warrior." Tez backed away, letting go. "Until we meet again."

Quinn smiled. Warrior. Yes, that's what he would like to be remembered as. He turned away to give Yasmin and Tez privacy to say goodbye. He stared down at the peaceful, exhausted face of his own female.

She'd done what he couldn't. She had climbed the trees and fought the wilds just to kill the last dangerous obstacle between them and their family.

He knew it was the only thing she could do. There was no other option in her mind. He loved her for that strength and passion.

She'd changed everything.

"Let us go," Yasmin said quietly, walking up next to him. He nodded. That was another woman who changed everything. Maybe he'd been blind growing up, to ignore that many Druids were non-violent and kind; maybe he just had met all the wrong ones, unlucky in his experience. Yasmin changed him. He respected her. She was about to do what no Druid had ever done, especially not one from the depths of the Amazon.

They moved quietly and quickly in the night. They were only slowed by Sawyer's sleeping form in his arms, which he was careful not to jostle. Sombra walked directly at his side, as if she couldn't bear to go far from her unconscious Magi.

"You didn't say anything about wanting Camila's body as proof," Yasmin finally said as dawn crept up.

"No. I have a feeling they will believe us when we tell them," Quinn explained. He would rather carry his mate than drag a body or carry a head. "I have you. They won't call you a liar."

"Good point." She sighed, nodding. "What is home for you?"

"Why?" He frowned.

"Curious."

"A...big white house on a few square kilometers of land where no one bothers us. We live far enough away from any cities that I can go out into our woods and feel alive. Sombra will have lots of space to run, I hope. Shade and Scout have never complained, and I keep them away from the locals. There's no Druids nearby, so the territory is mine, I guess." Quinn missed it. He loved the wildness and expansive nature of the Amazon, but he missed his plot of land, his white house, his garden, and his lean-to.

Home.

"And this team?"

"They are also home, yes. Vincent, our leader. He's dark, like Sawyer. They are well-suited in that way. She grew up with two of my packmates, Zander and Jasper. Good men, but very different from each other. She and Zander argue a lot, but she once told me that they love each other so fiercely that they fight with and for each other." Quinn took a deep breath. "Elijah. He's a cowboy and my closest friend. I consider him a brother in some ways and a convenient lover in others. He's a happy man, but he's protective as well."

"Over?" Yasmin sounded genuinely curious.

"Me. Her. The team. He's a kind man." Quinn missed him. As he held Sawyer, he also missed Elijah. He knew his cowboy, if alive, was probably worried sick over them. He privately, for a moment, hoped that the separation convinced Elijah to finally admit his feelings for their female. "We're all hers, in the end."

"Excuse me?" Yasmin laughed. "Really?"

"Yes and she's possessive. Once hers, you stay hers. I fought it for a long time, but she's hard to fight against, even when she doesn't know there's a battle." Quinn smiled down at her. "I thought I could never love because I had never loved before." Not like he did her.

"Oh, I knew you were lost the moment you woke up. I assumed you were mates, by what Sombra had told me. How she saved you from Camila."

"Now we are," Quinn whispered. "She has four mates now and she'll have a fifth before the year is up. Elijah is fighting harder than me...well, he's not even fighting, he's just running. He's admittedly being a coward about it. He loved someone once and lost that person. Now he cares again and is scared."

"Love is scary," Yasmin agreed softly. "He doesn't love you?"

"Probably in some ways, the ways I understand. Brotherly, friendly, just as a physical lover, but he and I have never been so devoted to be mates, only family."

"All love is love, Wolf. Pack, family, lover, friend. *Child.* It's all the same love."

"I know that now," he murmured, still looking down at Sawyer's face. "I know that now."

An hour later, Sombra snarled and Sawyer stirred uncomfortably. Quinn stopped walking and lifted soft earth to make her a bed raised from the bugs of the undergrowth.

"Is she okay?" Yasmin knelt next to Quinn as he laid her down.

"I don't know," he answered. "I don't know."

Sombra continued to snarl at Sawyer's tossing and turning body.

32

SAWYER

Nightmares came at the most inconvenient times, Sawyer realized, as darkness loomed on her. She was too exhausted to wake up.

She was drained and tired, which took her back to the end of a hard assassination. She burned out trying to get out. The guards she hadn't wanted to kill had chased her out right after she killed their master.

Now she was in front of her own.

"You. Got. Caught." Axel snarled out every word.

"I'm here, and they don't know it was me," she tried to explain.

A hand cracked across her face, hardened by the shield Axel always wore in her company unless she was unconscious. Stumbling, she hit her knees. She still had blood on her hands from the kill.

Blood on her hands...

She closed her eyes as Axel grabbed her hair and pulled her up.

"You gave away who sent the killer. They all know you're mine! Now I have to play damage control, tell my other allies why I had him killed, or they won't trust me. Politics, stupid bitch, you need to remember the politics!" He threw her away with her hair and she fell back to the ground, the marble of his home in Rome.

Something brushed against her mind. A feline. She gasped. Midnight was gone. There was no...

Sawyer snapped in lucidity. Sombra. Sombra was waiting for her to get up, to wake and go home. Her warrior Magi was scared in her sleep, and she didn't understand what evil was hurting her Magi.

Sombra could help her become lucid enough. That was fucking amazing. She had another ally in her fight for her peace of mind.

Sawyer smiled. Axel was still raging. No. Nightmare-Axel, not the real man.

She laughed. Why had she ever feared this man? She had just killed a fucking Druid. What the fuck was Axel compared to that, except a bad fucking memory?

Axel threw out a kick and Sawyer grabbed his ankle. She yanked it hard and brought him to the floor with her. She jumped on top of him and wrapped her hands around his neck.

"I'll fight you every night," she snarled down at him. "But I refuse to be fucking scared of you anymore."

With her hands around his throat, she pulled up and slammed him into the marble. Over and over. The shield broke and his head cracked open.

"I'll fight you, then I'm going to wake up and kiss one of the men I love. You can go to hell. One day, you won't even have power here."

She pulled herself out of the darkness.

～

SAWYER WOKE up with a start and grinned at the confused Quinn and Yasmin beside her. Sombra climbed into her lap.

"It was a nightmare," she quickly explained to them. "I'm fine. Sombra helped me."

"Good." Quinn sighed in relief. "I was scared you might be poisoned or bit by something."

"Tez wouldn't have missed that," Yasmin sternly said to him.

"I still worried," he mumbled, looking chastised.

"How close are we?" she asked as she stood up. Sombra basically glued herself to Sawyer's leg, with the intention of never leaving her alone again, even in sleep. She would watch her Magi while she slept now. Protect her.

Sawyer's heart swelled.

"Only a few more hours, I think," Yasmin told her. "Can you walk? Need more rest?"

"No, we're getting back to that fucking camp." Sawyer was on a mission. Nothing was going to keep her from seeing it through. Her men would be in that camp, dead, or they wouldn't and would hopefully be alive.

But she needed those answers, not more rest.

"Thank you for carrying me," she whispered to Quinn, taking his arm as they continued to walk.

"No reason to make you walk the entire trip when I could carry you. I will always help carry you."

"As long as you accept that I'll return the favor," Sawyer reminded him.

"Of course." He turned and placed his lips to her temple.

Sawyer knew the exact moment they were close to the campsite. She could smell it.

"Oh god," she said in a muffled tone thanks to the hand she put over her mouth.

"I will collect dog tags and then bury the bodies. They

are too old to try and take home." Quinn was grim. Yasmin gasped when they walked into the camp and saw the destruction.

"You survived this?" she asked, looking at Quinn and Sawyer.

"It was like a horror movie," Sawyer whispered. She looked up and gagged. The bodies were still in the trees. "Quinn..."

"I'll get all the dog tags for the families and IMAS. You breathe."

"I'm going to our section of the camp and..." She was off to look for very specific bodies.

"Of course," he murmured to her.

She walked through the destroyed campsite, her pulse racing. The world was quiet around her, too quiet for her. She left Quinn to the grim task of the other bodies, her eyes trained on their old tents.

How long ago was that night? It seemed like ages, a lifetime. New York felt like a distant memory. Home felt like a dream that was never real.

She stumbled to the tents and pulled open the flaps. No bodies. There were no bodies in the area. She even searched the bushes and growth nearby, hoping they had not been dragged away.

Some tiny piece of hope began to form in her chest. She didn't realize how much she had thought they died. She closed her eyes for a moment.

They got out. She repeated the words like a prayer. They got out.

She found their old bags and began to collect them. These were their things. She treasured them. Bags of clothing, snacks, personal items. She was inside the tent

Elijah, Zander, and Jasper had been sharing that night when she found it.

Elijah's sketchbook.

She snatched it quickly. Of all the things, she wasn't going to let that get lost. She would give it back to him. She held it to her chest. It was the only real personal item any of them had brought here. She wondered if he even noticed its absence if he was alive out there, hoping for Sawyer and Quinn to leave the Amazon.

"Your team was smart to leave," Yasmin commented. "To run and get out."

"Yes, they were," Sawyer agreed softly, keeping the sketchbook to her chest. She felt that little piece of hope for them grow. Were they tucked away in a hospital somewhere? Healthy? Did any of them get hurt? They had been secure when she ran out into the night for Quinn. "Quinn?"

"They are none of the bodies I can find," he called back to her. "They should be alive."

She placed a hand over her eyes. Her chest was tight, her shoulders shaking. She didn't let Yasmin touch her, backing away from the Druid that tried to comfort her.

"I'm fine." Sawyer turned away, clutching the sketchbook like it was a precious treasure. To her, in that moment, it was. She should have asked Quinn to try to track Elijah with it, but she couldn't bear to part with it. It seemed too important.

"We can walk back to the village. Seven days, though we can shorten that time by moving faster and walking through the nights," Quinn spoke as he walked over to her and Yasmin. She could hear the jingle of dog tags. So many. He held one out to her and she took it slowly, terrified. He'd said none of them were her team but...

It was hers.

Sawyer Matthews

IMPO

Her Registration Number. 59045673.

"Oh fuck," she mumbled. She touched her neck. She wasn't wearing it anymore. She'd never noticed. "I wonder where the one in my boot went..."

"You didn't have any when I found you. Either of you." Yasmin shrugged. "They will be lost forever, it seems."

"It seems," Sawyer whispered, pushing the dog tag into her pocket.

"Yasmin, can you bring any bodies out so I can bury them?"

"Of course, Wolf."

Magic filled the air. Cleaner than Camila's. Peaceful, but still it felt wild to Sawyer. She understood what Quinn had meant. The magic felt the exact same, with only minute differences based on personality. The same but different.

Then the earth shook.

Bodies were pulled into their graves, forever a part of the Amazon. Only their names would go home.

"I shall take over this area when I return," Yasmin promised. "I will make a memorial to this place, a symbol that we should never let these horrors happen again."

"Thank you." Sawyer and Quinn said it at the exact same time.

"We should get moving. No reason to stay here with the stench. The fight was..." Quinn frowned. "Six days ago?"

"Something like that," Sawyer confirmed. "The survivors, if they moved back towards the village, could still be on the path."

"They might have already made it out, but it would be

the first place anyone starts their search for us." Quinn sighed.

They started moving on in silence, leaving behind the horrors of the campsite. Sawyer was glad to see it go. They didn't bother grabbing tents to use, but Sawyer grabbed their personal bags. Between the three of them, the team would at least get their things back, even if they were a bit ruined.

When the sun began to dip below the horizon, they stopped for rest. Yasmin made a hut of vines for them. Sawyer built a fire. Quinn went out and took down a capybara for a meal with Yasmin's blessing. Sawyer had the fire going when he was back. He and Yasmin butchered the animal together while Sawyer just sat on an earth spot Quinn had made to be chairs.

Sawyer looked at the sketchbook, fighting her own curiosity. She wanted to keep moving, to get it back to him, but they all needed sleep. They had been running ragged for days. Yasmin and Quinn hadn't slept since before Camila. They needed to rest.

"He doesn't have to know," she whispered to herself, her hand trailing over the cover of the black, leather-bound sketchbook. She tried to convince herself not to, she really did, but her curiosity won.

She opened it slowly, trying to be gentle with the wet pages. She hoped it wasn't completely ruined. She didn't want to see Elijah's beautiful work ruined. That would be her excuse if he asked if she looked through it. She was checking on it.

She saw Quinn's face first. Stunning, with his signature and rare smile; his eyes were bright, even in black and grey. It was a little blurry from the water, but Sawyer could still see the skill and time Elijah had put into the image. Sawyer didn't dare touch it, for fear of ruining it.

The next page was Quinn again. Sculpted back and scars and the perfected toned ass. Sawyer resisted an immature giggle. If she could draw, she would pick similar subject matter.

Nearly the first third of the sketch book was only Quinn, then it changed. She started showing up. Tired. Fighting. Her hair flying while she danced around the ring.

Her over a book with Quinn, smiling at Quinn as he read the text.

Her eyes watered again. Elijah was fucking around, he had to be. He'd made her look beautiful.

The next page was her smiling at something that was obviously funny. The page after that was her and Zander shoving each other in some argument, or maybe they were just roughhousing.

One of her curled up in a recliner in the basement, watching a movie.

The rest of the sketchbook was just her. Her face, her body, posing, doing mundane things, real and imaginary moments. Sleeping, awake. Clothed and nude. He even added her scars to the ones where she was undressed.

Her heart pounded. There were nearly twenty pages empty at the end, but that was all. Everything in the book was a dedication of sorts to her and Quinn. All of it. Nothing for work.

It should have freaked her out, but instead, it just made her miss him. It also made her feel precious and beautiful. She blinked hard several times.

"God. Why am I crying so much?" she growled out, rubbing her eyes after she closed the sketchbook. It was probably the physical stress of the mission making her feel emotionally raw. She knew the reason for it, but she had never cried quite this much, and it was beginning to seriously annoy her.

"Sawyer?" Quinn frowned at her as he left Yasmin, who began cooking meat for them. She threw out large chunks of raw meat, including a leg, and Sawyer watched Sombra, Shade, and Scout each grab a piece and carry it away. Sombra sent Sawyer a bolt of delighted happiness.

"Sombra is happy for the meat," she told Yasmin, ignoring Quinn for a moment.

"Capybara is her favorite. She'll need to find something new when she leaves with you. This might be the last time she ever has it," Yasmin explained. Sawyer loved and hated that the Druid knew more about her animal bond than Sawyer did.

"Where are your bonds?" Sawyer had yet to see them.

"Oh, I'm taking a few of my smaller ones," Yasmin answered. She looked up and Sawyer's eyebrows raised high as two monkeys dropped down. A parrot of some sort landed on Yasmin's shoulder. They weren't big predators, but having three was a show stopper. "I'm leaving Sombra's mother to protect my children. You would like her, I think, but she and Sombra haven't gotten along since Sombra hit her adult years. Sombra doesn't take well to her mother's authority anymore."

"Of course she doesn't," Sawyer mumbled, glancing over to the black jaguar that was devouring the raw leg.

"Sawyer?" Quinn was annoyed. She looked up at him and smiled.

"I'm fine. I got nosy and looked through Elijah's sketchbook. I'm just feeling a bit...emotional."

"He is a skilled artist," he told her, sitting down. They both watched the fire and Yasmin turned meat over on the wood with a practiced hand. "I could have told you what was in the sketchbook. He will not be happy you looked."

"You knew?" Sawyer put the sketchbook in her lap and looked at him.

"He normally enchants his sketchbooks so they can't be opened, but a strong enough Magi can force it and break the enchantment." Quinn shrugged. "I got nosy one day as well."

"You probably were just wondering what sort of secrets he had that he was trying to protect."

"Yes. The same reason I snooped around your room when you first came to live with us," Quinn admitted.

Sawyer smiled. How things changed. He'd been so withdrawn from her at the time, so far from her, so feral. A wolf on a leash held by a toddler, watching her like his next meal.

"Here," Yasmin said, offering them each a piece of cooked meat. "No dishes. You'll need to eat with your hands."

Quinn didn't seem concerned, taking the meat and tearing a piece off. Sawyer didn't question it. When in Rome and all that shit. She took her own piece and hissed at the heat. It didn't seem to bother Yasmin or Quinn, so she sucked it up and bit into the giant rat meat. Capybaras were the largest rodent in the world, she knew that. Sawyer was eating rat in the Amazon with a Druid and Quinn fucking Judge.

The places her life took her were beginning to get a bit outrageous.

"I'm sorry the fight was so hard on you," Yasmin finally whispered.

"Excuse me?" Sawyer frowned.

"I could have helped more but I held back," Yasmin

disclosed gently. "I disagreed with Camila's use of the animals and putting them in danger, and I didn't want more to die in the fight. I understand why so many died, so you could put her down, but I wasn't willing to put more in danger. Wild animals should not fight in wars made by humans."

"I understand." Sawyer hadn't even thought about it. She did what she needed to do and that was it. "No worries. You don't need to apologize. I get it. A lot of living creatures died, not just humans."

"The ecosystem here is fragile and any more could have had serious repercussions." Yasmin sighed. "I just wanted to explain, now that it was over."

Silence fell over the camp.

It was over, and Sawyer didn't really care who had done what. It was just fucking time to get the hell out of this god damn rainforest.

After they ate, Sawyer walked into the new vine hut and curled up to get sleep. Quinn tentatively laid next to her and she rolled to put her head on his chest. Yasmin laid on the other side, falling asleep quickly, with her bonds crowding around her.

Sawyer fell asleep to Quinn playing with her wild, untamed hair, his steady breathing better than a lullaby.

THE NEXT MORNING, they were off in silence. There was no reason to stop their progress for another couple of days and Sawyer worked hard to keep the breakneck pace that Quinn and Yasmin were pushing.

Then Yasmin stopped.

"Hold," she ordered, tense. Quinn began to growl, and

Sawyer wondered if he was going to shift down into his wolf form. She didn't see him use it very often, but his other magic was probably better in a big fight.

Sawyer unsheathed her kukri, hoping it wouldn't be needed. They were so close to getting out. She had no magic. She didn't know if she could handle another fight. It would have to be Quinn and Yasmin.

"Put your hands in the air and identify yourself!" a masculine voice yelled out.

"No," Yasmin said with boredom. "I don't think I will."

Vines yanked soldiers from the trees and out of bushes. Sawyer's eyebrows wanted to leave her forehead.

"I'm Yasmin, Druid of the Amazon. I'm escorting Quinn and Sawyer to safety. You are?"

One of the soldiers was pulled closer. He was pale and Sawyer wanted to laugh.

"Gunnery Sergeant Dennis, Team Ares, IMAS Spec Ops," he answered.

"Release them," Quinn grunted. "They are good guys."

The soldiers all dropped to the earth.

"I'll recommend not threatening things you find in this area. They tend to fight back," Yasmin told the soldiers, smiling.

"Special Agent Quinn Judge?" The gunnery sergeant looked from Quinn to Sawyer then Yasmin. "We're here to find survivors and finish the mission."

"Mission is complete and successful," Quinn told him. "The Druid Camila, who killed the people of the villages and was pushing her territory out, is dead. Yasmin has agreed to play diplomat and go to New York to meet with the WMC to discuss ways of stopping this from happening in the future."

"Well, damn," the soldier sighed out. "Any other survivors?"

"Not that we've found," Sawyer answered. "Quinn..."

"I have the dog tags of those who died in the camp," Quinn supplied, pulling them from his pocket. Sawyer hated seeing how many of them there were. "I also buried the bodies. They had been..."

"You don't need to finish that. Thank you for these," Dennis replied, taking the dog tags and handing them off. "I take it you are all trying to get out of here?"

"Damn fucking right," Sawyer mumbled. "Done playing in the goddamned dirt."

"Come on. We have transports. We've only been coming in for a few days and we've been taking it slow, since we didn't know the threat level."

"Threat level is now low. We can move quickly," Quinn informed him.

Sawyer followed her teammate through the Spec Ops team, continuing their long walk out of the jungle.

They were so close.

33

ZANDER

Zander paced in the hotel room he and Jasper had been given.

Days without word from the Spec Ops team in the jungle. He hoped they weren't dead too. He really did. They were ballsy men, jumping in when they saw the destruction of the group that went before them.

"Elijah still angry at us?" Zander asked, hearing the door open. He knew it was Jasper.

"Yes, but since Vincent is letting him stay here in Brazil, he's feeling a little better. He's still worried out of his mind." Jasper walked in, fell on his bed and proceeded to pull off his prosthetic.

"We're all worried out of our minds, but..." Zander shook his head.

"We'd just get killed running out there," the golden boy finished.

"Yeah..." Zander took a deep breath. Hardest decision of his life. Leaving hell to save people. The healer in him knew he made the right decision, but his heart and passion were furious with him. Conflicting sides.

He'd gone with the healer half-knowing it was the thing Sawyer would have wanted him to do, but he still hated it. He should have been out there to heal her if she needed it.

"Have you seen Vincent?" he asked Jasper, who was laying out on his bed, with his shirt off now. Zander didn't blame him. It was fucking hot.

"He's been at the embassy for the last couple of days, talking to James and others. He and Varya are really the only two who are willing to tell outsiders what happened. The soldiers? They are all wrecks. Vincent is trying to keep us out of it."

"What do those fucks in New York want?" Zander glared over at Jasper, annoyed.

"They want to know why the only two unaccounted-for members of our team are the ones who need to be accounted for," he answered softly. "There's a sneaking suspicion, it seems, that Quinn and Sawyer took the chaos as a chance to run."

"God damn it," Zander snapped. "Are they serious? We were slaughtered. Quinn was right. Seventy-five percent of the entire fucking mission party is dead, and they think Sawyer and Quinn ran for their freedom? They probably fought for their goddamned lives and..."

"Zander, we can't think they're dead yet. We can't."

"What else am I supposed to think?"

"That Quinn and Sawyer are the two strongest members of this team, both in experience and magic. That Quinn is epically powerful for a Magi, and Sawyer is downright fucking ruthless when she's in a hard fight." Jasper sighed, and Zander saw sparks, not real, dance in the air. He watched them; Jasper never used his illusion magic. It was rare, and normally only when he was insanely bored.

"I know." He looked away from the pretty little sparks

and looked at Jasper again, who was playing with a small illusion above him. Fake black smoke swirled. If Zander touched it, nothing would change.

"Get some sleep. You're burned out and need it," Jasper ordered him.

"I am," Zander sighed, pulling off his shirt and falling onto his own bed. He'd burned out on the hard hike out of the jungle. He'd been fighting it. He once again tapped into his life force a little too much to keep everyone alive and with their limbs.

He and Rodriguez couldn't save them all, but they had saved as many as they could. Not enough, but they did their best.

Zander's eyelids were heavy, and he was half-asleep as Jasper began to sing softly. A hidden talent, Jasper's singing was something that happened so rarely that he often forgot the golden boy could. It had been years since the last time he heard the golden boy's voice in a quiet moment. Zander only heard it on accident, when he was trying to sleep. Jasper never shared it openly.

Zander, as the soft singing lulled him under, wondered if Sawyer knew he had such a voice.

"ZANDER, GET UP!" Jasper ordered loudly. Zander groaned, shaking his head. "Damn it, there's news. Team Ares is back. They have them. Zander, they have Sawyer and Quinn."

He had never woken up so fast. He promptly rolled out of the bed, scrambling for his shirt. Jasper was already running out of the room.

Zander gave up on his shirt and found shoes instead. He broke out into the hallway and saw Jasper at the elevator.

They were too high to try going down the stairs. Fourteen floors. The elevator was faster.

Elijah was next, nearly running into Zander. They glared at each other, then grinned, hugging tightly.

"Vincent said he'll meet us at the embassy. Once Sawyer and Quinn are checked for injuries, we're flying out immediately," Jasper called down to them. "Zander, get your shirt. Elijah, put your clothes on."

Zander looked at the cowboy. He was only in his briefs. Elijah laughed, pushing back into his own room. Zander was shaking his head, grinning, as he went back in his room and found his shirt. They didn't have any other clothes, theirs lost in the jungle. At least things were in New York for them. Zander knew this entire thing wasn't over, but they were about to at least go back to their own country - one step closer to home.

He met Elijah and Jasper at the elevator. They took an SUV from the mission to the embassy and found Vincent waiting for them at the door.

"They'll be here in about an hour. I told Jasper. Figured you would all want to shower," Vincent said, smiling.

"Fuck that," Zander replied, walking inside. They could smell his dirty ass; he didn't care. Elijah was laughing at the world. It seemed everything was funny to the cowboy now. After days of his cranky ass, Zander was genuinely relieved to see Elijah smiling.

They were led to a meeting room to wait in quiet. They stayed silent, but he could feel the excitement in the air.

Sawyer and Quinn were coming back to them. They were alive. He needed to see it to believe it, but now he had hope. He hoped they were in good health, because if they weren't, he couldn't help them. Well, he could. He'd probably kill himself in the effort, but he would help them if they needed it.

"Do you know anything about their status?" Jasper asked Vincent, who nodded.

"They seem healthy and Team Ares says they have a few surprises in store for us and our superiors, but wouldn't elaborate."

Zander nodded slowly. Good. They seemed healthy. That was good. He wrapped his arms around himself. They were coming back and they didn't need him to heal them. He leaned back in the chair, his eyes drifting closed again. He knew it was exhaustion driven by his burn out.

He was woken up by Jasper again, this time calmer, a whisper that they were nearly there. Zander nodded, his heart immediately starting to race.

He began to worry about something else, something he knew better than to worry about. Would they hate the team that left them? Would they really understand? Did they see Zander and Vincent deciding to get everyone out as a betrayal?

Zander followed everyone out of the meeting room and down in front of the embassy.

He saw the Humvees drive up.

It had been over a week since he last saw them, his lover and his friend. Even Vincent was getting antsy.

The Humvees stopped.

Zander was getting annoyed.

Soldiers poured out, but still he didn't see Quinn or Sawyer.

"They brought back a Druid," Elijah whispered in awe. "Shit."

"I feel her," Zander snapped. "I don't care."

"It's not our problem anymore," Vincent reminded

them. "It's absolutely not our problem. We're taking them, we're leaving for New York, wrapping up, and going home."

Zander nodded in agreement.

Then he saw her. She was beautiful and *alive*. Quinn was next and glued himself to her side. He ignored how tired they looked, ignored how Sawyer stumbled slightly. He ran for her.

"Sawyer," he gasped, wrapping his arms around her waist.

"Zander!" she cried out happily, holding him as well. He spun her.

She was *alive*.

"Sawyer, I'm sorry," he began quickly. "I had to make a decision. We didn't know where you and Quinn were, but people were hurt, and many were dying and I had to..."

"It's okay," Sawyer cut him off, slapping a hand over his mouth. "You're alive. The team is alive. We're alive. It's okay. You made the right decision." She moved her hand away again and he nodded slowly.

"I thought I failed to save you. I trusted you and Quinn to help yourselves, but I've been living in fear that I failed both of you." He needed to admit it to her. He had to.

"Thank you. Stop worrying. See? We trust each other, and things work out." She pulled back. He released her slowly, his heart feeling less poisoned by his own hard decision. He watched her hug Vincent, then Jasper. Zander's eyes drifted to Quinn and Elijah, who were holding on to each other like their lives depended on it.

They moved inside to the meeting room again, where Zander watched Vincent break, grab Sawyer and pull her into a kiss that should have been private. Even Zander felt some heat rise over his cheeks as Elijah coughed in the corner to break it up.

"I'm so glad you're alive," Vincent whispered to her. "I love you. Don't do that again."

"I love you too, and I'll try not to," Sawyer retorted, grinning. She looked over to Zander as he sat down. She settled in next to him. "I love you too. I should have said it earlier, before this. Zander Wade, I love you. I'll always fight my fucking hardest to come back to you. To you, Jasper, Vincent, all of you."

"I love you," he murmured back. He'd been hoping to hear those words for weeks now, and she'd never returned them. Now she had, and he felt like it was all fucking worth it.

"Someone open the door again," Quinn ordered.

Jasper pulled open the door and Zander chuckled at the wolves scrambling to get inside.

They were all stunned into silence by the massive black jaguar that jumped onto the table.

"Everyone, meet Sombra. She's a nightmare, but she's mine...like nightmares tend to be," Sawyer told them all, reaching out to rub the big cat's belly.

Sombra rolled onto her back so Sawyer could really scratch the barrel chest.

"You have a new animal bond," Vincent said, as if he was trying to make himself believe it. Zander couldn't blame him. It was a very big cat, and of all the things that happened on this mission, this had been...a completely unconsidered possibility.

"I do, and our next guest is the one who named her." Sawyer grinned and pulled her cat, causing the jaguar to growl. "Get off the fucking table, Sombra. Seriously. I want to eat real food on it before we leave."

The second growl was louder than the first but Sombra

got up, hopped off the table, and lay down near Shade and Scout.

Zander was still just blinking. His girl got herself a fucking jaguar for a new animal bond. That was telling.

"Next guest?" Elijah asked loudly, sounding concerned.

"Everyone meet Yasmin, Druid of the Amazon," Quinn announced, pointing at the woman who stood just outside the door. Zander leaned over to see her out there and watched her walk in. She had to be nearly in her forties, healthy, but not young like they were. "She saved our lives after Sawyer injured Camila and rescued me."

"Sombra led us to her and her husband healed us," Sawyer continued to explain.

"I can tell them." Yasmin sounded like a patient mother, looking over her two favorite children in Sawyer and Quinn. "After they healed, we made a plan to find Camila, finish your mission - which was best, since I knew the younger Druid needed to be put down. Then I accepted Sawyer's offer to visit the WMC."

Zander sank further into his chair and Sawyer patted his arm reassuringly.

"She's nice," she whispered to him. "She's not the enemy."

"And Camila? The one who attacked, I presume?" Vincent closed the door again, since Jasper had moved to sit down.

"Yes. She's dead now." Yasmin remained peaceful, but Zander had the sneaking suspicion that she was nervous and uncomfortable. Maybe since she was locked in a big steel and marble building, like Quinn once was very uncomfortable with it. "Thanks to Sawyer, really. She's the one who did the important fighting."

Zander choked on his tongue and spun to look back at

Sawyer. He narrowed his eyes at her and realized she was completely burned out as well and must have gone into her life force. Her cheeks were sunken, there were dark circles around her eyes, and her hair was limp and dull. She had.

"This mission can be marked as successful," Sawyer told them all. "That whore is dead, no worries."

"Good...to know..." Vincent seemed dazed by the new information. Zander didn't blame him. Vincent liked his control, and this was all completely out of his control now.

"She escorted Quinn and I out of the rainforest and now we are going to escort her to New York. Then I'm going to laugh in D'Angelo's face. Good plan? Good." Sawyer didn't leave anyone a chance to argue with her, and Zander wasn't feeling foolish enough to. He would let her take over the world now if she was just alive to do it. He didn't care anymore, as long as she was alive.

He knew that would change in a week, but he figured they both needed a respite from arguing.

"Eat, then leave," Quinn corrected. Zander chuckled as Sawyer growled at Quinn and he playfully growled back.

They were hanging out too much, but this time it had been his fault. He was the one who made the decision to leave them alone in the jungle together.

34

SAWYER

S awyer nearly kissed the concrete of the urban jungle known as New York City. When their private jet landed and she was allowed off the plane, she nearly started dancing in joy. She would take it any day over the hell of the Amazon. She was finally back in her element.

Yasmin stayed closed to her and Quinn, with her own animals all hanging on her. Sawyer knew it was for comfort. The Druid didn't know anyone that well, but she had fought with Quinn and Sawyer. Sawyer had no way of helping her, but Quinn held some understanding for the Druid's feelings about being in the middle of a city.

They made no stops at the hotel. They were ushered into vehicles and driven straight to the WMC.

Standing on the steps in front of the impressive building, Sawyer only felt proud.

"Fuck you," she said to the building softly. "I win."

"Sawyer, come on," Zander called out at her near the door. She looked to her side and smiled at Yasmin.

"Are you ready?"

"Were you really ready to fight Camila?" Yasmin asked in return.

"Absolutely not," she admitted, her smile turning into a grin. "But there's only one way to get what you want, in my experience."

"To fight for it?" Yasmin raised an eyebrow at her.

"Damn right."

Sawyer led the Druid up, Quinn flanking Yasmin so the Druid felt safe. Their animals were all around them. Jaguar, wolves, monkeys, and a parrot. They were probably quite the sight. Shadow, Druid, and Wildman with a fucking zoo around them.

"We can't go with you in the Council Chamber," Vincent explained once they were inside. "We're to report to our own meeting. I'm sorry, Yasmin."

"It's fine," Yasmin replied kindly. "I know your mission is now over. Go home and enjoy it."

"Thank you," Vincent said loudly, bowing his head to her. Softer, he continued. "And thank you for protecting them. It means the world to me."

"They are special people," Yasmin reminded him. Sawyer swallowed a lump of emotion as Yasmin turned to her. The Druid extended a hand to her, but she shook her head, refusing the hand. She wrapped her arms around Yasmin and held her for a moment. "Continue to be strong, jaguar."

"Be safe, Druid," Sawyer said in return.

Quinn and Yasmin whispered some words to each other outside the Council Chamber doors, then the team left her there to fight her own battles. She needed to convince the WMC that they needed to take a more active role with non-Magi governments to respect the territories of Druids around the world, or things like this would continue to happen. The Amazon was just the hotbed for the issues and it made Yasmin the expert on the situation.

Sawyer glanced back one more time to hear gasps as Yasmin was introduced to the crowd inside that chamber. Then the doors closed.

Sawyer hoped everything worked out.

They got onto an elevator and went up. They were led to a meeting room and Sawyer heard Vincent laugh.

"James!" Vincent called out.

"Oh my god, you all are going to give me a fucking heart attack," James bitched as he closed them all in the room with him. Then he hugged Vincent and went down the line, even grabbing Quinn and then Sawyer, who patted his back uncomfortably. "Great work out there," he whispered to her specifically. "I'm so fucking proud of you."

Her heart did several thumps. She was pretty fucking proud of herself too.

"What are we looking at now, James?" Vincent asked without any more preamble.

"Nothing. D'Angelo is about to come in and shake your hands and live up to her end of the deal. Your outstanding work down there has gotten you an ally. Enjoy it." James stopped and pointed at Sawyer. "She still doesn't like you, but she's been ecstatic that *her idea* of sending the team down to the Amazon has worked out so well. If you let her have the glory, I think you'll find she's a strong person to have on your side."

"I like that she thinks this is a win," Sawyer muttered darkly. "Like thirty soldiers died down there."

"To the Council, that's abstract. People die on IMAS missions," James reminded her.

"Fuck them. They don't know what happened in those woods." She was agitated suddenly.

"They don't. They also won't read the reports. To them, the Druid who was hurting people is dead and you brought one back for politics. Mission successful." James sighed. "Tell me, though. I want to hear."

Sawyer looked up into his grey eyes, wondering if he really did. The genuine caring on his face was real.

"We'll tell you," Quinn offered, grabbing her and pulling her to a seat. "We'll tell you."

Sawyer had heard all of it as Vincent recounted his half of the team's situation to James. James had already known that part of the story as well. He listened and nodded, reading over the reports Vincent or someone must have already sent in.

"Quinn? Sawyer? Your side?"

Sawyer looked at Quinn. He nodded and launched into the beginning of the fight that night, the one where he found a soldier named Peters on watch being eaten alive. His watch partner was never found. His section ended when he was taken down and gored open enough to nearly knock him unconscious as his wolves fought for their own lives. He remembered the jaguar jumping off him and vines overcoming him, but he was bleeding out too much and the pain from his bonds were keeping him from focusing on anything.

Sawyer continued when she ran off to look for him, leaving the team to protect themselves and the remaining soldiers.

When she relayed how she found Quinn and got a hit on Camila, James was clapping softly.

"Very good. And you met your new animal bond there." James' eyes trailed and hit Sombra, who laid at Sawyer's feet.

"I did, and I asked her to get me back to the team. Her and the wolves. Instead, she took us to Yasmin."

Sawyer explained the walk, how she fell and Sombra dragged her. How she woke up in Yasmin's village.

She skipped over what changed between her and Quinn. She and the entire team would deal with that privately at home. There had been strangers on the private jet that they didn't trust. Employees of the WMC, they could have reported back the unusual romantic situation they were all in, except Elijah.

"We can't tell people you killed Camila. It's a PR nightmare. Shadow capable of killing a Druid nearly single-handedly. That's a recipe for trouble. It would give a bigger name than you already have," James cut in when they finished the story of the fight. "Sure, you were all working together, but you did it. You climbed up there and killed her through all of her defenses. You got a blow on her by yourself before that. There's no way we can have that get out."

"There's no stopping it. Yasmin is down in the Council Chamber now, relaying her story to a majority of the WMC," Vincent told him, shaking his head. "It's going to get out and probably leak Sawyer's identity with it. There's no way people will be able to keep it a secret."

Sawyer cursed softly. Damn. This would be the most infamous thing she'd ever done. She could read the headline now. Shadow kills rabid Druid in Amazon rainforest. Tagline? Under her picture or Yasmin or something even better: Sawyer Matthews, once infamous criminal now working for the WMC and IMPO. Is she truly on our side with so much power?

It was funny, in a way. Sawyer really wasn't the strongest Magi to ever walk the earth. She had a neat combination of abilities than lent themselves to being very good at getting in and out of dangerous situations. She'd been lucky enough to have an above average power level and incredibly deep Source. But she wasn't a god or anything.

This would make some think she might be.

"We'll worry about it later," Sawyer cut them all off. "It's not out yet. There's no stopping it, and I want to go home. Get fucking Dina in here so I can tell her she can kiss my ass, then let me get the hell out of here."

"I've already given all your things to the Magi who will make your portal home." James reached out and tentatively patted her arm in a fatherly way. "I'm glad you all came home. You know that right?"

Sawyer took his hand and squeezed. She and James barely knew each other, but she could imagine in his position, he only had them to look out for. They only had him looking out for them. James was like an older teammate, and also a dad watching his adult kids run off and get themselves into shit everywhere they went.

"Let me see where she is," James broke the silence and stood up. He left them sitting in the room. Sawyer leaned on Elijah next to her, who stiffened.

"What's up, Cowboy?" she asked him softly.

"Nothing. Glad you're both alive," he answered stiffly. She frowned.

He'd been avoiding her since they got out of the Humvees at the embassy. He didn't even hug her and just hung out with Quinn for most of the trip to New York. She needed to get his sketchbook back to him, but it was in her bag. She would remember when they got home.

"Elijah?" She moved off him, but he didn't have the chance to respond. The door opened back up for Dina D'Angelo to walk in, looking relieved.

"Welcome back, everyone. I'm glad to see you all in good health," she greeted them. Her eyes fell on Sawyer. "I'm not going to keep you long. You came back alive and succeeded the mission when it wasn't required. With the losses the party faced, it would have been acceptable to declare a mission failure and back out. We would have allowed all of you to go home, but you finished it anyway."

"It was the only way to get home." Sawyer sighed. "Even discarding the mission, getting through Camila was the only way out of that jungle."

"Ah. I'm sorry for that. The general and I agreed that we should have listened to Special Agent Judge's advice initially. The mission was rushed, and not taken seriously enough. I just sat in for a few words of Yasmin's talk down below. We have been vastly underestimating the power of our Druids. We need to work better with them, keep them in our communities and work with them. We should no longer ignore them until there's a problem."

"No, you shouldn't," Quinn agreed darkly from his place in the back of the room. Sawyer saw Dina's eyes shoot up to him and away.

"The deal stands," Dina continued. "I will never again push to have you taken away from this team. It seems you work outstandingly well with them, and you are a great asset to our government. Have a nice day. Everyone, you can go home now. There's a Magi waiting to portal you to Atlanta, where we know your vehicles must still be waiting on you."

"Dina," Sawyer called out before the Councilwoman left the woman.

"Sawyer." Dina turned back to her, a little pale.

"Next time, admit you're wrong before you get a bunch

of people killed." She met the woman's gaze. "I'm not willing to do this for you a second time."

"Of course." Dina left.

"Damn it, Sawyer," James growled.

She shrugged. She wasn't going to let Dina walk out without thinking she didn't have a lesson to learn.

He sighed at Sawyer's indifference. "Come on. Let's get you all home."

Sawyer had never heard better words. Elijah jumped away from her quickly and left the room first. She frowned at his back.

What the hell?

35

ELIJAH

Elijah fell on his bed and breathed in his own scent in the room. He fucking missed it. He missed home so goddamned much. He missed his fucking bed, his space. Everything.

He didn't even bother unpacking. His bags were all over the floor, scattered about. One from the jungle that Sawyer and Quinn had saved. The two he'd taken to New York. Only one of his things didn't make it.

He'd been drawing in his sketchbook that night before passing out. He'd left it in the tent. It was gone now. He had others, but he would still miss that one.

A scratch at his door had Elijah getting up. He wondered which one of the damn zoo this was.

He pulled his door open to see the big-ass black jaguar. Sombra pushed past him into his room and he glared at her.

"Really? Don't you have a Magi to bother?" One he was desperately trying to avoid. He just couldn't. Leaving her out there in that rainforest had made him realize he hopelessly in love with her, and he sure as fuck wasn't ready for it. He'd promised himself he'd tell her if she was still alive, and then chickened out the moment he saw her at the embassy.

Now he just needed to relax and have some space. Sombra barging into his room meant-

"Damn cat!" Sawyer growled, pushing in as well. Elijah just held his door. He closed his eyes. He couldn't handle Sawyer right now. He couldn't handle his feelings. "Come on. We're supposed to go out and get you into the woods so you know about the territory, then I can go the fuck to sleep."

A growl had his eyes open again and he glared at the jaguar on his bed. Sombra was rolling all over it, probably shedding more than the wolves.

"Sombra," Sawyer snapped. "Let's. Go."

Sombra hissed as Sawyer tried to pull her cat off Elijah's bed. He heard claws rip into his blankets and sheets.

"All right!" Elijah roared.

Sawyer jumped and backed away. Sombra laid down defensively.

He wrapped an arm around the cat's body and lifted her. "Get. Out. I'm going to sleep, you two."

"Sorry," Sawyer mumbled, and Elijah dropped Sombra in the hallway. The jaguar looked completely guilty. He'd done the same to the wolves before. He knew this wouldn't be the end of it. He yanked his comforter off his bed and thrust it at Sawyer when he was back at his bed.

"She can fucking keep it if she keeps those damn talons out of my mattress. Convince her to keep her claws sheathed in the house."

"Of course," Sawyer agreed softly, taking the blanket. He watched her bury her face in it for a moment, but he refused to think much of it. He was tired. He needed some peace and quiet. "She tried breaking into Vincent's room as well, but he stopped her before she jumped on the bed. She finds the mattresses and how bouncy they are really funny."

"She's never been in a normal house." Elijah remembered now. It was going to be exactly like the adjustment with Shade and Scout, but with those two, he also had to teach Quinn a lot. At least Sawyer was just dealing with a very curious cat and not three feral creatures. He rubbed his temples, nodding. "Just...go. She can sleep in here with me if she wants, but she needs to keep her claws put away."

"I'll make sure she knows." She was nearly out of his room when she stopped. He spit curses in his head. "I need to bring you something, so don't pass out yet."

"Hurry," Elijah groaned.

He sat on his bed, now without a blanket, and waited. He had an extra for when he did laundry, but he was too tired to grab it from the closet.

Sawyer ran back in, holding something.

"Here. I found it in the campsite. I just never found a good time to give it to you. It's been damaged, but-"

Elijah snatched his sketchbook from her, amazed that it was really in front of him. He ran his fingers over it.

"Did you open it?" he asked softly, hoping she said no.

"Yes. I wanted to make sure it wasn't ruined," she admitted. She was lying to him, but he didn't call her out. She had just been curious and they both knew it. "You do beautiful work."

"Thank you, Sawyer," Elijah whispered. He put it down on the bed but didn't look back at her.

He'd never been scared of something he felt before, but this scared him. Loving her scared him. She was dangerous - her life was dangerous, even without being with the IMPO.

She made dangerous decisions and got into dangerous situations like she didn't know any other way.

"Good night, Cowboy," Sawyer murmured to him, backing away.

"Have fun with Sombra," he called out to her as she closed his door.

Unlike every other guy on the team, Elijah had done the committed relationship thing before.

He'd loved someone who'd died too young, and he saw her and felt how he felt; she lived such a dangerous life that she could possibly die on him too. The jungle had only proven that. He was terrified of jumping in and admitting it, only to lose her one day.

Elijah tried to sleep, he really did, but two hours later, he was still just laying next to his sketchbook, cranky. His mind was working too hard to convince his heart to quit with whatever the fuck it was doing.

He jumped out of bed and stumbled down onto the back porch, finding Vincent there doing exactly what Elijah wanted. Smoking a cigarette.

"May I?" he asked gruffly.

"Here," Vincent sighed, holding out his pack.

Elijah took one and lit it as he took his first drag. "What are you doing out here?"

"Watching them," Vincent answered, nodding his head to something. Elijah looked out and swallowed hard on another wave of emotion he couldn't deal with. "They found something in the jungle I don't think any of us expected."

Sawyer and Quinn were laughing as Sombra pinned Shade, then turned to pounce on Scout.

"How did you find out?"

"Kaar sent me an image of the kissing. He's decided to continue to spy on Sawyer and now her new animal bond.

He's a freak, but he saw it. I'm thinking those two will tell us tonight at dinner. It's not a big deal." Vincent took another pull on his smoke before continuing. "It's nice to see, really. Quinn seems to have figured out something. I'm not sure what, but he's seemed different since he walked out of the jungle with her. More comfortable."

"Yeah…" Elijah sighed. It was everything he'd ever wanted for Quinn. Find someone who loved him for exactly who he was. Someone who could understand him in some way. He figured Sawyer probably knew more about Quinn than him now, which should have upset him, but he was just happy to see them happy.

He was only worried about the scene for one reason.

"You're out of excuses, Elijah," Vincent told him. "Completely out of excuses. You need to get your head on straight and admit your crush on her before you lose your chance."

"We have time," he reminded Vincent with a bite. "Three months of vacation time, to be exact. They can't call us in unless there's a legitimate emergency."

"Have you noticed that those tend to follow us around now?" Vincent raised an eyebrow at him.

"Fuck." He looked away from his friend. "I'll handle it."

"I can't have you hung up on her and not thinking straight, unwilling to deal with it. That shit after we got out of the Amazon, Elijah? It can't happen again."

"I know," he agreed. He looked back out to Sawyer and Quinn. Sawyer was walking to them, but Quinn pulled her back and kissed her. Elijah watched his arms wrap around her waist and hold her for a long time.

It took a few tries, and even Elijah was chuckling a bit when Sawyer finally got free from Quinn, who just followed her like a puppy to the back porch.

"Smoke?" Vincent offered her innocently.

Elijah didn't like the look on her face.

Sawyer took the pack of cigarettes and shook her head. Then she crushed them.

"Wha-"

"I'm quitting," she told them. She snatched the cigarette hanging from Vincent's mouth and then reached for Elijah's. He just let her take it, putting it out so she didn't burn herself. "So are both of you."

"Why?" Vincent looked offended.

"Because I'm tired of plants that can kill me," Sawyer answered with a smile. Elijah watched her put the cigarettes in the ashtray, then she took the ashtray. "Understand?"

"Yes, ma'am." Elijah couldn't resist giving her a response. He looked away though when she looked at him.

"Sawyer."

"Vincent."

The standoff was real.

"Fine. I understand your reasoning," Vincent agreed. Elijah knew that their Italian was going to go and find his other pack. He was going to smoke in secret. Vincent had been a smoker since he was seventeen. Sawyer was going to have to fight to get him to quit.

"Awesome," Sawyer said brightly. "I'm leaving Sombra out here and going to pass out. Oh, and you've probably noticed, but Quinn-"

"We noticed," Vincent said kindly, leaning to kiss her cheek. She kissed him back. "Just want you happy, remember?"

"I do," Sawyer whispered. She looked at Elijah. "I'm not going to step in on what you guys have either."

"Thank you," he said honestly. That was a big gesture. He looked at Quinn, whose eyes danced with ideas.

Elijah would have been down with his body. He was now scared for his heart. The two pieces of it were in love with each other and he was caught, too scared to jump in with them.

Elijah had never been a coward until he met the bravery and fight in Sawyer Matthews.

He watched them go inside and stayed with Vincent. "Are you going to quit smoking for her?" he asked as the sun dropped.

"I'm going to try, I think," Vincent conceded, shrugging. "Elijah, talk to her."

"I will."

He had time. Elijah wasn't concerned. Three months to figure himself out, and her and Quinn. They'd survived hell and had time off.

DEAR READER,

Thank you for reading A Nature of Conflict!

This was an exciting book to write. I dove in and was so ready to take my team to the Amazon and throw them against some bigger issues. Sombra was a secret I kept from the moment I started writing. I knew Sawyer was going to get a big cat that was strong like she was and I hope you enjoy her addition to the team. Sombra promises to bring trouble!

There's two more books. Only two. I hope you keep with me and Sawyer to see how her saga continues and ends. There's things brewing for them. Book Four will be called An Echo of Darkness. I hope you're ready. I have a feeling the team isn't.

Whether you loved or hated the book, please consider leaving a review. Every review, even just a few words, is appreciated.

PS: To those who really wanted some Quinn love. You're welcome.

ABILITIES

Note:

It's important to remember that every Magi is unique. Two Magi could have the same ability and use them in different ways due to their personal strength levels.

Example: Sawyer can walk through a thick wall with Phasing but another Magi may only be able to pass through a thin door and push an arm through a window for a short time.

Ranking Code

Common- C, Uncommon-U, Rare-R, Mythic- M

- Air Manipulation-C- The ability to manipulate the element of air or wind.
- Animal bonds-C- The ability to bond with one to five animals. A person with this ability can feel emotional currents of the animal and use the animal's senses by inserting themselves in the animal.
- Animation-C- The ability to make inanimate

objects do tasks for time periods. I.e. Dancing
brooms

- Blinking-U- The ability to teleport short
distances (10-20 feet) within eyesight.
- Cloaking-U- The ability to become invisible.
- Dream walking-U- The ability to walk through
the dreams of others and go through the person's
subconscious to reveal secrets and memories to
the person.
- Earth Manipulation-C- The ability to manipulate
the element of earth.
- Elemental Control-M- The ability to manipulate
all elements and all combinations of them.
- Empathy-C- The ability to feel the emotions of
others without touch.
- Emotional Manipulation-U- The ability to feel
the emotions of others and manipulate them
with touch.
- Enchanting-C- The ability to enchant physical
objects with specific properties, such as never
losing a sharp edge for a blade.
- Fire Manipulation-C- The ability to manipulate
the element of fire.
- Healing-C- The ability to heal physical wounds.
- Illusions-U- The ability to alter an individual's
perception of reality.
- Magnetic Manipulation-U- The ability to control
or generate magnetic fields, normally a very
weak ability.
- Naturalism-C- The ability to control the growth
of plant life and identify plants' properties.
- Petrification-R- The ability to freeze a person's

movement without harming them by touching them.

- Phasing-C- The ability to walk through solid objects with concentration.
- Portals-U- Temporary holes through time and space to travel nearly instantly. (Not time travel)
- Reading-R- The ability to read the abilities of others, requires touching the individual.
- Shape-shifting-U- The ability to take the form of one animal, not chosen by the Magi.
- Shielding-C- The ability to create force fields that block physical interaction.
- Sound Manipulation-U- The ability to manipulate sound waves.
- Sublimation-R- The ability to transform into a gaseous form, normally looks like black smoke.
- Telekinesis-C- The ability to move objects physically with the mind.
- Telepathy-U- The ability to send thoughts to others for silent communication. Cannot invade the thoughts of others. This is a one-way ability, unless the other person also has telepathy.
- Tracking-R- The ability track a single individual by having a item that belongs to said individual.
- Water Manipulation-C- The ability to manipulate the element of water.

IMPO AND IMAS

Both organizations have a rank structure, but the IMPO is more relaxed than the IMAS.

International Magi Police Organization

Officer - Low level law enforcement officer

Detective - Case investigator isolated to the city they are assigned to.

Admin - Paper pushers, secretaries, assistants.

Lawyers - Self-explanatory. Magi lawyers who are experts in Magi law.

Special Agent - Case investigator that travels globally and carries out long-term investigations such as crime lords, internationally known criminals, and serial killers. Report to handlers and always work as a team.

Handlers- Normally retired Special Agents that act as liaisons between the Asst. Director/Director and Special Agents.

Assistant Director - Second in charge of the IMPO.

Director - The head of the IMPO. Reports directly to the WMC.

International Magi Armed Services

Chain of Command: 1 is the lowest rank,7 is the highest.
Generals report directly to the WMC.

Enlisted

E-1, Private (Pvt)
E-2, Private 1st Class (PFC)
E-3, Lance Corporal (LCpl)
E-4, Corporal (Cpl)
E-5, Sergeant (Sgt)
E-6, Gunnery Sergeant (GySgt)
E-7, Master Sergeant (MSgt)

Officer

O-1, Lieutenant (Lt)
O-2, Captain (Capt)
O-3, Major (Maj)
O-4, Lieutenant Colonel (LtCol)
O-5, Colonel (Col)
O-6, Lieutenant General (LtGen)
O-7, General (Gen)

IMAS Spec Ops

Special operations (or special forces). Teams are named for
gods and goddesses of war. (Ex. Team Ares or Team Mars)
Soldiers of all ranks may apply for the Trials. Only the best
succeed.

ABOUT THE AUTHOR

KristenBanetAuthor.com

Kristen Banet has a Diet Coke problem and smokes too much. She curses like a sailor (though, she used to be one, so she uses that as an excuse) and finds that many people don't know how to handle that. She loves to read, and before finally sitting to try her hand at writing, she had your normal kind of work history. From tattoo parlors, to the U.S. Navy, and freelance illustration, she's stumbled through her adult years and somehow, is still kicking.

She loves to read books that make people cry. She likes to write books that make people cry (and she wants to hear about it). She's a firm believer that nothing and no one in this world is perfect, and she enjoys exploring those imperfections—trying to make the characters seem real on the page and not just in her head.

She *might* be crazy, though. Her characters think so, but this can't be confirmed.

You can join her in being a little bit crazy in The Banet Pride, her facebook reader's group.

facebook.com/kristenbanetauthor

twitter.com/KristenBanet

instagram.com/Kbanetauthor

ALSO BY KRISTEN BANET

Made in the USA
Middletown, DE
09 February 2021

33429685R00245